Praise for October

"Sixteen installments in
Guire proves that her ca
mains unparalleled. This
planted since the very be
jaw-dropping revelations. . . magic, may-
hem, and mystery is fully pr McGuire continues to push her world's boundaries and her hero's limits. [*Be the Serpent*] proves a wholly satisfying payoff for longtime readers."
—*Publishers Weekly*

"These books are like watching half a season of your favorite television series all at once."
—SF Signal

"McGuire's newest October Daye novel (following *When Sorrows Come*) places the titular hero in the center of dealing with the foundations of Faerie itself. . . . The latest reveals from the ever-expanding history of McGuire's world still hold surprises, while previous plot threads are closed off to prepare for the latest cliff-hanger. This action-filled urban fantasy series shows no signs of slowing down."
—*Library Journal* (starred)

"I can't believe McGuire can come up with another adventure as riveting as this one. But then, I say that after every book in this series."
—SFRevu

"McGuire's ability to pack cascading disasters into a single book is showcased here, with a satisfying number of threads picked up from earlier in the series (most recently, *When Sorrows Come*) and woven into something both inevitable and surprising. Fortunately, McGuire has proven again and again that she can follow up a cliffhanger ending with spectacular payoffs, and fans will find the path to the cliff well worth the effort."
—Booklist

"The top of my urban-paranormal series list! I am so invested in the worldbuilding and the characters. . . . The romance is real and awesome, but doesn't overshadow the adventure."
—Felicia Day

DAW Books presents the finest in urban fantasy from Seanan McGuire

The October Daye Novels

ROSEMARY AND RUE
A LOCAL HABITATION
AN ARTIFICIAL NIGHT
LATE ECLIPSES
ONE SALT SEA
ASHES OF HONOR
CHIMES AT MIDNIGHT
THE WINTER LONG
A RED-ROSE CHAIN
ONCE BROKEN FAITH
THE BRIGHTEST FELL
NIGHT AND SILENCE
THE UNKINDEST TIDE
A KILLING FROST
WHEN SORROWS COME
BE THE SERPENT
SLEEP NO MORE
THE INNOCENT SLEEP

The InCryptid Novels

DISCOUNT ARMAGEDDON
MIDNIGHT BLUE-LIGHT SPECIAL
HALF-OFF RAGNAROK
POCKET APOCALYPSE
CHAOS CHOREOGRAPHY
MAGIC FOR NOTHING
TRICKS FOR FREE
THAT AIN'T WITCHCRAFT
IMAGINARY NUMBERS
CALCULATED RISKS
SPELUNKING THROUGH HELL
BACKPACKING THROUGH BEDLAM
AFTERMARKET AFTERLIFE*

The Ghost Roads

SPARROW HILL ROAD
THE GIRL IN THE GREEN SILK GOWN
ANGEL OF THE OVERPASS

**Coming soon from DAW Books*

SEANAN McGUIRE

BE THE SERPENT

AN OCTOBER DAYE NOVEL

Cover illustration by Chris McGrath.

Interior dingbats created by Tara O'Shea.

Map by Priscilla Spencer.

Edited by Sheila E. Gilbert.

DAW Book Collectors No. 1924.

DAW Books
An imprint of Astra Publishing House
dawbooks.com
DAW Books and its logo are registered trademarks of
Astra Publishing House

Printed in the United States of America

ISBN 9780756416874 (mass market) | ISBN 9780756416881 (ebook)

First edition: September 2022
First mass market edition: August 2023
10 9 8 7 6 5 4 3 2 1

For Mars.
All this time, and we're still dancing.

ACKNOWLEDGMENTS

All right: here we go again. It's been sixteen books, and we're getting to another of the events that's been planned since the beginning, thus proving that a) sometimes playing a very long game works out in your favor, and b) I have absolutely no chill when it comes to plot and pacing. I am overjoyed that we're finally here. I can't wait for you to see what's in store.

There's no point in writing a book if no one's going to read it, and so the fact that you're all still here—or just now joining us for the first time, depending—is a constant honor and delight. Thank you for coming with me on this weird, twisty, seemingly endless journey into the depths of Faerie. Like the two books before it, *Be the Serpent* was composed and completed during a near-universal lockdown, and the escape it provided me has been invaluable. I hope that it can do the same for you.

Big and ongoing thanks to the people who have been here for me every step along the way, including my D&D parties, all of whom are very good about my insistence on only playing Tiefling magic-users, the Machete Squad, the entire team at DAW Books, and my agent, Diana Fox, who has continued to go above and beyond all expectations in making sure that Toby's adventures continue not only to be written, but to make sense to people outside my head. This is not always the easiest of tasks!

Thank you to my entire convention support swarm, for coming together for the first time in two years to make Worldcon in DC a wonderful experience for all involved; to Vixy, who stands up against an onslaught of email with compassion and grace; to Manda, for making sure I eat even when everything but salad is just too much trouble; and to Wish, for keeping me from climbing the walls and crying out of isolation. Thanks to everyone who has played Dungeons & Dragons with me during these days of awkward Zoom games and virtual dice, and to Shivam, who has welcomed me back to the *Magic the Gathering* community with all the warmth I could have hoped for. Thanks to Shawn and Jay and Tea, to Phil and Mars and a whole list of people, all of whom I adore utterly.

My editor, Sheila Gilbert, makes so many things possible, as does the patient work of Joshua Starr, who emails me to nag when I let things slip. Diana Fox has discovered the ability to Discord message me at midnight, while I continue to love Chris McGrath's covers beyond all reason. All four of my cats are doing well: Elsie, Thomas, Verity, and Megara thrive on my being home constantly, and finally believe that they're getting as many Rocking Lobster cat treats as they properly deserve. Finally, thank you to my pit crew: Christopher Mangum, Tara O'Shea, and Kate Secor.

My soundtrack while writing *Be the Serpent* consisted mostly of *ruin, The Horror and the Wild,* and *Love Run* by the Amazing Devil, endless live concert recordings of the Counting Crows, and the soundtrack to the *Beetlejuice* musical. Any errors in this book are entirely my own. The errors that aren't here are the ones all the people listed above helped me fix.

Now let's go. There are questions to be answered, and problems to be solved, and time is shorter than you think it is . . .

OCTOBER DAYE PRONUNCIATION GUIDE
THROUGH *BE THE SERPENT*

All pronunciations are given strictly phonetically. This only covers races explicitly named in the first sixteen books, omitting Undersea races not appearing or mentioned in the current volume.

Adhene: *aad-heene*. Plural is "Adhene."
Aes Sidhe: *eys shee*. Plural is "Aes Sidhe."
Afanc: *ah-fank*. Plural is "Afanc."
Annwn: *ah-noon*. No plural exists.
Arkan sonney: *are-can saw-ney*. Plural is "arkan sonney."
Bannick: *ban-nick*. Plural is "Bannicks."
Baobhan Sith: *baa-vaan shee*. Plural is "Baobhan Sith," diminutive is "Baobhan."
Barghest: *bar-guy-st*. Plural is "Barghests."
Blodynbryd: *blow-din-brid*. Plural is "Blodynbryds."
Cait Sidhe: *kay-th shee*. Plural is "Cait Sidhe."
Candela: *can-dee-la*. Plural is "Candela."
Coblynau: *cob-lee-now*. Plural is "Coblynau."
Cu Sidhe: *coo shee*. Plural is "Cu Sidhe."
Daoine Sidhe: *doon-ya shee*. Plural is "Daoine Sidhe," diminutive is "Daoine."
Djinn: *jin*. Plural is "Djinn."
Dóchas Sidhe: *doe-sh-as shee*. Plural is "Dóchas Sidhe."
Ellyllon: *el-lee-lawn*. Plural is "Ellyllon."
Folletti: *foe-let-tea*. Plural is "Folletti."

Gean-Cannah: *gee-ann can-na*. Plural is "Gean-Cannah."
Glastig: *glass-tig*. Plural is "Glastigs."
Gwragen: *guh-war-a-gen*. Plural is "Gwragen."
Hamadryad: *ha-ma-dry-add*. Plural is "Hamadryads."
Hippocampus: *hip-po-cam-pus*. Plural is "Hippocampi."
Kelpie: *kel-pee*. Plural is "Kelpies."
Kitsune: *kit-soo-nay*. Plural is "Kitsune."
Lamia: *lay-me-a*. Plural is "Lamia."
The Luidaeg: *the lou-sha-k*. No plural exists.
Manticore: *man-tee-core*. Plural is "Manticores."
Naiad: *nigh-add*. Plural is "Naiads."
Nixie: *nix-ee*. Plural is "Nixen."
Peri: *pear-ee*. Plural is "Peri."
Piskie: *piss-key*. Plural is "Piskies.'
Puca: *puh-ca*. Plural is "Pucas."
Roane: *row-n*. Plural is "Roane."
Satyr: *say-tur*. Plural is "Satyrs."
Selkie: *sell-key*. Plural is "Selkies."
Shyi Shuai: *shh-yee shh-why*. Plural is "Shyi Shuai."
Silene: *sigh-lean*. Plural is "Silene."
Tuatha de Dannan: *tootha day danan*. Plural is "Tuatha de Dannan," diminutive is "Tuatha."
Tylwyth Teg: *till-with teeg*. Plural is "Tylwyth Teg," diminutive is "Tylwyth."
Urisk: *you-risk*. Plural is "Urisk."

Kingdoms of the Westlands
Kingdom of Frozen Winds
Kingdom of Warm Skies
Kingdom of Evergreen
Kingdom of Leucothea
Kingdom of Silences
Kingdom of Starfall
Battle of Silences
Kingdom of the Mists
Kingdom of Painted Skies
Kingdom on the Golden Shore
Kingdom of Angels
Kingdom of Copper
Priscilla Spencer

ONE

June 11th, 2015

Bear welcome in your eye, your hand, your tongue.
Look like the innocent flower,
But be the serpent under it.

—William Shakespeare, *Macbeth*.

IT HAD BEEN A normal night, melting into a normal morning. Then the sun had glinted off the pond and the world had twisted around me, going from clear, comforting sameness to chaotic murkiness as the water that was my natural environment suddenly and convulsively rejected me. I couldn't breathe. I couldn't *breathe*, and so I thrashed, trying to find a way to survive when nothing was the way that it was supposed to be, nothing was the way I understood it, everything was wrong and I was going to die, and I *understood* that I was going to die, and that was wrong too, everything was wrong—

I woke with a gasp, sitting halfway up in bed before the arm draped across my waist tightened and dragged me back down, forcing me into the pillows. Normally, I'm not into words like "forcing" being applied to me, especially not where my bed is concerned, but Tybalt had been sleeping beside me for long enough at this point—and wasn't that sentence something of a miracle in and of itself?—to have learned the difference between "Toby is getting up to use the bathroom" or "Toby is getting up because she hears the boys breaking something downstairs in the kitchen" and "Toby is pulling away because she just had a horrible dream and isn't sure where she is yet, I need to anchor her or she'll stab someone who doesn't deserve it."

Taking a deep, shaking breath, I sank deeper into the mattress, trying to get my heart to stop racing like it thought it could pound its way right out of my chest. Tybalt made a small, protesting sound and nestled closer, neck bent until his forehead was pressed against my shoulder. At least he was bipedal this morning. Now that he truly thought of the house as his home, he had a tendency to completely relax while he was sleeping, and sometimes that meant changing forms in the middle of the night. Going to bed with a human-sized man and waking up with an extra cat can be a little disconcerting.

Only a little, though. I knew he was Cait Sidhe when I married him—one of the fairy cats, as comfortable on four legs as he was on two. Honestly, on the days where I woke up without a bipedal husband hogging the covers, I just counted my blessings in a different direction.

Husband. Even after almost two full months of being married in the eyes of Faerie and the world, it was still strange to think that word and mean it. We'd only been legally married in the human world for about three weeks, having taken that long to get around to the courthouse wedding I'd been threatening from the beginning, but with that out of the way, the last of the big aftershocks of our marriage seemed to be receding into the rearview mirror.

Wedding? Survived, despite the small matter of a coup against the High King and a bunch of doppelgangers trying to kill us all before the ceremony could be performed. Performed by the sea witch herself, even, making me the second member of my immediate family to have her preside over our marriage vows—with the first being Simon Lorden, the man who was legally my father in the eyes of Faerie, despite biologically being a distant cousin at best, thanks to us both being descendants of Oberon. If someone bothered to untangle our family tree, they'd probably find proof that I'm actually his aunt or something, which only gets more ridiculous the more I think about it. But that's Faerie for you. Making sense is something that happens to other people.

Reception? Survived. Enjoyed, even, thanks to the efforts of our friends and loved ones, and Kerry's truly awe-inspiring cake. Honestly, I wasn't sure which I'd enjoyed more, getting the time to actually sit down and eat a proper meal without getting stabbed, poisoned, or called away to deal with some sort of monster infestation, or watching my colony of semi-adopted teenagers eating themselves into a cataclysmic sugar high. Luckily, I didn't have to choose. I got to have them both. An impossible luxury in a life all too frequently defined by bloodshed and chaos.

Honeymoon? Survived. Tybalt and I had taken the Tuatha Express to the Kingdom of Angels in Southern California, where we'd spent a very pleasant week splitting our time between Disney's Grand Californian Hotel, the two nearby theme parks, and—for one tense and somewhat irritating evening—the Court of Angels, where Queen Regent Amalia and Crown Prince Theunis had served us dinner, both looking deeply uncomfortable the entire time, which I suppose made sense for a Crown Prince and his Regent playing host to a known king-breaker whose only other visit to their Court had been to announce the death of their previous king and force a thirteen-year-old boy onto the throne. The kid was younger than my own squire, and hadn't been able to bring himself to look me in the eye once after the formal offers of hospitality had been made and accepted.

But a night in the Court had been the true, if unspoken, price of having a honeymoon in a Kingdom other than the one I lived in. I've gone and picked up a bit of a reputation for sticking my nose where it doesn't belong, thanks to both an absolute lack of patience for pureblood bullshit and my tendency to boot lousy or illegitimate monarchs off their thrones. I'm currently at three, "and counting," as my squire likes to say, usually when he's trying to annoy me. If we wanted to do Disney, we had to allow the local monarchs to host us, and I had to make nice the whole time, no matter how much it grated.

Fortunately, Tybalt had courtly manners enough for both of us, and it had been worth it for the picture of him the Park cameras had captured on their racecar ride. I was considering making it into a nice tapestry for the front hall. Only not, because I can't sew, and any weaver who took that commission from me would find an angry King of Cats breathing down their neck about five minutes later. I know my limits.

We were down to the last item on that particular list: marriage. We were surviving it so far, and now that the wisps of my dream were clearing away and the frantic hammering of my heart was beginning to ease, I felt like I was going to survive this day, too. And that was a good thing. Pureblood fae live forever if nothing kills them, but I'm still part human on my father's side, and a natural death could still be on the table for me. And I wasn't ready for that.

Of course, I also heal like there's some sort of prize to be won for doing it faster than anyone else, so if I did have a heart attack, I'd probably just come back to life with a ringing headache—the one thing my ridiculous recovery speed *doesn't* reliably protect me from—and the vague feeling that something had gone horribly wrong.

Carefully, I eased myself out from under Tybalt's arm and slid to my feet, stretching my arms over my head, both to unkink my spine and to remind me that I was a biped now, allowed to do biped things. Tybalt oozed into the warm spot left by my departure, burying his face in my pillow. Usually, like any sleeping cat, he either woke up at the slightest motion or slept with such total dedication that nothing short of an earthquake would disturb his slumber. I smiled, leaning over to stroke his brown-and-black striped hair before I padded toward the bathroom.

My unpleasant mental wakeup call was explained when I snagged my phone from atop the dresser, where I'd plugged in: the date glared from above the time, seeming to threaten and accuse in equal measure. June 11th. Six years to the day since I'd woken up face-down in a shallow pond at the Japanese Tea Gardens in Golden Gate Park, choking on water my body had abruptly forgotten how to breathe and gasping for air I no longer knew how to need.

That was the day I got my identity back. I didn't get the life I'd been living up until that point back. Magic can only do so much, and what was lost while I was in the pond was lost forever.

Not that I'd trade the life I had now for the life I had then even if someone were to somehow make me the offer—and with Faerie being what it is, somebody eventually might, even if they couldn't actually do it. The fae are big on making promises they can't keep. But all things considered, this was my least favorite day of the year. You'd think the day I'd gone *into* the pond would carry that distinction, but when it happened, I hadn't known just how much things were about to change, or how hard everything was going to become.

When the spell broke, though . . . when the spell broke, that was when I'd known that I was screwed.

But I should really start closer to the beginning if I can. My name is October Daye, Knight of Lost Words, official Hero of the Realm of the Kingdom in the Mists, the fae demesne roughly paralleling the mortal lands known as the San Francisco Bay Area. My father, Jonathan Daye, was a human; my mother, Amandine the Liar, is the Firstborn daughter of Oberon—yes, *that* Oberon—and Janet Carter—yes, *that* Janet.

We don't do family reunions, but I bet they'd be fun, in the "entrails all over the lawn" sort of sense.

Humans and fae aren't the same species, but they're close enough that, like lions and tigers or dogs and wolves, they can sometimes reproduce. When that happens, you get changeling kids like me, caught between two worlds, forever dancing along the borders of both of them. I don't know whether it helps or hurts that the human world doesn't know Faerie exists, while Faerie tends to view the human side of things as a useful junk shop to steal ideas and artifacts and sometimes children from, all while looking down on it from the vaunted height of being immortal and magical and self-absorbed.

Anyway, I was born while my mother was married to Simon Torquill, meaning that even though he's definitely not the man who fathered me, Faerie considers him my legal parent. And since he divorced my mother, and I sided with him in the separation, Faerie now considers him my *only* legal parent. He remarried almost immediately—like, same day, not even an hour later, which I guess would be the new dictionary definition of "rebound" if not for the fact that he married a couple he'd been close to and cared about for well over a century. Faerie makes timespans weird sometimes. Just go with it. These days he lives in the Undersea Duchy of Saltmist with his Merrow wife, Daoine Sidhe husband, and my older sister, August, the only other Dóchas Sidhe in the world.

I never said this was going to be easy to follow.

Simon and I get along pretty well now that he's not, you know, married to my mother and spending all his time doing the bidding of his evil asshole of a former boss, Eira Rosynhwyr. But before we made peace, he was basically the monster under my bed, and that whole pond thing I mentioned—the thing that's left me with the occasional horrific nightmare and what looks likely to be a lifetime case of hydrophobia—was his fault. Eira wanted him to kill me. He, knowing he was sort of my father if not quite exactly, couldn't bring himself to do it. But he also couldn't disobey her directly. So when he couldn't get out of confronting me in front of his handler-slash-lover, Oleander de Merelands, he went for an old pureblood method of removal. After all, when you're going to live forever, turning your enemies into something they don't want to be is a great way to get rid of them for a few decades, and when the spell wears off, well. It's not like they really lost anything, is it? No harm done.

So he turned me into a fish. A koi, to be specific. And rather than letting me suffocate on the hostile air, he'd pushed me into the water and saved me in the only way he could. And maybe he really hadn't had a choice, but he'd been laughing when he did it, and that still haunts me.

I spent fourteen years in that pond. Fourteen years for my two-year-old, mostly human daughter to grow up thinking I'd run out on her as soon as the challenges of motherhood became more than I could handle; fourteen years for my carefully constructed mortal life to fall apart. When the spell had finally broken and dropped me back into myself, I had been completely lost, thinking I would never be able to rebuild . . . thinking I'd failed everyone I'd ever cared about.

Now here I was, six years later, with a man in my bed who I'd have sworn hated me when I went into the water, a blood-sister under the sea and a heart-sister in the bedroom down the hall, and two boys who might as well be my sons just one room down from her. Raj didn't technically live with us, since he was going to be the next King of Cats just as soon as his Regent decided he was ready to challenge Tybalt for the crown, but he was here more nights than not. He knew his responsibilities were going to take up a lot more of his time soon, and more, he knew that Quentin wasn't going to be with us forever. We all knew that.

I had mostly been able to not think about it until my wedding, which took place in the knowe of Quentin's parents, the current High King and Queen of the Westlands, aka the faerie bosses of North America. And yeah, the math on that makes him the current Crown Prince, meaning that one day not too far in the future—like within the next nine years—he'll have to go back to Toronto and take up his adult duties. Which will suck for all of us, but maybe for Raj most of all. I'm Quentin's knight and surrogate mother figure. Dean is Quentin's boyfriend. Raj, though . . . Raj is his brother.

I made my way to the bathroom and clicked on the light, squinting in the glare. Being afraid of water doesn't exempt me from the need to shower, although I draw the line at baths. I left the door open. Cait Sidhe don't share the feline dislike of getting wet, and if the sound of the shower woke Tybalt, there was a chance he'd come to join me. Sometimes it's nice to take chances.

Fae are more nocturnal than humans, meaning we tend to keep hours a lot closer to human teens than human adults. Waking up before noon would normally have meant climbing back under the covers and trying to steal a few more hours of peace before something exploded or tried to stab me or otherwise complicated my life. Not an unreasonable fear, either; I seem to have a calling for chaos, and it finds me even when I don't go looking.

But today, I would have been up soon, with or without the nightmares to serve as an unasked-for alarm. Because today, in addition to being the six-year anniversary of my return from the pond, was the day I'd been called to attend formal Court at Queen Windermere's knowe in Muir Woods, where I'd stand witness and provide testimony as Rayseline Torquill's parents petitioned to have her woken from her enchanted slumber.

I had to wonder if Luna requested this date out of the mistaken belief that being reminded of my own lost years would make me more sympathetic to her daughter's plight. Her daughter, who had been elf-shot on the same day as *my* daughter, Gillian, who was only in the line of fire because Raysel kidnapped her and put her there.

Gillian had been born mostly human, but had still been partially Dóchas Sidhe, despite growing up completely ignorant of Faerie. All that had changed on the day Raysel grabbed her and dragged her into danger. My then-boyfriend, Connor, had been killed trying to save her, and he died believing he'd failed, because Gillian was too human to survive being elf-shot.

For a pureblood like Raysel, elf-shot meant a hundred-year nap. For a changeling like Gillian had been, it meant a quick, painful death . . . or would have, if not for the fact that me being Dóchas Sidhe gives me a certain measure of control over someone's blood. I offered my daughter the choice she'd been denied before, the choice between Faerie and a mortal life, and when she chose humanity, I pulled Faerie out of her veins, taking the poison with it. I freed her from my world to save her life, and that was due to Raysel's actions.

Of course, Gillian ended up being elf-shot *again* some time later, and had been transformed into a Selkie in order to save her life. She wasn't a Selkie anymore, having been transformed a second time, into one of the Roane, but she'd never be Dóchas Sidhe—or human—again. Those paths were lost to her. And I could trace those losses back to Rayseline. I'd agreed to speak at her trial. That didn't mean reminding me of how we'd come to be in this position was a great plan.

Sadly, Tybalt didn't come to join me as I scrubbed the last of my slumber away and rinsed the shampoo out of my hair. He was still sleeping peacefully when I stepped out of the bathroom, wrapped in a towel, and moved toward the dresser.

It was the sound of the drawer sliding open that finally caused him to crack one eye open, watching lazily as I dug for something to wear.

"Not dressing nicely for Court?" he asked.

"The sun's up, and we have to walk through Muir Woods to get to Arden," I said. "Unless you feel like maintaining a don't-look-here from the parking lot to the top of the trail, I should wear something that doesn't look out of place in a national park."

He yawned extravagantly. "Or you could let me carry you through the shadows, as befits my lady wife."

I threw a pair of socks at him. "Try again, kitty-cat. I just washed my hair, and I don't want to get there with icicles on my head."

Tybalt batted the socks aside. "I don't understand why you would refuse a faster, safer means of travel with such regularity."

"Can't go through the McDonald's drive-through on the Shadow Roads, and the boys are riding with us." As my squire, Quentin had a vested interest in the proceedings. As Tybalt's heir, Raj had much the same. And Dean, Quentin's boyfriend—who was now also my little brother by marriage, one of the many, many things I try not to think about any harder than I have to—had been one of the others kidnapped by Raysel on the day when she was elf-shot. She cut his finger off to send a message. I still wasn't sure which side he'd be speaking for.

Ugh. The only thing worse than attending a formal Court is attending a formal Court where I'm expected to participate in legal arguments. Normally, I come in, get into a fight with the nearest noble, stab something, and leave. It's very efficient and dramatic and entirely inappropriate when you're trying to convince the Queen to authorize the early awakening of someone who may not have broken Oberon's Law in a way that anyone would hold against her, but who had definitely behaved in an inappropriate and impolite manner, possibly racking up several charges of offense in the process.

Including the one she was expecting me to make. Which was going to be its own big barrel of bullshit, and now I got to wade through it. Tybalt, Quentin, and May all knew about it, which meant Raj and Jazz almost certainly did too. None of them had told me not to do it. That didn't make me any less anxious.

I dug out one of my oldest pairs of jeans and a black T-shirt with the Paxton Gate logo on it, pulling them briskly on. Tybalt was out of the bed by the time I had my jeans buttoned, and in the bathroom as I was belting my knives around my waist.

For years, the two I carried were a silver one gifted to me by a girl named Dare who thought I was going to be her hero, and an iron one given to me by Acacia, the Mother of Trees, when she realized I had to be the one who killed her husband. I'd been forced to stop carrying the iron knife after my blood shifted one time too many and left me too fae to handle it safely. I could push myself back toward humanity—my magic allows it—but Tybalt would kill me if I did that on purpose, and honestly, I wouldn't blame him. I'm still trying to stay at least a little bit human, but at this point, making myself more mortal would just mean making myself more vulnerable, and risk taking me away from another family. I'm not going to do that.

Today would be the first day I carried two knives to Arden's Court. The first, the silver, was familiar. The second was relatively new, although it felt natural and easy in my hand, and was made of a material I still hadn't identified. In a very real way, it was the only gift I had received on my actual wedding day. Contrary to mortal customs, purebloods believed gifts should be given in private when possible, rather than forcing the recipient to perform gratitude for an audience. Wedding gifts were still showing up almost daily, making my front porch a constant surprise and my dining room a maze of boxes.

The knife was different. I hadn't even realized it *was* a gift at first; I'd thought it was just something I could use to cut the cake. But when I'd tried to return it, the Luidaeg had interceded, explaining that once her father—you know, *Oberon himself*—handed someone a weapon, it was a grave insult to hand it back, and did I really want to insult my grandfather, the Lord of All Faerie, on my wedding day? Was I that eager to become something genuinely unpleasant and leave Tybalt functionally a widower?

I was not. And so now I carried a gift from the father of us all on my left hip, sharp and deadly and ready to be used.

But no pressure.

My life got weird at some point, is what I'm saying, but I wouldn't have it any other way. Tybalt emerged from the bathroom impossibly already dressed, which meant he'd probably popped over to the Court of Cats long enough to retrieve one of his apparently unlimited pairs of leather pants, combining them with a plain white shirt of a style that would have looked more contemporaneous on the set of a BBC period drama than the streets of San Francisco. We made an odd couple. But then, we always have.

"Are you ready, little fish?" he asked, voice mild.

I smiled, pulling my wet hair back with a scrunchie. "I'm always ready to go with you," I said, and leaned in to kiss him, and together we left the room, heading for the chaos yet to come.

TWO

ONE NICE THING ABOUT packing the car with teenagers: the chaos of going to formal Court pales before the chaos of shepherding two teen boys, a Fetch with the metabolism of a hummingbird, a centuries-old King of Cats, and myself through a McDonald's drive-through. May and Tybalt are the co-presidents of the "make Toby eat something already" fan club, and Quentin is vying for officership in their next election.

May being May, it wasn't impossible that the elections might become reality someday, if they weren't already. Her sense of humor is . . . let's go with "unpredictable." She's earned it. As my Fetch, May has all my memories up until the moment of her creation as a distinct entity, and fragments of all the people whose memories she consumed while she was still a night-haunt. The biology of Faerie is exciting and about as reasonable as May's idea of what is or is not funny.

Fortunately, McDonald's was already serving lunch by the time we swung through, and we found ourselves bound for Muir Woods with several sacks of cheeseburgers and fries, boxes of chicken nuggets, and filet-of-fish sandwiches.

The ice cream machine was even working, meaning we had milkshakes to keep us occupied during the drive.

Raj, having finished his own milkshake, was leaning into the front seat trying to snatch Tybalt's out of his hand. Both of them were laughing. I was inclined to let them have their fun: with Raj so focused on his training these days, he didn't get many opportunities to play, and while he had made it clear that he wasn't going to follow the classic Cait Sidhe system and exile his uncle when he took the throne, he and Tybalt weren't going to be able to spend time together after that. Not the way that they were used to.

At the same time, I was trying to navigate a full car through midmorning traffic, with a don't-look-here spell on the vehicle to keep anyone from noticing that we were apparently on our way to some sort of science fiction convention. It was working; none of the other drivers seemed to see us. That meant I needed to pay even more attention to the road. Don't-look-heres reduce collisions, since people instinctively realize there's something they need to steer around—it's handy—but if I had to hit the brakes suddenly, the delay the spell caused could get us rear-ended.

Then Raj hit my arm, nearly dousing me in my own milkshake, and I scowled at both of them.

"Boys!" I said, more sharply than I meant to. "Can we *please* get to Court alive?"

"You and May would survive," said Quentin helpfully. "You're both basically indestructible."

"Yes, but I would be very sad and very cranky and your parents would dedicate the rest of their lives to figuring out a way to kill me after all," I said, and caught Quentin's sour expression in the rearview mirror.

He'd been cranky and lashing out since we got back from Toronto. Fortunately, I knew it wasn't about me marrying Tybalt; it was about the fact that he hates being reminded that he's not really my son. One day he'll have to go back to his real parents and take up his duties as Crown Prince of the Westlands. I shrugged, mouthing "sorry" to the mirror, and he sighed and looked away. Even if he hated it, it was reality, and he couldn't glare it out of existence.

If glaring at things made them go away, the world would be a very different place.

Raj stopped trying to take Tybalt's cup and sank back into his seat, lower lip shoved out in a pronounced pout. "You said we're supposed to share," he said, petulantly.

"I am sharing," said Tybalt. "This is my share. You had your share. It's been consumed."

"Everyone just eat your fries before they get cold and turn evil," I said.

"Are we there yet?" asked Raj.

"I will sit on you," said May. "Jazz had to work, which means there's no one here to tell me to behave myself. So don't make me sit on you."

He snorted and stole some of her fries.

The merry chatter continued all the way to Muir Woods, where the parking lot was open and almost entirely full of ordinary, visible cars. I pulled into one of the few available slots, and as we got out of the car, May cast another don't-look-here over it, to keep us from being noticed if we were here after the sun went down. I shot her a grateful look. She smiled at me.

"I got you," she said. "I always got you. You know that."

"I do," I said, and meant it.

That was what really made this day different from the day six years ago when I'd woken up alone, afraid, and abandoned in the Japanese Tea Gardens: these people, all these people, had my back. No matter how bad things got, they had my back, and I knew it, and they wouldn't let me forget it. I had a *family*. This wasn't even all of it.

It was still a strange and heady thing, feeling like I belonged somewhere, and it buoyed me through the park gates and along the trails that led to Arden's knowe. Knowes—better known in the human world as "hollow hills"—are built in places where the nearest realm of Faerie, the Summerlands, and the human world intersect. They exist almost entirely in the Summerlands, paying very little attention to silly things like "physics" and "geography," but their roots are sunk in mortal soil, letting them serve as points of passage between the two worlds.

If we had come at night, the trees would have been

alight with pixies. They were sleeping now, waiting until it got late enough that the humans went away and it was safer for them to go about their business. Not that humans could see them under most circumstances, but a windshield will take out a pixie as surely as it will a butterfly. Not worth the risk.

We followed the pre-set trail into the shadow of the redwoods and through the carefully curated and manicured recreation of the wilderness that dominated this place before the arrival of first the fae and later the European settlers. The humans were doing their best to preserve what natural beauty they had left, and we weren't here to interfere with it.

We went around a bend and found ourselves alone on a stretch of trail, safely sheltered from view by the topography of the terrain around us. Conveniently, a nearby tree's roots had grown in a ladderlike series of tiers, providing a reasonable passage up the rise.

Park rules tell us to stay on the trails. This was a trail of sorts, just a more private one, protected by something stronger than a few rules. Humans who passed this point wouldn't see the easy way up, and would need to scramble through briars and patches of poison oak if they wanted to climb the seemingly hostile hillside. We began our climb easily, single-file, and as we went higher, the air softened and brightened around us, signaling the point where we weren't quite in the Summerlands, but weren't quite in the human world anymore, either.

At the top of the hill, we stepped into a wide clearing in the redwoods, at the center of which grew a truly massive tree with double doors standing open in its trunk. Figures stood to either side of the entryway, dressed in the royal livery of the Mists. Neither of them was particularly familiar, which was unusual; usually Lowri, the captain of the Queen's guard, could be found in one of the sentry positions. I guess everyone gets a few hours off.

The guards nodded to us as we passed by, but didn't ask us to stop or present our credentials. At this point, basically everyone in the Kingdom knows who we are, and they don't want to attract more of our collective attention than strictly necessary. I'd be offended, if it weren't so damn convenient.

The air changed again when we stepped over the threshold into the impossibly extended interior of the tree, marking our final transition to the Summerlands. The dizziness that followed the transition only lasted a few seconds, more like vertigo than anything else. I may never get used to how much *easier* it is to travel between the worlds now that I'm not as human as I used to be. It's not fair. Changelings already suffer on so many levels; they don't need an extra layer of difficulty in getting to what ought to be a sanctuary.

But then again, when has Faerie ever been "fair"? The closest we come is the name, and honestly, the name's pretty misleading. Tybalt looked to me, trying to measure my disorientation. I smiled, shook my head, and kept walking.

The arrival chamber led into a long hallway paneled in carved friezes showing important moments from the Kingdom's history. They change depending on the mood of the knowe. Today they were showing a lot of Court scenes, including the trial where the false former Queen of the Mists sentenced me to death. Not my finest moment.

I didn't recognize a lot of the others, but I've never made a practice of studying the history of formal Court in our Kingdom. As we approached the door to Arden's receiving room, the mystery of where Lowri was received an answer: she was right outside, polearm held to block the door.

"Halt," she said. "Who goes there?"

The temptation to say something snarky was strong. Tybalt cleared his throat and looked at me semi-sternly, making it clear that this wasn't the time. Party pooper. With a sigh, I said, "Sir October Daye, Knight of Lost Words, and Squire, Quentin."

"No title yet," said Quentin.

"King Tybalt of the Court of Dreaming Cats, and Heir, Rajiv," said Tybalt.

"Prince of Cats," drawled Raj.

As our wards, the boys didn't get to introduce themselves. May, however, was an adult and expected to present herself. She smiled serenely at Lowri. "I was a member of this Court when last I entered this room on formal grounds, and I stood before your King Windermere as one of his charmaids, well known and well beloved. They call me May Daye now, and you would do well to let us in."

Lowri paled. "You don't have to go being all terrifying and Fetchy about it," she grumbled, raising her polearm so we could go inside. "You may pass."

"You started it," said May, with her usual sunny smile. I ignored her, shooting Lowri an apologetic look as I moved to push the door open.

I'd been hoping since this was an early Court—it was barely two o'clock in the afternoon and we were already getting started, making this the fae equivalent of a six a.m. traffic court appointment—we'd have the room mostly to ourselves. Just us, the accused, and the witnesses for both sides.

No such luck. I opened the doors on a zoo.

Not quite literally. Faerie has its share of what Chelsea sometimes calls "petting-zoo people," normally right after Raj has stolen the toppings off her slice of pizza and she's getting ready to beat him with a pillow, but that doesn't make us animals. Still, the room was filled almost to capacity, bodies crowding both sides. I paused in the doorway, proceeding forward only when Tybalt placed a hand at the small of my back and pushed me along ahead of him, guiding us toward an open space in front of the dais holding Arden's throne.

As our sole Queen, she sat alone, a tall, beautiful woman with long purple-black hair pulled over one shoulder and styled with an artful twist of silver blackberry briars whose thorns looked as sharp as the real thing. They echoed the silver brambles embroidered into the purple-black velvet of her dress, wrapped around and entangling her until she looked as much statuary as sovereign. She turned her attention to me as we entered, mismatched metallic gaze implacable and unwavering.

"We're not late, are we?" I murmured.

The question was intended only for Tybalt, but the enchantments meant to carry the words of today's witnesses were already in place, and had apparently targeted me as soon as I stepped inside: they picked up my words and flung them around the room, filling the space with my anxiety.

Arden's expression softened. "No, Sir Daye, you're right on time," she said. "My apologies. A formal Court is an overwhelming thing, and as you have just returned from your marriage journeys, it may be more than you were expecting."

I had a deeply antagonistic relationship with our former Queen. Thus far, I've managed to stay on mostly good terms with Arden. I reminded myself of that as I pulled away from Tybalt and strolled toward the open space that had been so clearly left for me. The rest of my group moved to join the crowd. Impossible as it seemed, given everything, this didn't directly concern them.

Oh, indirectly, it concerned them from fifty different directions at once, but in the immediate "were you there, do you have to testify" sense, nope. I was on the hot seat alone for this one.

Arden watched me, evident sympathy in her eyes, but didn't speak again until I stopped before her throne and bowed. Proper courtly etiquette is one of the few lessons I learned from my mother that hasn't turned out to be some sort of nasty trick designed to eventually screw me. I may be crass, but I can bow with the best of them, holding my back perfectly straight and my right leg extended just so, until Arden said, with warm sincerity, "You may rise, Sir Daye."

I rose.

Her throne was the only one on the high dais, but she wasn't entirely alone. A second, smaller throne sat on the tier below hers, slightly behind and to the right. Her brother, Crown Prince Nolan, was seated there, wearing a doublet that matched her dress, a coronet on his purple-black hair and an expression of vague perplexity on his face. He'd been asleep when all this was going down, and it had to have felt a little bit like someone trying to recount the plot of a movie he hadn't seen, then expecting him to follow the sequel.

On her left were two ornate chairs that very distinctly

were not thrones, one occupied by a man whose platinum hair was streaked with bloody red, the other by a woman whose long, straight hair started dirty blonde at the roots and darkened as it went on, leaving her ticked like a tabby's coat, with black taking over the last six or so inches. Matching tufts of fur topped her ears. She looked almost more feline than Tybalt, which I've always found somewhat humorous when I stopped to think about it. She snuck me a little wave, and I cast a smile her way. Madden, the Queen's Seneschal, and Cassandra, both the Queen's Chatelaine and my honorary niece.

Arden didn't have a large Court yet. She hadn't had the time to assemble it, having held her father's throne for just under three years. In pureblood society, that's barely the blinking of an eye. But she did all right with what she had, and since she mostly didn't grow up in Faerie—when the false Queen seized the throne, she sent Arden into exile in the human world, where she'd been a bookstore clerk for decades—it was pretty impressive how quickly she'd adjusted.

The rest of the crowd made up for the sparseness of the dais. One side of the room was occupied by what looked like the entire population of Shadowed Hills, including my liege, Duke Sylvester Torquill, and his wife, Luna, who was glaring daggers at me across the space between us. I didn't quite understand why. Luna isn't my biggest fan these days, but I'd promised to speak in Raysel's favor, had already done so once, and was planning to do the same today. There was no way Luna knew what else I was planning to do. If she had, she would already have been attacking me.

The other side of the room was packed with denizens of the Undersea. What looked like most of Saltmist was there, as were the Roane who had formerly been the Selkies of Half-Moon Bay. Duchess Dianda of Saltmist stood toward the front of the group, in a long blue dress that reflected all the colors of her more customary fins and scales, with her oldest son by her side. Neither her husbands nor her younger son were in evidence. That was too bad, even if it made sense—Peter couldn't hold a two-legged shape long without aid, and it wasn't comfortable or easy for him even when he had the help he needed to get there. I still wasn't sure how he'd been able to attend my wedding. And I wouldn't have come either, if I'd been Simon, knowing what this Court was intended to resolve. I'd still been looking forward to seeing them, and maybe talking Simon into coming back to the City for a burrito after all this was concluded. Even if things dragged out all beyond reason, we should be done before dinner.

I focused on Arden, taking a deep breath. She inclined her head.

"You may speak," she said.

"Forgive me, Your Majesty, but are we ready to begin? This is a little more formal and a little less catastrophic than I'm used to, and I'm not quite sure what I'm supposed to be doing here . . . " A light titter ran through both sides of the room, more pronounced on the Undersea side. I didn't flinch. Not knowing all the rules of this sort of thing means getting it wrong sometimes.

It had taken me a long time to realize, but the manners and etiquette my mother drilled into me weren't designed to make me a productive member of Court. She didn't teach me diplomacy, or how to organize a wedding, or what questions I could ask a Queen. She taught me to curtsey and demur, lessons I converted to bowing and demanding basically the day I got my title. If she couldn't keep me away from Faerie completely, she'd been preparing me to be a servant.

Thanks, Mom. What a wonderful legacy you tried to leave me.

"Not quite," said Arden. "We're waiting for one more witness, and then we can get started."

I blinked, looking around the room. Gillian was with the Roane, half-concealed behind Elizabeth Norton, looking anxious about the whole situation. I couldn't blame her. She wasn't expected to testify today, but we were talking about waking up a woman who'd almost killed her, and maybe my greatest failing as a mother is that that sentence isn't "*the* woman who'd almost killed her." Being my kid is hazardous sometimes. It's not fair. Dean was with Dianda. I looked back to Arden.

"Who?" I blurted.

The door opened behind me. I turned.

The Luidaeg, immortal, terrible, terrifying sea witch, was stepping into the room. As usual when she didn't feel like being fancy, she was working hard to make sure I couldn't be the most informally dressed person in the room, barefoot in denim overalls, with no socks or shirt in evidence. Her dark, curly hair was pulled into pigtails, one over each shoulder, and secured with electrical tape. Everything about her was perfectly human. Even her ears were rounded, normally a decent indicator of whether or not someone has any fae blood in them.

She looked toward the rest of us and smirked. "I was aiming to be late," she said. "Did I manage it?"

"By several minutes, yes," said Arden. "Congratulations. We have all waited on your pleasure."

The Luidaeg smiled, showing teeth as serrated as a shark's. Even when she looked completely human in every other regard, she rarely bothered with her teeth. "Good." She turned back to the door, which she was still holding open with one hand, and even at a distance, I could see her face soften. "Don't worry. If anyone's in trouble here, it's me, and Queenie wouldn't dare to discipline me, even if she had the authority."

The same spell that made my voice fill the room was working on hers. Unlike me, she didn't seem to mind. No one else said a word. When the sea witch wants to be a little bit of a jerk, it's best to just sit back and let her.

I don't remember her being this active when I was younger. Yeah, I spent a lot of time and energy avoiding most of Faerie, but she was the story fae parents told their children to frighten them into behaving. It's hard to be fundamentally terrified of a woman who wears overalls without a bra because she doesn't like underwires, eats ice cream straight from the carton, and most of all is so devastatingly lonely that when I started coming around and treating her like a person, instead of like a terrifying force of nature, she encouraged me to keep doing it. So she must not have been around enough for the scary to wear off until after I got back from the pond.

She plays chess with Quentin. Sometimes he even beats her, and rather than transforming him into something unpleasant in punishment, she seems pleased by the fact that he's not only improving, he's not afraid of her. Given that he'll run the continent someday, this is either a good thing or proof that I've completely destroyed his sense of self-preservation.

A smaller figure stepped into the room, anxiously smoothing her white eyelet lace sundress with her hands before reaching for the Luidaeg. The Luidaeg took the girl's hand in her own and started toward me, leaving the door to swing shut behind her.

Only not quite, as an orange hand caught it, and Poppy slipped into the room. In turn, the Luidaeg's Aes Sidhe apprentice held the door for a nondescript man with antlers sprouting from his brow. Oberon, King of All Faerie, was here.

And almost no one seemed to notice him, their eyes locked on the Luidaeg as she led Karen Brown across the floor toward us. Given how hard he was working to fly under the radar of all the people who would very much liked to have known that he was back, I had to wonder whether he'd have allowed the door to slam in his face if Poppy hadn't been there to catch it.

I wonder a lot of things where Oberon's concerned. He left us centuries ago, after a failed Ride—disrupted by my grandmother—resulted in the loss of one of his wives. Maybe if it had happened immediately, I'd understand a little better, but it didn't. He had time to plan his exit, lock the doors to deeper Faerie, and start a relationship with my grandmother, although he was gone before my mother was born. Titania vanished at the same time, and the dominant theory has always been that Oberon did something to her, forced her to go away in order to maintain the balance in Faerie. No one really knows for sure.

For a people with the capacity to live forever, the fae sure are bad at keeping track of our own history. It turns out the conscious mind can only hold on to so much memory at one time—more than that and everything starts getting jumbled up and curdling, turning into a useless soup of facts and fancies. So even the oldest purebloods tend to view anything that happened more than a few hundred years ago as something out of myth and legend. They remember the things that mattered to them personally. The rest just . . . drops away.

The Luidaeg stopped next to me, hand still wrapped tight around Karen's. Calmly, she looked at Arden and said, "I am Antigone of Albany, known in this modern time as the Luidaeg, mother of the Roane, binder of the Selkies. They fall beneath my power and my protection. I have agreed to waive my right to demand the Torquill girl's life in recompense for my charge's death. Her existence was possible only because my own brother felt the need to prey upon children, forcing her mother into an impossible decision. The Blodynbryd are vegetable in nature. It should have been no more possible for her to have a child with one among the Daoine Sidhe than it is for a human to grow wings and fly away without magical aid. Much of what Rayseline did was no fault of her own."

The room seemed to hold its breath.

"When last this matter was raised, I stood before you and said I would not see the girl awakened until the time was right. I was and am aware of the pain this caused her parents. I was and am also aware that both her parents are going to live forever, and she's only been asleep for four years, while my boy will be dead for the rest of time. Even if I have no intention to demand justice for Connor O'Dell's loss, a little more time drowned in dreams seems like a more than reasonable price to pay."

On the far side of the room, Sylvester covered his mouth and looked away, while Luna glared at the Luidaeg like rage alone would be enough to destroy her. It wouldn't. You need silver and iron wielded together to kill one of the Firstborn, and I hate that I've lived the sort of life where I have to know that.

"But that was a different time," said the Luidaeg, and glanced at Karen, who was watching Arden with a fixed, unblinking gaze, not acknowledging her sister at all. Cassandra was doing much the same. The two of them get along just fine, but Karen is a known oneiromancer, a kind of Seer that hasn't been seen in Faerie in centuries. Seers of any kind are almost impossibly rare, which is what makes it so odd that two of the five Brown children have demonstrated divinatory talents. Cassandra is an aeromancer, reading the future in the movement of air. Not many people know that. Putting a little distance between herself and her oracular sibling when they have to appear in public together helps her keep her secret.

As to why she'd need to, most of the Seers in Faerie are gone, wiped out years ago. Only the Roane and the Kitsune were able to survive, and the Roane only survived in part. No one's ever confirmed exactly why everyone who can see the future would be targeted, but I'm willing to bet Eira Rosynhwyr had something to do with all of it, not just with the destruction of the Roane. She doesn't like things she can't control.

"I would see everyone directly harmed by her actions. I would hear them consent to this," said the Luidaeg. "As Connor's Firstborn, I still retain that right."

"Of course," said Arden, with surprising grace for a Faerie Queen being ordered around in her own knowe. Then again, no one was going to lose respect for her because she backed down in front of the sea witch. Being Firstborn doesn't come with a title, but it comes with power. Lots and lots and *lots* of power. Some, like my mother, are still new or reclusive enough that no one knows enough to be afraid. Others, like the Luidaeg, have cut a large swath across our history, and we know damn well that they can wreck us if we get in their way.

The Luidaeg stepped back, and Arden gestured to both sides of the crowd. One by one, the people who were directly impacted by Raysel's actions came forward, first Dean, then Gillian, and finally Luna. The Luidaeg cocked her head, looking critically at Luna.

"Didn't realize I was also calling for the parents," she said. "You want to rethink this, rosebud?"

"No," said Luna. "The first sign that my daughter had lost her way in the dark was her attempt to poison me, her own mother, at the bidding of your sister."

Even she wasn't willing to say Eira's name. It didn't matter that the woman was sleeping in a sealed skerry, almost impossible to access without walking the Rose Road and petitioning the missing Queens—which implied that Maeve, at least, had to be answering and give a damn what happened to us—before you could reach Eira's bier. She was still Firstborn. She still might hear us.

The Luidaeg nodded, very slowly. "So we're going to say all of Rayseline's actions should have bearing on this decision, not only those undertaken on the day when she was elf-shot?"

We were moving into dangerous territory. I shot a helpless look at Arden. She met my eyes with a tiny shake of her head. No, this wasn't normal. No, Courts weren't supposed to begin with the presiding monarch having control wrested away from them. No, she wasn't going to intercede. If the Luidaeg wanted to run this show, the only person in this room even remotely powerful enough to take it from her was Oberon, and as those of us who knew he was here had all seen, his hobby seemed to be standing back and watching as his descendants broke things. He wasn't going to help.

Someone had to do something, or this was going to get real ugly. "I'd rather not legislate Raysel's entire existence, if you're cool with that," I said. "She was hurt, very badly, and then she was misled. Her actions were still her own."

"Yes!" said Luna, seizing on the part of that that I *least* wanted her to be seizing on. "She was damaged, and she was misled! And the one responsible is here, in this room, today!"

So Simon *was* at Court? It made sense, all things considered, but it probably hadn't been his best decision ever. Since he wasn't being charged with violation of the Law and was now technically resident of another Kingdom—Saltmist is a part of the Undersea Kingdom of Leucothea—he wasn't required to attend.

But the crowd parted, and two men moved through it, both Daoine Sidhe, one redhaired, the other with hair the coppery color of bronze, covered in a light layer of verdigris. That's not as odd as it might seem; the Daoine Sidhe never met a color they couldn't incorporate into their ridiculously over-bright aesthetic. Their hands were locked together, and the redhead looked like he was going to be sick.

I shot him a reassuring smile. His expression softened, some of the fear slipping away. Simon still wasn't used to people being kind to him when they didn't want something, doubly so when that kindness came from me, the daughter he'd never asked for and really had nothing to do with.

They stopped with the other witnesses, Simon not letting go of Patrick's hand as he faced Luna. "I'm here, sister," he said.

"I'm not your sister," she spat.

"Oh, did you and my brother divorce? I'm so sorry, we don't always get the news down in the Undersea. Or is that the true purpose of waking dear Rayseline so early? So that she might approve your separation? I highly recommend it. Divorce is quite freeing, really." He looked past her to Sylvester, still surrounded by the crowd on the other side of the room. "It allows one to pursue so many new opportunities in life, and a change might do you good."

Sylvester flushed and looked away. Luna narrowed her eyes, watching her brother-in-law with a fierce hatred that was almost enough to startle even me. "Shut your mouth. I asked you to come forth to admit what you did to my daughter."

"It ranks among my greatest shames, and since my senses have been returned to me, I've made no effort to conceal it." Simon looked, not to Luna but to the Luidaeg, meeting her gaze without flinching. "Many years ago, to save the heart and hope of the man I loved best in all the world, I surrendered myself to your sister, Lady, whose name I dare not speak, lest it attract her attention even now. She was my Firstborn, and I was helpless before her desires. Whatever she asked of me, I would do. And still I fought, long and long, to remain my own man as best I could, until the day my daughter disappeared. That was when she owned me, utterly and without exception. I became her creature, and what she demanded, I did, without hesitation. I never killed for her. The woman to whom I was given did. My hands are not completely clean."

"But you never broke the Law, failure," said the Luidaeg. She somehow managed to make that cruel nickname sound almost kind, like she was reminding him that he had failed to fully become a monster. It was a nice trick. Tilting her head very slightly to the side, she asked, "What does this have to do with Rayseline Torquill?"

The Luidaeg can't lie. A question, by definition, can be misleading, but it can't be entirely false. I realized she was giving Simon the opportunity to tell his side of the story before the gathered Court, something he might otherwise never have had, since he hadn't broken the Law; many of these people had been at his wedding to Dianda and Patrick but still considered him a monster.

His breath caught, gaze dipping toward the floor. "Must I?" he asked, in a defeated tone.

"Yes," said the Luidaeg, much more gently. "You must. You live beneath my waters now, and I am one of the few threats your lady wife can't fight on your behalf. Now answer me."

"My . . . my keeper wanted to see my brother's strength disrupted. He strayed too far from what she desired in the Daoine Sidhe, and he had married the child of one of her greatest enemies. She saw the opportunity to harm a wayward child of her own line and a descendant of Maeve at the same time, and she ordered me to dispose of my brother's wife, to end her like the beast she presented herself to be. The child as well, if I could take them together without being seen."

Sylvester gasped, the sound small but somehow huge at the same time, even beyond what the spell should have been able to amplify. Luna didn't even blink.

Simon continued: "She intended their deaths, that was clear, but as she failed to directly and explicitly order them . . . I had little ability to twist my keeper's orders, but I did what I could. Beasts, when disposed of, must be kept in cages, and that was what she had technically ordered me to do. I began spinning a spell to hold my target in a space as good as death. My keeper always liked it when I chose to be cruel for her. I thought . . . " He paused, throat working as he swallowed. "I thought she would be proud of me for causing so much pain."

The grief in his voice was raw and unmistakable. Luna's expression didn't soften. Sylvester looked away.

Simon kept talking. "I still had free passage of my then-wife's land, and when next Luna stepped foot there, I was waiting. I would have preferred she not have the child in her company, but she did, and as Oleander was with me, if I stole away the woman and spared the girl, she would have killed her for the amusement of it. So I had to take them both."

This was a part of the story I hadn't heard before. I blinked, listening attentively.

"She and her daughter were picking wildflowers," he said. "They wandered from the border of my brother's land onto the edge of Amandine's, and we were waiting for them. We hadn't done anything to lure them. We couldn't. Sylvester would have known in an instant if I tried anything, and I was not prepared to confront my brother. So we saw our chance, and grabbed them when they were vulnerable, and swept them away. I used Luna's blood to open a channel to the Rose Road, and we walked it to the domain of Blind Michael, who had known Oleander once of old."

That was news to me. Had she been one of his children? Had she fallen into that dark and corrupted forest and escaped it somehow, or had she come to him as a fellow monster, if a lesser one? The room was rapt, watching him, and Simon deflated slightly under the collective weight of the Court's gaze.

"He granted us a vial of his blood, laughing at the request. I doubt he would have laughed if he'd known who we ultimately served, but in the moment, he seemed to find the idea of locking his runaway daughter in a prison he played a part in creating more than amusing enough. He asked . . . " He stopped then, and swallowed. "He asked for his granddaughter, in compensation for the child he had lost. He said she would be happy in his halls, and I knew he lied, and so I lied in turn, and said that the girl's imprisonment had been a part of our agreement with my mistress."

So it could have been worse. Raysel could have grown up in Blind Michael's hands. "Wait," I blurted. "Acacia didn't know Luna had a daughter."

"We spoke to the monster, not the matron," said Simon, sounding almost relieved to be talking about something other than his own misdeeds. "Oleander felt it best to avoid her eye, for fear of tipping off a war between the Firstborn, with us at the center."

"Oh." It made sense. I just didn't like it.

"So we took the monster's blood and followed the Rose Road into the dark, where I used what he had given us and the spell I had prepared together to weave a pocket realm capable of sustaining both itself and the lives of those inside it," Simon continued. "Time would pass there. The realm would provide basic sustenance. But there would be no light, no variance, nothing to distract or allow for any form of escape. I believed my mistress would free them in short order, when she had wrung the concessions she desired from my brother. And in honesty, I had saved their lives. I was in her thrall. She didn't leave me with much capacity to care."

He was looking at the floor by this point, talking without pause or any real inflection. He sounded like a man defeated.

"My brother engaged my wife's second daughter, who was legally my own but wanted none of me, and knew nothing of what I might be to her, to find his missing family. He tasked her to track me, and my mistress again saw an opportunity. She commanded us to remove October from the situation. Those were her exact words. 'The girl troubles me. Remove her.'"

His voice finally broke. He lifted his head, turning to look at me. "I thank Oberon every day for the binding he placed on his child, forbidding her to do direct harm to those he had claimed, and for the fact that he claimed your mother before he left us. She couldn't order me to kill you. And I couldn't disobey a direct order. Saving my brother's wife and daughter had spent the last of her good graces; she would never have tolerated a second refusal from me. Had she ordered me to kill you, I would have had no choice. I'm so sorry."

THREE

LUNA SMIRKED, THE EXPRESSION of dismayed displeasure she'd been wearing throughout this story giving way to something smugger and more self-satisfied. So this was why she'd asked if we could hold Raysel's second appeal on the anniversary of my return from the pond. She'd done it to hurt Simon, not to hurt me. Oh, I was probably acceptable collateral damage in her eyes—Luna and I hadn't exactly been getting along for the last several years—but this was all aimed at hurting him.

From the look on her face, she expected that admission to upset me. I glanced to the Luidaeg for permission, then walked toward Simon, still standing hand-in-hand with Patrick. Both watched my approach warily, but neither of them moved again.

"Fuck her," I said, and put my arms around Simon's shoulders, hugging him from the side. Startled, he let go of Patrick's hand and put his arms around me in turn. I looked at Luna as I spoke. "She wanted you to kill your sister-in-law and niece, and you didn't. She wanted you to kill me, even if she couldn't say so in as many words, and you didn't. Your Firstborn tried to make you break the Law, and you managed to evade her at every turn. You're not on trial here, and even if you were, I'd find you innocent."

Simon made a choked noise and said nothing. Luna glared at me.

The Luidaeg cleared her throat. "October is correct. We're not here to audit the crimes of Simon Lorden. Why have you asked him to present a recounting of what he did to your daughter? His crimes are well documented and known, and have been paid for tenfold."

"If he hadn't broken her mind in the dark, she would never have done the things she did," spat Luna.

"And if my sister hadn't used her influence over her own descendants to control him, he would never have taken her," said the Luidaeg. "This is a game that can go on forever, little rose, and some of its roots are deep and poisonous. Or do you want your own crimes held up to the light? Of you, the failure, and your child, only you have unquestionably broken the Law. Would you prefer this day become an accounting of everyone's past transgressions?"

Luna recoiled. "I'm not the one under discussion here," she spat.

"I'm sure Hoshibara's parents wish you were," said the Luidaeg. "Or that you would be, one day. Regardless, I still fail to see what Simon has to do with Raysel's choices. She made them after she was free, she made them willingly, and she acted of her own accord."

"She was working with Dugan," I said, not letting go of Simon.

"Yes," said the Luidaeg. "And Dugan was working with my sister's puppet queen. But there's never been any evidence that my sister directly influenced Rayseline's actions, or that they even met in person. Raysel made poor choices. She made dangerous choices. She still acted of her own free will. Does anyone contest this?"

Luna looked like she wanted to. Unfortunately, the only piece of evidence she had left to present—that Raysel had also been working with Oleander, who had a much closer relationship to Evening—wasn't going to do her any favors, since Raysel was directly responsible for Oleander's death.

She could still be charged with that violation of the Law, even with the Luidaeg and the Roane allowing her clemency for both Connor's death and the death of a Selkie woman I had never met.

Raysel hadn't known at the time, and neither had I, but Selkies were close enough to human that elf-shot was fatal to them. She was a killer, absolutely. She had also been using a weapon she believed was safe to aim at her own kind.

Finally, slowly, I let go of Simon, looking to the Luidaeg. She nodded, and I said, very clearly, "No. I do not contest that Rayseline Torquill acted of her own free will when she abducted my daughter, Gillian Marks, from her home with intent to do her damage."

"I do not contest that Rayseline Torquill acted of her own free will when she stole my sons from what should have been safety and imprisoned them, intending to do them damage," said Patrick. "Her puppeteers hoped to start a war. Had they succeeded, I would be calling for her death."

Luna looked like she wanted to say something. Showing rare restraint, she didn't.

"She was definitely acting of her own free will when she cut off my finger," said Dean, holding up his left hand to show the gap between his middle finger and his thumb. It had healed cleanly, and the scar tissue shone in the light. Making eye contact with Luna, he said, "She knew what she was doing. But we understand violence in the Undersea, even if it's unusual on the land. I knew what she was doing, too. I hold a lot of grudges. I don't think they're enough to leave her sleeping."

"Without her, I could have been—I don't even know what I could have been, and now I never will," said Gillian. "But I'm happy. I have Firtha, and the Roane, and the whole wide sea. Without her, I'd be a different person. I like who I am enough not to regret it."

"All right," said the Luidaeg. She looked to Arden on her throne. "The last time we stood here, I listened to everything said, and to the holes where nothing could be spoken, since the failure was still asleep in his own bower, and I refused. As sea witch and Lady of the Lake and mother of the Roane, I refused to see the child who had done me and mine such injury awakened."

"Yes," said Arden, apparently feeling like she was allowed to rejoin the conversation at this point. "You did. Have matters changed?"

"The time was wrong before," said the Luidaeg. She set her hand on Karen's shoulder. "The tides have shifted, and the girl can wake now, if Your Majesty agrees."

It was nicely done, the little reminder that she knew Arden was in charge here: she might be Firstborn, but this wasn't her Kingdom. Arden nodded, settling back in her throne.

"The evidence has been presented, and as no one stands before us to charge the girl with violation of the Law, she can be awakened as soon as the tincture is prepared."

Beside her, Cassandra cleared her throat. Arden glanced over, eyebrows raised.

"Something to say, Miss Brown?"

"Only that Walther anticipated this might be the outcome, and left a sufficient dose to wake her when he went to work this morning." She reached into her tunic, pulling out a small bottle filled with glittering pink liquid. Walther had been refining and improving his elf-shot cure since he first developed it. The earliest iterations had required constant refrigeration to stay stable. Now they could sit at room temperature for hours.

Before he went to work, huh? Maybe Walther and Cassandra's relationship was even farther along than I'd thought. Well, good for them. They deserved something nice for themselves.

"Then all we need to do is send a healer to Shadowed Hills so it can be administered, and she can be awake before sunset," said Arden. The room continued to watch her expectantly. She sighed. "Right, the formal part. I, Queen Arden Windermere in the Mists officially declare Rayseline Torquill's slumber at an end; she may be awakened, free to rejoin Faerie and her family."

"We don't have to send anyone to Shadowed Hills," said Luna, gathering a bit of her wounded dignity about her, like she thought it might change things somehow. She turned to the group that had accompanied her, and they parted, spreading out in what I'm sure was meant to be some sort of grand reveal. It was a reveal, at least to me. Grand, however, is very much up to the onlooker.

Instead, I had one question: "How did you get a *glass coffin* all the way to Muir Woods?"

Luna turned back to me as Sylvester's knights carried her sleeping daughter toward us. "Magic, of course."

"Sure of yourself this time, weren't you, rosebud?" asked the Luidaeg, tone utterly mild.

"I had no intention of being denied again," said Luna. "Had you attempted to refuse my daughter's awakening, I would have raised an objection."

The Luidaeg lifted an eyebrow. "And how do you think that would have gone?"

"Thankfully, we're not going to find out," I said brightly. "Because we're going to wake her up, and no one's going to go out of their way to upset the *sea witch* right now, right? I, for one, don't want to see what happens when you summon an entire ocean into a receiving room."

I'd be fine, probably. One of my wedding gifts was a guarantee from Amphitrite, Firstborn of the Merrow, that neither I nor Tybalt nor any children I might have would ever suffer death by water. Amphitrite being Firstborn, and non-malicious Firstborn at that, I was pretty sure that protection would extend to Quentin and Raj, as my "sons." And May is literally impossible to kill. That didn't mean I wanted to find out for sure, or that other people couldn't be hurt if the Luidaeg lost her temper.

"Do you really think I'd do something like that?" asked the Luidaeg.

"Yes," I said—in harmony with Dean, Gillian, and Quentin, who had moved closer when the formal structure of the moment started breaking down.

Rather than looking upset with our lack of faith, the Luidaeg smiled and took her hand off Karen's shoulder, gesturing for her to join me. Karen yawned broadly and wandered to my side, slumping lightly over to lean against me. At seventeen, there was considerably more of her to lean than there used to be, and she looked tired every time

I saw her. I'd expressed my concern about it to the Luidaeg several times, since she seemed to be serving unofficially as the woman's apprentice; sea witch or no, I wasn't going to have her exhausting my honorary niece.

It had taken until my third attempt for the Luidaeg to answer with anything more than vagueness and handwaving. But that time, she had looked at me, calm as the sea before the storm, and said, "She's an oneiromancer whether I train her or not, October. She'll probably be asleep twenty-two hours a day by the time she stops growing. She'll wake up to eat and relieve herself, then go right back to sleep. By the time she's a hundred, even that won't be true waking, just sleepwalking from one moment to the next. That happens whether I teach her to control her power or not. That happens whether I let her be a normal girl as long as she can or not. But this is my only window for teaching her how to control what she is. She's tired because her magic makes her tired. I'm not letting her rest because she's going to have centuries where that's all she can do. Got a problem with it? Take it up with Faerie."

That had been enough for me, because the Luidaeg can't lie: if she said she was doing what she could to help Karen while it was still possible, she meant it. So I just put my arm around the girl, helping to prop her up, and let her lean against me as her older sister descended the dais, Walther's cure in hand, and moved toward the group.

"I'll call for a healer, then," said Arden, trying to maintain some illusion of control over the situation.

"No need, Your Highness," said Luna, and curtseyed deeply to our mutual Queen. "We brought our own."

"Er, hi," said Jin, stepping through the crowd. She stopped at a polite distance to curtsey but never took her eyes off the Queen. "Um, wow. I had somehow managed not to be in a room with you up until this point, Your Highness. And . . . you look so much like your father. I'm sorry."

I blinked. Jin had been here for the convocation where the elf-shot treatment was approved for use by the collected monarchs of our neighboring Kingdoms, but looking back, I couldn't remember a time when she and Arden had been in the same room. I could remember times when I'd been yelling for Jin, trying to get her to come and solve a problem, and been unable to find her. Had it been because she was avoiding our Queen?

Arden blinked. "Come again?"

"Oh, oak and ash, I'm sorry. My name is Jin. I served in the Court of your grandparents when it was new. I, um, may have encouraged your father to court your mother when he didn't think it was possible. You knew me when you were a child. I looked very different then."

That, at least, wouldn't be a surprise to anyone. Jin is Ellyllon, and Ellyllon molt every few years, shedding their faces and forms and exchanging them for something new. Judging by the way her skin had started to pale in the last year, she was approaching the point of her next molt, and we'd all have to learn her face over again. For her, that's just normal. That's the way the world is supposed to work.

Arden, however, stared. She'd been outside of Faerie for long enough that sometimes things that seem ordinary to the rest of us are revelations to her. "Jin?" she asked. "Really? You mean you survived the earthquake?"

From her tone, what came next could be either tears or a declaration of treason. We got the first. Eyes bright, she waved a hand and vanished from her throne, reappearing next to Jin and wrapping her arms around the other woman as she sobbed into her shoulder. Jin embraced her back, and the two of them clung to each other.

More fun things about a world where people habitually live for centuries: there's a whole lot of buried history just waiting to blow up in your face. I turned to Luna, who was staring at the pair, open-mouthed. "Your healer is unavailable," I said. "I've administered this tincture before. May I . . . ?"

Luna desperately looked like she wanted to tell me no. The impulse visibly warred with her desire to have Raysel awake as soon as possible. Finally, grudgingly, she said, "Yes."

Taking the bottle from Cassandra's hand, I moved into the crowd around the coffin. It was made up of familiar faces, only about half of whom were willing to meet my eyes. I swallowed the urge to rage at them for their cowardice. We were knights of the same hall, they and I, and would be unless and until Sylvester released me from his service. We had sworn fealty to the same hand, pledged our loyalty to the same command. How dare they act as if I had no business walking among them? Just because I was currently banned from the space that should have been my safety, that always had been before?

It wasn't right and it wasn't fair and Sylvester was violating at least a dozen rules of hospitality by refusing to let me come home. Tybalt could probably have named them all, detailing all the ways in which my liege was failing me. He wasn't Sylvester's biggest fan and never had been, even when we'd been on better terms. And that wasn't why we were here, because there was no degree of rudeness or neglect that could have been enough to justify punishing Raysel for her father's actions.

Etienne was closest to the coffin. He *did* meet my eyes, giving a small nod before he opened the lid, which swung as easily as if it were made of nothing but dust and moonbeams. Raysel was exposed to the open air for the first time since being removed from her parents' knowe.

Most people, when elf-shot, wake up looking exactly the way they did when they went to sleep. Elf-shot puts adult purebloods into something that's closer to a state of suspended animation than actual slumber, since for them, the end of childhood means the cessation of physical changes. They live, they get shot, they sleep for a century, and they wake up with nothing more to show for it than dusty skin and maybe a sore back. I don't know what would happen if someone elf-shot a pureblood child. I've never heard of it happening intentionally, and we have a treatment now. So what would happen now, today, is we would wake the kid up, and then I would kick the crap out of anyone who thought it was a good idea to elf-shoot them in the first place.

It wasn't going to be like that for Raysel. When she'd gone to sleep, she'd been perfectly balanced between Blodynbryd and Daoine Sidhe, and that had been a large part of the problem. As I said before, the fae *aren't* human. We're something else entirely, but sometimes we can have children with human beings—or with each other, when our biology is closely enough aligned to make it work. Not every kind of fae is compatible with every other kind. As a Blodynbryd, Luna wasn't truly a mammal, more a rosebush that had grown to echo a woman's form and function. She wouldn't have been able to have a child with Sylvester, who was Daoine Sidhe, and as mammalian as they come, except that she had stolen the skin of a dying Kitsune girl in her father's forest. Magic being what it is, the change had been more than just skin-deep.

Even Luna hadn't been able to transform herself enough to become completely mammalian, but she'd become close enough to have a daughter with Sylvester, and Raysel had been born delicate, primed to shatter under the kind of abuse her uncle subjected her to, because her body had been at war with itself. Purebloods have lots of stories about something they call "changeling madness," where the minds of changelings tear themselves apart because they can't handle the strain of being mortal and immortal at the same time. Maybe that happens and maybe it doesn't: I've seen plenty of changelings with issues, but given that we're treated as a disposable underclass by our own society, constantly marginalized and shoved aside, I think that's less biology and more generational trauma. No. I think those stories come more from edge cases like Raysel's, children who should have been impossible, inevitably falling to pieces as time puts more and more of a strain on seams that should never have formed in the first place.

So after Raysel was elf-shot, I had used blood magic to go into her dreams, and I had offered her the Choice only the hope chests and the Dóchas Sidhe can grant. I had offered to make the slow war between the two halves of what she was come to a peaceful end, by removing one of the combatants from the battlefield. She had gone to sleep appearing mostly Daoine Sidhe, save for the slant of her ears, the softness of her features, and a faint pinkness at the roots of her hair. She was waking up the rest of the way there. Her bones were sharper now, her ears more pointed, and her hair redder.

She looked like a female version of her father, and I only

hoped she'd take it as well awake as she had asleep. I bent carefully over her, opening the bottle in my hand, and pressed it to her lips, sliding one hand under her head to lift it up and allow gravity to encourage her to drink. The trick to giving anything orally to an elf-shot victim is keeping them from choking in the process.

Something about the magic in the mixture allows them to swallow rather than letting the liquid run back out of their mouths. The room fell quiet as the seconds passed, me pouring the liquid drop by drop into Raysel's mouth, her sleeping peacefully on.

Finally, loudly, Luna demanded, "Why isn't it *working*?"

And Raysel opened her eyes.

They were the clear, pale gold of acacia honey, rimmed in a thin line of darker gold, and slightly unfocused as she blinked and tried to recover her bearings. Finally, she pulled away from me and the liquid I was still dripping into her mouth, swallowing one last time as she sat up in her coffin, looking around the room.

I took a step back, tilting the bottle up so as not to pour the rest of the mixture onto the floor. She didn't need to drink the whole thing for it to be effective; according to Walther, as soon as a sleeper woke, that was it. The spell was broken, and their body would clear the last of the poison with the tincture's help. If more mortal medicine worked like that, we'd have fewer issues with their hospital system.

Luna made a choked sound and shoved me out of the way in her rush to get to Raysel's side. Raysel blinked in confusion as Luna yanked her into a fierce hug. The confusion was probably twofold: the last time they'd both been awake, Luna had still been wearing her stolen Kitsune skin. This pink-haired, white-skinned woman was a stranger.

But the smell of her magic was the same, and Raysel was entirely Daoine Sidhe now. She inhaled and relaxed, allowing Luna's embrace to continue and even lifting her own arms to join it. As she did so, she looked over her mother's shoulder at me and mouthed, "You promised."

Shit. Maybe it was cowardly of me, but I'd honestly been

hoping she would have forgotten. Despite that, I had taken steps to prepare in case she hadn't. I turned to face Arden. She was no longer clinging to Jin. Instead, the two of them were standing a foot or so apart, holding hands and talking quietly.

I squared my shoulders and took a deep breath before asking, "Is this Court still open?"

Arden glanced in my direction, looking briefly like she didn't understand the question. Then she shook her head to clear it, dropping Jin's hands, and said, "Of course, Sir Daye. What can the Court of the Mists do for you?"

She was using her customer service voice. Unsurprisingly, she wasn't happy to be interrupted. Well, I wasn't happy to be doing the interrupting, and Sylvester and Luna weren't going to be happy about what I was about to do, so at least the misery was getting spread around.

"As Rayseline Torquill is awake, I wish to officially claim offense against her for the abduction and assault upon my daughter."

A gasp filled the room, uttered in unison by almost everyone present. But not me, not Tybalt, and most importantly, not Raysel.

Arden blinked, eyebrows climbing as she took in what I'd just said. "Are you sure, Sir Daye?"

"I am."

Claiming offense is an old fae tradition that seems to have arisen mostly because we don't have much in the way of actual Laws. We have a lot of traditions and rules of etiquette, but we don't have a system of formalized and codified justice. Given what a shitshow justice is in the mortal world, maybe this is better. I don't think so, though. I think it has just as many problems, and even less accountability, since at the end of the day, the buck stops with the local monarch and whatever they decide.

Anyway, claiming offense against someone means expressing what they did to wrong you, what you want the consequences to be, and letting the local authorities decide how it's going to work out. I don't fully understand it, and I've usually been on the receiving side, not the initiating. Luna made a small sound of barely suppressed rage behind me. Sylvester stepped toward me, one hand up, like he thought he could make me retract the words.

"She doesn't mean that, Your Highness," he said, sounding almost desperate. "Sir Daye is obviously just confused. She would have spoken to me, as her liege, if she meant that—"

"When?" I asked, spinning to face him. He stared at me in obvious confusion, golden eyes so much like his daughter's that it hurt to look at them. "When would I have spoken to you, Sylvester? You've banned me from Shadowed Hills, even though I've done *nothing wrong*, and you don't answer the phone when I call. Did you think I was going to send a letter, maybe? Tie a note to a pixie and make them play go-between? You can't shut me out and then act surprised when you don't know what I've been doing! I am *not* confused. I came here today to wake Raysel if the Queen allowed, and to claim offense against her as soon as she was able to speak in her own defense."

"I can't," said Raysel, voice a little creaky from disuse, but still clear and carrying. "I did what she says I did. I caused harm, and it doesn't matter if I understood that I was doing it, it still happened. Her claim is valid. I have no defense for myself."

"No," snarled Luna. She appeared next to Sylvester, moving fast, looking at me with such venomous loathing in her eyes that I took a half-step back. How did we get here? How did we go from her being the closest thing I had to a mother figure to her looking at me like that? I didn't know, not really, but I knew there was no going back.

"No," she repeated, stabbing her finger at me like she thought she could do actual damage with the gesture. "You *can't* claim offense against my daughter. You're a *changeling*. You don't have the authority."

"Luna . . . " Sylvester began.

She turned her glare on him, and he quailed. "Don't say anything. You may like to pretend she belongs in Faerie, that she deserves her position and her place, but we both know she's mortal. She's here on sufferance. She can't claim offense against a pureblood. It's not *allowed*." There was a malicious triumph in her last word.

"Perhaps not," said Tybalt, voice low and dark and barely above a growl. "But none can contest my place in Faerie, and the girl Rayseline harmed is my daughter by marriage. If you will not allow my lady to claim offense, then I will claim it on her behalf."

Luna narrowed her eyes. "You have no claim on the girl, and she has no claim on your titles or bloodline. I refuse to allow the pretense that you're allowed to claim offense for her."

"Gillian is pureblooded Roane," said Tybalt. "Will you really claim Faerie's justice does not apply to her?"

"She wasn't when she was injured," snarled Luna. "She was the changeling daughter of a changeling woman, and she has no right to our justice for transgressions committed when that was so."

The Luidaeg was watching this all go down, looking faintly amused, which is never as good a thing as it might seem. Oberon was also watching, from the back of the crowd. He looked more distressed. I couldn't bring myself to feel bad for him. I wanted to shake him and shout for him to fix this. We were his descendants, in some cases literally his children, and he was the one who'd overseen the creation of this whole stupid system! He should have been stepping in to make it better, or at least to make it less broken, and instead he was lurking around the edges like a stray dog who wasn't sure whether they'd be welcomed or whipped. And I was getting damn tired of it.

"Then maybe you'll allow *my* claim of offense," said Dianda. She sounded almost chipper about it, like this was the most fun she'd had in weeks. She strolled languidly over to stand next to Dean, who hadn't said a word through this whole exchange. "She abducted and mutilated my oldest son. She stranded my youngest son away from the water long enough that he could have suffered serious damage. Much longer, and this would be a very different sort of trial. I'm less forgiving than the sea witch. I wouldn't waive the charges of murder." She looked to Arden. "I know I'm not your subject, but in this matter, I'll place myself at your command. May I have my justice?"

Arden nodded, slowly. "You may claim your offense."

"But—" began Luna.

"Duchess Torquill, I may run a casual Court here, but I am the Queen in the Mists, heir to Gilad, who had been heir to Denley, first King in the Mists. My word is law within these halls." Arden looked coldly at Luna. "If this is not something you can live with, perhaps you should seek another Kingdom. Be aware, however, that if you depart, the fact that multiple of my citizens and one of my neighbors have attempted to claim offense against your daughter will travel with you, and you will find no harbor among my peers."

Luna visibly deflated. Sullenly, she said, "I apologize, Your Majesty."

"Excellent." Arden looked to Dianda. "The transgression against your house was a terrible one. What amends would you ask of the girl?"

"She will spend a year in service to Sir Daye's household, and return to her parents' halls at the end of that time only if she and Sir Daye both agree that her debt has been paid," said Dianda. "I would take her home with me, but I think her presence might discomfort one of my husbands. I'm still trying to get him to believe that we're not going to get rid of him the moment he becomes inconvenient; bringing in a lady's maid designed to remind him of what *that woman* made him do strikes me as unkind."

"Sir Daye? Is this acceptable to you?"

Of course it was. We had anticipated Luna's objection and arranged for Dianda's intercession beforehand, in case she also objected to Tybalt. "It is," I said.

"You'll have to feed and house the girl. It seems unfair to place an additional burden upon you in the name of delivering satisfaction."

"I have a guest room," I said. "My home was a gift from my liege, Raysel's father, and is more than large enough to house her as well. May already cooks almost everything in industrial quantities. Feeding Raysel won't be a problem, and as long as she's not allergic to cats, we are a more than suitable environment."

"Then the claim of offense is granted and fulfilled," said Arden. "Rayseline Torquill, for your actions against the

House of Lorden and the Duchy of Saltmist, you will spend the next year of your waking life in service to Sir October Daye. You will live in her home, and you will enter the Duchy of your parents only in her company. At the end of that time, if you both agree, you may return to Shadowed Hills. If you do not agree, your service will continue. Do you understand?"

"I do," said Raysel. She had climbed out of her coffin at some point, and was standing next to Etienne, her hands behind her back, her chin high. "I am grateful for the opportunity to make amends for some of the damage I have done."

"You can't intend to let Sir Daye make off with our daughter when she's just been awakened!" snapped Luna. "It's unreasonable to expect that from her! Or from us! She deserves the chance to recuperate from what she's been through before she begins a year of senseless servitude! Just let us take her home, and—"

"And spread the offense my house claims against *her* to your entire Duchy?" asked Dianda. "I specified that she was not to return to Shadowed Hills without Sir Daye's company until both agreed her debt had been repaid. Or are you finally allowing October to come home?"

Luna stopped dead, eyes widening as she recognized the walls of the cage she had just built around herself. If she let me come back to Shadowed Hills with Raysel, she was admitting my banishment had been purely for her comfort, and Sylvester wouldn't have an excuse to shut me out again—especially not now that I clearly had an army of purebloods willing to claim offense on my behalf if I wasn't allowed to claim it for myself. I hadn't done anything wrong. He was my liege. Locking the doors against me broke a dozen rules of hospitality, and she knew it.

So did Etienne. He looked deeply relieved by Dianda's question, shoulders relaxing. He glanced at Raysel, who was perfectly still, the only motion a small muscle in her jaw that kept twitching.

"I don't . . . She allowed . . . Why are you involving yourself in this matter?"

"Because your precious little petal hurt my boys," said

Dianda. She raised her voice slightly, even though the amplification spell on the room meant it was entirely unnecessary. "No one hurts my boys."

Patrick put an arm around Simon's shoulders, pulling the other man close, glaring at Luna in a way that made it perfectly clear how many names were on that list.

"And because Toby's family," continued Dianda. "Unlike some people, I acknowledge that sort of thing. Sorry if that makes you uncomfortable. It's just how I was raised."

"The sea is not meant to involve itself so directly with the land," said Luna.

"Did you miss the part where I just said Toby was family?" asked Dianda. "She's my husband's kid. That makes her mental health my problem, and you're trying to damage her mental health, which means I have to deal it with it. So yeah, I'm allowed to involve myself, because Toby's involved, and *my son* is involved, and you're being sort of an asshole right now, I hope you understand that."

"Root and branch, this better not be the way we kick off a war," I muttered—or tried to, anyway. The amplification spell caught that, too, making it way louder than it needed to be.

Luna shot me a scandalized look. "I wouldn't drive Faerie to *war*," she said.

"I don't know, sort of seems like you're trying," said Raysel. "Sir Daye claimed offense against me because I asked her to."

Luna gasped. "How—You've been asleep. You couldn't ask anyone for anything."

"You sent her into my dreams to change the balance of my blood, to make me one way or the other," said Raysel. Her voice was clear, but her hands were starting to shake. She'd told me once that it was easier for her to think when she was asleep, when she had the time to figure out what she was going to do or say next, and we were running up against the edges of the confrontation as she had scripted it for herself. "You were fine with me making choices while I was asleep then."

"I did it to save you," said Luna. "Your body was tearing itself apart. I shouldn't have been able to have you, my little rose, my little treasure, and once your blood figured out that it was impossible, it wanted to let go. So I turned to your father's knight and asked her to remake you in an image that could survive."

"She gave me a choice, Mother. She asked what I wanted to be, and I chose Daoine Sidhe, and I'm not sorry. I can feel my magic starting to wake up, now that it's not spending all of its time fighting just to keep me alive. It's amazing. I think . . . " She kept looking at her mother, the muscle in her jaw jumping even harder. "I think I can be happy."

"So be happy with us," said Luna, desperately. "Be happy at home."

"I'm not sure I can." Raysel finally dropped her gaze to the floor. "You expect so much of me, and you don't see me the way I am now that I'm not your perfect little girl. You don't know who I am. *I* barely know who I am. I need to be somewhere else for a while, and right now, the best somewhere else is with October. So I asked her to claim offense when Father sent her into my dreams a second time, so that I could go someplace where I'd know I was safe, and might be able to sleep at night. You know. Without someone having to elf-shoot me first."

Silence filled the room after Raysel finished speaking. I already knew everything she'd just said, and even I hated the weight of it. I looked to Simon, who looked like he was going to be sick. Everything that had been said about why he'd done the things he'd done was true, but at the end of the day, even without Evening forcing his hand, he would have chosen to hurt Raysel if it meant getting August back. He'd been trying to save his daughter, and he'd seen another man's child as a reasonable exchange.

Maybe that's the way it always works. Someone else's child is always an acceptable form of currency. It's only when we start to see the consequences of those choices that we understand how much harm we've done.

"This Court is still active," said Arden, voice carrying like a shout through the silence. She barely needed the magical amplification. "Duchess Lorden's claim of offense has been heard and accepted, and will not be altered. Rayseline Torquill, you may, if you desire, have one hour's time to speak privately with your parents, but the choice of whether or not to return to Shadowed Hills is no longer your own. You will return there unaccompanied only when Sir Daye declares your debt repaid, and even then, only once a full year has passed. Do you understand?"

"I do," said Rayseline.

"Is there any further business for this Court?"

Surprising no one, there wasn't. With an expression of deep relief, Arden nodded.

"Then go peacefully and in the understanding that the rose and the tree will stand watch over us all until we meet again. This Court is closed. Our business is discharged. You may now away."

She clapped her hands and turned to face me, smiling. "Open roads and kind fires," she said, voice no longer magically amplified. "I'm pretty sure you're going to need them."

FOUR

IT WAS NO SURPRISE to anyone when Luna and Sylvester—the first glaring daggers, the second refusing to meet my eyes—bundled Raysel up and swept her away as soon as Court was finished. It was a bit more of a surprise when Etienne went with them but Jin stayed behind, falling into a muttered conversation with the Queen, Arden still seated on her throne, Jin's wings beating almost constantly.

I had better things to worry about, like moving to the side of the room with my own small group. "You did beautifully, Di," I said. "I was hoping things wouldn't have to go that far, but I still really appreciate it."

"And here I was hoping they'd go a little farther, and I'd have an excuse to kick that woman's teeth in."

"Aren't you normally all about the punching?"

Dianda shrugged. "I'm supposed to have legs for 'etiquette' reasons when I attend one of your land events, unless I'm trying to make a point. I may as well use them for something."

"Fair enough."

The Luidaeg, who had been watching our conversation with a predator's rapt interest, interrupted to say, "Wait, you *planned* this?"

"We did," I said. "Raysel really did ask me to claim offense against her, and I said I would, but a promise made in a dream isn't necessarily binding. I had to ask my family if they were okay with it."

"I'm not thrilled," said Quentin. "She hurt Dean. But that was before we were dating, and I don't think—Shadowed Hills isn't a great place to need someone to take care of you. It's better for Chelsea, because Bridget understands how to be a mom, and Etienne doesn't think he already knows everything, but it was pretty bad for me, and I was just a foster. I can't imagine sending Rayseline back into that when she wants out. And Dean said he'd be okay with it, as long as I didn't expect him to sit next to her during movie nights."

Meaning Raysel would be invited to movie nights. Interesting.

"I have no ground on which to stand when it comes to chiding my lady for the adoption of strays," said Tybalt. "Not only is it a habit in which I myself have been known to indulge, but without such inclinations, I might not be married to her."

"You were never a stray," I said. "A pain in my ass, sure, but not a stray."

"I'll always vote for mercy when I can," said May.

"That's . . . You know, coming from you merry band of fools, that's impressive as hell," said the Luidaeg. "I half-expected you to let her parents whisk her away and lock her in a tower like a fairy tale princess, ignoring the part where she needed a lot more help than she was ever going to get there, and turn her into your next great enemy. You're learning."

"She's going to get whatever help she needs," I said firmly. "Arden knows a couple of therapists who are aware of Faerie and equipped to deal with some of the weirder shit we have to live with. Raysel's going to have a door she can close and someone who won't judge her to talk to and she's not going anywhere near her parents unless she wants to."

"Which means I won't be dropping by uninvited until she can look at me without flinching and I can look at her without wanting to vomit," said Simon.

I turned to blink at him. I'd known he wouldn't be able to hang around Raysel without upsetting her, and we'd already discussed some of the ways to help with that. I hadn't been expecting himself to voluntarily exile himself from the house.

"We can meet somewhere in the City," he said. "It'll just take a bit more planning on our part. I know you're allergic to the concept, but I also know you're capable of it. It's best for everyone involved. Everyone deserves to feel safe."

"Yeah," I agreed. No burritos today. But maybe burritos tomorrow?

And then Karen, who had been standing quietly to the side, her eyes focused on nothing specific, screamed.

The amplification spell was gone, but the acoustics of the room were still made to help people communicate with large groups: they grabbed the sound, bouncing it from wall to wall until it seemed like the loudest thing that had ever existed. The Luidaeg recoiled, visibly startled.

"Karen?" she asked.

Karen didn't seem to hear her. She was clutching at the sides of her face, bending almost double as she screamed.

The smell of redwood sap filled the air, sharp and resinous, as Arden appeared in front of the wailing teen, eyes wide with alarm. "What's wrong?" she demanded. "What's going on?"

Under any other circumstances, it would have been nice to see her becoming comfortable enough with Faerie to open a portal in order to travel less than twenty feet, instead of walking like a normal human person. With Karen still screaming and the rest of us absolutely unsure of why, "nice" wasn't exactly on the table. Even the Luidaeg looked alarmed, which was alarming in and of itself.

Then the door slammed open and Cassandra came staggering into the room, tears streaming down her face and one hand pressed hard against the side of her head, like she thought she could do something to stop some terrible sound the rest of us couldn't hear. She shot me one sharp, panicked look as she stumbled to her sister's side and dropped to her knees, the two girls clinging to each other.

Karen's screams dwindled into sobs. She buried her face

in Cassandra's hair, crying like her heart was broken, like she thought the world was ending—like the world had already come crashing to an end.

We had two Seers in the Court in the Mists, and both of them were terrified and all but incapacitated in each other's arms. Slow dread spread through me like blood soaking into silk. I raised my head, meeting the Luidaeg's eyes, which had gone glass-green in her shock, shifting colors to mirror her mood.

"Queenie can drive, and I know where the house is," she said, voice rougher than it normally was. She put her hand on Karen's shoulder, keeping herself anchored to the two girls. The Luidaeg was a Seer too, I remembered—and she didn't seem to have Seen anything. Only the Brown girls, still crying and clinging to each other, had.

Oh, this was bad.

"Right," I said, catching her meaning. I dug my keys out of my pocket and threw them to Simon before I spun on my heel, raising my arms toward Tybalt. "Carry me through the Shadows? We need to get to the Brown house, *now*."

"Of course," said Tybalt, and swept me off my feet into his arms, a gesture that could have been romantic under other circumstances but was currently nothing but practical. This was the best and fastest way for us to move. Arden would bring the car, but she couldn't be our means of transit, not when we might be charging into danger. Protect the Queen. Slay the monsters. Isn't that the hero's job?

"Raj and I will follow you," yelled Quentin, as Tybalt ran across the room toward the nearest patch of shadow. I flashed my squire a thumbs-up over Tybalt's shoulder and took a deep breath at the same time.

We plunged into darkness and cold.

My fondness for driving when it's an option isn't just about being able to go through a drive-through if the urge takes me: it's a desire to avoid the Shadow Roads whenever I can. They may seem kinder to the Cait Sidhe, but to me they're airless and cold, a freezing void where I could easily be lost forever. Just before our wedding, Tybalt had been elf-shot in the process of pulling me into the shadows, and had dropped me when he lost consciousness.

I still had nightmares about that moment. I hadn't been particularly comfortable traveling via Shadow before I was stranded there, however briefly, and now . . . let's just say it wasn't in my top ten favorite ways to get around the Bay Area. But it was faster than taking the mortal roads, and there was no traffic, and it meant we weren't risking one of the only monarchs I actually *liked*. Tybalt ran while I huddled against him, feeling my lungs begin to burn as the air ran out, ice crystals forming in my hair. Going into the shadows when I've already been bleeding is an experience—one that I've had too many times to be comfortable with it, and one that I was distantly relieved not to be having now.

I was resolutely thinking about everything except for what we might find when we broke back into the light. For something to impact Karen and Cassandra, and only Karen and Cassandra, so violently, it had to be focused on the Brown household. If it had been something that impacted a larger percentage of Faerie, I had to assume other Seers would have picked up on it—or at least the Luidaeg, since she'd been standing right there.

Good. Focus on that. Focus on the idea that this would be a small crisis, something I could deal with that had upset the girls but wasn't going to be catastrophic. It wasn't going to be the end of the world.

Tybalt tensed before taking a final leap, out of the shadows, back into the light. He put me down as I sucked in a large, desperate gulp of air, coughing to clear the ice crystals from my lips and nose. It always took a few seconds for my eyelashes to thaw enough for me to open my eyes, and when they did, I saw that we were standing in a suburban backyard, green grass and a tall wooden fence surrounding a surprisingly elaborate play structure made entirely of treated wood. No metal at all, not even in the swing set—the swings were on ropes, old-fashioned and safe for fae children.

I turned to face the house. The sliding-glass back door was closed, and the curtains were undisturbed. Everything looked perfectly normal. Appearances are deceiving more often than I would prefer. I took a step forward and stopped dead.

I smelled blood.

"Tybalt," I said, voice gone low. He snapped to attention, instantly focused on me. "I need you to go to the front of the house and see whether you can see anything. Check whether the cars are here. Then come back."

A cat prowling around the front yard would be less suspicious than a strange woman, and he wouldn't need to spin any illusions—a Cait Sidhe in cat form is indistinguishable from an ordinary cat. The same couldn't be said of either of us as bipeds. He still narrowed his eyes, hands flexing.

"I promise not to go in the house until you come back, unless I have no other choice."

Some of the tension left his shoulders, and he nodded curtly before turning and stalking toward the fence. His form flowed smoothly downward as he moved, until, with no clear point of transition or in-between forms, a tabby tomcat stalked in his place, tail lashing.

I watched him go, waiting until he had squeezed under the fence before I approached the house. I'd been telling the truth when I said I wouldn't go in unless I felt I didn't have the option of waiting, but that didn't mean I was going to stand idly by.

I was stepping onto the concrete patio outside the door when I caught another whiff of blood. It was fresh and sharp, with an underlying trace of peppermint. I stopped where I was, closing my eyes as I turned to follow the scent. When I was sure I knew where it was coming from, I stopped turning and opened my eyes again.

The house was behind me. I was facing the small redwood "castle" Mitch and I had spent an entire weekend building, back when Cassandra was still young enough to fit inside, and we had believed Gillian was going to grow up alongside the Browns, one big screaming mass of children. The blood I smelled was inside the castle. I swallowed, hard.

Well, I'd told Tybalt I wouldn't go into the house. I hadn't said anything about going into the castle. I moved toward it, slow and easy, one hand going to the silver knife at my hip. Drawing the knife I'd received from Oberon felt like an escalation in a way I still couldn't quite put a name to.

"Hello?" I called, once I was close enough to see if anything moved in the shadowy inside. The smell of blood got stronger the closer I drew. I could distinguish two sources now: the peppermint primary, and a secondary ribbon of fresh warm milk. Most people's magical scents will have two primary components, but this wasn't that. Two people had been injured, both fae enough to have magic of their own.

"Little fish, what are you doing?"

The voice was pitched low and came from directly to my left. I stiffened, then forced myself to relax. "Do you really think it's a good idea to sneak up on the woman with the knives? You don't recover from being stabbed the way I do."

"Perhaps not, but I move faster than you do, and you've yet to successfully stab me." Tybalt moved forward, into view, his eyes fixed on the castle. "I remember someone promising me she wouldn't go into the house."

"This isn't the house, and I'm not inside it."

He gave me a look that promised future retribution for that attempt to skirt the rules, then turned his attention back to the castle. "Then we're on this side of the yard because . . . ?"

"I smell blood. Fresh. I think whoever's bleeding is inside the castle." Raising my voice a little, I called, "Hello? This is October. Whoever's inside the . . . playhouse, I need you to come out. Right now."

There was a scuffling sound, followed by a wavering near-teenage voice calling, "Aunt Birdie? You promise?"

"What is it with people trying to make me promise things today? Yes, Andrew, it's me. Tybalt is with me. Are you hurt? I smell blood."

The Brown kids understand the way my magic works better than most people do, at least in part because their mother has been my best friend since we were children. To Andrew, the fact that I was easily ten feet away and claiming to smell blood wouldn't be anything unusual. If anything, it might be reassuring. See? Aunt Birdie is playing bloodhound again. Everything's normal.

There was a long pause before he said, voice gone very

small, "Not as hurt as Tony is. He won't wake up, Aunt Birdie. He got us both outside, but now he won't wake up."

I gasped a little, looking to Tybalt. "Can you lift him?"

"I don't think I can."

"Well, I don't think I can fit inside the playhouse, especially not if you're already there. Can you lift him enough to get him out?"

"We're not *coming* out until you can say for sure that she's gone!" His voice rose throughout the protest, until it became a wavering screech that faded into sobbing.

Oh, this was bad. "She?"

"The bad woman. She's inside the house. She—I wasn't—I tried, but I wasn't fast enough, I'm so sorry, I should have been faster. I tried. I tried." The sobbing got louder, making it almost impossible to understand what he was saying.

"Okay, Drew, I just need you to tell me one thing, okay?"

A sniffle. "What?"

"Is Tony breathing?"

The pause that followed went on for long enough that my stomach clenched painfully. Finally, voice small, Andrew said, "Y-yes. He's breathing."

"Okay. Then I need you to stay right where you are, hold on to your brother, and wait. Tybalt and I are going to go inside the house, and if there's a bad woman there, we'll make her go away. Do you understand me?"

"Yes."

"Will you stay?"

"Yes. I'll stay here." He sounded younger and younger the longer our conversation went on, less the ten-year-old boy he'd grown into and more the child he'd been during the years I missed, when I was living a drowned life and he was growing up without me.

"Okay, buddy. We'll be back as soon as we can. Tybalt?" I turned to face the house. "We can't wait for the others to get here. Not when we don't know how hurt Tony is." Sending Tybalt in in his cat form wouldn't help. He couldn't give medical aid when he didn't have thumbs, and we hadn't gone to Court with a full first aid kit.

"I understand." His tone was flat, but he didn't object

when I started moving, only paced me step for step, clearly intent on following me inside. Our relationship had begun with him following me into danger because it amused him, grown into him trying to keep me out of danger because it distressed him, and finally matured into him following me into danger because if I was going to insist on doing it *anyway*, he might as well be there to back me up. It was a progression I genuinely didn't mind. Oh, I might say I'd have been happier if I'd never needed to go into danger in the first place, but that never works. Better to go in with support.

Nothing moved as we approached the house. When we reached the door I paused, glancing to Tybalt. "I sent you to check for cars."

"I did."

"And?"

"One, in the driveway."

Meaning either Mitch or Stacy had been home when everything went wrong. Anthony wasn't quite old enough to get his license yet, and while Karen was, her oneiromancy came with a side order of unpredictable narcolepsy. Sometimes she literally couldn't wake up. In the interests of not killing herself or anyone else, she had elected not to learn how to drive. She had looked shaken enough when I asked if she was certain that I was pretty sure she'd seen something in her dreams that made her not even want to take the chance.

Asking the color of the car wouldn't help much. Technically, Mitch and Stacy both had their own vehicle, but in practice, they swapped back and forth, depending on who was picking the kids up that day and needed the bigger back seat.

"Okay, so either Mitch or Stacy is probably inside," I said. "Remember that if one of us is taking the hit, it needs to be me."

Tybalt didn't look happy, but he nodded without complaint. It hurt him to watch me run into knives so that they wouldn't be free to use on him. He still understood the logic of it, and you don't survive as long as he has without occasionally letting logic take the wheel.

I have a key to Mitch and Stacy's front door, but I didn't

want to risk attracting attention by going around the front. Gingerly, I reached out and tested the back door. It shifted when I pulled, scraping in its tracks. The sound wasn't huge. It was still enough that anyone inside would know we were coming. I paused to consider our options, and decided I didn't care. I had two hurt kids and the air still smelled like blood.

Mind made up, I yanked the door open with one prolonged scraping noise and stepped into the house, almost reeling as the smell of blood hit me properly for the first time. Oh, there was blood in the backyard, and plenty of it, but that was in the open air. This was blood that had been trapped inside with no way for the smell to dissipate and nowhere for it to go.

Peppermint and milk still underscored the smell, but the scent of cloves was much stronger, almost stronger than the blood itself. I gasped as I caught my breath, glancing over my shoulder to Tybalt. "Jessica," I mouthed, and he nodded, understanding me at once.

Mitch and Stacy had five kids. That's all but unheard-of in Faerie, where the purebloods have traded living forever for a birth rate so low that some couples can be together for centuries before they manage to conceive. That's part of why changelings like me keep happening. Purebloods desperate for the chance to be parents may see a half-human child as a way to practice and prepare themselves for the kid that will actually matter, the one they hope will come along someday. It's hard not to take that personally. Mitch and Stacy were both changelings, and that gave them the added fertility to keep filling their house with babies.

Stacy had been thinking about trying again, now that Cassandra was living in Muir Woods and Karen was talking about going to live with her sister as soon as she turned eighteen. Since "going to live with her sister" meant moving into Arden's knowe, no one really had a problem with the idea. It wasn't like college was an option for someone who seemed increasingly inclined to sleep for eighteen hours a day, and moving into a giant impossible castle isn't like shoving yourself into your older sister's cramped one-bedroom apartment.

Three girls, two boys. We knew where the two boys were, and the older girls were both in Arden's hall, sobbing endlessly. The blood in the air smelled like the youngest of the three girls, Jessica, who was twelve years old and still afraid of the dark after what had happened to her in Blind Michael's lands. He'd taken Andrew and Karen too, but Karen's trauma had been at a slight remove, due to his having seized her sleeping self rather than her physical form, and Andrew had been young enough at the time that he'd virtually recovered. Yes, Blind Michael proved that monsters were real, but I had proved that monsters could be destroyed. As long as Andrew knew where I was, he was okay.

And now the air inside his house smelled like his sister's blood, and another monster was in the mix, and I hated it completely. Nothing was supposed to touch my family. Nothing was supposed to touch my people. Ever.

The smell was coming from the living room. Beckoning Tybalt to follow, I moved slowly deeper into the house, hands on my knives, scanning my surroundings for motion or signs of danger.

The lights were out, casting the house into pleasant dimness despite the sunny day outside, but my surroundings were familiar enough that it didn't slow me down. The carpet was thick and brown, swallowing the sound of our footsteps. Framed pictures lined the walls, mostly family snapshots, interspersed with a few posed portraits. The most recent was from the previous summer and showed the whole family, Cassandra included, standing on the trail at Muir Woods, bright, sincere smiles on their faces. They looked so happy, so *perfect*, that it hurt to look at them that way when the smell of blood was hanging in the air, and they weren't happy anymore.

Another smell overwhelmed the blood and cloves when we were about halfway down the hall, strong enough and startling enough to stop me dead in my tracks. My feet suddenly felt like they were rooted to the floor. I didn't want to keep going. I didn't want to be here anymore. Every scrap of sense I had was screaming for me to flee, to get out of here and run as fast as I could for the hills, and to never, never look back.

"October?" Tybalt's voice was close to my ear, pitched low to keep from carrying, but still virtually a shout in the still, quiet air of the hall. "What's wrong?"

"Can't you *smell* it?" I didn't do nearly as good a job as he did of keeping my voice down. If he sounded like he was shouting, I sounded like I was screaming, and any hopes that we hadn't been heard were pretty well eliminated. I still couldn't hear anyone else moving. Maybe that was a good sign. It didn't feel like one.

"I smell the blood."

"No. Not the blood." Magic has a scent, and every person's magic is unique. Even two magical traces that are superficially identical—say two people whose magic smells like apples, which isn't uncommon among close family members—are actually entirely different if you have the nose for it. Which most people don't. But me, lucky me, being able to pick out and identify the individual strands of someone's magical signature seems to be part and parcel of the standard Dóchas Sidhe starter pack, whatever *that* means. There have only been two of us that I know of, and it's not like August and I have had a lot of heart-to-heart conversations.

Tybalt probably wasn't picking up on the scent of cloves in Jessica's blood, meaning he didn't know for sure who'd been hurt. I almost envied him that ignorance. I could only muster up the focus for "almost," because the majority of me was screaming inside my head, demanding to know why the fact that it clearly had the votes wasn't causing me to turn and run for the door. I didn't want to be here. We shouldn't be here.

Because over everything, drowning out the scent of blood, hung the scent of roses. Not modern, cultivated roses, and not wild roses, either: this was the smell of an old rose, the kind of strong rosewater perfume that people have been dabbing on their wrists and pouring into their bathwater for centuries, the overwhelming, cloying scent of closed rooms and stuffy manners. It smelled ancient in here, unspeakably old, and I choked on it, unable to keep moving forward.

Tybalt's hand at the small of my back urged me on. "I don't know what's stopping you, but whatever it is, I can't smell it," he said, very softly. "I only smell blood, and the distress of your family, and know we need to continue on if we want to know that your people are safe."

"Right. Right." With him preventing me from turning and running, I was able to finally unroot my feet from the floor and continue down the hall, passing rooms with closed doors that smelled of neither blood nor roses, and offered me no answers.

Then I reached the end of the hall, where it emptied into the living room, and I was running after all, but not out of the house. No: I was running as fast as I could for a heap in the corner, a discarded pile of limbs and destruction that was barely recognizable as the broken shape of a twelve-year-old girl.

There was blood everywhere. The carpet squelched under my feet as I ran. Still, I hoped, despite the smell of blood and roses hanging over everything, despite the utter, condemning silence of the room, I hoped, because letting go of hope means letting go of everything.

When I reached Jessica, I dropped to my knees beside her and rolled her onto her back as gently as I could. You shouldn't move someone who's that badly hurt, but part of me was hoping that if I jarred something, she would move or at least moan, proving she was still alive. She didn't. Her skin was cold to the touch, and her open eyes stared blankly at the ceiling, not seeing anything. She was never going to see anything ever again.

I was the one who moaned, soft and low and almost stunned, too shaken by what I was seeing to do anything else. This little girl, who had called me Aunt Birdie like all her siblings did, who had run and danced and seen so much of her brief childhood's joy extinguished in Blind Michael's lands, who had been struggling ever since to find her way back into the brightness that was hers by right . . . this child, this *baby*, had stopped her dancing.

"If we'd been much slower, the night-haunts would already have come and gone," I said dully, dragging my fingers across the blood-soaked carpet.

"Are we going to wait for them?"

It was a good question, even if it would have seemed utterly ridiculous to most people. The night-haunts are the vessels of Faerie's dead. They eat the flesh of our fallen, and something about consuming their bodies and their magic at the same time allows the night-haunts to take on their faces and personalities . . . at least for as long as the person those things originally belonged to had lived. They'd get twelve years out of Jessica. Twelve years, during which she'd still think like herself, still dream like herself, but wouldn't age or grow, wouldn't ever be anything but the child she'd been when she died. Wouldn't ever get the life she should have had.

Everyone in Faerie knows the night-haunts eat our dead, leaving clever mannikins behind for the humans to find, keeping the fae from being discovered by the mortal world. Fae flesh doesn't rot, so without the night-haunts, we would cover the world in our remains. Thomas the Rhymer's famous river of blood was literal when Faerie really went to war, since pure fae blood didn't curdle and rot away the way human blood would have. And on that horrifying thought . . .

I lifted my blood-wet fingers and looked at them, trying to keep breathing as regularly as I could. The night-haunts know everything a person knew, right up until the moment of their death, and since they aren't *really* that person, sometimes the night-haunts can tell you things the person couldn't, or wouldn't, because they don't care the same way. But dealing with them is dangerous. Everyone knows they exist. Almost no one knows what they really are. They're our own collective haunting, and it hurts to look at them.

"I don't think they'll know anything she didn't," I said. "And their patience with me is pretty thin these days."

The night-haunts aren't what we'd call big fans of company, or of dealing with the living. They'd prefer to be left alone, as a rule. And tempting as it was to let them come and transform this horrible scene into something a step removed from me, we didn't have the time to wait.

All I had to do was put my fingers in my mouth, and we'd

have whatever answers Jessica could give us. All I had to take was the easiest, most reasonable step in the world. And I would, just as soon as I could make my hand stop shaking. My eyes burned with the tears I couldn't let myself shed yet, not until we knew what we were dealing with.

We had two little boys in the backyard—Anthony would probably hate being thought of that way, but it was technically true, and felt *very* true right now—and we didn't have a lot of time. There was a car in the driveway, but I couldn't smell any other traces of blood or hear anyone moving.

"Check the garage," I said, still staring at my fingers.

"October—"

"*Check it!*"

Recognizing the borderline hysteria in my voice, Tybalt moved away, leaving me alone with the body of the child I'd been able to save once, but hadn't been able to protect in the end. "Oh, oak and ash, Jessie, I'm so sorry," I whispered, and stuck my fingers in my mouth.

Magic lives in blood, and memory lives on in magic, at least for the fae. As soon as Jessica's blood hit my tongue, the living room changed, a veil of red falling over it and the lights coming on, as the angle of the sunlight through the curtains shifted to about an hour earlier. I closed my eyes, taking the last of my sensory input out of the situation, and surrendered myself to the memory.

It was easier than it should have been to fall into the red light of her last moments in this world, easier than it should have been to let go of myself and become her from tip to toe. The resistance I would have expected from a changeling's blood wasn't there. Instead, there was a warm, soft ribbon of inky darkness, pulling me in like a poet pulls a rhyme, slotting me perfectly into the scene.

"Mom?" I haven't heard her moving around since she told me to go to my room. She was really upset when I told her Anthony came in late last night. I wasn't trying *to get him in trouble! I swear I wasn't! It's just she asked why he wasn't out of bed yet, and when I said it was because he'd been out until almost dawn she got all quiet and asked me where I thought he'd been. And she's* Mom, *when she asks questions with that look in her eye, I* can't *not tell her the*

truth! So I told her he'd been out with his girlfriend, and she got real quiet, and then she said "Girlfriend?" in this funny voice that didn't really make any sense. He's older than me! He can have a girlfriend if he wants to have one! Cassie has a boyfriend, and Karen sort of maybe has a girlfriend, but Mom never wants to talk about any of us doing anything like that. It's gross anyway. I don't know why anybody would want to waste their time that way.

But she said to go to my room, and then something broke, and now I don't hear anything. I don't like it. I tried taking down one of my books to ask it what's going on, but Cassie says I'm not as good at reading the future as I ought to be yet, and none of the poems it opened on made any sense. "And You As Well Must Die, Beloved Dust"? "Death Is a Dialog Between"? "Because I Could Not Stop for Death"?

That's silly. Nobody's dead *here, and Auntie Birdie isn't supposed to come over until next week. No one ever dies when she's not around. And my book knows she's coming. It wanted me to read "An October Garden," and that's all autumn and dead roses, so it felt like that was about dying, too. I don't like it.*

I broke out of the memory with a shudder and a gasp. So she'd been a Seer like her sisters? Practicing some form of rhapsodomancy from the sound of it—reading the future through poetry. Poor sweet baby. She'd been right in the end, even if she hadn't been able to see it until it was too late. Death had come to her house, and I had come along right after, and now she was gone and she would never know how right she'd been, and it was entirely unfair.

I dragged my fingers through the sodden carpet again, sticking them back in my mouth and bringing the red blood memory crashing back down. It was even easier this time, coating my vision in red and my tongue in the taste of cloves and pine resin.

"Mom? Mommy? Can I come out of my room now?"

Still nothing. But then the front door opens, and I hear Drew talking so fast he's stumbling over his words. He's all full of bubbly, telling Anthony about the game of Pokémon he won at lunch, and Anthony's saying the right things, like he really cares. He's always done stuff like that.

Then Anthony yells.

"Who the hell are you and what are you doing in my house?" He sounds really scared. "Drew, get behind me! Mom! Mom!"

I don't want to come out of my room, but my book said someone was going to die today maybe, and maybe it wasn't wrong after all. Karen says you can make the future be different if you move fast enough and don't pretend it can't be changed, and I want to be like Karen, I want to be fast and sure and brave, like Cassie, like Auntie Birdie. So I slam open the door of my room and run out to see what's happening.

Anthony is in the living room with Andrew behind him, and there's a lady there. I don't know her, but I know she scares me. Just looking at her, she scares me.

What scared *me* was that even though I could see everything else Jessica was looking at, I couldn't see the woman she'd seen. It was like that portion of her memory had been wiped away, leaving a blurred shadow where the attacker should have been. But the red overlay of her thoughts was fading, leaving me back in myself. I dimly realized that I was crying, tears running hot down my cheeks. I ran my fingers through the blood one more time.

She has something in her hand. It's—that's a knife! That's a really scary knife! And Anthony's still trying to push Drew toward the hall, and she's stabbing him, she's hurting *him, and he's screaming, my big brother is screaming! So I do the only thing I know how to do.*

I find my brave, and I pick up my book, and I run across the room, and I hit her with it as hard as I can. It's not hard enough, but it distracts her long enough for Anthony to grab Drew and toss him down the hall, and there's still a knife in his side, like he's Auntie Birdie, like he thinks he can't be hurt. I hit her again, and she looks *at me.*

Oh, I wish she hadn't looked at me. I wish this lady never saw me, not ever, not once, because I know her and I can't know her and I won't *know her.*

Blood magic isn't an exact science. Despite the clarity with which Jessica thought "I know her," I still couldn't see her assailant, or get any sense of who the woman might have been, apart from someone who smelled so strongly of roses that it was choking me.

It was choking me, and she was choking Jessica. Even at my remove from her memory, I could feel her hands clasp around Jessica's throat, the girl dropping her book as she scrabbled to unlock the woman's fingers, to take one more breath of air. I wanted to break out of the memory—I wanted to leave before I risked following her into death. I couldn't do it. As soon as I let go, she'd be gone, and I'd never see her again.

My sweet, silly, bratty, traumatized niece. I wasn't ready to say goodbye. I was never going to be ready.

"W-why?" choked Jessica.

I don't know what I was expecting. Malicious laughter, maybe, or bestial shrieking. Instead, a hand was withdrawn from her throat, and as the knife slid into her side, a calm, unfamiliar voice said, *"Leave nothing behind. Be the serpent, be the shadow. Be nothing, or never come home."*

"Ah," sighed Jessica, and closed her eyes. Her heartbeat was slowing, her lungs aching as the last of the air left them, and there was a stabbing pain in her side, and another in her chest, and—

And I broke the memory with a gasp, opening my eyes on the blood-soaked living room and the crumpled body of a little girl who had died trying to be a hero for her brothers. I pushed myself to my feet. Tybalt was already behind me, and he didn't flinch from the blood on my hands as I collapsed against him, trusting him to hold me up.

Everything was falling apart so quickly.

FIVE

NO MATTER HOW UPSET I was—and I was plenty upset—I couldn't allow myself to wallow in it for more than a few seconds. All too soon, I was pulling away from Tybalt, sniffling and wishing I could wipe my tears away without getting blood all over my face. "Any sign of Stacy in the garage?" I asked, voice thick.

Neither answer would be a good one. Either she was dead or she was gone, but there was no way she'd stood idly by while someone broke into her house and assaulted her children.

He shook his head grimly. "No."

"Okay. Okay. Maybe the person who . . . the person who killed Jess, maybe she took her for some reason?"

"It's possible."

I took a step back, standing up as straight as I could manage under the circumstances. "Okay. I need to wash the blood off my hands before I go back to the boys, and I need you to go wait out front for everyone else to get here."

"I assume we still wish to avoid attracting mortal attention?"

"Yeah. Come out the back door with me, go cat, and go sit at the foot of the driveway." No one would think it was odd for a stray cat to be hanging around in the middle of the day. Colma is full of strays. And while Mitch and Stacy didn't have any pets, they did have five kids, two of whom they were still homeschooling. Any one of them could have been encouraging a stray to hang around.

It was good logic. It held. And I held on to it as I made for the bathroom to rinse Jessica's blood off my hands, scrubbing for as long as I dared. Tybalt stayed close. He wasn't going to argue about splitting up once we were outside, but it was clear he didn't want to leave me alone in here again. After what I'd just seen—what I'd just halfway lived through—I didn't want him to. I can be a little self-destructive sometimes. That doesn't make me a fool. If there was any chance at all the woman who'd killed Jessica was still here, I wasn't going to let myself be caught alone with her.

Jessica had fought. When that woman was holding her down and squeezing the life out of her eyes, she'd fought, as long as she could. She might have been able to fight hard enough to get away if not for the second knife, the one that had disappeared with her killer. But while it was possible a human forensic team might find differently, I hadn't felt her draw her attacker's blood. The roses were entirely a by-product of whatever magic this woman had used to get into the house. I might be able to follow them anyway.

Not until we finished dealing with the boys.

Once my hands were clean, I pushed past Tybalt out of the bathroom and made for the back door with him in close pursuit. I was so grateful for his presence that it was almost a physical ache behind my breastbone. When had he become so predictably my anchor?

I could never have guessed how important he'd become to me, and I to him, in just six years. And if I was lucky, I'd never do anything to make that change.

The smell of blood still hung in the backyard, fainter now, as if the bleeding had mostly stopped. We approached the little castle cautiously, stopping far enough away that we hopefully wouldn't frighten the boys.

I crouched, pitching my voice soft and gentle as I called, "Hey, guys, Auntie Birdie here. Some friends are on the way with my car, and they'll be able to take you someplace that's safe. But right now, I need to look at Tony's injuries. Sweetie, I know how he got hurt. I know why he's bleeding. And I need you to let me see."

There was a long pause, followed by a scuffling sound before Andrew's round, worried face appeared in the castle window, eyes open so wide that I could see the whites all the way around. He had a streak of blood on his right cheek. "You swear?" he said.

"I swear," I said.

"Pinkie promise?"

"Need to come close enough to touch pinkies for us to do that."

Andrew hesitated, clearly pondering this. He looked further up, focusing on Tybalt. "She's telling the truth?"

"I don't know precisely who's coming, although I could hazard some fair guesses, but October gave her keys to her father before we left Court. Your sisters were there with us. I'm sure they're very worried about you."

I didn't want to go into the topic of sisters right now, not with Jessica dead in the living room. She'd died in the mortal world: when the night-haunts came for her, they were going to leave a perfectly realistic human corpse behind. Andrew didn't need to see that. Neither did Anthony. They were kids. Let them be kids a little bit longer before they had to face the fact that their world had just changed forever.

Andrew sniffled, looking from me to Tybalt and back again before he appeared to make a decision. Slowly, with exquisite care, he crawled out of the castle and onto the grass. There was blood all the way down his side, staining his shirt, but none of it looked like it was his. All the blood that *did* seem to be his had come from a long scrape along his left forearm, probably banged against something in the rush to get out of the house and into the castle. Lots of opportunities to take off a layer of skin when you're not paying attention during that sort of headlong flight, and most people don't heal the way I do.

"Hey, buddy," I said, smiling warmly at him. I spread my arms and he flung himself into them, shaking as he huddled against me. I hugged him for almost a minute, breathing in the scent of his skin and the mingled dry straw and milk scent of his magic. Then I pulled away.

He made a frantic sound and scrabbled to hang on to me, grabbing at my shirt and clinging. I pushed him gently back. "Hey, buddy," I said again. "Hey, you need to go to Tybalt for a second, okay? I need to check on your brother."

Andrew kept fighting to hold on to me. Anthony shifted positions inside the castle, shoes scraping on the wooden floor. "I'll be right out," he said, voice considerably weaker than it usually was. He sounded like he was fading, poor kid. Blood loss will do that. At least he was awake. I'd been getting worried.

I stopped pushing Andrew off of me for a moment, and he clamped down on me like a limpet, clutching tightly. I stroked his hair with one hand, and I waited.

The scraping sound came again, louder this time, and Anthony pulled himself into the light, offering me a weak smile. I didn't even have to push Andrew away again. Tybalt was already plucking him off of me, bundling the boy into his arms while I dove for his brother.

"I don't look *that* bad, do I?" asked Anthony, chuckling a little, like he was making a funny, funny joke. Then he coughed, barely covering his mouth with his hand. It came away even bloodier than before. He looked at it, blinking. "Oh. I guess I do."

"Yeah, buddy, you do," I said, on hands and knees beside him. His shirt was drenched in blood, darkest around the wooden hilt of the knife that was still jutting from his side. He followed my gaze down to the wound and managed a wan smile.

"Learned from watching you," he quipped, smile becoming a grimace. "Don't pull out the knife, it just means everything it's keeping inside can come *outside*, and that's bad for most people."

"Hey, you haven't seen me get stabbed that many times," I said.

"Mom talks about it every time you do," he said, and coughed again, eyes going unfocused. "She'd like you to . . . stop . . . "

"Hey. Hey." I didn't want to touch him when he was already injured, but I reached over and shook his shoulder anyway. "I need you to stay awake. Arden's bringing the car. She can take you back to Muir Woods as soon as she gets here. We have healers there."

"Arden?" Anthony's eyes had been drifting shut. On hearing the Queen's name, he opened them and looked at me quizzically. "You mean like the Queen?"

"Not *like* the Queen, the *actual* Queen. Come on, buddy, stay awake. You're going to get the royal treatment."

"You're so . . . weird." His expression softened. "Should have listened to the wind this morning. It was saying bad stuff was going to happen."

"The wind?" I looked over my shoulder to Tybalt, who looked as confused as I did, then back to Anthony. "What do you mean, 'the wind'?"

"You know how Cass tells the future from the air? Doesn't have to be moving. Can be inside, even, if she needs to be. She got the better end of the deal." He coughed again, closing his eyes. "I need wind. Me and Bert from *Mary Poppins* . . . "

"Oak and ash, kiddo, can you *all* tell the future?" Two Seers in a family was strange. Three was pushing the bounds of logic. Four was . . . four was impossible.

"I don't read air," said Andrew, crouching next to me and locking his arms around my neck.

Tires screeched to a halt on the street in front of the house. The scent of musk and pennyroyal drifted slowly over me. Tybalt had shifted to his cat form and was presumably going to meet the rest of our group before they could go inside and see what was in the living room.

I relaxed a little. Backup was exactly what I needed. "Oh, good, I was going to be—"

"I only see the future when I look at a fire, but I don't like to look at fire. It still makes my dreams all tangled, like when that bad man took us away."

I froze. Five kids, five Seers. How was that even possible?

Answer: it wasn't. This couldn't possibly be happening.

The back gate slammed open and feet pounded across

the grass toward where I was kneeling with the boys. I twisted to look over the shoulder not being blocked by Andrew. Cassandra was almost to us, moving fast.

Arden was behind her, running more slowly, Tybalt inexplicably in her arms—still in feline form. And behind them, Simon and Quentin. As odd groups to come running to my rescue went, it was definitely not one I could have predicted.

Cassandra actually shoved me aside as she tried to get to her injured brother, and so I stood, lifting Andrew as I did. He was almost too big for me to lift, and he wasn't making it any easier by hanging off me like a deadweight, burying his face against the side of my neck in sudden shyness.

"Hi . . . Cass," said Anthony, audibly pained.

"What did you *do*?" she demanded. Looking wildly around, she added the one question I didn't want to answer yet. "Where's Jessica?"

"Inside," I said. She looked from Anthony to me, meeting my eyes. I gave a small shake of my head.

Watching realization wash across her face was worse than being stabbed myself. She crumpled inward on herself, seeming to age and get younger at the same time. Then she turned back to her brother and stroked his forehead with one hand. "Hey, buddy, you remember Queen Windermere?"

"Hi," said Arden, stepping up beside me. She put Tybalt down, smiling at Anthony. "I'm the Queen. You must be Anthony. It's a pleasure to meet you properly. Your sister is a favorite of mine."

"I'd get up, but I've lost a lot of blood, and I feel real bad," said Anthony. He winced. "The wind said not to come home today. I thought it was being dramatic again."

"You have to learn that the future's never being dramatic when it tries to tell you something, you goober," said Cassie, sounding like she was on the verge of tears. I wasn't feeling too steady myself.

"Can he be moved?" asked Arden.

"Don't ask me," I said. "I can always be moved."

"It should be reasonably safe," said Simon. "Just don't

jostle the blade too much and it can be removed once he's been transported."

"Good. Your Highness?"

"On it," said Arden, and stooped to help Cassandra guide Anthony to his feet. He hung between them, limp, head dangling. "Toby, can you put the other one down?"

"If he'll let me." I bent until Andrew's feet were on the ground. He whimpered, trying to climb back up me. "Hey, buddy. Hey, hey. I need you to go with your sister and the Queen, okay? Karen's waiting for you in Muir Woods. You'll be safe there."

"I don't *want* to!" he wailed. "I want to stay with *you*!"

"Hey, Andy," said Quentin, moving up on my other side. "Remember me?"

Andrew lifted his head and looked suspiciously at Quentin, sniffling. "You're Quentin," he said. "You're Aunt Birdie's squire."

"I am. And we were in Blind Michael's lands together, a long time ago. You and me, we got into a lot of trouble, and Toby saved us. That's what she does. But to save us, she had to go to some really dangerous places, and she got hurt a lot while she was there. Your brother's already hurt. I don't want to make your sisters deal with you both being hurt at the same time. So please, will you go with Cassie and the Queen, so they can get you someplace that's safe? Just for right now?"

Andrew's suspicion faded into simple dubiousness, and he finally let me go, stepping uneasily over to take Cassie's free hand in his own. She looked at me with desperation in her eyes.

"I'm going to do what I can," I said. "Get them safe, and get Anthony's wounds looked at. Hurry."

"We are," said Arden, and flicked her fingers. A portal opened in the air in front of her, carrying the scent of redwood sap and blackberry flowers, and she stepped through, tugging the Browns with her.

"Jessica's dead?" asked Quentin, as soon as the portal closed.

I nodded, not trusting myself to find my words.

Simon blinked, asking blankly, "Jessica?"

"The youngest of the Brown girls," I said. "Mitch and Stacy have—*had*—they had five kids. Three girls, two boys." Now they had two of each. If Jin was still in Muir Woods, then I knew Anthony was going to be okay, at least physically. Having faith in Jin has served me well so far, and I didn't see any reason to change that now.

But for the moment . . . "Simon, what are you doing here?"

"You threw me the keys, and I know how to drive," he said. "I thought you might need another blood-worker to hand, depending on what was happening." He ducked his head. "I suppose I thought you were asking me along, on some level. My apologies if that wasn't the case."

Maybe I had been. It was the only reason I would have thrown him the keys and not Arden, or the Luidaeg. "Patrick's okay with this?"

"Patrick's just happy I wanted to do something without someone to hold my hand," said Simon, wistful fondness in his tone. "I haven't been exactly what you'd call adventurous since our marriage, and I think I'm starting to worry him. It may seem as if something inside me has been permanently destroyed."

"Has it?" asked Tybalt, with surprising mildness.

"I don't know," said Simon. "So I'm sorry if I've crashed your adventure. We're only about three miles from the ocean. I can call a cab and see myself back to Saltmist, if you'd prefer."

I shook my head. "Don't be ridiculous. You're here, and we have a big problem to deal with."

"Jessica's dead," repeated Quentin. It wasn't a question this time. It wasn't even a complaint. It was a slow, horrified acceptance. "Toby, what *happened*?"

"I don't know yet," I said. "Something terrible. There was a woman—a woman Jessica didn't know—in the house, and she attacked the boys when they came home from school. Jessica was in her room. She didn't see the woman arrive, or her mother leave, but when she heard her brother yelling, she came out of her room and she tried to defend him. The woman, she had a knife—"

"Yes, we saw that," said Simon. "Was there only the one injury?"

"Not counting Jessica, yes. The intruder stabbed Anthony, and she didn't have time to pull the blade out before he got away. He was able to get Andrew to the backyard while she was . . . " I paused to take a breath. "While she was murdering Jessica."

"Her blood told you all this?" asked Quentin. "How close to her death did you get?"

"I rode her blood as far as I could," I said. "It's not the same as keeping her from dying alone, but it was all I had. She wasn't in pain at the end. She barely felt the knife go in. Simon, when the woman you used to work for faked her own death, she was able to edit the memories in the blood she spilled so I wouldn't see what had actually happened. Do you know any magic that would let someone do that?"

"My keeper was rightly proud of her ability to manipulate blood, saying blood was the foundation of all magic, and her mastery over it proved she was more valuable to Faerie than any other of her mother's descent," said Simon, in the measured, careful tone he always seemed to adopt these days when he couldn't avoid talking about Evening. It was like he was worried that saying the wrong thing would summon her from the bier where she lay elf-shot and make her everybody's problem again.

He knew her better than anyone I could think of except for the Luidaeg. If he was worried about that, so was I. "Part of her pride was in the fact that no one else could do what she did," he continued. "Not her descendants, not her siblings, no one's hands but hers. Is there . . . " His voice hitched with obvious horror, but he forced himself to continue, asking, "Is there any chance . . . ?"

"No," I said, without hesitation. "I smelled the woman's magic while I was inside the house. Roses, yes, but roses are so damn common in Faerie that they might as well be a default setting. Instead of flashing twelve o'clock, we smell like Grandma's perfume. These weren't the right kind of roses. They weren't *hers*. And there was no snow. If it had been her, there would have been snow. When it's her, there's always snow."

"Hence the name," said Quentin.

Simon looked only slightly mollified. "Did you catch anything else?"

"No, I was sort of focused on the dead kid," I snapped, and immediately felt bad about it. I glanced at the house. "I could go back in. The night-haunts will have come and gone by now, and someone should be there when Mitch gets home. We know where all the kids are, thank Maeve." I almost wished I didn't. I would have been happier believing Jessica was missing, rather than dead and gone forever. I paused. "But I don't know where Stacy is. I'm guessing the car in the driveway is hers, since Jessica remembers her being home before the attack, but she isn't here."

"Was she—?" asked Quentin.

I shook my head. "No. All the blood in the house belonged to the kids, and she hadn't done any magic large enough to make an impression. She almost never does." Stacy's more human than most changelings, being only about a quarter fae. As with many thin-blooded changelings, the fae blood she did have was so attenuated that I had difficulty fully catching hold of it and had never fully identified her lines of descent. Her parents had both died when we were children, leaving her in the care of her grandparents, both pureblooded Gwragen whose dislike of changelings had kept them from inquiring too deeply into our activities during the day.

I paused. I hadn't thought about Stacy's grandparents in years. My own official relationship to Simon made some things make a lot more sense, like how two purebloods could have a changeling child—which Stacy's mother must have been, for her to be as human as she was. Either one of them could have had an extramarital affair and chosen to claim their daughter, bringing her home to be raised as their official child until she became old enough to be inconvenient and needed to be swept off to the side with the rest of the changeling riffraff.

That might also explain why Stacy's grandparents had never seemed particularly upset, on the rare occasion when the topic of their daughter had come up; she'd been an embarrassment to one of them and an unwanted burden to the other.

There are a lot of things I don't much like about Faerie. The way it chews up and destroys its changeling children makes the top of the list.

Regardless, Stacy's fae blood being as thin as it was meant that she'd never had much in the way of magic. She could manage basic illusions and a small amount of the hearth magic that Hobs, Brownies, and the like used to manage noble households, but nothing on the level of what a full Hob could achieve. Come to think of it, Mitch was the one with Hob heritage; she was part Barrow Wight, and . . .

And I didn't know what else. That was weird. Regardless, I focused more closely on the house. "Come on," I said. "We should make sure it's safe before Mitch gets here."

"Don't worry, Simon, I'll protect you," said Quentin amiably, as we started moving toward the door.

"That's very generous of you, young squire," said Simon.

"Dean would be pissed if you died and he wasn't here to watch," said Quentin.

"Quentin," I said, aghast. Simon, on the other hand, actually laughed. He sounded honestly amused, too, not like he was trying to pass my squire's rudeness off as an attempt at humor.

Quentin frowned at him, verging on a pout. "What's so funny?"

"I understand your anger better than you might think," said Simon. "Had someone done to my Patrick, or to Di, what I did to your swain, I would find myself in a terrible temper. The fact that it was intended as a temporary measure does not change the fact that it was an assault, and would it not cause trouble among both our households—and imply a tighter bond than I think you may wish to be tied with—you would be well within your rights to claim offense against me."

"Oh, great, there's two of you," I muttered to Tybalt. He laughed.

It felt odd to be laughing and joking as we walked toward the place where an honorary member of my extended family had died, but sometimes laughter is the only thing that keeps you from crying. Jessica needed me to find the woman who had killed her. I hadn't been fast enough to save her, and that was the only thing I could have done better up until now.

Time for us to wait for her father to come home. I wanted to call him, but right now he existed in a world where all five of his children were alive. I wanted him to stay there even more than I wanted to pull him into my world. He'd get here soon enough, and once he did, there would be no going back for him.

The smell of blood and roses was heavy in the still air of the house. I led the others down the hall to the front room. The real Jessica was gone, replaced by a perfect human replica crumpled exactly as she had been. I knew it wasn't the actual corpse, which made it easier to look at the carnage. Simon, oddly enough, seemed to share that ease, while Tybalt moved to look out the window and Quentin made a choked sound before heading off to check the kitchen.

Simon and I circled the body, careful to avoid the edges of the bloodstain. "Whoever killed this girl went to far greater extremes than were necessary," he said.

"Yeah, she wasn't a big kid, and she wasn't armed, except for a book of poetry that should be right over"—I looked around, finally spotting the heavy book Jessica had been toting on the floor near the front door—"there." Retrieved, it was even heavier than it had seemed in her hands, the pages carrying the faint clove and pine resin scent of her magic. I sniffed them, trying to commit the scent to memory. She wouldn't be spinning any more spells, not after this.

Simon watched quizzically, but didn't comment, just waited for me to walk back over to him before he said, "The knife remained when the boy was stabbed. There's no knife in the girl."

"No. It wasn't here before the night-haunts, either, but I felt it go in while I was riding her blood."

"Forgive me if this question seems indelicate, but how close to a death can you come before it overwhelms you?" I glanced up, blinking at him. He was watching me, a small grimace on his face. "Amy—your mother—always had trouble breaking the connection after a certain point. She said it was as if they wanted to pull her with them into darkness, and she had to find a method of resistance."

"I've never ridden all the way to a real death," I said, uncomfortably. "I thought I had, once, but it turned out the person I'd been riding with wasn't dead at all."

"But how close?"

"Why do you want to know?"

Simon flushed, turning his face slightly away. "I never expected your sister to choose me in the divorce," he said. "To be honest, I never expected to survive a divorce, even if I were foolish enough to attempt one. Amy . . . Amy doesn't like to surrender things she feels belong to her."

"Yeah, I know from that one."

"When August spoke my name over Amandine's, I was thrilled, and I was terrified." Simon shrugged. "I think I have a better sense of how to be a father than Amy has of how to be a mother. I understand that people aren't pets at the very least, and that puts me above her in terms of both mercy and understanding. But I have no idea how to teach or protect a Dóchas Sidhe."

Ah. "And you think I do?"

"I think you're mostly self-taught, but that you have direct access to your own magic, and as the two of you present, at least externally, as the same variety of fae, your experiences should translate." He shrugged. "She's a grown woman. She can seek her own tutors if she feels she needs them. But she's still shaken by what she's been through, and when she asks questions, I don't always know the answers."

"Ah." I resumed circling the mannikin that had replaced Jessica's body, studying the position it had fallen into. Everything was consistent with the scene as it had played out in her memories, and with a death brought on by choking and blood loss. The poor girl had never stood a chance.

Simon didn't know the answers, and I would have given them to him if I had, but I didn't know them either. August and I legally shared a father, thanks to the weird and occasionally incomprehensible structure of Faerie's system of inheritance and lineage, but we biologically shared a mother. Amandine the Liar, Last among the Firstborn. She was the youngest known child of any of the original Three, and like all Firstborn, she was what Walther liked to irritably refer to as "biologically unstable."

Not that Walther actually *liked* to discuss the Firstborn. As a man of science, they annoyed the hell out of him, because at the end of the day, the Firstborn don't make any scientific sense. Every one of them is unique, sometimes to the point of displaying dominant traits from things that aren't fae at all, like Acacia, who is essentially a very talkative tree, or Diamont, who was born looking more like a boulder than a boy, and only uncurled himself to become the Father of the Bridge Trolls after his mother had left him by the banks of the Glomma, believing him to be a statue in earnest. Things like that used to be common enough in Faerie that even the Firstborn themselves don't know how many siblings they have. Maybe Titania was gardening, or maybe she was planting a new sister. Maybe Maeve was singing a catchy tune, or maybe the eight notes of the refrain were a new brother who hadn't yet figured out how to have a physical form. Things like that.

Anyway, each of the Firstborn is unique, and it's not until you get to their kids, people like me, two steps removed from the roots of Faerie, that you'll start to see consistency. Whenever one of the First has a kid, whatever attribute they were born to bring to Faerie will be amplified in that child, intensified and made more pronounced. Amandine was born when the Queens were newly lost, and when the hope chests were already fading into legend. Faerie seems to know what it needs, and what it had needed in that moment was someone who could bend blood to Faerie's benefit. Hence the only blood-worker more powerful than Eira Rosynhwyr. And all Amandine's kids—both of us so far—showed the same abilities, if dialed down from her own, and seemed to have inherited very little from our fathers.

August and I would breed true from here. Any kids we had would be Dóchas Sidhe, and so would their kids, and so on, and so on, until our descendants were as common in Faerie as any other type of fae. Thanks to our specific magic, we wouldn't even need hope chests to keep from functionally breeding the bloodline out of existence after two or three generations of marrying humans or other types of fae in order to avoid marrying immediate siblings. Odds were good that if Amandine had a third kid, they'd be Dóchas Sidhe like us, if slightly different, since no two children of a Firstborn are exactly the same.

Odds were also good that she could create a whole new descendant line if she went out and found herself someone other than a Daoine Sidhe or a human to get knocked up by.

Does it make perfect sense? No. Does Faerie ever make perfect sense? This much, at least, is consistent: every Firstborn exists to fulfill a function in Faerie, and they fulfill it through their children. Someone like Amandine, who managed to stop at two—that we knew of—is an oddity. Most Firstborn count their children by the dozen. August and I both being her daughters, born within a short period, meant that our magic was probably almost identical.

"There's pancake batter all over the floor in here," said Quentin, sticking his head out of the kitchen. "It looks like someone dropped a whole bowl of the stuff."

"Any footprints?"

"Not that I've seen so far."

A mess in the kitchen was probably a clue to where Stacy had gone. There was no way she would have stood idly by while someone was attacking her kids, or hidden while Jessica threw herself into danger. A scenario was beginning to put itself together in my head. Something had happened outside the house, close enough to catch Stacy's attention while she was in the kitchen, but either quiet enough or far enough away that it hadn't been noticeable from Jessica's room. Maybe a neighbor yelling, or someone knocking on the front door and startling her. She'd dropped the pancake batter and—

And nothing. That didn't make any sense. Stacy would have needed to be in real and immediate danger to make that kind of mess and just leave, especially with one of the kids in the house. If I hadn't known where all five of them were, I would have been afraid something had happened to one of the children. As it was, I *knew* something had happened to one of the children. I just didn't know *what*.

Carefully, I walked around the bloodstain on the carpet, leaving Simon to study the body as I joined Quentin in the kitchen. He hadn't overstated the mess. Pancake batter covered most of the floor, drying in long, sticky streaks along the nearby cupboards. What he hadn't mentioned was that the stovetop was still on, scorching the bottom of Stacy's grilling pan, probably badly enough that she'd have to buy a new one. After today, that was the least of her problems.

I reached over and snapped the stove off, taking note of the little bowls of chocolate chips, blueberries, and strawberry slices on the counter. "She wasn't expecting to go anywhere," I said.

Quentin looked at me, swallowing hard. His eyes were very bright. He had been in Blind Michael's lands with Jessica and Andrew. While he'd never seemed particularly close to the younger Brown kids after that awful experience, it wasn't the sort of thing somebody could just forget about because it was over. He and Raj were basically brothers because of what they'd been through together. For him, this had to be like finding out the horror movie you'd survived when you were a kid was suddenly getting a sequel.

"Hey," I said, more gently. "Do you need a hug?"

He nodded wordlessly, all but throwing himself across the puddle of pancake batter to lock his arms around my shoulders and squeeze me close. He was taller than I was. That was still jarring sometimes. I was so used to thinking of him as my teenage sidekick, had been so comfortable looking at him through that lens, that it was weird to look at him any other way.

But he was going to be twenty-one before Samhain. He was only nine years away from being expected to return to Toronto, declare his majority, and take up his position as his father's heir. He was an adult.

Time isn't fair. Never has been, never will be. It's a lot like Faerie that way.

I put my arms around Quentin and hugged him back, taking a moment to ignore the horrific situation still unfolding all around us. The smell of roses had even reached into the kitchen. It wasn't as strong here as it was in the living room, but it explained why I hadn't picked up on the smell of charring metal before Quentin found the stove. It was hard for me to smell anything above the roses.

A car pulled into the driveway. I let go of Quentin and stepped quickly out of the kitchen, heading for the front door. I made it there before I heard Mitch's key slide into the lock and the knob began to turn.

I positioned myself so my body would hopefully block the worst of the bloodstains, taking a deep breath. Everything was about to be very real, whether we were ready for it or not. As if a dead child wasn't real enough. Tybalt moved to stand behind me.

The door swung open. Mitch Brown blinked when he saw me, surprised but not shocked by my presence. "Oh, hey, Toby," he said. "Stacy didn't tell me you'd be coming by today. Hey, Tybalt. How's things in the king game?"

"Very nearly retired," he said, sounding only slightly subdued.

Mitch laughed. "Good to hear. You need some time to breathe before the next time this one gets you into trouble."

Simon came up behind me on my other side, the three of us effectively blocking Mitch's view of the living room. Mitch blinked.

"Duke Torquill?" he asked, blankly. "Why are you in my house?"

"Can we talk on the porch?" I asked, before Simon could answer and make things even more confusing for the poor man. Mitch's day was about to get a hell of a lot worse. We didn't need to draw it out.

Mitch blinked again. "Sure," he said, and took a step back, out of the doorway. "What's going on . . . ?"

Tybalt and Simon followed close behind as I stepped onto the porch, Simon muttering under his breath. It wasn't until I smelled smoke and apple cider twining around us that I realized what he was doing, and shot him a grateful look over my shoulder. Anyone passing on the street would see Mitch talking to three perfectly normal human people, and not a bunch of escapees from a fantasy novel.

Illusions are an incredibly useful tool, even if they do make my ears itch. I resisted the urge to scratch, focusing instead on Mitch, who was looking increasingly bewildered.

He was a tall man, especially for someone of Hob descent, and like all Hobs or part-Hobs, he was solidly built, fat layered over muscle until he had the basic physique of a barrel, or a throwing caber. His hair was sandy brown, a few shades lighter than my own, in that same "colorless dishwater" family, and his eyes were bluish gray. When we were kids, Stacy used to swear he was the most handsome man in all of Faerie, and I'd never quite been able to understand the appeal. These days, I got it a little better.

I would have shattered him beyond repair if I'd been the one he fell in love with, and he would never have been able to hold me up. Still, there was something to be said for a person who radiated rooted solidity. I just hoped that I wasn't about to destroy that forever.

"Have you heard from Stacy today?" I asked.

Mitch shook his head. "No," he said. "I was doing the ordering all afternoon, and I haven't been checking my phone. Why, did she call you? Is something wrong?"

I took a deep breath. "No," I said. "She didn't call. I was at Arden's Court—today was the day of Rayseline's appeal and—"

"Did they let you wake her up?" he interrupted. "That poor kid. I always thought she was going to be a part of our chaos, you know, and then everything went wrong. Begging your pardon, Your Grace."

I blinked. I had forgotten he thought that we were here with Sylvester. It seemed so improbable to me now, after everything we'd been through, that I hadn't even considered the possibility that he wouldn't realize the man behind me was Simon. Nothing else made sense.

"No pardon needed," said Simon graciously. "Dearly as I love the girl, she isn't mine, and as a large part of what went wrong, I would be dishonest to object to it being named as such."

Under other circumstances, I might have laughed at the look on Mitch's face as he realized who he was talking to. Given everything else that was going on, I couldn't even crack a smile. "Mitch, this is my father, Simon Lorden.

Simon, this is Stacy's husband, Mitch. He and I have been friends since we were kids."

"Charmed," said Simon, graciously. "I appreciate your past kindness to October."

I rolled my eyes. "He's taking the 'allowed to have a friendly relationship with me' thing very seriously, as you can see."

"Indeed," said Mitch, sounding only a little confused. It made sense. He mostly knew Simon as my liege's estranged brother, the man who had put me into the pond. The irony of spending this particular anniversary in Simon's company was not escaping me. "Toby, what's going *on*?"

"There's been an incident," I said, grimly. "I was at Court when Karen and Cassandra started screaming. Did you know . . . ?"

"That my daughters could see the future? I did." He sobered as he looked at me. "I didn't know *you* knew about anyone but Karen. We made the decision, as a family, to keep those talents hidden from everyone else a long time ago. I'm sorry that had to include you."

"I understand." And I did, even though it stung. I wasn't family, not really, and they were changelings trying to raise their children and get by without attracting too much attention from the Courts. I had always been more deeply entangled with pureblood politics than was normal for a changeling, thanks to the one-two punch of my mother and my relationship with Sylvester Torquill, and they had been protecting their kids from the possibility that news of an unprotected changeling Seer would get out and they'd find their children snatched in the night by the local nobles.

Changelings have very few rights in Faerie, and we don't even culturally view kidnapping as a crime, not the way that humans do. Messing with fae kids is a quick way to wind up elf-shot or down a few limbs, but it won't get you imprisoned or even arrested. When someone snatches a pureblood kid, there's usually some form of punishment. Can't say the same for changelings.

Karen's wild talent had been discovered during the fight to recover the kids from Blind Michael, and anyone who might have thought it was a good idea to snatch her in the aftermath had been deterred by the presence of the Luidaeg, who had made it very clear, very quickly, that no one was touching Karen Brown but her. Sometimes it's good to have a monster in your pocket.

"I didn't know about Cass until recently," I said. "But both girls were screaming and distraught, while the Luidaeg didn't seem to realize anything was wrong, so I assumed that whatever was happening, it had to be very localized, and I came straight here."

Mitch looked past me to the house, seeming much more nervous than he'd been a few seconds before. "October, where is my wife?"

"I don't know." I put my hands up, palms toward him, warding him off. "She was gone when we got here. Tybalt and I searched the house, and there was no sign of her."

"She was making pancakes," said Quentin. "She dropped the batter on the floor, so I think she left pretty fast."

Mitch blinked at him. "And didn't wipe it up? Oh, God, did one of the kids get hurt?"

"Her car's still here," I said. "And . . . yes. I'm sorry, Mitch, but yes. Whatever happened before we got here . . . Anthony's been stabbed. He's in Muir Woods now. Arden took him there to see a healer."

The color drained out of Mitch's face. "Anthony—he was picking up Andrew from his day camp program. Is he . . . ?"

"Andrew's in Muir Woods with his brother, but he's fine," I said, keeping my voice as reassuring as I could. I was about to run out of reassuring things to say. Might as well keep it going as long as possible. "He was upset and freaked out, but he's not hurt. I'm sure Arden and Nolan are spoiling him rotten by now. They like kids."

Even if they didn't, the Luidaeg was there, and Madden, and so many others who would be happy to step up and help a ten-year-old boy.

Mitch paused, clearly doing some mental math. It wasn't hard. There were only five pieces to be counted. "Toby, why won't you let me go inside?"

"I needed to talk to you first."

"Cass and Karen were with you at Court," said Mitch.

"Anthony's there getting medical care. Andrew is with him. My wife is missing. Toby, where is Jessica?"

I swallowed, hard, and forced myself to meet his eyes. "I'm so sorry. It was too late by the time we arrived."

Realization washed over him like a terrible wave, draining the rest of the color from his face. His breath came faster and faster, going from normal to hyperventilation in a matter of seconds, and then, without saying a single word, his eyes rolled back in his head and he collapsed to the ground.

SIX

"YOU DON'T HAVE MUCH experience at this, do you?" asked Simon, looking at the unconscious man in front of us.

"It's not normally a part of my job!" I snapped. "I'm a private detective! People hire me to find out whether their significant other is cheating on them, or to help them untangle custody disputes! Dead people aren't usually a part of my day-to-day."

"And yet I've seen you handle far too many corpses for my own comfort," said Tybalt, moving behind Mitch and hoisting the other man off the ground.

"Not when they're the children of close personal friends of mine," I said. I knew I had handled that poorly, even by my own somewhat loose standards, but I hadn't known what else to say, or how else to say it. It was a situation I'd never wanted to be in, and never dreamt I might be. And where the hell was Stacy?

"Where should we put him?" asked Simon, moving to support Mitch's other side.

"Quentin knows where their bedroom is, and there shouldn't be any blood there," I said. "Get him to his bed. He should wake up someplace safe and familiar."

They nodded, and the three of them went back into the house, Quentin pausing in the doorway to look at me.

"You coming?"

"In a second," I said, and reached into my jacket pocket, fishing around until I found my phone. Portable phones are a lot more common in the mortal world than they are in Faerie, where human tech doesn't always work reliably, but our friend April has been trying hard to get us all up to modern standards. I tapped the screen to wake it up, then scrolled through my starred contacts until I found Stacy's name.

If I'd been thinking more clearly, I would have tried this sooner. I raised the phone to my ear, listening as it rang. "Come on, pick up," I said. If she picked up, she could explain everything. She could tell me where she'd gone, why she'd left in such a hurry, why she'd run out without her car or her daughter. It wouldn't bring Jessica back, but it would give me a chance to try telling someone else without getting it quite as wrong this time. It would be a second chance to be a good friend.

The phone rang and rang and rang, until it clicked over to voicemail. Stacy's cheerful voice began telling me to text, because she never had time to listen to her messages anyway, and I hung up.

I don't do voicemail or answering machines. I have my reasons.

Instead of texting, I called again. And again after that. On my third try, the line clicked and Stacy said, "Hello? October?"

"Stacy!" I started crying as soon as I said her name, unable to stop myself. The relief and grief were too immense, and they overwhelmed me. I put a hand over my face, staggering to the side until my hip hit the porch rail and stopped me. "Are you okay? Where are you?"

"I'm at the grocery store," she said, all puzzled bewilderment. "Is something wrong?"

"Which one? We'll come and get you." It would be a tight squeeze getting all of us into the car, but Tybalt could ride in cat form, or could run ahead to Muir Woods with Simon while the rest of us drove.

"The Safeway in Daly City. Toby, what's going on?"

"I'll tell you when we get there, okay? Just stay where you are. Can you promise me that? Promise me that you'll stay right where you are until I can come and get you."

"I promise," said Stacy, still sounding bewildered.

"Good. I love you. I'll be right there." I hung up and slipped the phone back into my pocket before opening the front door and stepping into the house.

The living room was empty and no one was screaming, so I guessed that Mitch was still unconscious. I walked down the hall to the bedroom where he was laid out on the king bed he shared with his wife, eyes closed and face pale, my companions arrayed around him like the spokes of a deeply distressed wheel. As usual, Tybalt was the first to notice my arrival.

"October?"

"Hey. How is he?"

"He hasn't woken yet. That may be a mercy. I'm not sure there was any truly gentle way to tell him what had happened, but . . . "

"But I botched it. Yeah, I know." I shook my head. "This isn't news any parent should have to hear, and it isn't news any aunt should have to pass. I wish he were awake."

Tybalt's eyes narrowed. "I know that tone. You would ask me to do something inadvisable, were he awake."

"But you can't carry an unconscious man through the shadows," I said. Mitch couldn't hold his breath if he didn't know he needed to, and the last thing we needed to do was suffocate him getting him back to Muir Woods. "Do you think Arden will kill me if I call to ask for another taxi run?"

"If she does, will you stay dead?" asked Quentin. His tone was honestly curious, but there was a gleam in his eye that turned it cutting. I eyed him. He glowered back for a moment before his shoulders sagged and he relented. "Sorry. I shouldn't—I'm sorry. It's just not fair that everyone else in Faerie stops their dancing and is gone, and you always get better."

"Would you prefer I died and stayed that way?"

For a moment, he almost seemed to ponder that. Then

he shrugged, shaking his head. "Nah. You'd be even more annoying if you were one of the night-haunts."

"I love you too." This post-Toronto snippiness was getting annoying, but it was understandable under the circumstances. I gave him a one-armed hug before turning my attention to Tybalt and Simon. "I found Stacy. She's at the grocery store."

"Without her car?" asked Simon.

"Maybe she just needed butter or something. If she'd dropped her pancake batter, it's conceivable that she might have been out of something small that she needed to re-make it."

Conceivable, but not logical. If she'd just been going to get an ingredient for lunch, why had she been gone so long? Why hadn't she taken her car? Why hadn't she cleaned up the batter first? Why would she have walked to a store more than three miles away instead of borrowing something from a neighbor? And why hadn't she turned off the damned *stove*? None of the pieces I had came together to make any sort of sense.

Simon looked dubious. Tybalt moved closer.

"Wherever you go from here, I go with you," he said.

"Did I even imply any different?" I asked. "I don't want to do this without backup, Honestly, I don't want to do this at all, and I don't even know what 'this' is yet. Opinions on the Arden thing?"

"You may as well make the attempt," said Simon. "I can't imagine angering the Queen would make our situation any worse than it is right now."

"You really haven't been hanging out with Toby for very long," said Quentin. "She can always make things worse."

Shaking my head at that brutally honest assessment of my talents, I pulled my phone back out of my pocket, selecting another name from my contact list. How did we get by before cellphones? Even in Faerie, a land rich with magic and possibilities, they've made things so incredibly much easier that I can't believe we got by without them for centuries.

Arden picked up on the third ring. "This better be important," she said, voice tight.

"Hello to you too, Your Majesty," I said. My tone probably wasn't as deferential as it was supposed to be when talking to a queen, but then, it never really is. I don't so much do "deference." "Is everything settled over there?"

"You mean, do I have three hysterical Seers haranguing my borrowed healer—will you be mad at me if I refuse to give her back? She was my father's before she went to work for Duke Torquill, and I need a court healer—for information on their brother? If that's what you mean, then yeah, everything's settled."

"So you're not currently helping with the treatment?"

"Not at the moment—Oh, fuckery. You're going to ask me to give you a ride, aren't you? Don't you have Tybalt with you?"

"I do, but I also have Mitch, and he passed out when he heard the news."

"Toby kinda fumbled telling him about Jessica," called Quentin, voice pitched to carry.

I glared at him. "That's real nice, Quentin, yes, please tell the Queen how bad I am at my job."

"He passed out?" asked Arden.

"Cold," I said. "And even if he woke up, I don't think he's safe to drive. But I found Stacy, and I need to go get her, and we're sort of out of room in the car. Can you please come and get him?"

She sighed, deeply. "You're not the sea witch. You don't get to just order me around."

"That's why I'm asking nicely. I can beg if you want me to. Or I can call the Luidaeg and ask her to tell me the secret hero password that makes you come and carry the man whose daughter is dead and whose wife is missing to safety."

Arden made a small sound of irritated dismay. "Please don't call the sea witch. I just got her out of here, and if she comes charging back, you know I'm going to have to deal with the repercussions for weeks."

"We're still at the house in Colma," I said.

"Where?" she asked, and I could hear her in the hallway. Damn teleporters. They make the rest of us look slow.

"Hang on." I clicked off the phone, sliding it back into my pocket, and yelled, "We're in here!"

The bedroom door opened. Arden slipped inside, pausing as she looked at Mitch. "I don't think I can lift him on my own," she said.

"Yeah, I get that," I said. "Simon?"

"Gladly so," he said. "This has been a fine adventure, but I haven't the stomach for as much of it as I once did." He moved to pull Mitch into a sitting position, gesturing for Arden to get the man's other side. "Please be safe, for the sake of my heart if nothing else. I know your close companions have had plenty of time to grow accustomed to the way in which you throw yourself at danger, but I'm still new to being allowed to worry openly."

"Haven't found anything that could kill me yet," I said, with as much cheer as I could muster.

Arden moved into position under Mitch's arm, the two of them hoisting the man to his feet. She looked at me flatly, lips pressed into a hard line. "Please don't start thinking you can call every time you're in a tight spot," she said. "I'm happy to help, for Cass's sake, but I have a Kingdom to run."

"I really appreciate it, Your Majesty, and it's not going to become a regular thing," I said.

She nodded, sketched a circle in the air with her free hand, and was gone, taking Mitch and Simon with her. I saw a slice of the receiving room in Muir Woods through the portal before it slid closed, and the three of us were alone in a house that smelled of blood and roses.

I held my hand out to Quentin. He dropped my keys into my palm.

"Come on," I said, and made for the hall.

They followed me through the house, none of us stopping to look at the body that resembled but wasn't—had never been—Jessica. The Browns had been in this house for over twenty years. They'd raised five children here. They'd been happy here. And as I took my last breaths of the heavy living room air, I knew they wouldn't be coming back any longer than it took to pack up the stuff they absolutely couldn't do without.

We'd have one of the Bannicks in to do the cleanup—maybe Elliot from Tamed Lightning, maybe someone else—and there would be no signs that anyone had ever died here. A single Bannick is worth a dozen human crime scene cleanup teams, and the fact that Jessica's death hadn't alerted the human authorities meant there would be no traces of her left. Twelve years wasn't long enough by any measure. It felt almost criminal that it would end with her total disappearance.

It couldn't be helped. Adding a murder investigation to the agony Mitch and Stacy were already going to be experiencing wouldn't make things better for anyone, and it would make so many things worse. I stepped out of the house for the last time, Quentin and Tybalt close behind me.

My car was parked halfway across the driveway, and Mitch's was parked behind it, like an accusation. I winced, pausing to peer into the back seat before unlocking the driver's-side door and sliding behind the wheel. The car still smelled faintly of fried potatoes. Had it really been so recently that the world seemed like it was going to keep making sense for the whole day? Things fall apart so quickly.

Tybalt got in next to me while Quentin took the back, and the click of seatbelts buckling was the only sound until I started the engine and pulled away, leaving the house, the blood, the mess, the mystery all behind.

It wasn't a long drive to the Safeway where Stacy was waiting for us. I pulled into the parking lot and scanned for a space, fighting to keep my breathing slow and level. Quentin leaned up between the seats.

"What are you going to do?" he asked.

"Find out why she left in such a hurry, tell her there's been an accident, and give her a ride to Muir Woods," I said. "We all know I'm bad at this, but I'm also her best friend. She might take it better from me."

"I can go to the Court of Cats and call for Juliet while you make the drive," offered Tybalt. I blinked at him. We're not joined at the hip or anything, but he rarely offers to leave me alone when there's an emergency in process. Something about me running off and almost getting myself killed every time he takes his eyes off me causes him an unreasonable amount of stress. Maybe he didn't see Stacy as a threat?

That would make sense. She was a thin-blooded changeling who had just suffered a terrible loss and had never shown any particular skill at either offensive magic or outright combat. Julie and I survived our childhood at Home by being meaner, faster, and less discerning than our peers. Stacy did it by being too sweet to kill, sticking to the shadows and staying out of the way whenever possible. She'd just . . . never put herself into the line of fire. If anyone was going to hurt me, it wasn't going to be her.

"That would be fabulous," I said. "If the two of you can meet us in Muir Woods, I'd really appreciate it."

Tybalt nodded, a corner of his mouth quirking upward in a smile. "You're my family now," he said. "You're allowed to say 'thank you.'"

"Not in front of the kids."

Quentin leaned up between the seats again. "I see a spot!"

It was near enough to the front that I'd be able to find her quickly. I pulled in, pausing to check my reflection in the rearview mirror. As I had suspected, Simon's illusions had gone with him when he left with Arden. That was fine. I dragged my fingers through the air, tangling them with almost imperceptible shadows until it felt like I was moving my hands through cobwebs, then chanted, lightly, "Boys and girls come out to play, the moon it shines as bright as day, leave your supper and leave your sleep, and you'll get grounded for a week."

The cut grass and copper scent of my magic rose to fill the car, bright and bloody in its own way, then burst and showered down over us, leaving my skin tingling. I checked my reflection again. I looked perfectly human, with nothing about me that would stand out in a crowd. Looking over my shoulder at Quentin confirmed the same was true of him.

I turned my attention to Tybalt. He was watching me, a small, fond smile on his face. "Be safe," he said, and fell backward. It should have ended in him leaning against the car door. Instead, he vanished into the shadows that had gathered there, wrapping them around himself like a cloak as he transitioned onto the Shadow Roads.

"Come on, kiddo," I said, pulling my keys from the ignition and getting out of the car. Quentin followed, and together we approached the Safeway.

Walking toward a large supermarket—especially a supermarket that was part of a large grocery chain where I was once gainfully employed—shouldn't come with as much anxiety as it did in that moment. Shoppers passed us, bags in hand and phones to ear, ignoring us utterly. This was just a day to them, and nothing unusual or important.

The doors opened on our approach, welcoming us into the air-conditioned interior. As usual in urban grocery stores, there was a colony of pixies buzzing around the produce department, unseen by the mortal shoppers, armed with tiny spears and knives that they were using to carve away chunks of overripe fruit. I know pixies have natural magic that keeps them from being seen by humans. I've never been able to understand how this extends to them stealing food in plain sight without attracting attention. Maybe it's something like a don't-look-here, just automatic and unbreakable.

Like most modern Safeways, there was a Starbucks toward the front of the store. I walked toward it, gesturing for Quentin to follow me, and there, in the small seating area, was Stacy, sipping on some sort of iced coffee drink. My knees almost buckled at the sight of her. She seemed perfectly normal, untouched by the chaos of the day, her purse on the table next to her hand and a few smudges of pancake batter on the front of her shirt. If she could look this normal, the world couldn't have changed that dramatically.

And Jessica was still dead, killed by a woman whose face I couldn't see who reeked of roses, and no amount of normal was going to change that, ever again. I swallowed hard and walked over to Stacy's table.

The thought that Stacy could have been magically compelled to harm her own child had occurred to me, seductive in its simplicity, repulsive in its impossibility, but seeing her told me it couldn't be the case. There wasn't a speck of blood on her, and I didn't smell it, even as I got closer. She would have needed bleach to wash it away so completely that I couldn't pick up on it, and she hadn't done that. Her hands, blessedly, were clean.

She looked up at my approach, smiling placidly. "Hey, Toby."

"Hey, Stace," I said. "You mind if I sit down?"

"Not at all. Oh, hey, you brought Quentin with you. Hello, Quentin. It's nice to see you again."

"I've been around," said Quentin, sounding distinctly uncomfortable. He hadn't seen Stacy since the wedding, where he'd been transformed into a Banshee boy whose own situation had been dire enough, once, that he'd sold his very essence to the Luidaeg in exchange for something she'd never named. If he was still around, I hoped he was doing well, and if he wasn't, I hoped he'd had a good life. But I guess that's never guaranteed in Faerie, or anywhere else.

"It's been so busy since the wedding," said Stacy, mildly.

I frowned. "Stacy, why did you come to the store?"

She blinked at me.

"What do you mean? I needed to go to the store, or I wouldn't have come."

I pulled out the chair across from her and sat. "But you don't have any groceries," I said. "And you left your car at home. What did you need so badly that you couldn't even take the car?"

"Oh," she said, with vague confusion in her tone. "I don't . . . I don't know. I must have needed something, or I wouldn't have gone." She blinked again, and some of the fog cleared from her gaze, replaced by the first traces of alarm. "I was making pancakes. I don't think I turned the stove off."

"Don't worry, I got it," I said. "You'll need to buy a new pan, but the house isn't going to burn down."

"You're so good to me." She shook her head, clearly still bleary. "I don't know *why* I needed to leave so quickly, just that I *did*. I remember talking to Jessica and telling her to go to her room when she talked back to me, and starting pancakes so they'd be ready when the boys got home, and then . . . and then I was here, and I knew this was where I needed to be, and then you called and said to wait, so I got a coffee and sat down so you could get here." She blinked again, slowly. "I think there was something I had to do, and

I think I did it, and now it's done, and so I can sit down and rest."

That sounded like a compulsion spell to me, and one that was better designed than the one Simon had hit Quentin with not all that long ago. This one had clearly come with a beginning, a middle, and an end, and was sophisticated enough to have wiped itself away after it had served its purpose. That wasn't great. Trying to be casual about it, I leaned forward and breathed in deeply, searching for traces of someone else's magic.

SEVEN

"TOBY? TOBY, WAKE *UP*!"

Someone was shaking me, which didn't make sense. Neither did the fact that my eyes seemed to be closed, when they'd been open less than a second before, or the fact that I was sprawled on something hard and cold. My head ached like I'd been slinging illusions around all day without a pause to consider my magical reserves, and that didn't make sense either. I don't get magic-burn like that anymore. I haven't since I rebalanced my blood to make myself more fae than human.

"Toby!" The person shaking me was starting to get really serious about it, shaking so hard that if I'd had a spinal injury or something, they would have been hurting me worse. I groaned and opened my eyes—or tried to, anyway. They were strangely resistant to moving, like they'd been glued shut.

At least the groaning seemed to reassure the shaker that I wasn't dead. They stopped bouncing me quite so vigorously, which my pounding headache appreciated. I relaxed, slipping back toward unconsciousness.

Wait. Hadn't I just been doing something? Something

that felt like it was really important and probably at least a little bit time-sensitive?

My eyes finally opened, and I immediately slammed them shut again as the glaring overhead lights of the Safeway blasted my retinas. I groaned and rolled onto my side, only abstractly relieved when my body was willing to obey that particular command.

"What the hell—?"

"You *scared* me," said the voice I now recognized as Quentin's, as he jerked me roughly into a sitting position and wrapped his arms around me in something that resembled a hug only in the sense that constrictor snakes technically hug their prey. He seemed determined to squeeze the life right out of me.

I opened my eyes a second time, patting him unsteadily on the back. "I'm okay, kiddo," I said, and I was, except for the headache and the fact that I was on the floor, with no idea how I'd ended up there.

A crowd had gathered. They were mumbling and staring, but they weren't freaking out, which meant that either my illusions had managed to hold or Quentin had reinforced them when he saw me go down.

He squeezed me tighter for a moment—something I wouldn't have been sure was possible before he did it—then let me go, sniffling as he pulled away.

"You're going to have to get a tougher skin if you want to keep coming with me on errands," I said, offering him a forced smile.

He briefly looked like he wanted to start squeezing me again. Instead, he stood, offering me his hands, and I let him pull me to my feet.

Stacy was still sitting calmly in her seat, sipping her iced concoction like nothing had happened, like she wasn't surrounded by a ring of both humans and anxious, hovering pixies while her best friend sprawled on the cold linoleum floor. I frowned at her. None of this had been normal, but her behavior was what put it over the edge into completely beyond the pale.

What had I been doing when I—oh, right. I'd been about

to check for traces of the compulsion spell that had sent her here in the first place. Magic lingers. For someone to hit her with a spell that strong, they would have needed to leave a layer of it clinging to her skin like cheap perfume. If I could just pick that up, I could figure out what we were dealing with. I started to lean toward her again.

Quentin grabbed my arm, jerking me back. I turned to frown at him.

"What's that all about?"

"That's what you were doing right before you passed out," he said, tone borderline frantic. He glanced around at the humans who were still watching us with the vague interest every crowd has for a car crash, clearly censoring his words. "I think somebody spilled some bleach or something. Something that *smelled bad* and made you fall down."

"Oh," I said. I should have realized that faster, but my head was still throbbing, and the light was still burning my eyes. "Stacy's never had much of a sense of smell, and she's been a little off since we got here. Maybe somebody *did* spill something."

Muttering and alarmed, the humans began moving away, not wanting to emulate my journey to the floor. I pulled away from Quentin, standing on my own, wishing the throbbing in my head would stop. I heal quickly enough these days that any pain lasting more than a few seconds is a major distraction and deviation from the way the world is supposed to work.

"Hey, Stacy," I said, as gently as pain and disorientation would allow. "Come on. I'll take you to Mitch and the kids."

"All right," she said, grabbing her purse as she stood. "It's very kind of you to give me a ride home."

"They're not at the house."

She raised her eyebrows. "No? Well, I suppose Mitch has a car, so they can come and go as they see fit."

I took her arm, guiding her out of the store, the pounding in my head getting stronger until it transitioned into a feeling of generalized nausea, like I was going to throw up all over everything. Normally, that would have been annoying but not problematic, since I'm not great about remembering to eat. After today's McDonald's run, it could be the sign of a big mess coming. I dug my keys out of my pocket and passed them to Quentin.

"Get the doors unlocked and make sure the back seat's clear," I said.

He nodded and ran off to do just that.

We all have our little weird tics and twitches. One of my big ones is checking the back seat for intruders. I came by it honestly—an assassin camped out in my back seat once, and nearly managed to do their job before I trashed my own shocks getting away, and then I'd gotten shot for my troubles. Not my favorite day ever, and unlikely as it was to happen again, if checking the car before I got in was a way to avoid it, I was going to do that.

"You can ride up front if you want," I said to Stacy. She made a noncommittal humming sound and let me guide her to the vehicle, where she got in obligingly enough, putting on her seatbelt without being prompted. Given how out of it she seemed, that felt like a good sign.

Quentin handed back my keys as we both got into the car. The afternoon sunlight was glaring off the windows, making the inside of the car virtually invisible to anyone who happened to be looking in. I still locked the doors before snapping my fingers to release the illusion making us look human.

Nothing happened.

"That's weird," I muttered, and snapped again. Still, nothing happened. "Hey, Quentin, weird question maybe, but what do I look like to you right now?"

"You have that human face that makes you look too much like May on," he said. "Why? Did you forget what your own illusions look like?"

"No." I could feel my magic, curled like a cat in my belly, warm and comfortable and present. That alone kept me from panicking. "Just having trouble finding the release, that's all."

In the rearview mirror, Quentin looked as human as I did. He met my eyes and frowned, quizzical and displeased. "Maybe you hit your head in a new way?"

"Great. If there are specific injuries that can jam my illusions in the 'on' position, Tybalt's never going to let me hear the end of it." I started the car, finally pulling out of the space. Another car dove in as soon as I was clear, showing all the normal urgency of a mortal shopper presented with good parking. Never cast a don't-look-here when you're in a grocery store parking lot. The spell will keep people from explicitly noticing your presence. For a person on foot, it will usually avoid collisions. For a moving vehicle, it will do the same, and since healthy traffic doesn't come with a lot of desire to play bumper cars with strangers, it works out okay.

Disappear in a parking lot, and suburban shoppers will crush you into a ball of tinfoil before you have a chance to realize that you've made a mistake.

My ears itched with the weight of the illusion I inexplicably couldn't dispel. I scratched idly as I turned the car toward the freeway onramp, trying not to think too hard about what my inability to undo my own spell meant. I've been caught flat-footed by the inability to cast before; as a changeling, my magic is limited, and as a descendant of only Oberon, I don't get any of the ease with illusions that comes to descendants of Titania. Maeve's children didn't get the illusions either, but their magic moves through water, making them more protean. While I, or a Daoine Sidhe like Quentin, would use a shield of something that didn't really exist to hide ourselves, a descendant of Maeve might actually change the shape of their exterior form.

Fae are always fae on the inside. Even I can't turn someone human unless they have mortal blood from the beginning for me to work with. But the outside can look like basically anything, given the right magic.

So my magic being unreliable was nothing new. It getting stuck actually *working*, though; that was a little weird. I tried to focus on the road.

Stacy waited until we were on the highway before she spoke again. "Where are we going?"

I glanced at her. She was holding her purse in her lap, hands folded atop it, looking out the windshield with an absolutely placid expression on her face. She'd been placed under a powerful compulsion charm, forced to leave her house, stranded in a grocery store with no idea why or what she was supposed to do there. She'd come to, only to find her best friend the chaos magnet standing over her, saying her husband and children were inexplicably not at home. She should have been worried. She should have been at the very least confused. And instead, she was perfectly calm.

I very badly wanted to check her for traces of unfamiliar magic before they'd had a chance to fade away. Whatever had been done to her must have been done from close up, or the smell would have been all around her like a cloud of cheap perfume. But given that the last time I'd tried to identify the spell she'd been under, I had promptly passed out on the Safeway floor, it seemed better to keep driving and not risk losing consciousness while I was operating a motor vehicle.

"Muir Woods," I said.

"Oh. That's nice." Stacy smiled, settling in her seat. "You say Mitch and the kids are there? Cassie works there, you know. She really likes our new queen."

"Queen Windermere is doing an excellent job so far," I said. "She's definitely an improvement over the last one."

"I think the last one doesn't count, since we found out she was an imposter," said Quentin.

"Still held a throne for like a hundred years, and she was only the third person to be in charge of the Mists," I countered. "She'll definitely be in the history books, or she would, if we wrote them. The Library will keep a record of her."

"Queen Windermere is Tuatha, isn't she?" asked Stacy.

I glanced at her, blinking. "Yes, she is. That's an odd question."

"I was just thinking, most Tuatha don't go looking for crowns. They leave that sort of thing to the Daoine Sidhe. Oberon wanted his children to be heroes. He told them they should be heroes. So why does a Tuatha want to be our queen?"

"I think mostly because her father was our king, and she loved him a lot and wants to take care of the kingdom he cared about," I said. "And why he was king, well, from what I understand, *his* father founded the kingdom, back when the fae were first fleeing to North America to get away from one another. So maybe there just weren't any Daoine Sidhe around who wanted to do that much paperwork."

"Odd," said Stacy, and yawned, putting her head against the window. "I'm tired now. Wake me when we get to Muir Woods, okay, Tobes? I'm going to get a little bit of sleep while I still can."

"Sure, Stacy. You rest." I met Quentin's eyes in the rear-view mirror. He looked as concerned as I felt. But without a way to identify whatever spell she was under, there wasn't much else we could do. I kept driving.

It was edging toward rush hour, but we weren't quite there yet, and the roads between Daly City and Mill Valley—the human city closest to Muir Woods—were relatively clear. It would have been worse earlier in the day, when tourists would have been streaming over the bridge to see the redwoods.

Quentin and I rode in silence, letting Stacy sleep. It was honestly something of a relief. I didn't know what to say to her. I'd been intending to tell her about Jessica, to prepare her as much as I could for what we were about to find, but I hadn't been able to figure out how to begin, not when she was so clearly disconnected. It was almost like she'd been drugged.

The parking lot was halfway empty when we got there. I pulled into a space and leaned over to shake Stacy awake with one hand. She lifted her head almost immediately, turning to blink blearily at me. "Are we here?" she asked.

"We're here. Come on, I'll walk you up. Quentin, can you get the car?" Under the circumstances, I didn't trust myself to cast a don't-look-here and not lose the car forever.

"On it," he said, and started chanting a sea shanty under his breath as I got out and moved around the back of the car to help Stacy with her door. I made sure to focus on the car itself the whole time, since a good don't-look-here would mean losing track of it as soon as I took my eyes away. The smell of heather and steel rose in the background, then burst . . . and nothing changed.

I blinked, looking purposefully away, and then back again. The car remained exactly the same. "Quentin?"

He got out. "Yeah?"

"Can you see the car?"

He turned purposefully away, scanning the trees, before turning back and looking directly at what he shouldn't have been able to see. "Yeah, I can. Toby, what the hell?"

"I don't know. Maybe you cast the spell wrong?"

He gave me a withering look as I helped Stacy out of the car. "It's a *don't-look-here*. I've been casting those on my own since I was *five*. I didn't cast it *wrong*."

"Well, I felt the magic, so I know you pulled it. Try again."

"We dug his grave with a silver spade, walk him along, John, carry him along, his shroud of the finest silk was made, and he still managed to get bloodstains all over the damn thing when he rose from the dead and ate the vicar," chanted Quentin rapidly, yanking his hands through the air and concluding by slamming them against the roof of the car. The smell of his magic rose and burst around us, thick with anger and too strong for the spell he was trying to cast.

The car's outline didn't even waver. I stared at him. He stared at the car. Stacy gazed off at the trees, entirely unconcerned.

"Toby . . . "

"Yeah, I see it," I said, grimly. "Come on. We need to talk to Arden, and we have a few hours before the park closes." The whole point of hiding the car in the parking lot was keeping myself from getting towed if we were still here when the sun went down and the state police declared Muir Woods off-limits to the public. As long as we were reasonably quick, we'd be in and out before that happened.

As we approached the gates, I picked up a few dead leaves and twined them between my fingers, whispering a fragment of an old ballad as the smell of my own magic rose around us. There was a sick, twisting feeling in my stomach. I already knew this wasn't going to work. I also knew that I had to try.

When we stepped up to the ticket window, I offered the leaves to the man taking tourist money, a bright, guileless smile on my face. He looked at them and frowned.

"What's this supposed to be?" he asked.

"My son was just saying this place looked like something

out of a fairy tale, and in the fairy tales, you can usually pay your way with dried leaves." I smiled brightly at the man, making sure to dimple as hard as I could, trying to project "single mother trying to pick up dates in inappropriate places." It wasn't a role that came naturally, but it was one I'd needed to play a few times when I was on the job. Even the best investigator gets caught by their clients every now and then.

Whatever I was selling, this guy wasn't buying. He gave me an exasperated look, glancing to Quentin as if he expected the boy to be embarrassed—and to be fair, Quentin knew how to play his part, looking intensely uncomfortable and then stepping halfway behind me. "Sorry, lady, we only take cash."

"Well, it was worth a try," I chirped, pulling my wallet out of my pocket and extracting a few bills. A handful of change later, the three of us were inside, walking briskly down the wooden path toward the entrance to the knowe.

"What did you try to do, Toby?" asked Stacy.

"I was attempting fairy gold," I said. "It should have worked. That's such a low-powered illusion that it's never shorted out on me before. We need to get to the knowe. Something's really wrong."

It wasn't just the sudden failure of my magic—and Quentin's, too, based on the issues he'd had concealing the car. It was the headache still pounding behind my temples, steady as a heartbeat but ten times as loud. Every time it pulsed, I felt like I was about to barf, and I wanted to sit down and close my eyes almost more than I could say.

Quentin shot me a concerned look, clearly catching the pain in my expression. "Are you okay?"

"Not really. I've had a headache since the Safeway."

"But you—" He caught himself. "Right. We need to get to the knowe."

We led Stacy along the marked pathways to the place where the way up to the knowe would open for us—or where it was supposed to open, anyway. There was nothing there. When I looked up the side of the hill, I didn't see any easy ladder of interlaced tree roots, only an endless tangle of brambles and poison oak, leaves spreading in sharp-edged precision. I stopped in the middle of the trail, staring upward.

"Quentin?"

"Yeah?"

"Are we in the right spot?"

"We should be, yeah. I . . . Do you think Arden moved the door?"

"To be honest, I'm not sure she can." Knowes are half-architecture, half-living things. They're planted by fae hands, and their first structures are built in the ordinary way, with tools and raw materials and effort, but at a certain point, they start to grow and change and have their own opinions about things. I've been able to shortcut several potentially dangerous situations by appealing to the buildings I've been in, and they seem to appreciate being talked to nicely. The knowe at Muir Woods was opened by Arden's grandparents and sealed itself when King Gilad died, refusing to be used by the pretender to his throne. It had waited, patiently, for her to return, opening only once it was told she was alive by the Luidaeg, who couldn't lie. But Arden and her knowe were still getting to know each other, and it would be a while before they had the sort of relationship where asking for major restructuring made sense.

Plus, why would she have moved the door when she knew I was on the way over? It didn't make sense. I pulled my phone out of my pocket.

"What are you doing?" asked Quentin.

"Calling for backup." I tried to think of who I knew for sure was in the knowe at the moment. Arden, but she might kill me if I called again, or at least ask me to do something I'd find unpleasant and annoying. Cassandra, but she was a little busy at the moment. Raj didn't have a phone. Tybalt did have a phone, finally—reminding him he could use it to call me when I wandered into danger and didn't tell him exactly where I was going had actually convinced him to take the plunge—but even April couldn't arrange reliable reception in the Court of Cats, and if he was still working on getting Julie to the knowe, I didn't want to interrupt.

May had a phone. Sometimes the fact that May had all of my memories up until the moment of her "birth" could be really inconvenient. Because May had a phone, but she also had all my love and affection and lifelong attachment to Mitch and the kids, and I didn't want to distract her from them right now if I had any other option.

Phones are such a new thing in Faerie. How did we get so dependent on them so quickly?

"That reminds me," I muttered. "We're going to need to get Rayseline a phone if she's going to be living with us." One more thing for the long, long list of adjustments we'd be making. I frowned, then opened my contact list, finally raising the phone to my ear.

"Hello?" said Simon. "October? Is everything all right?"

"I'm not entirely sure," I said. "Did Arden move the front door?"

"No. Why would she have done that?"

I pinched the bridge of my nose. "I don't *know* why she would have done that, but I'm down on the trail with Stacy and Quentin, and the path up isn't here, so I don't know how we're getting in."

There was a long, bewildered pause before Simon said, sounding alarmed, "I'll be right there," and hung up.

I lowered my phone, tucking it back into my pocket, and turned to Quentin. "Simon's coming to get us."

"Why'd you call *him*?"

"Because I knew he'd be here, and I knew he'd be free to come out and get us." Stacy was looking at the side of the hill, head slanted slightly to the side, like she was watching something I couldn't see. I was suddenly direly afraid that she was.

"Hey, Stacy?" I stepped closer to her, pitching my voice a little higher, like I was talking to someone who might fall apart at any moment. "What are you looking at?"

"Why don't we just go up the stairs?" She pointed to the spot where the path up should have been, finger steady enough to make it clear she was pointing at the lattice of roots. She turned to blink guilelessly at me. "I don't understand."

"Whatever's stopping me from dropping our illusions seems to be keeping me from *seeing* them, too," I said. "So I can't see the trail up, and neither can Quentin."

"Nope," he agreed. "And it's sort of existentially terrifying in a way I don't really know how to express, so I'm going to keep standing here and looking pretty."

"You're good at it," I said, reassuringly. "Just a few minutes and Simon will be here."

"I don't like waiting for Simon Torquill to come to my rescue," he grumbled.

"Lucky for you, we're not," I said. "Simon Lorden, on the other hand, should be coming down that hill at any moment."

Stacy wrinkled her nose but didn't say anything. Since she'd been the one to make sure he had a role to play at my wedding, it seemed a little odd for her to react that way. I wanted to ask about it. Before I got the chance, Simon was stepping off the side of the hill, face flushed and shirt askew. He looked as human as we did. Standard protocol for entering the mortal part of the park, at least during the daylight hours.

"Can you really not see the way back up?" he asked, focusing on me.

"Nope." I shook my head. Quentin was looking increasingly freaked out, which wasn't fun.

Simon stepped fully onto the path. "That's not normal."

"No, it's not." I raised an eyebrow. "Can *you* see it?"

"What?" He turned and looked back the way he'd just come, sudden tension in his shoulders. It grew as he stared. "I can, but it's *flickering*, like it doesn't want to be seen. October, what—?"

"If I knew, I wouldn't be standing here trying to hold it together," I said. "Come on. Let's get inside before someone has a total panic attack and we have to deal with the park rangers."

I offered him my hand and, when he took it, reached back to offer the other to Quentin. As soon as Simon's fingers closed around my own, I saw the trail bloom into being where I would have sworn it hadn't been before, an easy pathway through the brambles and toxic vegetation. Not to be left out, Stacy reached for Quentin's other hand, and with Simon at the lead, our little group began making our way up the hill.

A new problem waited at the top, where Simon let go of me. I could see two people standing in the clearing for no apparent reason, but no sign of a doorway in the tree behind them. Neither of them was armed, either. They looked strangely formal for two people hanging out in the woods, but not like guards on duty. And while there was no reason for them to be disguised when they were in a place that mortals generally couldn't even *find*, they both looked perfectly human.

This was bad. "Quentin . . . ?"

"I see it too," he said unsteadily, stepping up next to me.

"Is something wrong?" asked Simon.

"Neither of us can see Faerie right now." I turned to him. "Do you know how to mix faerie ointment?"

"I do, but my lab is back in Saltmist, and that's a long way," he said. "If the Queen has a lab that I can utilize, I'd be able to mix something up for you, but if not . . ."

"Dean has one at Goldengreen," said Quentin. "Marcia can't see anything without faerie ointment, so he has to make sure she has a steady supply. One of the Silene who lives there serves as an unofficial Court alchemist."

"Most of Count Lorden's Court dislikes me, for good reason," said Simon. "I'm not sure I would be allowed access to any equipment he has there."

"We can figure something out," I said. We were in enough trouble. We didn't need another reason to be miserable right now.

The guards had finally noticed us. They looked in our direction, frowning. I didn't recognize either of them.

"October?" called the woman. Her voice, at least, was familiar: Lowri. She waved us over. "Everything okay?"

"Nope," I said, almost violently cheerful as we approached. She blinked. I shrugged. "Just being honest. Mind if we come in?"

"Not at all," she said. "Queen said to expect you."

"One small problem," said Simon, apologetically.

I turned to look at him.

"What now?"

"I can't see the door."

Well, crap.

EIGHT

AFTER SIMON'S PROCLAMATION, IT had only taken a few seconds for Lowri and Nolan—her current fellow guard—to swing into action, Nolan waving one hand oddly in the air before seeming to step just out of view. The smell of his magic rose, but I never saw the portal, or anything that would have led me to think magic was real if I hadn't already known about it. Lowri moved toward us. I put up a hand.

"Stop there!"

She stopped obligingly, looking puzzled. "October . . . ?"

"Simon was fine before he took my hand," I said. "Whatever's going on with us, it seems to be contagious."

"What is?" asked Stacy, sounding politely bemused. "Aren't we going to go inside?"

"In a second, Stacy."

Contagious to everyone but her, which would have been interesting if this hadn't been such a serious situation. It couldn't be connected to having human blood, or I would have been able to see everything clearly. Simon had been born a changeling and turned fully fae before he was old enough to consent, while Quentin was the son of a changeling woman who had similarly given up her human blood, in her case for the chance to marry a king. So all three of the people affected were connected to humanity in some way, even if some of those connections were attenuated.

But Stacy was more mortal than any of us. She had never asked me to change her blood, and I had never offered. She'd seemed so happy as she was that there really hadn't been any point to reminding her that she was never going to be considered a full part of Faerie, and we had time before old age was going to make it a pressing issue.

It was still a little odd that I'd never even thought to ask her, not even on the rare nights when we'd gone out on the town with Kerry and done our best to fit in with the shrieking human college girls, slamming fruity cocktails like our lives depended on it. We talked about everything. When I'd lost my virginity, she'd been the first person I wanted to tell about it. There had never been a major development in my life that I hadn't discussed with Stacy. So how was it that I'd discovered a way to make *her* life easier, and I'd never brought it up?

"I can still feel my magic," said Simon, looking down at his hands and flexing his fingers like he was trying to feel the illusions he couldn't actually see. "It's *here.* I just can't see it."

"Lowri, are you wearing a human disguise right now?"

She shook her head. "No."

"Great. So I can't even see the parts of Faerie that the humans *can* see."

Looking alarmed, Lowri took another step backward, putting more distance between us. Quentin was starting to breathe rapidly, clearly on the cusp of some sort of breakdown. I put a hand on his shoulder.

"It'll be okay," I said. "Look, Stacy's fine. We'll figure this out."

Nolan reappeared, once again seeming to step out from behind something, rather than through any sort of magic. This time, a woman was with him, dark-haired, dressed in jeans and a sweatshirt. Despite her rounded ears and rebalanced color palette, she was obviously the Queen. And being Arden, those could very well be her real clothes, not an illusionary construct like the ones on the guards. That was almost reassuring, which was nice, since absolutely nothing else was.

"October!" She rushed toward us. "What's going on? Nolan says you can't see the door."

"You shouldn't touch us," I said, almost apologetically. Even for me, telling a Queen she's not allowed to do something is a little awkward. Sure, I'm great at overthrowing them when they get out of line, but Arden was doing her best to do right by us, and hadn't gone in for any massive violations of anyone's autonomy—at least not that I was aware of.

Arden stopped, several feet still between her and Quentin. "Why?" she asked, warily.

"I can't release my illusions," I said. "I can feel my magic, but when I try to tell it we don't need it right now, it won't let go. And I can't see the pixies, I couldn't see the trail up the hill, and I can't see the door into the knowe. Are you wearing a human disguise?"

Eyes wide, Arden shook her head.

"No, I didn't think so. So yeah, I can't perceive Faerie at all right now. Neither can Quentin."

"Neither can I," said Simon. "It vanished somewhere between guiding October up the hill and stepping into the clearing. You all look perfectly human to me right now, which is more mundane than what would be seen by an actual human."

"More concerning, too," I said. "Do you have anyone in your household who makes steady use of Faerie ointment? It might help to counter whatever's happening to us."

"I can see just fine," said Stacy. "I really don't understand what's going on. You said Mitch and the kids were here? Is something wrong?"

Arden's eyes widened as she turned to stare at me again. I gave a quick shake of my head, hoping her time in retail had left her with enough common sense not to say something silly like "You mean you don't *know*?" or—worse—"Sorry, your daughter's dead."

To my immense relief, Arden said, "Mitch and the children are inside the knowe, but if October and the rest of you have somehow been infected with a condition that's preventing you from seeing properly, I can't let any of you inside until we know what's actually going on."

If it wouldn't have been treason and I hadn't been married, I could have kissed her.

The air in front of the big tree shimmered, briefly distorted like a special effect out of a bad science fiction movie, and another woman joined us in the clearing. This one looked like a human teenager in denim coveralls and stompy black boots, dark, curly hair pulled into pigtails and secured with strips of electric tape. She glared at the lot of us before demanding, "Well? Were you planning to come inside any time soon, or is it just going to be a day where I have to babysit and you people hang out leaving me to take care of everything? Again?"

"Luidaeg." I sighed heavily, in relief. "We have a problem."

"And what's that?"

"We can't see Faerie."

She blinked. Unlike Arden, she didn't look odd at all as a human. She actually looked more like herself this way than she did in most fae guises. The majority of fae have ears that are pointed to one degree or another—one of the few things the movies get right. The Luidaeg doesn't, or if she does, she's always hidden them well enough that no one knows. Most of the time, she goes around looking human from tip to toe, completely veiled in mortality. It's a gift that seems unique to her, even among the Firstborn. Oberon was able to hide as a human man for decades, but when he did that, he didn't know who he was. Now, he could dim himself to the point of becoming unnoticeable. Not quite the same thing. Still impressive, just . . . not the same.

"At all?"

"Nope." I shook my head. "I can feel my magic respond when I call it, and I can smell spells the way I normally do, but they're sort of . . . removed. Like I have a bad cold or something." Except that an actual cold wouldn't stop me from smelling magical signatures. Magic isn't smelled in the nose, exactly. Faerie is weird and we just go with it.

"Really." She moved closer, eyes narrowed as she peered

at us. Stepping back again, she snapped her fingers. "Queenie."

"Please try to show some basic respect in the presence of my staff," said Arden, moving to stand next to the Luidaeg. "I know it's not easy for you, but I have to live with these people when you're not here."

"Do I look as if I give a shit? I know you've let your little chatelaine's boy-toy set up an alchemy lab off the kitchens. He's a smart fellow, he'll have the basics on hand. Go get me half a dozen eggs and a bottle of foxglove extract."

"Those aren't mine," said Arden. She took a step back when the Luidaeg turned to look at her with narrowed eyes. "Except for the part where they're in my knowe and I'm the Queen here and so I can make a case for anything he's left here being mine by right of I'm the Queen and also I can buy him replacements if he gets really snotty about it, be right back." She took another step back and was gone, disappearing like someone had made an edit to the film we were all living through.

This was getting old, and rapidly so. "You know, I've been human enough to need fairy ointment and it was never this bad," I complained.

"Well, it wouldn't have been, would it?" asked the Luidaeg. "That was just mortality. It's not the human world's fault that it's not the same as ours. People frequently can't see things that don't concern them. We could be standing at the intersection of twenty different flavors of reality and only seeing the two where we have any business being."

Well, that was an unsettling thought. I blinked. "Okay, so?"

"So normally, humans *can* see our world, because cutting it out completely breaks theirs a little bit. It's better for them to see people with pointy ears and funny eyes who can do things they can't than it is to see things just happening for no reason. This isn't that. This is what we used to call a Llangefni screen, back when they actually happened, which they don't anymore."

I raised an eyebrow. "Except that if one of them *is* happening, they clearly *do*. What's a Lang-have-knee screen supposed to do?"

"That may be the worst Welsh pronunciation I've ever heard," said the Luidaeg. "It's a Llangefni screen. A form of illusion used mostly on women who'd been serving as midwives or wetnurses to fae children."

"Ah." Not all pureblood women lactate. Again, some of them are trees, or rocks, or birds, once you start really looking at them on a biological level. But all fae children nurse. It's not the smartest thing biology has ever done to us. And some women's milk just never comes in. That happens to humans, too. Wetnurses used to be a lot more common, back when it was easier to abduct a human woman and make her look after your babies. "But didn't we *want* them to see the fae?"

"Up until a point, yeah. That's why fairy ointment was developed. Unfortunately, for it to be stable, fairy ointment has to be *really* stable. The stuff could last for years. And we had some issues with human women falling in love with the fae world, to the point where they didn't want to go home when their terms of service were done."

"Okay . . . " Fae households stable and wealthy enough to not only seek but support human wetnurses would probably have seemed like a massive improvement over the mortal world in the same time period. I'm not a historian, but Faerie has always been better about things like "sufficient food," "clean water," and "heat." Plus from what I understand, the human wetnurses were generally treated very well. Better than changelings in the same time period, at the very least, and my standards may be low, but that's good enough for me.

"Others were happy to go home but wanted to be able to come back to Faerie on their own, which meant being able to see the doors. So they stole pots of ointment on their way out the door, and they hid them until they wanted to come back. We couldn't have that." The Luidaeg shook her head. "The wetnurses were one of the only times I can think of where Faerie has gone to the human world for resources *without* being awful and predatory about it. Oh, some people could be—they'd use compulsion spells to woo away women with babes of their own, and leave their families frantically trying to find a way to nurse a child whose mother had disappeared—but for the most part, no one wants their precious, long-awaited baby being cared for by someone too spell-mazed to make decisions for themselves. It was better to woo and bribe and convince. It shouldn't have been a shock when some of them didn't want to go back, and yet somehow, it was. So the Llangefni screen was developed. It's a complicated illusion. Instead of returning the nursemaids to the normal version of the human world, where they could potentially have used their knowledge of Faerie and any ointment they'd managed to steal to work their way back inside, they'd be cut off completely."

I must have looked appalled, because she snorted and said, "This was the kind way to cut them loose. Before the Llangefni screen was perfected and taught, people were killing them or putting their eyes out, and I feel like both of those choices are a little worse than saying 'Sorry, you don't work here anymore, we'd like you to stop trying to crawl in through a window.'"

"My mother was one of those women," said Simon, voice gone stiff.

"Yeah, and your father and your other mother were weird for keeping her around after she finished feeding your sister," said the Luidaeg. "I'm not saying they were *wrong*, or that they shouldn't have done that. I liked your mom. I only met her a few times—we were already well on our way to withdrawing from the daily business of Faerie by that point—but she was sweet, and kind, and she deserved the life she got to have. Fact remains that she was hired to do a job. If the Torquills had decided, when it was done, that they no longer wanted a human around the place, they would have been justified in putting Celaeno out, and doing whatever they felt necessary to keep her away and keep our world concealed."

"So how the fuck did we run into one of these 'Llangefni screens'?" I asked. "It was just me, Quentin, and Stacy when this started, and none of us knows how to cast an illusion that powerful. Much less one that's contagious, since Simon's got it now too."

"I don't know," said the Luidaeg. "I can think of a few ways, but most of them would only really apply in Europe.

As to why your father and your squire have been affected, I'm sure you can think of a reason if you really work at it."

Meaning it *was* the fact that they had close human heritage, even if it had been removed. But half of Faerie has human heritage these days. Anyone with a surname, really. And that's most of us.

"We are not in Europe right now," said Simon.

"I noticed." The Luidaeg's voice was dry, but not wholly unsympathetic.

Arden reappeared, clutching a small wicker basket. The Luidaeg stuck her hand out imperiously, and Arden passed it over for inspection.

"What took you so long?"

"Sorry, but Walther didn't set his alchemy lab up with the expectation of having it raided," said Arden. "I don't exactly spend a lot of time there, and I didn't know where anything was."

"Huh." The Luidaeg put the basket on the ground, after taking out a small glass bottle, and took a step back. "Well, this should do, and if it doesn't, I can officially say that this isn't my problem. I'm only doing this because Karen needs her mother, and we can't let you people inside the knowe while you're under a Llangefni screen."

"A what?" asked Arden.

"Tell you later," said the Luidaeg. "Stay where you are." She hauled back and threw the bottle at the basket of eggs as hard as she could. Something magical must have happened, because from my perspective, with all view of magic currently blocked off by an inexplicable illusion screen, the bottle slammed into the eggs and vanished rather than breaking any of their shells. In the aftermath of this impossible event, the eggs turned a pale purple, like they were being prepared for a very pastel Easter egg hunt.

The Luidaeg retrieved the basket and picked up an egg, balancing it thoughtfully in her hand. "The humans have a lot of stories about how you get rid of changelings," she said. "But what most of them really meant is 'how to stop seeing the changelings that are already in your home, because your wife went stepping out with an elf knight down in the roses last spring.' And if we reverse those techniques, we can break down a Llangefni screen."

I blinked. "Meaning what, exactly?"

"Meaning you four need to hold still—sorry, Stacy, but even if you don't seem to be affected, we can't risk you carrying an infectious illusion into a space that the mortal world doesn't actually believe exists."

"Could this thing destabilize the knowe?"

"Probably not. Knowes can't catch a screen, anyway. But since someone under a Llangefni screen isn't supposed to see a knowe, much less enter one, I don't think it's a good idea to let someone go inside where they might remind the parts of the shallowing that technically coexist with solid material in the human world that they aren't supposed to be there. Faerie survives conflicting with ordinary physics by staying under the radar and not attracting more attention than absolutely necessary."

"Okay," I said. I wasn't sure I entirely followed her, but it also didn't matter, because me not understanding what was going on wasn't going to change the situation.

"Good," said the Luidaeg, and threw an egg at my head.

I flinched, but not fast enough to stop it from smacking me in the forehead and breaking there, sending egg goo and bits of shell running down my face and into my eyes. I reached up to wipe it away, and my fingers found nothing to remove, sliding over clean, dry skin. Instead, there was a sensation like cobwebs being brushed away, and when I blinked—several times—my vision was clear. The Luidaeg still looked exactly the same. Arden and Lowri, on the other hand, looked like themselves, which was an astonishing and welcome change.

"You should probably wash your face," said the Luidaeg, throwing an egg at Quentin. "Foxglove isn't a great thing to leave in your eyes long-term."

"Right," I said. One more thing to test: I snapped my fingers, and felt my magic respond, dissolving as it finally realized I was asking it to do something. Quentin's face returned to normal. Simon, who was also properly pointy-eared and inhuman, didn't, since he'd never been under an illusion in the first place. "Okay, that was unsettling and stupid."

"Yup," said the Luidaeg, continuing to throw eggs. "I'll probably be really freaked out in a little while, once there's time to sit down and think about the implications. No one's needed to cast a Llangefni in *years*. Maybe centuries at this point. I don't know of anyone who still *can*."

"Right." Simon and Quentin were looking around them with refocused eyes, clearly seeing the same things I had. I turned to Stacy, offering her my hand.

She took it hesitantly. Like the rest of us, there was no outward sign that she'd just been hit in the face with an egg. Magic is weird sometimes.

"Let's go see Mitch and the kids," I said.

She smiled, hesitantly, and came willingly enough as I led her through the open door into the knowe. One nice thing about Faerie's general dislike for thanking people: no one thought it was rude when I walked away from a monarch and one of the Firstborn without thanking them for helping me. Or if they did, they didn't say anything about it.

Simon and Quentin followed us without protest, stepping into the cool, dark, impossible hall. The transition was even easier than usual, maybe because I was still dosed in the Luidaeg's latest solution to ridiculous fae magic.

"Does the sea witch do you a lot of unasked-for favors these days?" asked Stacy.

"Only when she can get away with it," I said. "Her bindings are very specific, and she can help her friends when she can justify her actions as selfish. In this case, I'm guessing the fact that she's taken Karen as an apprentice means getting you into the knowe qualified as a selfish act, and the rest of us just got helpful spillover."

"But I could see the door the whole time."

"Yeah. I don't know how to explain that." Or how we'd been enchanted in the first place. The moment when I'd collapsed on the Safeway floor seemed like the most probable time for this to have all started, even if the illusions Quentin and I had both been wearing at the time made it difficult to pinpoint.

I paused, blinking. My head didn't hurt. My headache had gone away when the Luidaeg hit me with an egg, which was a ridiculous sentence to even think, and yet seemed to be the actual situation. Right, so the Llangefni screen had been connected to the headache, and getting rid of one had resolved the other.

"Where are Mitch and my children?"

"Simon?"

"We took them to the children's quarters," said Simon. "They're largely unoccupied at the moment, as there are no young children in residence, and they seemed like the safest place for people who were experiencing distress."

"What do you mean, 'experiencing distress'?" Stacy's voice was getting louder, and she looked like she was on the verge of starting to yell at people. "October, what is *happening*? What is going on? How did I wind up in that Safeway? I don't remember leaving my house. I was making pancakes, and then you were calling me, and I was at the store. Did I walk that whole way?"

Okay, so the Luidaeg's egg-throwing party had cleared up the compulsion spell. What fun. "All good questions," I said. "Stacy, why weren't you asking these things before?"

"None of them seemed important before!"

So she'd never lost sight of Faerie, only of the things that actually mattered. Everything about this just got more and more concerning. "Simon, you go ahead and lead us to the children's quarters. I don't know the way, and I don't think we want to spend any more time wandering aimlessly than we absolutely have to."

Stacy glared. "No, we don't," she said, voice sharp. "Take me. To my family."

"Of course." Simon moved to the front of our little group, continuing along the hall with the rest of us in pursuit. I fell to the back to walk with Stacy.

She was glancing rapidly from side to side, studying every aspect of the hall around us. The carvings on the walls were showing a procession of funerals, bas reliefs of night-haunts on leaf-husk wings filling the swirls of the scrimshaw sky. It was morbid and unnerving, and I brushed the wall with my fingertips as we walked along.

"Hey," I murmured. "Do you think you could maybe dial it back a bit? You're pouring it on a little thick, and it's not particularly kind."

The next set of carvings showed the founding of the Kingdom, Gilad's parents moving through the redwoods, the knowe opening. Ordinary, calm, children's-museum glimpses of history. I smiled at the wall.

"That was cool of you, and I appreciate it."

I returned my eyes to the front to find Stacy looking at me oddly. I shrugged.

"I don't know if not being allowed to say thank you extends to the architecture, but I try to err on the side of caution," I said. "I don't want to offend the knowes."

"You are *so weird*," she said, but fondly, like the expression of my weirdness was a welcome distraction from her concern. "Toby . . . what's going on? Why are we in Muir Woods? Why didn't I care before this?"

"I think you didn't seem to care because the thing that was keeping the rest of us from seeing Faerie or accessing our magic properly was keeping you from reacting the way you should have," I said, as delicately as I could. "I knew you cared. You just couldn't access the feeling directly."

Stacy looked, if anything, even more alarmed. "How does a spell keep me from feeling something?"

"I don't know. How does a pill keep someone from being depressed, or tired, or anything else? Brains are weird and complicated, and if you can use science to change the way they work, of course you can use magic to do the same thing." Magic and science have a lot of overlap in their results, especially where biology is concerned. If there's a magical equivalent of nuclear fission, I don't want to know about it.

"Oh." She thought for a few seconds. "Well, I care now. Toby, what's going *on*?"

"Today was the formal Court where we discussed whether or not to wake Raysel," I said.

She gasped. "Oh, Toby! I wanted to be there. I'm sorry I couldn't be there."

"It's all right. I didn't ask you to come." I hadn't asked her mostly because I'd known that if I asked, she'd show up, and if things had gone poorly, I hadn't wanted one more witness to our failure.

"Still."

She squeezed my hand, and I smiled at her, feeling terrible at the same time. Her daughter was dead, and here I was letting her reassure me, rather than getting to the point. "Karen was there, with the Luidaeg, and Cass was there in her role as Arden's chatelaine, and they both had some sort of . . . I don't know. Some sort of attack, and started screaming that something was wrong. So Tybalt and I went to the house."

"Did something happen? Toby, are the kids okay?"

I took a deep breath. "Most of them. Anthony got hurt, and we sent him back here to see a healer—I haven't seen him since then."

Simon glanced over his shoulder at us. "Jin was able to stop the bleeding and remove the weapon. He should recover fully."

That was one good thing about today. We didn't have enough of those to hold on to. I closed my eyes for a moment, still walking, trusting Stacy's hand to keep me steady. I'd been doing that for most of my life. When everything else dropped away, there was always Stacy, reaching out to keep me from losing my balance completely.

"Anthony was hurt getting Andrew out of the house," I said, and opened my eyes before I walked into a wall. "He wouldn't have been able to get away from the woman who was attacking them, but Jessica intervened to stop her brothers from being hurt. She was a hero, Stacy. I need you to know that. I saw what she did, and she was a hero."

"You saw . . . you mean you rode her blood, don't you. You mean you *drank my baby's blood* so you could *watch her memories*, because she couldn't tell you herself." Stacy yanked her hand out of mine and stopped walking.

I stopped in turn, facing her, feeling strangely unmoored without her hand in mine. She glared at me, face pale except for bright spots of color in her cheeks.

"Why couldn't she tell you herself? Toby, where is my daughter? Where is *Jessica*?"

I took a deep breath, resisting the urge to close my eyes.

She deserved to know that I was seeing her when I said this. "When the Root and Branch were young, when the Rose still grew unplucked upon the tree; when all our lands were new and green and we danced without care, then, we were immortal. Then, we lived forever." Stacy's face fell, the last drops of color draining away, and she looked, briefly, like she was going to collapse. I didn't stop. I couldn't stop. I owed this to her. I owed this to Jessica, to a little girl who had never done anything wrong, who had run out of time long before her time was done.

"We left those lands for the world where time dwells, dancing, that we might see the passage of the sun and the growing of the world. Here we may die, and here we can fall, and here my darling Jessica Brown, daughter of Mitch and Stacy Brown, has stopped her dancing."

"No," moaned Stacy. "No, she can't—you can't—this *can't*—" She stopped, the third negation still hanging on her lips, and just stared at me, waiting for me to say that this was some kind of senselessly cruel, unnecessary joke. Like I could take it back.

I would have if I could. Instead, I half-shrugged, helplessly, and said, "I'm so sorry, Stacy. I'm so damn sorry."

"What . . . what *happened*?"

"I don't know yet. Someone broke into your house. I know it was a woman; I know her magic smelled like roses. She attacked the boys, and Jessica, she had this book of poetry, and it told her she needed to be afraid—it told her someone was going to hurt her brothers if she didn't intervene. So she intervened. She broke up the fight, and she gave Andrew and Anthony the time they needed to get away. The woman killed her. I don't know why she attacked your children."

The stranger's voice, filtered through Jessica's blood memory, whispered in my ear: "Leave nothing behind. Be the serpent, be the shadow. Be nothing, or never come home."

It didn't make any sense. Why should it? Nothing else about this day made any sense. There was no real reason to expect a murderess's words to change that.

"We're here," said Simon, breaking the silence that

stretched between me and Stacy like a thin ribbon of unspoken promises and unanswered prayers. We both turned to look at him. He had his palm pressed to a plain door in the hallway wall. Had it been there a moment before? I wasn't sure. The knowe was trying to help, in its slow, quiet way, and I was grateful for that.

"Stacy, are you ready?" I asked.

"No." She shook her head, wiping her cheeks with the flats of both hands. Tears kept streaming from her eyes, making the gesture pointless. "But I don't think I ever will be. Mitch and the kids are in there?"

"All four of them were when last I checked," said Simon.

"All right," she said. "I'm so . . . Toby, I'm so sorry you had to see that. But you'll find her, right? You'll find the woman who hurt my baby?"

"I will," I said. "I promise. I will find her, and I will do my best to make sure you get to face her. You have my word." My magic rose and then settled around us, sealing the promise with a level of formality that Faerie itself would enforce. If necessary.

"Thank you," said Stacy, and pushed past Simon, opening the door and slipping silently inside.

The three of us who were left in the hall looked at each other, silently, not one of us wanting to enter that room without an invitation, not at all sure where we should be going instead. I've dealt with a lot of horrible things during my time as a hero of the realm. The death of a little girl who considered me family was a new, and terrible, one on me.

Finally, Simon cleared his throat. "My spouses have returned to Saltmist. They expect me to join them later. Rayseline is still here, waiting for you to take her home. I believe your Fetch has elected to stay with her for the present, until such time as you are available to drive them both back."

"Cool," I said. "Oak and ash, Simon, what are we supposed to do? How am I supposed to handle this?"

"I don't know," he admitted. "Disappearing children are something I have a reasonable degree of experience in. Dead ones . . . the idea is unthinkable."

"Maybe the Luidaeg can help."

Quentin wrinkled his nose. "Stacy doesn't find the Luidaeg comforting the way that we do," he said. "She's not likely to take another Firstborn shoving her nose into the family business very well."

"I don't have any better ideas," I said. I turned, heading back the way we'd come. Both of them followed me.

"Where are you going?" asked Simon.

I sighed heavily. "To tell the Queen we have a murderer in our midst. Again."

The fun never stops, even if sometimes, the dancing does.

NINE

ARDEN WAS BACK IN the receiving room, although the Court had cleared out. It was just her and Nolan, her on her throne with her laptop balanced on her thighs and her legs curled up to brace her heels against the arm, him sitting on the floor, leaning up against the spot where the interior designer would probably have expected her feet to go. Not even Madden was in evidence; the royal siblings were, for once, entirely alone.

Arden looked up when we slipped into the room, concern writ broadly across her face. "Is Stacy all right?" she asked, half-closing the screen of her computer.

"No," I said. "How could she be? Her daughter just died."

"You're right. That was a terrible question."

The knowe had provided a pitcher of hot water and several soft facecloths on a small table near the door. I grabbed one, using it to wipe the foxglove out of my eyes, gesturing for Simon and Quentin to do the same before I turned my attention back to Arden.

"If you have any more lousy questions, ask them now," I suggested. "I can take it, and that way you're not asking Stacy."

Arden pursed her lips and exchanged a glance with her brother. "How are *you*?" she asked.

I laughed unsteadily. "Well, I have to take the girl who tried to murder my daughter home and get her settled in my guest room, and then I have to find out whether my best friend since childhood needs me to help her organize her own child's funeral. I assume you've already given Cassie whatever time off she's going to need?"

"I told her she was relieved of her duties until such time as she felt capable of taking them on again, and she got that look she gets when the air's trying to tell her something and she doesn't want to listen, and told me it wasn't going to take as long as I thought it would, unless it was going to take all the time there was left in the world." Arden shook her head. "I wish we hadn't lost so many of the oracles. I feel like Cassandra would be a lot easier to understand if she'd been able to train under another Seer."

"And if she'd been able to openly admit to having the gift," I said. I didn't need to explain to Arden why Cassandra being a changeling Seer meant she was in even more danger of abduction and compelled service than a pureblood would have been. Any noble who wanted to command her loyalty could just threaten her family, without concern that they'd be breaking the Law if they made good on their threats.

That horrifying thought led me to a question I hadn't wanted to consider, much less ask: "Has anyone been asking about her recently? Or Karen?"

Cass's talents were still relatively unknown outside Arden's circle of close friends and advisors. Quentin and Simon both knew, as did Nolan; if they hadn't, I had all faith Arden would have waited until she got me alone before saying anything. She's careful with her people. Careful enough not to make that sort of a mistake. I guess having your parents assassinated and your brother elf-shot for decades teaches the value of discretion.

Karen, on the other hand, had appeared at the convocation of Western nobles as the Luidaeg's apprentice, and her gifts had been well established to the quorum before the dust had settled. Everyone who cared to know knew there was an oneiromancer in the Mists. She was publicly under the Luidaeg's protection, and most people wouldn't be willing to risk offending the sea witch even to get themselves a Seer . . . but did the nobility of the inland Kingdoms understand the threat the Luidaeg represented? Or the threat she *could* represent if she ever decided to stop dealing with the descendants of her siblings like we were equals and unleash the full potential of an elder Firstborn?

Proximity to the ocean doesn't define her power. It just makes her happy. There's water everywhere, and they used to call her the Lady of the Lake. If someone had hurt Jessica to get to Karen, the Luidaeg was going to make them sorry, and as a Firstborn, she was functionally above the Law. Maybe she could be charged with a violation and maybe she couldn't, but unless her father wanted to get involved, she wasn't going to be punished for anything she did.

"Not in my presence," said Arden. "People know Karen can see the future in dreams, but I don't think they realize how *much* she sees, and it's not like she usually volunteers the information. I think she's less of a Seer and more of a messenger in some ways."

That fit with what I knew of Karen's capabilities. She could enter the dreams of anyone sleeping—including the increasingly rarer victims of elf-shot, the ones who, like Raysel, had been left asleep even after the cure became available. So while she *could* see the future, she only seemed to bother when it was immediately important to someone she cared about, or when it impacted her directly—like, say, someone killing her baby sister. She wasn't a useful all-purpose Seer. She was useful in other ways, and it was absolutely believable that someone might attack her family to get to her, which was part of why the Luidaeg had been so public about staking her claim after Karen's abilities became more widely known. Mess with the oneiromancer, mess with the sea witch.

"So this probably wasn't an attack on her family to get to her," I said. "Simon, I know your old employer wasn't big on Seers."

"That's a mild expression of her hatred of them," he said. "According to her, oracles betray Faerie with every breath, because when they lay down a prophecy, they strip away the freedom of anyone who hears it. I always found her fondness for Oleander mystifying, given that the Peri Oleander was descended from carry some small gift for prophecy themselves."

"Yeah, got that firsthand." Oleander had spouted a bunch of prophetic nonsense at me before she died, and my life being what it is, I was sure it was all going to matter eventually. I pushed that thought aside, watching him. I had to ask. "Did she tell you why she did what she did to the Roane?"

"Tell me? Sweet girl, she *gloated* about it. Any time she could turn the conversation's tide to her past crimes, she did, and gleefully. Taking the Roane from her sister was a point of very greatest pride to her. She did what she did to take the prophets from the sea and the children from their mother's arms, and near as ever I could tell, those reasons were equal in her eyes. She was nothing if not efficient." He shook his head. "But if your question is whether she wanted the oracles destroyed, the answer is yes. She very much did. She also claimed responsibility for the reduced numbers among the Lamia, for the isolation of the Peri, and for orchestrating the destruction of the Ysengrimus."

"The who?"

"Exactly." He shook his head a second time, like a horse trying to dislodge a fly. "The fact that you smelled roses concerns me—but there was no trace of snow, and she's never been able to conceal the winter's touch upon her workings. What's more, she slumbers still."

"Are we sure?"

"I am." He looked at me, unblinking. "If she were awake, she would have come for me. I have stronger claims on me than I did when first she took me, but I don't know that they would be strong enough to stop her. All the ocean might not be enough to stop her. And if she comes for me again, if she threatens my family again, I'll go with her willingly rather than risk harm coming to them. There's little enough I can give in payment for the grace they've given me. Not being placed into harm's way by my presence may be the whole of what I have to offer."

"Wow," said Quentin, before I could say anything. We both turned to look at him. "Can I be there when you tell Dianda that? Because I really want to watch her beat your ass. And I know you haven't told her yet, because if you had, there's no way you'd be walking around under your own power."

"My lady wife would never strike a partner in anger," said Simon, sounding less horrified than offended on her behalf.

"No, she wouldn't," said Quentin. "Dean's had to relearn a lot of rules about when you should and shouldn't hit people since he moved to the land; they're way fonder of punching in the Undersea. But he's never hit me, not once, and he says that's not a thing they do down there. If Dianda hits you, it's because you've earned it by being an asshole, not because you're a misbehaving husband."

"It's bad that I almost find that a relief, right?" I muttered. Finding out that my brother wasn't into pain as a part of his love life was more than I'd really wanted to know.

We can't always get what we want. Simon sighed. "I know," he said, looking away. "I'll do it all the same, to protect my family. If I go quietly, she may not claim August."

"So she went out of her way to destroy oracles, and the house smelled like roses, but not *her* roses," I said, trying to get us back on track before this got any more awkward. "Not Maeve's roses, either, or Amandine's. Why are so many people in Faerie rose-scented? Was someone trying to cut corners on the toy line?"

"There's a playset I'd like to see," said Arden. "A modular Muir Woods, complete with royal household, and maybe a Madden with actual transforming action."

"You'd get in trouble because all the kids would want a Queen of Faerie doll with fancy dresses, not jeans and sweatshirts," I said.

"Like you're one to talk," said Quentin, and laughed nervously.

It felt weird to be laughing this soon after Jessica's death. Which reminded me. I turned to Arden. "You have a Bannick on staff at this point, right?"

"Not on staff as such," said Arden. "Your friend Danny, the taxi driver? He knows a lady. She comes by when I need someone to do some deep cleaning."

"Okay, so we call Danny before Mitch and Stacy leave here," I said. When Arden looked surprised, I shrugged. "Jessica died in the living room, and she didn't die cleanly. There's a lot of blood. The night-haunts have been and gone; they left a manikin behind, but the body's already been consumed. We're going to need someone to clean the place if we don't want Mitch and Stacy dealing with the stress of a human murder investigation on top of everything else."

Human wisdom would assume one or both of Jessica's parents had been complicit in death, especially without anything to point at somebody else. I wasn't terribly worried about the physical evidence I and the boys would have left behind; with the exception of Simon, we'd all been there before, and I was pretty sure Simon's fingerprints weren't going to show up in any human database. We'd be fine. They wouldn't be.

Arden nodded, slowly. "That makes sense. It doesn't sit right with me, though. Someone should know what happened to her."

"And someone will," I said.

The door to the receiving room slammed open and a blond man in a brown tweed jacket and jeans raced into the room, bringing the smell of ice and yarrow blossoms with him. His magic was still high, crackling in the air around him like he'd just been threatened in some way, and he nearly fell over as he came skidding to a stop in front of us, hands clenching and unclenching as he stared first at Arden, then at me. His eyes, blue enough to look like a special effect out of a Hollywood movie, were wide and unfocused, unseeing. He knew we were here. He knew who he was looking at. He might not fully understand what that meant.

"Where is she?" he demanded, voice peaking and cracking on the last word. "Where's Cass?"

"Walther, hey," I said, holding up my hands placatingly. "Did someone call you? Are you okay?"

"Cass," he repeated. "I want you to take me to her. I

want you to take me to her *right now*!" He was yelling by the time he stopped, and his hands were no longer clenching; instead, he had balled them into fists, although at least he wasn't threatening to hit me. Yet. I had the feeling that was next on the agenda if I didn't get him to her before he had to escalate.

"She's with her family," I said.

He blinked slowly, eyes seeming to focus for the first time. "All of them?"

"Not all of them," I said, grimly. "I'm guessing she called you?"

He nodded.

"We weren't fast enough for Jessica," I said. "I'm sorry."

Walther blinked again, eyes filling with tears before he turned his face away. "She was just a kid," he said.

"I know. She was a good kid."

"She'd finally stopped wetting the bed. She was excited about finishing middle school and going to a real high school."

All the Brown kids were homeschooled with a group of other changeling kids until they reached high school age and went to the local school system in order to learn how to move in the human world. Having a diploma at the end didn't hurt, either; Cass had been able to use hers to go to college, which had put her in the position to meet Walther outside my sometimes-ridiculous sphere of influence. Karen was a year away from graduation, and still plugging gamely away at her classes, even as it got harder and harder for her to stay awake as much as she needed to.

"Toby . . . what *happened*?"

"We still don't know," I said. "Someone threw a compulsion spell over Stacy and got her out of the house, then jumped the boys when they came home. Jessica had been in her room. She heard the noise and came out to intervene, and the woman . . . she hurt her, Walther. She hurt her real bad. Jessica Brown has stopped her dancing. She's with the night-haunts now."

"So she bled," said Walther. "You had access to her memories. You must have seen what happened. You have to know."

"But I don't," I said. "Whoever hurt Jessica, they didn't show up in the blood memories. I could smell their magic—it was a woman, and I heard what she said while she was killing Jess. But I never saw her face."

"Did—?"

"I think Jessica did, yeah," I said. "I didn't stay to talk to the night-haunts. Maybe I should have. Maybe I should call them back and see what they can tell me. Her memories must have had time to settle within the flock by now."

"You promised to stop doing that," said Quentin. "They're not a toy. If you keep messing with them, they're going to eat you."

"Maybe," I said. "Maybe I deserve to be eaten, if I can't tell Stacy what happened to her little girl."

"Maybe you do," agreed Walther roughly. "That doesn't mean it would help. You'll have to find another way."

"There was another issue," said Simon. Walther and I both turned to look at him. "A complicated and currently unfashionable illusion called a Llangefni screen was thrown over October when she went looking for Stacy, and transferred from her to several others, myself included. Infectious illusions are . . . They're not outside the realm of the possible, but they're difficult in ways I can't easily articulate. I'm not the most powerful illusionist in Faerie, but I served under a woman who very well may have been, and she taught me many things that can take advantage of the level of power I *do* possess. I couldn't spin that illusion. I doubt my old mistress could have done it easily, if she could have done it at all."

"Which means there's absolutely no chance Stacy did it, and we need to assume it was somehow tied to the compulsion spell she was under," I said.

The door opened again, and we all looked around to see who was coming to join us. The Luidaeg stared back before she sauntered fully inside and toward the throne, Oberon—as he so often was—following in her wake.

We held our tongues until she reached us, when Arden set her laptop fully aside, rose, and bowed. "Luidaeg," she said.

Like most of the Firstborn, the Luidaeg technically has

no title. She pre-dates the feudal system we mimicked from the humans, and never saw the point in chasing crowns. So for her, the title she had been given by Faerie itself when she stopped using her given name with most people was the polite form of address. Everything else was just frills.

Arden didn't acknowledge Oberon at all, and from the way he relaxed, I suspected that was what he'd been hoping for.

And in that instant, like a balloon being pricked with a pin, my patience for whatever game it was he'd been playing burst and drained away, and I stalked toward him, shoulders tight, eyes narrowed. The Luidaeg turned to watch me go, lips slightly pursed, like she was reserving judgment on my actions until she knew exactly what they were.

Every step made me angrier, until I was standing right in front of the tall, unassuming man with the antlers on his brow, the man who was the father of us all, both symbolically and—in some cases—literally. I tilted my chin up so I could meet his eyes.

"You," I said.

"Me," he agreed. Arden jumped, looking at him for the first time since he'd entered the room. She hadn't been ignoring him before, I realized; she hadn't been able to see him until he'd decided to allow her to.

"You need to cut this shit out," I said, voice hard and louder than I had intended.

He blinked. "I'm sorry?"

"You need to *stop*," I said. "You fucked it all up. You get that, right? We were fine. Faerie was flawed but it was *fine*, and then you left, and we all started eating each other alive. Your kids are killing each other. Somebody hurt a little girl I considered part of my family, and I don't know what I'm going to do about it—I just know that nothing I do is going to make it right, because there is no making this right. She's dead, and she's gone, and the only people who might be able to help me are the night-haunts, and *they* asked me to stop summoning them all the damn time. So congrats, asshole. You fucked it all up by leaving, and then you came back and you didn't do anything to fix it. You need to stop. You need to start helping us."

He blinked again, more slowly this time, and his eyes seemed to truly focus on me for the first time. There was a distant, primal menace in his expression, something older than I was by such a vast degree that the part of my mind responsible for registering fear and transmitting it to the rest of the committee barely even recognized it as a threat. That was nice. Normally, I'm way too foundationally aware when I'm daring something bigger than me to knock me down a peg. This time, I knew it, sure, but I didn't *know* it. The gulf between us was too enormous.

No one else was saying a word, not even the Luidaeg. They were all just watching as I tried to pick a fight with Oberon, the man whose power was as great compared to that of the Firstborn as theirs was to my own.

Sometimes I'm a damn genius.

"What did you just say to me, daughter of my daughter?" he asked, voice a low, warning rumble.

"I *said*, you fucked up royally when you walked away from the people who needed you, whatever reason you may have had at the time, however good of an idea it may have seemed, and I *said* you're still fucking up right now, today, by coming back and not stepping up to do your damn job," I snapped. "You're *Oberon*. You're the King of *All* Faerie, not just some puny Kingdom here or demesne there. You could stop this. But you don't. You walked away from your kids when they still needed you, you left us all trapped here on Earth for reasons literally no one has ever been able to explain or figure out, and now that you're back, you just want to, what? Watch television with Poppy and eat all the Luidaeg's ice cream? You have a *job* to do. You need to start *doing* it."

He inhaled slowly, looking at me the whole time, and the part of me that had been steadfastly refusing to see how dangerous he genuinely was suddenly seemed to realize what I'd been doing for the last five minutes and panicked in the back of my mind, quietly, so as not to set off the rest of my limbic system. Big help, there, brain. Couldn't have reached that conclusion, oh, *before* I started mouthing off to the man who created us all?

Finally, in a low tone, he said, "You are so much like

your grandmother sometimes. I forget how quickly things change in your mortal world. I thought you would remember why I left the way I did. I thought you were being polite out of consideration for what I'd been through, what I'd lost." He looked to the Luidaeg. "Annie, is she telling the truth? Do you truly not understand why I locked the doors?"

She shrugged. "I've been trying to tell you, Dad. You just didn't want to listen."

"I see." He looked back to me. "As to why I don't simply solve your problems for you, if you had a tank of very small creatures, mice or fish or fleas, and they had a problem, and they somehow managed to express that problem to you, would that mean you could magically fix it? Every time? Oh, if the problem was large enough for you to see, if there was a cat among the mice or a hunting snake among the fish, you might be able to intercede, but if the problem was more to a scale with them, who were so much smaller than yourself, you might well be left standing helplessly by, however much you wanted them to be safe and cared for. I can grant the large strokes of what will aid you, but the fine details are too far beneath me for my aid to help them."

"Don't start a campfire with a nuke, got it," I said.

"But as to why I locked the doors . . . the Summerlands grow from fae presence. They are a skerry created by the sheer weight of our descendants gathered together, like a film of sweat left by a hundred soldiers running in the summer sun. They are a natural phenomenon, and they will always expand to contain you all. The deeper realms, the ones farther from this world and its physical laws, they formed from myself and my wives, or from our direct descendants, and without us to keep them safely tamed, they could easily turn feral and consume anyone too weak to take them back in hand. I locked those doors because without us, you would never have survived. You would have been destroyed."

I stared at him. So did everyone else in the room. In that moment, you could have heard a pin drop—or the whisper-soft sound of a Cait Sidhe stepping out of the Shadow Roads. I turned. Tybalt was standing near the edge of the shadows behind the throne, one hand on Julie's shoulder, the tiger-striped changeling looking far more winded than her adoptive uncle, who traveled through the shadows almost as easily as he breathed. Julie was Cait Sidhe, which meant the shadows liked her a lot more than they did me, but she was also human, and they would always push against that part of her.

"Toby!" she exclaimed, seeing me looking in her direction. She stepped out from under Tybalt's hand, rushing across the floor to my side, not sparing a second glance for Oberon. So he'd lifted the illusion of not mattering for those of us who were already in the room, and not for everyone? It was probably petty of me to be annoyed by that. We'd never get anything done if someone was stopping to go "Holy crap, that's *Oberon*" every five seconds. But it was still time, and past time, for him to be telling the rest of the family that he was back.

"Uncle Tybalt told me what happened," she said, as she hurried toward me. "How's Stacy holding up? Where are she and the kids? This place is a freakin' maze, even by pureblood standards—uh, no offense, Queen Windermere."

"None taken," said Arden, who sounded like she couldn't decide between shock and amusement. "I didn't build it. I didn't even plant the seeds."

"They're in the children's quarters," I said.

"I can take the young mistress to your friends, if you feel it would be appropriate to do so," said Nolan. He was probably a little bit desperate to be out of this deeply alarming conversation. He'd been standing by quietly enough that, to be honest, I'd almost forgotten he was there. Not the worst attribute in a Crown Prince who wasn't looking to inherit the throne anytime soon, really.

"Appropriate?" snapped Julie. "I'll show you appropriate."

"Julie." I put a hand on her arm, trying to soothe her. "It's okay. He wasn't trying to be a dick. He doesn't know us all very well."

"I know you better than is perhaps optimal for my health," muttered Nolan, probably more loudly than he'd intended to.

I ignored him. "He'll take you to them. Nolan, you remember Juliet of the Court of Dreaming Cats. You met her at the wedding. She grew up with me and Stacy. We've been friends since we were just kids. Stacy will be glad to see her."

Probably more so than she'd be to see me right now. Julie had a bit of a reputation as a street thug, but she wasn't known as a constant magnet for chaos the way I was. I couldn't see my presence as soothing.

"It would be my pleasure," said Nolan, moving to Julie's side and offering her his arm with an exaggerated flourish. She looked him frankly up and down, then smiled, slow and languid.

"You can take me anywhere you want, handsome," she said, taking the offered arm.

I released her, stepping back. Julie likes to flirt. Men, women, it doesn't matter—I've seen her flirt with and flatter a Bridge Troll to the point of convincing him that maybe the tiny, breakable cat-person would be a good choice for a coffee date. It's as natural for her as breathing is for me, and Nolan was the kind of guy who deserved a little enthusiastic flirting-with. Being a Crown Prince could be a real limiting factor on a guy's dating life, at least according to Quentin, who'd been warned extensively before leaving Toronto that he couldn't trust the motivations of anyone who knew who he actually was.

And it was natural for me to be focusing on trivial things while under this much stress, and I knew it. It's a tendency I've been wrestling with for as long as I can remember, like being able to step back and focus on the small will somehow make the large less massive.

Nolan transcribed a shallow arch in the air with his hand. Julie looked to Tybalt, and upon receiving his nod of approval, stepped through the portal that opened in front of her, vanishing at once.

Nolan moved to follow.

"Nolan," said Arden, before he could. He glanced back at her. "Just . . . be careful, okay? We don't know what's really going on. I don't want another of those Llangefni screens cropping up inside the knowe."

Nolan nodded and once more moved to follow Julie through his still-open portal.

"Wait!" shouted Walther, seeming to realize what was happening. Like most of the people in the room, he'd been too stunned by standing there and watching me yell at Oberon to have reacted before this. He ran across the room to Nolan. "You're going to Cassie?"

"I am."

"So you could have taken me there anytime?"

"Hey, Walther?" I said. "Maybe let's not start a fight with the Crown Prince in his own knowe, okay?"

Walther shot me a look so full of venom that if it could have done harm, it would have. It burned. "I just want to get to my girlfriend," he said.

"I understand, but we still have to follow the rules."

He snorted. "Because you're always such a rule-follower." Turning back to Nolan, he demanded, "Take me with you. I need to get to her, and there's nothing I can do here. She has to be devastated."

"Of course, Sir Alchemist," said Nolan gravely. "You have my apologies for not offering before."

He gestured to the portal, waiting for Walther to step through before he looked back at the rest of us, clearly waiting for another objection. Receiving none, he stepped through the portal, which closed behind him.

"What," demanded Oberon, "did the little Queen just say?"

"Didn't get around to that part when I was explaining why we needed to be here a little longer," said the Luidaeg.

Tybalt didn't look angry, just confused, which either meant he didn't know what a Llangefni screen was, or that he didn't see why having one in a knowe might be alarming. Either way, it was better than watching him realize I'd put myself in danger in his absence yet again. I'd take it.

Besides, I was basically waving a red flag at Oberon right now. Tybalt would have plenty of reasons to worry about me.

"There is none in this Kingdom with the strength or finesse needed to cast a Llangefni screen," said Oberon. "That is lost magic."

"Hang on," I said. "How can it be lost magic if half the people here know what it is, and know enough about it to be concerned?"

"Everyone here who knows about it is either old enough to have been here before it was lost, or a scholar of old magic, like the failure," said the Luidaeg. "As to how magic can be lost, look to the blood."

Simon's eyes widened, as if that had explained everything. "Of course," he breathed. "I've wondered about some of the older techniques, and how they could have been lost the way they have been, but that—that makes perfect sense."

"What does?" asked Tybalt, blankly.

I raised my hand. "You want to share with the rest of the class? Because I am not seeing anything here that makes sense."

"Magic lives in blood," said Simon. "I know you've borrowed magic from other lines by taking their blood as a source of power, rather than memory. I've frequently done the same."

"Etienne says we'll have to start working on that in my training soon," said Quentin, who didn't sound thrilled about the idea. "He also says that Duke Torquill isn't particularly skilled in that area, and we may need to find someone else who can instruct me."

"My brother always found the idea of taking someone else's magic as his own somewhat questionable," said Simon. "It could be used as a means for incriminating the innocent, since it enables the caster to leave traces of someone else's magic in a place where it shouldn't have been. But refinement of the magic that dwells in blood is at the base of much of alchemy, and it was important to me that I master the art."

"I used Caitir's blood to open a path out of the Shadow Roads, when she and Tybalt had both been knocked unconscious and I had to get us out of there before I suffocated," I said, slowly. "So yeah, blood."

"But you couldn't have done that without her blood being available to you in the first place," said Simon. "On your own, you can't open portals. Even now, even having done it, you can't do it again without the blood to carry the key and allow you to slide it into the lock. You're stuck without the blood."

"Still not following," I said.

"Llangefni screens require access to a type of illusion magic that hasn't been seen in a very long time," said the Luidaeg. She was watching Oberon fixedly, like a hawk watches a patch of grass where it's sure a rabbit has gone to ground. She wasn't blinking, that was for sure. "The Morgen could cast them, but the Morgen died out long ago. There just wasn't room in the rivers for one more clear tributary, and they merged with other streams and all their unique gifts were lost with the tide."

"So once the blood that had been harvested from the Morgen had all been used, the working became impossible," said Simon. "The magic was lost."

"My Summer Queen could cast the screens," said Oberon. "My Winter Lady never had the gift."

"Because Mom wasn't about illusions; she was about transformations," said the Luidaeg, sharply. "A Llangefni screen is all about tricking the eyes into not seeing what's actually there, and when it's cast on someone with fae blood, on convincing their magic that it's been released when it's really rising. It doesn't bind anyone's magic. It . . . redirects it. It *tricks* it. A Llangefni screen is a lie gone walking, and nothing stops it but tearing it down. I didn't speak for the Morgen when it became clear they were going to fade into memory and myth. I didn't want the things they could do to be preserved."

I blinked at her. The Luidaeg had talked before about descendant lines going extinct, and she had always, always been sorry. She had always, always regretted it. To lose a descendant line was to lose a part of Faerie forever, and to leave another of the First grieving as she had grieved. To hear her talk about extinction so casually, so clinically, went against everything I expected from her.

"The Morgen belonged to Liban, did they not?" asked Oberon.

The Luidaeg nodded. "She died before they did, or I might have fought to keep them with us," she said.

That eased a bit of my objection, but nowhere near to all of it. "So these Morgen people are all dead, and no one else can cast one of these screens?" I asked. "Just to be sure I'm on the right page here."

"There are things that are just normal abilities, so ordinary that we never bothered to name them, and then there are things like the don't-look-heres that got named because they were universal. The rarer abilities, like the Llangefni screens, are really more like techniques refined by and limited to specific descendant lines," said the Luidaeg. "With Titania gone and the Morgen swept away, that illusion should be outside the capability of anyone currently in Faerie."

"It's worse than that," I said, grimly. "Whoever killed Jessica didn't leave their own image in her blood."

"What?" asked the Luidaeg, more sharply than I would have expected. I blinked at her. She stared at me, face gone pale. "Are you serious right now? Choose your words carefully, October. This is important."

I took a half step backward, stopping when my shoulder bumped against Tybalt's. He was standing silently, just watching for now, clearly confused. Hell, *I* was confused, and I had more information than he did. It was a wonder he was keeping up as well as he was. "I'm serious," I said. "I went into Jessica's final memories, and there was a woman attacking her. I know Jessica *must* have seen her. There's no way she wouldn't have. She was looking in the right direction, her eyes were open, and she saw everything else that was going on, but she didn't see the woman who killed her—or if she did see her, her blood didn't hold on to it."

"Oh, *Mom*," breathed the Luidaeg. It sounded less like she was trying to identify someone and more like she was praying. She walked over to her father and hid her face against his shoulder, and somehow that was the most terrifying thing that had happened during a fairly terrifying day.

Oberon, for his part, raised a hand to stroke her hair, looking at me levelly, and asked, "Did the girl see or hear anything else? Anything at all?"

"The woman who attacked her, while she was strangling

her, she said, 'Leave nothing behind. Be the serpent, be the shadow. Be nothing, or never come home.'"

Oberon closed his eyes.

"Ah," he said. "Then this is to be my fault. I am so very sorry."

TEN

HIS ANNOUNCEMENT FELL INTO the room like a lead balloon, all of us staring at him in silent, open-mouthed shock—except for the Luidaeg, who left her face pressed against his shoulder, shuddering now, clearly terrified. That was somehow the worst thing yet, in a day that had started with a small victory before transforming into an endless parade of worse and worse events. A girl was dead. My best friend's family was broken. Raysel was awake and not yet safely tucked away in my house, where her parents couldn't get to her without going through a whole detachment of angry onlookers.

Killing a Firstborn takes iron *and* silver. Was it even possible to kill one of the Three? I was suddenly itching to find out.

"You need to explain yourself, right now, in small words," I said, voice tight. "I may have brought you home, but that doesn't mean I can't find a way to put you back where I found you."

Oberon, while clearly still upset, actually looked amused. "Are you threatening me, granddaughter?"

"Not sure about that one way or the other just yet," I said. "I kinda want to be, but my husband here would like to stay married to me for a little longer before I go and get myself smashed by something infinitely larger than myself."

"Quite," said Tybalt, in a strangled voice.

"So if you explain fast, I won't have to start something I can't finish, and you won't have to explain to your eldest daughter why you killed me after she said she was going to be the one to do it."

Simon and Quentin both turned to look at the Luidaeg. Neither of them had been there on that long-ago night where I'd met the sea witch properly for the first time, and she'd announced that when I died, it was going to be at her hand. From the looks on their faces, that was probably a good thing. I guess most people aren't that cavalier about the idea of being murdered by their friends.

As for Tybalt, he just looked resigned. That was fair. I made him agree to kill me once, when Oleander's poisons had been well on the way to convincing me that I was going to become a danger to everyone I cared about. And then I'd gone and married him. To him, it made a lot more sense that someone might threaten my life and then become a much bigger part of it.

Oberon sighed and sat down. There hadn't been a chair there a moment before, but as soon as his knees began to bend, a throne of twisted roots and bending branches sprouted from the floor, as old and weathered as if it had been there since the knowe was first opened. Some of the branches put forth small flowering twigs as he settled, and shelf fungus sprouted from the base of the throne.

Arden blinked but didn't object. Some people have a sense of self-preservation.

I am not "some people." I folded my arms and glared, waiting.

Oberon sighed again, more heavily. "Impatient," he said, looking at me. "Something else you share with your grandmother. My sweet Jenny never once met a mountain she didn't think needed to be climbed, and immediately. She never waited for anything in her life."

I was getting a little tired of being compared to Janet Carter, the woman who intentionally alienated me from my own daughter. Oh, right, and broke Maeve's Ride, somehow—through a mechanism I was hoping Oberon was about to explain—shattering the balance between our Queens, and throwing Faerie into disarray in the process.

"She's not the only person I'm descended from," I said, sharply.

"No, I have some blame to bear in your composition as well," he agreed. "You are definitely of my lines. I've always been a father to heroes." And he looked, oddly enough, at the Luidaeg, who looked uncomfortable in response.

"I don't think musing about the family is what October was hoping for," she said. "You said this was your fault, Dad. It's time you start talking."

Oberon grimaced, still watching her. "You used to have more deference when you spoke to me."

"You used to have the right to demand it," she said.

"I see." He turned back to me. "Faerie was once more than it is now, and less at the same time. My wives and I were born of the same source, like buckets drawn from the same well, but we were no true kin to one another. They claimed each other as sisters more out of the hope that a familial relationship would make it easier for them to share our world without destroying one another than out of any recognizable kinship, for there were no models for us to draw upon. We became, we began, and when we came together, a world was born. The deepest realms of Faerie spread out beneath our feet, establishing their firmaments in the great nothingness around us, and we walked paths that had not existed until we had need of them, on and on into the void, until we found this place, this 'Earth' of mortal lives and mortal meaning. Something we had not created. It gave us something to model ourselves after, for we had not once thought beyond the moment."

I wanted to ask about a dozen questions. I didn't want to ask anything at all. What he was saying made it sound like the Three were gods, created from nothing and creating in their turn, and I just didn't want to take that sort of step toward escalation. Super-powerful immortal beings, sure. Actual divinities? Nope, I'm good.

"We saw that the human families had children, and so we made children for ourselves," he said. "Some in the biological manner the humans were so very fond of, others through other means. We shaped them not, decided their fates not at all, but allowed Faerie itself—allowed the nebulous light of our birthing—to decide what most it needed, and so they were born to every form imaginable, as different from one another as snowflakes. They served us as we served Faerie, and all was peaceful, for a time. But while my ladies could make their children either with my aid or with the raw materials of the mortal world, they could not increase Faerie with each other. They could not coexist much of the time. Their hatred grew between them like a rose, bright and blooming and drawing blood with every opportunity it found. In time, they couldn't be near one another without falling to a rage. Maeve, who was always the calmest of us, asked only to be left alone when she was not with me, to be allowed to fill the fens and wilds of this bright world with her descendants, and to hear Faerie ring with their laughter. She was the first to take her children back into the worlds that had been birthed on our long walk, to show them the art of building skerries and realms out of the nothing, and to see them settled where she thought them safe. They built kingdoms without our presence, and without the looming threat of their cousins close to hand. Titania, on the other hand, loved her sister, but it was the love of a root for a bone, of a fox for a bird. She thirsted to devour everything Maeve was, to take it into herself and for her own, and to never see Faerie shared between them again. When I came to her, for we had long since decided that I would share the mortal year between them, she asked over and over again if I would stay, if I would eschew her sister's arms for her own, which smelled so much sweeter, which kept the same shape from hour to hour, from day to day. And when I refused, she set her children to destroying Maeve's. They began with the more bestial among them, the ones whose other parent could be in some way traced back to the mortal world and not to my bower, and they killed with bright abandon."

Oberon sighed, heavily. "It took far too long for me to

realize I needed to intervene. Children were an endless gift. We could always make more of them. But children became adults, ourselves cast again in miniature, and they were frustrated and angry that their gifts were so much less than our own. They could create continents, raise kingdoms, but we had birthed *worlds*. They could craft deeper realms for themselves out of the firmament we had already laid down, but they couldn't create out of nothing. They grew jealous. If they wanted to fight among themselves, it seemed unwise for me to stop them."

"What my father isn't saying, as he recounts the way he tried to become father of the year, is that not all of us *wanted* to fight," snapped the Luidaeg. "Titania's kids came into our homes and cut us down. They hunted us like animals, and when they couldn't kill us themselves, they turned the world against us. We fled into deeper Faerie because they were the ones who taught the humans to take up iron and silver. We learned to hide because they wouldn't let us be found. Faerie gives her newest residents the shapes she needs them to have, and the shapes they'll need to stay alive. It wasn't until Titania's descendants began waging war against us that we started to see forms like the Bridge Trolls, and the Ysengrimus, and the Gean-Cannah. Faerie readied us for war, because the war was already happening."

As she spoke, Oberon looked more and more depressed. I couldn't quite make myself feel bad for him. So much of what we'd been through sounded like it came from him being a shitty parent.

And we were getting off the point that we had come here to discuss. "What the hell does any of this have to do with the woman who killed Jessica?" I demanded.

"I'm sorry," said Oberon. "It's difficult for me to say. I thought I was acting in good faith, for the good of all Faerie. I may have been wrong."

"May have been?" asked the Luidaeg. "*May* have been? Are you kidding me right now, with your 'may have been'?"

He looked at her sorrowfully, agony in his eyes. "I saw no other way."

"Because you never wanted to," she snapped. "You were

so overpowered compared to everyone around you that when you ran up against a problem you couldn't resolve with the wave of your hand, you checked out. Get to the damn point, Dad. Everyone else has a time limit."

"Of course." He turned back to me. "The creation of myself and my ladies was not without consequence. The force which made us was lessened in the making, wounded, in a way, and it bled into the void without healing. We found we could stop the bleeding for a time, if we fed it lives."

"Lives?" I asked, blankly.

"As with the night-haunts, if it was given lives, it could endure. Their strength would feed and heal it, for a time. We couldn't go ourselves—it would reject us when we tried—and it seemed cruel to serve up our own children as payment for something they had no part in. So we turned to the mortal world."

"The Rides," I said, a piece of incomprehensible history falling into place. They had been a part of fae tradition when the King and Queens were still with us, one every seven years, alternating between Maeve and Titania. A grand procession from the Summerlands into deeper Faerie, always carrying one human with them, always returning without that human in their company.

The last Ride, Maeve's Ride, had been broken by my grandmother, Janet Carter, and kicked off the entire chain of events that led us here, to this room, with our long-absent King explaining our own past to us.

Pieces of this felt like things we should never have forgotten, things we should have been repeating between us over and over, enshrining them in memory. And then I remembered that while the fae aren't human, and purebloods can hold grudges on a geologic scale, they're still people. We're all still people. Asking them to remember things that made them look bad was asking them to behave in an unrealistic way. When you live for centuries, you have plenty of time to rewrite the past and make yourself look good.

"The Rides," Oberon agreed. "My Ladies agreed to alternate caring for and preparing their sacrifices. They took mortals who wouldn't be missed or mourned, and they had fourteen years to ready them for the end that was ahead. Fourteen years against a mortal lifetime was an eternity. We found the best results when they went willingly, and so my Ladies cared for them as true members of their Courts, cosseted and waited upon, and then, they would Ride to lands no human eyes were meant to see, and they would give their offerings unto the wound, and Faerie would endure for another seven years, strong and healthy and no longer dying by inches. But when my Jenny found herself attached to the latest human tithe and broke the Ride, Maeve was forced to go in his place. We had no other willing offering prepared. Titania had her sacrifice, but the girl was as yet only half-ready for her duties."

"Wait," I said. "I thought you couldn't go. I thought you said the injury would reject you."

"Yes, as a tree rejects a nail when hammered into the trunk. We could stop the bleeding for a time, but we would inevitably be pushed out again, no healing performed, no strength given up."

"And was 'for a time' more than seven years?"

His silence was more than answer enough.

"So what you're saying is that you set up a system of *human sacrifice* to cure a problem you created, whether intentionally or not, and then when someone stepped in to stop it, everything got fucked up?" I folded my arms, glaring at him. "Just so we're on the same page here."

"We intended no harm."

"But you did it, Daddy," said the Luidaeg. "Intent is fairy gold. It makes you feel like you've paid in the moment, but it turns to dust and leaves when the sun comes up and everyone sees what you've done. You did harm."

Oberon looked away from her. "Maeve went into the wound," he said. "The sacrifice was no longer willing, and no replacement could be found. The woman who had broken the Ride came to me demanding redress, and I was charmed by her boldness. Enough so that I listened to her, enough that I took her as my companion for a time. And through it all, Titania grew more bold, and more angry at the fact that she finally had everything she could have wanted—her sister gone, all Faerie hers for the taking—and still she wasn't happy. She had believed, truly, that in Maeve's absence, she would finally be content. She would be Queen of All Faerie, and none would be her equal, and she would be happy. But she wasn't, and the balance, which had already been disrupted by her sister's absence, was thrown ever more off by her temper. She raged, and she set her children more fiercely than ever against Maeve's, thinking that perhaps the peace she sought would be found in the extinction of her sister's memory."

He fell quiet, and the Luidaeg sighed.

"They were killing us like we were nothing," she said. "We had claws as sharp and spells as swift, but we lacked the hatred, and we lacked the intent, and again and again they pursued us, however far or fast we ran. We couldn't hate them enough to hold them at bay. We went to our father, begging him to intercede, begging him to do *anything* before we were wiped out. And then he was gone, and so was she, and while the attacks didn't stop—the children of Titania had learned their lessons too well to stop immediately—they did pull back to what they'd been before our mother disappeared."

"She would have destroyed Faerie in her quest to be the only Queen remembered or beloved," said Oberon. "She was already destroying her children. She knew nothing of what it meant to love the ones who depended on her for their own health and happiness. She knew nothing of parenthood."

Honestly, at this point, I wasn't sure he did, either. But I held my tongue, waiting for him to finish this towering, terrible story.

"So I cast her out." It was such a simple explanation for one of our greatest mysteries, one of the events on which the last five hundred years and more of our world revolved. I stared at him, saying nothing. It felt like there was nothing to say.

"I couldn't leave her to walk free, being who she was, being *what* she was, or no part of Faerie would be safe. She and Maeve had always balanced one another, and with one Queen gone, there was no balance at all. I couldn't keep her fully in check on my own, not with all of Faerie pressing me to solve their problems, and my own children seeking aid. The only way was by removing her from the field entirely. Her power has always been in the flowers, in her illusions. Water and blood both stood beyond her. I seized them both and bent them around her like a cage, and when she was well caught, I bound her."

"What did you do?" I asked, ashes and horror on my tongue.

Oberon, King of All Faerie, father of us all, looked at me levelly, and he was as great a monster as any of his descendants. "I made her less than she had been," he said. "I wrapped her in veils of blood and water until she could no longer stand, and then I cast her into the Faerie she had helped to create. I ordered her to leave no trace, to be neither seen nor found, until such time as she learned to be a part of Faerie without destroying it, or until her sister came home and I released her from her punishment. I set her into Faerie as a part of Faerie, and because the binding was built from water, it was self-sustaining, capable of endless renewal. Whenever she came close to being caught, she would remember herself long enough to rise and leave that life behind, then settle into another, like a flower that seeds itself from garden to garden, forever."

I stared at him. We all did. "So you're saying you turned Titania into someone else and threw her to the wolves of Faerie, enchanted to never be caught out for what she was?"

"Yes."

"And you made her undetectable? You made her look like she was just any fae?"

"No. Had I done that, she would have been a figure to be feared. She would have found a way to claim a crown as her own, as she always had before, and she would have been your sole and only Queen, even until the present day. I suppressed her memory of who she had been, who she truly was, and I disguised her as the least among you, that she could learn to survive the world we had created for our children. I hid her well, but there would always be times when she knew who she was, when she could choose to stop destroying Faerie and to be a willing part of it instead. That was the punishment, more than any other part of it. The knowing that she could break this cycle, if only she could figure out exactly how."

I turned to Tybalt. His eyes were wide and his cheeks were pale; if he'd had whiskers in his human form, they would have been pressed flat to his cheeks. I looked back to Oberon.

"Why did you order her to leave nothing behind?" I asked.

Oberon shrugged. "She was always the most determined of us to leave Faerie shaped in her own image, to be remembered and beloved. I gave her an existence where she could do none of those things. She had to remain small, and hidden, always."

"You're a bastard and a monster and everything that's about to happen is on you, but you're not the only one who's going to get hurt," I snapped, and spun around to face Tybalt again. This time he grabbed my arms and we fell backward into shadows, just the two of us in the black, airless void that loved him so well and tolerated me so grudgingly. He ran, pulling me along with him, and I did my best to keep pace, my hand tight in his.

We didn't have far to go to get back to the children's quarters. We stepped into the light and into a scene of intense destruction. Every piece of furniture in the room had been broken, the curtains yanked from the windows, the windows themselves smashed in. The smell of roses hung over absolutely everything, thick enough to be choking, almost too heavy for me to stand.

There was blood on the floor. Not much; a light smear, like you might get from a glancing wound. I stopped to breathe in deeply, picking up the scent of ice and yarrow.

"Walther," I said, twisting to look at Tybalt. "He and Nolan made it here before things got ugly."

"What do you think happened?"

I turned to look more slowly around the room, the first hot flush of panic fading to be replaced by grim acceptance of the situation. I didn't want to be right about this. There was no way I could be wrong. Not after what we'd already seen. Not seeing this room.

"I think," I said, slowly, "that Oberon hid Titania among

their descendants, and he bound her power to make it possible for her to blend. And then he walked away, and left her, with orders not to get caught and not even to know herself most of the time. So she hid, and she did the things that made sense for the people she became, each time. And sometimes, that would have meant those people got married and had kids."

Tybalt prowled around the room, checking under broken chairs and piles of fabric for signs of where the Browns and others might have gone. I could barely watch. This was all too much, and I was trying to wrap my head around it just as quickly as I could. Lives depended on my understanding.

"But she was still Titania," I said. "Still the Summer Queen. Any children she had would be Firstborn. New Firstborn, impossible to explain when both Oberon and the Queens were missing. And his spell ordered her to leave no trace behind. So when those kids got old enough to have kids of their own . . . "

I trailed off, unable to finish the statement. It hurt to even think.

Tybalt lifted his head and looked at me. "If her children had children of their own, they would have established their own descendant lines, and betrayed her placement," he said. "Five hundred years of families. Five hundred years of slaughterhouses."

"Five hundred years of killing her own kids to keep herself a secret," I said bitterly. "Hell of a way to make her a better person, don't you think?"

"You might be wrong," said Tybalt.

"Would both of us be wrong?" I asked. "This is a thing that makes no sense whatsoever, but it makes everything make sense if you step back and look at it like it's the truth. How did Stacy have five kids? Even being part human shouldn't have made her that fertile. Why did none of them look like anything we knew about their backgrounds? Why are they *all* Seers? Why did I never know exactly where she came from, or care enough to suss out the balance of her blood?"

Most of all, why had I never offered her the chance to

fully join Faerie the way she deserved to? The way I should have? It was like there were thoughts I shied away from having when Stacy was involved, patterns my mind simply wouldn't complete. It had always been that way, even when we were kids. There just hadn't been any reason for it up until now.

And now that there was, I wanted to scream.

"She's gone as well," said Tybalt. "Would they have taken her with them if she were the source of the trouble? Perhaps they've simply attracted the attention of this terrible punishment, and they run now as a family."

"You have no idea how much I want to believe you," I said, looking around the room one last time. "If this *is* Titania, the last time I tried to get too big a whiff of her magic, I completely lost the ability to see Faerie. Can you follow her trail?"

"And why should I not fear the same fate?"

"None of your ancestors were human. The spell she used on the rest of us wasn't made for you."

Tybalt used to yell at me for treating him like a bloodhound, back before my own ability to follow the trail of a person's magic had grown strong enough that I didn't need the help. Under the circumstances, me being the one to follow the magic wasn't a great idea. He nodded and shimmered, the smell of musk and pennyroyal rising as he disappeared, replaced by a large tabby cat. Lowering his head toward the floor, he walked straight toward the back wall of the room, stopped, looked back to me, and meowed.

"Okay." I walked quickly over, knocking on the wall as I checked for hidden doors. It's not as easy as they make it look in the movies. You don't get clear hollow spots or easy gusts of air. A really good hidden door will be exactly that—hidden. Otherwise, what's the point? Still, there will be signs, and a hollow space can never sound exactly the same as a filled one.

When I reached the end of the wall, there was still no sign that anything here was out of the ordinary. I stopped and frowned, then looked back to Tybalt. "You're sure?"

He meowed again.

Well, damn. "Okay. Time for Quentin's least favorite

habit, talking to the architecture." I turned back to the wall. "Hey. Toby here. I'm looking for my people. I think one of yours is with them. Are you hiding Nolan? I know he's your boy. I know you love him." That was a guess as much as anything else. The knowe had sealed itself off for a century rather than be held by someone outside of the Windermere family, reopening only when it knew they might come home. It made sense that it would love Nolan just as much, given how much it clearly cared for his sister.

Naturally, there was no response. But it felt like the room was listening, if a room can be said to listen. Sometimes the things I believe mean accepting some pretty weird stuff.

"I need to find them," I said. "I need to keep them safe. If I'm right, if what I'm afraid is happening is actually happening, then they're in danger, and I need to get to them as soon as possible. Please, can you help me?"

There was a click, and a door opened in the wall where I would have sworn no door had been a moment before. I glanced up at the ceiling.

"I'm so grateful," I said. "I can't say enough how important this is. If you need anything, just figure out how to tell me, and I'll do my best."

I ducked through the door into the short hallway on the other side, Tybalt on my heels, and the door slammed shut behind him, leaving us alone in the dark.

So pretty normal, really.

ELEVEN

THE AIR INSIDE THE hall smelled of blood, and not at all of roses. I decided to take that as a good sign, breathing deeply and closing my eyes as I followed the blood trail through the dark. I hadn't gone very far before I heard footsteps behind me and felt Tybalt's hand on my lower back, steadying me without urging me on.

"Do you truly think this is Titania?" he asked, voice low.

"Don't you?" After everything else, it was the only thing that made sense, and more, it pulled so many other things together into a coherent whole. Now that it was in front of me, it seemed inevitable, like we had always been intended to end up here.

The smell of blood was getting stronger. I could smell other blood traces beneath it, not as strong, but still present. Anthony, mostly. He'd been injured, and without my unnecessarily rapid healing, he still would be.

Sometimes I forget other people stay injured for more than a few minutes. I don't *like* that I forget it; it feels like the supernatural healing equivalent of those people who grow up poor, get access to a lot of money, and forget how much a gallon of milk costs. I have to be careful to treat other people like they're breakable without trending over into acting like they're already broken.

But my feelings don't matter when it's someone else's injury. Walther was actively bleeding. Anthony was hurt. I didn't have time to stand around being surprised by their fragility. I breathed in as deeply as I dared, focusing on blood rather than magic, and found a third trace, even fainter, that managed to smell effervescent and tingly. Jin was still with them. She'd been hurt at some point, but she was close enough to molt that the amount of blood didn't really tell me how bad her injuries were. Ellyllon who are preparing to shed their skins don't experience pain, or injury, the way normal people do—and for once, I was including myself in the "normal people" column. She could have been holding her guts in with one hand and still barely bleeding.

Faerie doesn't go out of its way to make anatomy easy, which is why we mostly don't have physicians. We have healers who use magic to do their jobs, midwives who use their hands and years of training, and alchemists who just sort of argue with the innate properties of the world around them until they get something that can act as a painkiller or a counteragent to a poison. Really, it's a miracle we've lasted this long.

Tybalt stayed close behind me as I prowled through the dark, his presence more reassuring than anything else could possibly have been. He was a defense and an exit if I needed one, and we had plenty of shadows to flee through. I kept walking.

The blood traces ended at another wall. I pressed one hand flat against it and leaned forward until my forehead touched the wood. It had been polished but never stained or treated beyond that; it still smelled of sap, as strongly as if it had just been hewn from a fallen tree.

"Hey," I said, voice low. "We already did this part. Can we just skip to where you let me in so I can help them? Please?"

There was a click. Nothing moved. I straightened and stepped back, giving the door room to swing open a few inches into the hall.

"I appreciate this," I said. "You're helping a lot."

On the other side of the door was another low hall, this one lit by a soft ambient glow from the ceiling, coming from spalted streaks in the wood itself. Spalting is caused by fungus getting into wood either when it's alive or after it's dead. Faerie has more than its fair share of bioluminescent fungus, and that gives our architects ways to arrange for at least faint light without actually expending magic. Plus it can look really cool, which was probably most of the logic behind this hall. I smiled a little as we walked, passing darkened doorways that smelled of nothing but dust and sap, following the scent of my injured friends.

This hall, at least, ended in an actual door. I hesitated to consider the best way to do this, then reached out and knocked, very lightly.

Something moved on the other side, quick as a whisper, away from the door.

"Hey," I called. "It's Toby. I'm here with Tybalt. We're coming in."

For the first time, I paused to consider the fact that no one else was likely to be able to find us. Quentin is more polite to the knowes than most members of the Divided Courts, but he's a little mortified when I make nice with them, and he was unlikely to think to try it—and even if he did, he didn't have the history to make the knowe do him a favor if it was even slightly unsure. Arden couldn't portal to us if she didn't know where we were. Madden could probably track us by scent, but he'd have the same issue Quentin did when it came to getting through the hidden doors.

Oh, well. Good thing I was used to working with minimal backup.

"Okay? You know we're coming in," I called, more loudly, and opened the door.

The room on the other side was small, square, and plain, with the only furnishings being a single bed and an old-fashioned wooden wardrobe. It was also intensely crowded, as it currently contained five Browns, Walther, Jin, and Nolan, plus now Tybalt and myself. This was the sort of room that would have felt cramped with five people. Ten was way too many.

Walther was gripping the broken-off leg of a chair like a club, and Anthony was stretched out on the bed, blood seeping through the bandage on his side and into the thin mattress. It would need to be replaced, and probably burned, since at this point I was pretty damn sure that all four surviving Brown kids were Firstborn. Their blood would be intensely valuable to blood-workers like Simon or alchemists like Walther, and did we really need prophecy in convenient lozenge form? We did not.

Everyone else was clustered in the corner of the room, as far from the door as they could possibly get, except for Karen, who was asleep on the floor at the foot of the bed, one arm tucked under her head as a makeshift pillow, and Jin, who was slumped against the wardrobe and—yes—holding one arm clasped across her midsection like she was struggling to keep something tucked away inside. I hate it when my guts want to be on the ground.

As one, the people in the room, sans Karen, turned to stare at me. I stepped fully inside to let Tybalt enter, then closed the door, before I turned and waved at them.

"Hey," I said.

"Aunt Birdie!" shouted Andrew, pulling away from his father and throwing himself across the room to wrap his arms around my waist and bury his face against my side. I lowered my hand to rest atop his head, feeling the blood that was drying sticky in his hair. Poor kid. Nothing about this day had been easy on him, and it wasn't going to get any better.

"Toby," said Walther, lowering his chair leg and straightening, swallowing hard as he tried to relax into a less confrontational position. "Are you—Is everything—What's going on?"

"I came here to ask you the same thing," I said. "Are you hurt?"

"You know I am, or you wouldn't be asking," he said, and held up his right arm, showing me the shallow cut that ran along the side from just above his elbow almost to his wrist. "How did you find us?"

"Followed the blood trail," I said. I looked to Jin, who had bled the least but was the most visibly injured person in the room. "How's Anthony?"

"I got the knife out, stopped the bleeding, cleaned and packed the wound and was preparing to regrow the skin, and then the Prince and the alchemist showed up, and everything went to shit," she said. She sounded exhausted. That wasn't really a surprise, all things considered. She had apparently run some distance with a horrific gut wound, and was now jammed into a too-small room with a bunch of kids who weren't hers and a few adults on high alert. Not what she'd signed up for when she'd agreed to accompany the boss to Muir Woods.

"He'll live," she continued. "In case you were worried about that. We need to get him better medical care at some point in the not-too-distant future, but right now, he's stable, and he'll stay that way as long as we don't ask him to move again any time soon. Were you followed?"

"No," said Tybalt, with absolute certainty. "Why has the Prince not removed you all to safety?"

"Because I can't," said Nolan, sounding more frustrated than anything else. "I delivered the alchemist to his lady—"

"Please, can we not call her that?" asked Mitch.

Nolan ignored him. "—and was about to take my leave when there was a very bright light. Terribly so, as if we had looked into the center and soul of a dying star. When the light cleared, the screaming began, and I found my magic quite beyond my reach." He sounded almost embarrassed by that, as if he were admitting to some unspeakable failing on his part.

"We grabbed the kids and ran," said Mitch. "Everyone was screaming. Stacy—did you see her? Was she in the hall?" His voice broke, in desperation and denial.

But was it really denial? Could he honestly be expected to look at the situation and go "Oh, my wife, who I've known since we were both kids, has secretly been Titania this whole time, and has decided to kill our children before turning into someone new and forgetting about me?" It was a stretch even for me, and I'd been standing there while Oberon basically drew me a road map to that inevitable conclusion.

Everything about this was terrible, and none of us was

going to walk away untraumatized. But right now, we had something bigger to worry about. I looked around at the others. "Can any of the rest of you reach your magic?"

They shook their heads in ragged unison, with Jin laughing dryly at the end.

"If I could get to my magic, do you think I'd be standing here with my guts in my hands?" she asked. "I'd have myself patched all the way back together and be working on the kid. But right now, it's not happening."

I gave her a closer look. Her skin, which had already been pale when the day began, looked like so much wax packed over the structure of her face and arms. Her wings hung limp behind her, and her flesh was starting to hang *off*. "Are you molting?"

"I want to be. I was already standing right on the edge, and a sharp-enough shock to the system when you're almost there should kick off the process. Everything inside me is getting loose and ready to drop away. But it can't quite let go. It's like something's holding it on, even though it shouldn't be able to stay."

Ellyllon biology is odd even by fae standards. Maeve claims them, but they work closely enough with blood that Oberon was probably also involved. Even so, this wasn't good. "This doesn't sound like what happened to us," I began.

No, but it was close, wasn't it? An absence of action instead of awareness; a reaching inward rather than a looking outward. I could see how perceiving magic and actually reaching for it might be connected. It was all in which part of the circuit got interrupted. "Okay," I said, slowly. "That's not great."

"You think?" asked Jin, and laughed again, this time with an edge of hysteria.

"Tybalt, can you touch the shadows?"

"I can," he confirmed. Then he sighed, heavily, fixing me with an unhappy look. "You're about to ask that I leave you once again, when the danger is both unknown and unknowable, aren't you?"

"We need to get these people out of here, and walking

back isn't an option," I said. "Maybe the Luidaeg still has some of those eggs. I promise not to go hunting for her while you're not here."

"We've made it this far into the latest nightmare without you being ripped open and bleeding out on the floor. If we could continue that state of affairs, I would be immensely grateful," he said, and kissed me quick before stepping into the shadows and disappearing, leaving only the faint scent of musk and pennyroyal behind.

I turned back to Mitch. We were in a room with the Crown Prince in the Mists, and both Jin and Walther were older than he was, but he was the father of the four children currently in here with us—three children and Cassandra, anyway, who was legally an adult in the human world, even if she was a few years away from being able to say the same in Faerie—and for the moment, I was willing to let him feel like he was in charge. That would change in a hurry if we entered a situation where we needed heroing. Once the heroism starts, I'm pretty much the boss of things.

"Tybalt will either be back with a way to put you all in contact with your magic, or with the sea witch," I said.

Mitch flinched. Not an uncommon reaction from adults in the Bay Area. Quentin and the rest of his gang were growing up weird because they thought of the Luidaeg as a friend rather than a sort of predictable environmental hazard. When I was his age, I thought of the sea witch as Faerie's greatest monster, a constant, lurking threat who could—and would—sweep me away if she was given half a chance.

Some of that was my mother, who never had a nice thing to say about her sister, even before I'd known the Luidaeg *was* her sister. But Sylvester had been the same way. Most of it was just natural fear of the Firstborn, created by the gulf between their power and our own and emphasized endlessly by the stories about them we chose to remember and retell.

Faerie is a world made up of incredibly long-lived people with equally short memories. It would be annoying if it wasn't so damn horrifying.

"I know she's been kind to Karen," he said, hesitantly,

"but she's still . . . well. She's still *her.* Is it really safe to bring her here when we're all defenseless?"

Mitch was scared and traumatized and had just lost one of his children. Cassandra might understand if I got snappy, and Karen was currently unconscious; Anthony and Andrew, on the other hand, didn't need to watch me picking a fight with their dad just because I was stressed.

Fortunately, I didn't have to. Jin barked bitter laughter, hand still clamped over her middle, and said, "Don't be stupid, Brown. We're *all* defenseless in front of the sea witch. If she wants us broken, we break. If she wants us bent, we bend. She's a nightmare walking, and the only reason we're still here is because she hasn't seen the value of getting rid of us. You flatter yourself by behaving as if she'd be a threat to you without good reason."

"Threaten to take Karen away from me, and you'll give me a good reason," said the Luidaeg mildly. I didn't need to turn to know that she and Tybalt were standing behind me. I turned anyway.

She was still in her human teenager guise. The electric tape around her left pigtail had come halfway unraveled, hanging down in a thick black curl that made her look vul nerable and so very, very young. Knowing she was older than everyone else in this knowe put together, with the exception of her father and possibly Titania, if she was still here, didn't change that. Her eyes had changed, however. They were the clear glass green she normally wore only when she was going among the Roane.

Those eyes were fixed on Mitch, studying him as intimately as a doctor would study a patient, mapping every inch of him and not approving of anything they saw.

Tybalt was beside her, his expression grim, his hands folded behind his back. He met my eyes and nodded, very briefly, but didn't move. He knew where he was supposed to be, and for once, it wasn't by my side.

"I . . . I would never," stammered Mitch.

"You would, though, if you thought you could get away with it," said the Luidaeg. "I've claimed her publicly, in front of kings and queens, but you'd still take her, because she's your child and you love her. You know *how* to love her. That's more than my parents ever managed. Love isn't always a good thing. Sometimes it's the worst kind of poison. Karen belongs to Karen. Absolutely. She's also old enough to know what she wants, and what she wants is to understand what she can do, and how it can improve her life rather than making it harder. My children were Seers, every one of them. I don't See constantly or clearly the way my brother Isengrin did. I still See with unclouded-enough eyes to be of service to your children, and they're going to need me. Karen was just smart enough to get in on the ground floor before I had to start charging."

She looked to Andrew and Anthony, expression grim. "If you want to study under me, you'll be more than welcome, but you'll pay for your tutelage as your sister has never been expected to. I won't apologize for that. You're no kin of mine, sons of Titania, and there's no one to claim you but our Lady of the Flowers, which she'll no more do than she will change her ways."

I blinked. But the questions I had didn't really belong in this moment. This was a moment for Mitch, the Luidaeg, and the children. The rest of us were onlookers, nothing more.

"Now, you've said nothing to actually offend me, and done nothing to actually incur my wrath," said the Luidaeg. "I think we can both agree to forget you looking at me like I eat the flesh of children, if you'll agree not to take them away from me."

"I . . . I won't take them," said Mitch.

"I'll hold you to that." The Luidaeg turned on her heel and stalked over to Jin. "Ellyllon," she greeted, briskly. "Ffion would not thank me if I treated with you poorly."

"Is she alive?" asked Jin, almost analytically. It took me a moment to find the hint of longing under her tone and realize that I was hearing the latest iteration of a question I'd heard a surprising number of times before. It was the way everyone seemed to inquire about their Firstborn when the Luidaeg mentioned them by name. Everyone but the Daoine Sidhe—on the occasions when the Luidaeg had interacted directly with one of them, they either seemed to already know Evening was still around, or wanted to preserve the illusion of not knowing for a little while longer. Anything to keep them from facing the reality of the woman who created them.

To my surprise, for once, the Luidaeg nodded. "When last I heard, yes, she was," she said. "She's shed her skin so many times that I wouldn't be able to pick her out of a crowd, but she always said she didn't mind that, said it would make it easier for her when the time came for us to fade into the background and let our children have the world. There's every chance you've seen her more recently than I have. There's also every chance she's died since the last time I looked. Your magic is bound, little Ellyllon. May I release it?"

"Please," said Jin, looking deeply relieved by the idea. "I'm not close enough to molt to feel no pain at all, and the pain I do feel is more than I would have chosen for myself. I've never been one of those who elects to shed a skin as brutally as possible."

"Then I suppose you honor Ffion by having a new experience," said the Luidaeg.

Jin laughed again. I could hear how much weaker she'd grown just since I got to the room. It was probably a good thing that she'd been hurt the most severely, given the way Ellyllon recover; that might even have been the reason why, if she'd jumped in front of a blow that could have been fatal for any of the other people in this room.

The Luidaeg reached out and ran her thumb along Jin's forehead. The skin opened in a bloodless line behind her hand, like she was unzipping the Ellyllon's face. Stepping back, the Luidaeg lowered her arm. "Try now," she said.

Jin took a deep breath, wings buzzing. Then she relaxed, relief flooding her face. "I can touch it," she said. "I can feel my skin softening. I should be . . . oh. I should be inside the wardrobe."

Gathering her dignity around herself, as much as a woman who was still holding her guts in with one hand could, she pushed away from the wardrobe, turned, opened it, and stepped inside, closing the door again behind her.

The Luidaeg watched, expression almost fond. Glancing to me, she said, "They don't like it when people watch them change. I can't blame them, really. It's pretty gross. Like cutting open a cocoon before the caterpillar is done being made of goo. I don't recommend opening that wardrobe before she's ready to come out."

Wet ripping sounds were coming from inside, disturbingly meaty. I shuddered and looked to Mitch and Nolan.

"What about them?" I asked.

"What about them?" she echoed, tone only lightly mocking. "I unbound the Ellyllon because she's the only medic in this place right now, and I need the children looked to. I can unbind the alchemist because technically I still owe him a debt of honor for unmaking my sister's pretty poison. He can draw on that for decades before we have to negotiate a new price. The little prince and the castoff, though? There's no way to justify treating them for free."

"Will our magic come untangled in its own time?" asked Nolan, solemnly.

"Wish I could say yes—really, really wish I could say yes—but no, it won't," said the Luidaeg. "This is an old trick, used to punish the members of my generation when we were disobedient or needed to be brought back under control. For someone of your strength, it will settle in your bones and blood, eating and eating until there's nothing left to swallow, and then you'll have no more magic than a mortal. Immortality is a magical function. Flesh isn't meant to last forever."

"So this is a death sentence."

"If not reversed, yes." The Luidaeg looked at him levelly. "You know I can't lie. What will you pay me to save your life, little prince? Make a fine offer and I'll consider it."

"I can't leave my sister," he said.

"But you'll leave her if you die."

"True enough, I suppose. Would my service suffice?"

The Luidaeg tilted her head. "No. Only your word."

"What word is that?"

"The first time she comes to you offering the crown, you must say no, for her sake. The second time, you must say no, for your own sake. The third time, you may rise and take your father's throne."

Nolan blinked before laughing nervously. "I'll never be King," he said. "If that's all you want from me, that's an easy-enough agreement. Am I required to take the crown if she offers three times?"

"No, but you will," said the Luidaeg. She turned to Mitch. "Your turn."

"No one's going to be offering me a kingdom any time soon," he said.

"That's true. You're an ordinary man, Mitch Brown, and you deserve none of this. So from you, I'll have your greatest gift and dearest burden." She smiled, and her teeth were sharp and plentiful. "I'll have your children."

"What?"

"I've been a mother in my day, and a grandmother well-beloved. I have the space to keep them safe, and the skill to teach them properly, as you know full well you never could. You must have realized by now that their magic doesn't follow any path you understand. So I'll save you and I'll have them, or you'll refuse me and die, and I'll have them anyway."

Mitch shook his head. "You can't be serious."

"Oh, but I have to be. I'm literally forbidden the sweet comfort of falsehood, thanks to a woman you know better than you think you do—a woman who lies better than any of us could ever dream to do. For me to be anything less than serious would be to violate the geas that binds me, and I'm sorry, but you're not worth the consequences of that choice. Not even for the sake of the children you're going to give over to my keeping, one way or the other. The only question is whether it's voluntary." The Luidaeg looked past him to Cassandra. "Tell your father, little chatelaine. Tell him that I only speak the truth."

"I'm sorry, Daddy," said Cassandra. "The Luidaeg can't lie." She sounded almost ashamed, like that was somehow her fault, or like she should have figured out a way to change the fundamental rules of Faerie for her father's sake.

"My life isn't worth theirs," snapped Mitch. "I'm not giving my children into servitude to have a spell that may or may not even exist unmade. My magic isn't very reliable. Never has been. So how do I know it's not out of reach because it doesn't want to come when I call it? Wouldn't be the first time, especially when I'm under stress. And even if this spell *is* real, I'm mortal. I'm going to die with or without magic."

"You'll die faster without it," said the Luidaeg.

"Maybe so, but I'll die knowing I never sold my children to the sea witch."

The Luidaeg sighed. "I'm *trying* to give you the best path out of this that I can. It's not easy. My geas doesn't want me to. It wants me to find a way to make you suffer, as if you're not already suffering enough, as if you're not going to be suffering even more as the next few days unfurl around you. None of this is your fault. None of this is something you deserve. And it's not fair in the slightest that you don't have a way to set it aside and say 'No, thank you, I'm an ordinary man who lives an ordinary life and just wants to kiss my children before I tuck them into bed.' You shouldn't be a part of this at all. You are, though. And yes, I would be teaching your kids anyway, but if I tell the magic I'm trying to *take* them, it will let me save you first."

"You have just reminded us of your inability to lie, milady," said Nolan, sounding anxious, which he probably was. Most people aren't that used to talking back to the Luidaeg. "If you say you'll take his children, are you not bound to do precisely that?"

"I never said I wouldn't take him too, or that I wouldn't let them stay in the home they've always known for as long as they wanted to, although that home may be less welcoming than they remember," she said, sounding frustrated. "Dad's *ass,* you people were less annoying when you were properly afraid of me and didn't try to negotiate or ask for clarification of perfectly reasonable portentous statements! Yeah, I'll have his kids. They'll learn to control what they can do under my tutelage, and he won't have the authority to tell them to find another teacher. But they'll have the free will to do it if they come to that conclusion on their own."

"Do it, Daddy," said Cassandra abruptly. She was looking at a point somewhere above the Luidaeg's head, her eyes moving in short jerks, like she was following the motion of something small and only partially visible. "She's the only teacher we have available, at least right now, and Andrew is going to need her really badly in a few years. The rest of us read air, one way or another, but he reads fire. Pyromancy isn't common outside the Burning Kingdoms, and their monarchs will come for him if he doesn't have a protector. He's not fireproof. It would be fatal. This is how you keep him safe. This is how you keep us all safe."

Mitch's face fell, his shoulders slumping, and for a moment, he looked very small, and very exhausted, which was strange in such a big man. He looked to me, not the Luidaeg, and asked plaintively, "How did this *happen*? Why is this happening to *us*?"

"If you're gearing up to blame Toby, don't," said the Luidaeg. "Your little chaos charm isn't the reason everything's going to shit right now. If anything, she's the reason it took this long for things to get as bad as they were always going to get."

Mitch stared at her. Then, with a convulsive shudder, he shook his head, turned once again to me, and demanded, "Where's Stacy? October, *where* is my *wife*?"

"Yeah, I'm not going to get through this," said the Luidaeg. She turned to Walther. "Okay, alchemy-boy, here's what I need you to pay: you will never unmake one of my workings, however little you may care for what it does, and if you and the little oracle have children, you'll give them over to me for training until such time as I'm finished with their education."

Walther blinked. "Us having kids without involving magic would be a neat trick," he said.

"Faerie," said the Luidaeg. "Neat trick or not, I've been a party to stranger."

He glanced at Cassandra. "Is it fair for me to agree to this, since it doesn't only concern me?"

"It is," said Cass. "Trust me, if it were possible for us to have kids, there's no one else I'd want responsible for their education. And even if we're not going to have kids, I want you around to keep not having them with me. *Please* agree to this, with my blessing."

Walther nodded before returning his attention to the Luidaeg. "Then yes, you have my agreement, with the small caveat that if I don't know something is one of your workings, I may unmake it out of ignorance, rather than intent."

The Luidaeg quirked a very small smile. "Negotiating with the sea witch? Oh, brave boy. So much braver than you think you are." She reached for him, and he didn't shy away.

As with Jin, she ran her thumb across his forehead. And as with Jin, it left a line where it passed, this one bright and beaded with blood. It was redder than it should have been, redder than rubies, and almost frothy, like it had been carbonated before it was released from underneath his skin. Walther hissed between his teeth, shoulders going tight with the effort of not pulling himself away from her.

The Luidaeg lowered her hand, shaking it a few times, like it had gone to sleep and needed to be woken. "Hey, Toby?"

"Yeah?"

"Don't drink that. He's bleeding out magic his body was never meant to hold, and it wouldn't be good for you."

It seemed odd to be offended under the circumstances, but I still managed it, at least a little. Snorting loudly, I said, "I'm not a damn vampire, Luidaeg. I can have self-control when I need to."

"Yeah, but you're not great at knowing what you should and shouldn't put in your mouth," she said. "This is a shouldn't."

"It doesn't look very appealing," I said.

"Ugh, flower magic." She focused once again on Mitch. "Last man standing. The kids aren't bound the way you are. I guess the blast wasn't set to take them down. So what do you say? Am I your new nanny, or are you going to die a slow and horrible death?"

"You said they'd have to pay you," he said, clearly grasping at straws for a reason to tell her no, she couldn't have the kids. No, his life wasn't worth it. "I'm not selling them into slavery."

"Why did we stop having a stable apprenticeship system?" The Luidaeg threw her hands into the air, eyes rolled toward the ceiling in an exaggerated plea for mercy from the universe. "There was a time when one of the Firstborn said they wanted your offspring, you handed them over with gratitude. And that was just 'I want them,' not even 'I want to teach them how to use their magic, which no one else they have access to is equipped to do, and maybe help them stay alive for fifteen minutes longer than they would have managed without me.' Yeah, the humans started acting like trade schools were somehow shameful, but they still want their air-conditioning fixed, so they can stuff it."

"Luidaeg," I said. "Come on. He's had a hard day."

"We've all had a hard day," she said sourly. Glaring at Mitch, she said, "I live in a house the size of everything I could possibly want, and it isn't very well maintained. So they'll be asked to do chores and work for me to balance out the time I spend on their education. Cleaning and cooking and service for scholarship. They'll still have time to be kids. They'll still have lives. And they'll survive to enjoy them."

"Basically, she's going to make them work in exchange for teaching them things they need to know," I said. "Come on, Mitch. Just agree. Don't leave them orphans."

"Orphans?" He looked alarmed. "Toby, *where's Stacy*?"

Crap. "I'm going to go and look for her as soon as we're done here," I said. "The faster you agree, the faster I can get back to work."

So maybe that was playing a little dirty. I couldn't track her through magical means, not without risking another Llangefni screen or this new magic binding thing, which seemed even worse, since the screen wasn't likely to kill me. And I wasn't actually sure how to start tracking someone by mundane means when their last known location was inside a knowe. Still, she'd been my best friend for almost my entire life. I owed her the effort.

I owed us all the effort. If she really *was* Titania in

disguise—if my friend had only ever been a mask worn by the worst of us—I needed to find her and, more importantly, find a way to *stop* her, before a whole lot more people wound up getting hurt. I owed it to the woman I'd always believed her to be. I owed it to her family.

I owed it to the Luidaeg, who had already suffered enough at Titania's hands, and didn't deserve to have it all turn against her again.

"All right." Mitch squared his shoulders, looking at the Luidaeg. "Unbind me, so Toby can get out of here and get back to *finding my wife.*"

"Be careful what you ask for," she said, and sighed, reaching up to run her thumb across his forehead. Again, it left a shallow slice behind, and as with Walther, the blood that bubbled up was overly red, too bright to be real. I breathed in the scent of it, and my stomach churned with revulsion.

There was no trace of his magic, or of Walther's, in the smell. Only the bright burn of roses, so many roses. Roses enough to choke the world.

"That should do it." The Luidaeg stepped back, then shifted to the side and repeated the process a third time, with Nolan. He beamed bright as anything as soon as she pulled her hand away, looking like a child on Christmas morning.

"Everything is back as it should be," he announced, joyously. "I can feel the whole of the world in my veins like lightning. Is there any place you would like to be, my lady sea witch? Only name the place, and I'll move mountains to have you there."

"I do believe you mean that," said the Luidaeg, sounding amused. "I'm good where I am for now. Why don't you get everyone to your sister? She's still in the receiving room unless something has changed while we were locked in here arguing about whether or not to save your damn lives, and I'm sure she's pretty panicked by now."

Nolan nodded and sketched a circle in the air with his hand, opening a portal to the room where, yes, Arden waited. He gestured for the others to step through. Anthony and Andrew did as instructed, Anthony leaning heavily on Andrew, while Cassandra scooped Karen off the floor as easily as if the other girl were made of dried leaves and straw, then stepped through with Walther beside her. In a matter of seconds, Tybalt, the Luidaeg, and I were alone with Mitch and Nolan, and the wardrobe that still contained Jin.

Mitch looked at me grimly. "Find her," he said, then stepped through.

Nolan hesitated, waiting to see if we were going to come. The Luidaeg made a little shooing motion with her hands.

"Toby's got the cat, and I've got feet," she said. "Get out of here."

"As I am bid," he said, and stepped through, the portal closing behind him.

The Luidaeg heaved a sigh as she turned to face me. "Well," she said. "You're nicely fucked now, aren't you?"

TWELVE

"NOT HOW I WOULD have put it, but that sounds pretty accurate to me," I said, and dragged a hand across my face. It didn't make me feel any better. "Is this actually happening?"

"Looks like it." She crossed to the wardrobe, rapping her knuckles against the wood. "You decent in there?"

"Halfway," said an unfamiliar voice, lighter and higher than Jin's had been when she went into the wardrobe. "Is it safe to come out?"

"Not sure I'd say that, but it's a lot safer than it was."

The wardrobe door cracked cautiously open, and a narrow face as unfamiliar as the voice appeared in the gap. Her skin was a rich medium brown, her eyes a few shades darker, and her hair darker still, verging on black in the low light. She glanced anxiously between us, then slipped out, wings buzzing in a constant expression of her nerves. They were longer than they had been, and looked closer to being able to support her weight, although they weren't quite there yet.

A few more molts and she'd get the sky back. Ellyllon are unique among the winged fae in that they start out able to fly, lose the ability as they grow, only to get it back if they manage to live long enough. It seems like a cruel trick for Faerie to play, but then, more and more, I suspect cruel tricks are the entire point.

"Where did everyone else go?" she asked.

"Back to the receiving room."

Jin made a sour face. "You know, I'm not sorry to have a body that changes every few years, but sometimes it can be real inconvenient," she said. "Like when you've just been reunited with someone you haven't seen since they were a kid. It's not the best way to have continuity of friendships."

"No, I guess it wouldn't be," said the Luidaeg. "Can you find your way back to the receiving room?"

"I don't know." Jin shrugged. "We were running and then there was a door none of us had ever seen before, but Walther was bleeding and Mr. Brown was in some kind of shock, and it seemed like a good idea to get out of there as fast as we could—"

"When did you lose track of Stacy?" I asked.

"The Prince came through with Walther in tow, and Cassandra ran to meet them," said Jin. "As soon as he put his arms around her, Stacy got very pale and asked them to move apart. He refused. She put her hands on the sides of her head and bent forward, breathing hard, like she was going to throw up on the floor. Mr. Brown ran to help her up, and then he hit the wall, and there was a very bright light, and the smell of roses, and she was gone."

"Was someone else there?"

Jin looked at me and frowned. "Yes . . . and also no. I don't know. It felt like someone else was there. Someone pulled Walther and Cassandra apart, and shoved the older boy and his father away, and then there was blood and everyone was screaming and we ran just as fast as we could."

"She's still holding on," said Tybalt, voice gone grim. "She's fighting. Luidaeg, is there any chance she wins this fight?"

The Luidaeg looked at him, and shook her head, answer in her eyes. "If my father did what he says he did, then no," she said. "The mirror's cracked. The curse is come upon her, and now is her time to either repent and rise or refuse and sink again, remade in a new image. Much like the Ellyllon, but with less purity of motivation, I think."

Jin blinked, wings buzzing and throwing glittering dust into the air all around us. I closed my eyes for a moment. If what the Luidaeg was saying was correct, and I believed the inevitable conclusion that everything we'd heard today was pulling us toward, then my friend was already gone. She was nothing more than a night-haunt, an illusion of the person I'd loved, worn like a mask over a far older and more terrible truth.

The Luidaeg seemed to follow the line of my thoughts, because when I opened my eyes she was watching me gravely. "Jin, you should go," she said.

"What? Why—"

"*Go*," snapped the Luidaeg, eyes flashing black as she turned to look at the anxious healer.

Jin swallowed, hard. "I'll see myself out," she said, and ducked for the door, all but running back into the hallway on the other side.

The Luidaeg waited until the door was closed behind her before she spoke again. "I saw my father hand you a knife at the wedding," she said. "I know he didn't take it back. Do you have it with you?"

"I do," I said, and touched the knife belted to my hip.

"Show me."

Pulling the knife from its sheath felt like a promise I didn't want to be making, as if by doing so, even when asked, I was committing to using it for its intended purpose. The Luidaeg held her hand out and I dropped the handle into her palm, letting her take the blade from me. She lifted it toward the light, squinting.

"Hmm," she said. "I think it's antler, rather than bone, but it should still work."

"Oh, go—Wait, *what*?"

"Antler. You know what those are, don't you?" She offered the knife back. I took it. "They're the handles on the stag. Not that I'd suggest grabbing them if you don't have a damn good reason, since the best-case scenario when you do that is being stuck on the end of a pissed-off stag. Bone would be better, but I guess Daddy has a renewable source for antler. He drops them every spring, right around Moving Day, and we used to use them for all sorts of things. There's a piece in every hope chest."

"You're telling me that I've been carrying around a *piece* of *Oberon*?" I demanded, staring at the knife in my hand.

The Luidaeg nodded, apparently untroubled. "He isn't good at showing people he likes them, but he must like you, if he's giving you one of those. He tends to keep them close, given what they're used for."

"What's that?"

"Murder, mostly." She said it so lightly, like it was nothing out of the ordinary. "Silver and iron for a Firstborn, silver and bone—or antler—for our parents. Not that we know that for sure, of course. It was just what the magic seemed to indicate, and what the oracles Saw, back when there were enough of us to ask."

I kept staring at the knife. I couldn't seem to take my eyes away. "So you're telling me this knife could—could—"

"Could kill Titania, if you used it correctly and caught her off-guard, yes, I am," said the Luidaeg. I finally looked up. She was watching me, eyes once more green as glass and filled with endless sorrow. "I know you don't want to hear this, and I know you may not believe me, but I don't want to be saying it, either. Stacy is gone. I can't even say that she's dead, because she never existed. Stacy was a pretty mask for an ugly woman to wear for a little while, and now that she's taken it off, it won't fit her anymore."

"Like Luna and Hoshibara," I said, lips numb. It felt like I was standing outside this scene and watching it unfold, like none of this had anything to do with me. Like I should have been able to smile politely, say, "No, thank you," and walk away, leaving everything exactly as it was before I got out of bed this morning.

"Very much like that," agreed the Luidaeg. "She became a child and she grew up with you so the mask would be a better fit, but the trouble with perfectly fitting masks is that they always crack when you take them off. She can't go back. But right now, while she's still bound to clean up the mess she's made, she might still be clinging, just a little bit, to who she was."

"The mess?" I asked. It was a silly question. I already knew the answer. I couldn't let myself know the answer. If I knew the answer, then all of this would be real.

I could feel Tybalt's hand on my shoulder, steadying me. This was already real. All the denial in the world wasn't going to change a damn thing, and the fact that I wanted it to didn't matter one little bit.

"The children," said the Luidaeg. She sounded sympathetic; she understood why this was so hard for me. It would have been hard for anyone. It would have been hard no matter who it was. The fact that it was Stacy just made it borderline unbearable. "She has to eliminate the children in order to do what she was bound to do."

"But—but she's already left a trace," I protested. "We know who she is, we know she's here. Can't that be enough?"

"You know compulsion spells don't work that way." The sympathy in her voice transitioned into genuine sorrow. She didn't want to be doing this any more than I wanted it to be happening. She shook her head. "Letter of the law, not spirit. He told her to clean up after herself until she became a better person, and when she got the signal to either come home or change again, she chose to change again. She's still Titania under everything else she's been and become. She's still the woman who told my sister there was no harm in eliminating monsters, and Faerie could only be improved by our absence. If she'd learned to be someone else, she wouldn't have reacted to the return of her memories by murdering her own daughter."

Jessica. Poor, sweet, silly Jessica, who had never fully recovered from what Blind Michael did to her, but had been trying so very hard to find her way back to us. Jessica, who was never going to make it all the way. I closed my hand around the hilt of my knife, sliding it back into its sheath, and looked at the Luidaeg.

"Stacy would never have hurt her own daughter," I said. "That means this isn't Stacy."

"And I need you to hold on to that," said the Luidaeg.

"She may still look like Stacy. She's still in flux, and parts of her will want to be the person she's grown accustomed to being. You need to keep yourself from giving in when it looks like she's someone you still love. She doesn't love you anymore."

I took a short, sharp breath. "You sure got used to this idea fast."

She shrugged. "I'm a lot older than you are. It's a lot harder to surprise me. Besides, you brought Dad home." At my blank look, she sighed. "My sister followed me here. I came here because the tides told me this was where everything was going to either put itself back together or go completely to shit, forever and ever, the end. Sylvester winding up here was a surprise, but it probably shouldn't have been; once my sister was here, Simon's arrival was inevitable, and there was no way his brother wouldn't follow him. They loved each other, once. Twins are rare enough in Faerie that they don't often choose to stay apart for long."

That sketched an interesting shape for my own potential future. I was no longer entirely sure I wanted to reconcile with Sylvester, not as long as he remained devoted to Luna. And so much was going to be guided by Raysel's recovery. Until she was ready to face her parents—and mine—we were going to be giving them all a wide berth.

"Put me, my sister, and Amy all in one place, and if I'd been thinking in terms of it being possible, of course Dad would be attracted to the same region. Janet followed her daughter, and even without knowing who he was, he followed everyone he remembered on some level that he loved. That sort of gravitational force was going to pull Titania in. As soon as you found him hiding in a shape we couldn't see, I began to wonder if my dear old stepmommy might not be nearby. I am truly sorry that she seems to have taken this particular form. You deserved better. *Stacy* deserved better. At this point, I wouldn't be surprised if you found Mom lurking under a rock somewhere. Or maybe a pier. She always did like the water."

"And you didn't think that maybe, I don't know, warning me would be a good idea?"

"Would it have changed anything? Would you have been

more careful? Would it have turned back time and made Stacy into someone you would ever—*could* ever—suspect of being an enemy?" The Luidaeg shook her head in hard negation. "She hasn't earned her release from Dad's spell yet. She'll come for the Browns. She'll destroy them all, if she's allowed. If you want to save them, you have to find her, and you have to stop her."

I took a slow breath. "And you have to help me."

"I do?" Her eyebrows climbed toward her hairline. "She's the reason I can't lie. She's the one who made it so I can't harm her directly, or any member of any descendant line she's officially claimed. Right now, this second, I could slit Karen's throat myself if I wanted to. All she has to do is say publicly that Karen is her daughter and claimed as such, and I won't be able to do that anymore."

"Did you want to?" I asked.

"Is that the point?" she demanded.

"It's not," said Tybalt slowly. "It never has been. To be forbidden something, even something you would never choose to do on your own accord, is a burden. I am a man and I am a cat, and neither of those things eats rocks."

That was such a random thing to say that I just blinked at him for several long seconds before I said, "Well, yeah. It would be hard to order pizza if you ate rocks."

"Oreads, on the other hand, eat rocks as a primary part of their diet. If you were to forbid me to eat rocks, I might look at you oddly, and would then go about my day, unchanged but annoyed. Forbid the same to an Oread, and damage them materially."

"How does that have anything to do with Stacy?"

"It would be rude of you to forbid me the swallowing of stone, even if you did so in jest," he said. "Our lady sea witch has never been in the business of killing children. By forbidding her to do so, Titania casts aspersions on her character, and prevents her defending herself at the same time."

"Huh." I love Tybalt more than I thought it was possible to love anyone but my own children, and sometimes it still feels like he's intentionally confusing. I shook it off and focused on the Luidaeg. "I don't need you to hurt her. I need you to help me find her. Which isn't going to be easy when she's not bleeding, I don't know exactly what she can *do*, and even picking up the traces of her magic seems to give her the ability to screw *my* magic all to hell. I need some sort of shield to keep her from touching me, or I'm never going to be able to track her down."

"Oh, is that all?" asked the Luidaeg, mulishly. "I don't have what I need to give you what you ask for while we're in Muir Woods, you realize. And even once we get back to my place, there's the matter of payment. You're asking me to give you protection from the mother of half of Faerie. That doesn't come easy, and what doesn't come easy doesn't come cheap, either."

"Don't I have any credit built up from helping you bring back the Roane?"

"That was clearing a debt that already existed. Overpayment buys you nothing."

We had entered into a new bargain shortly before bringing back her descendant line, if not her actual descendants: two of the three things she had asked of me had already been fulfilled. Simon Torquill was home, and safe, and protected for maybe the first time in his long and too-often-brutal life, and I had spent a very pleasant day at her house, eating ice cream and increasingly surreal sandwiches while she bled me into a variety of jars and vessels. Honestly, it would have been enough to qualify as a vacation day, if not for the fact that I healed so quickly she'd needed to keep stabbing me every minute or so for the entire occasion.

I looked at her in silent pleading.

The Luidaeg winced, glancing briefly away. "She bound me, and I can't set someone against her who intends to do her harm," she said.

"I won't hurt her if she's still Stacy," I said quickly.

"No, if you want my help, that's when you *have* to hurt her," she said. "Titania has never claimed Stacy Brown. Her blood may be a beacon shining through the woman's self and seeming, but they aren't the same person, not really, not below the surface. Because Titania never stood before Faerie and claimed Stacy as her own, I can still help you hurt the woman, where I can't help you hurt the queen."

I blinked. "That's not even splitting hairs. That's twisting a technicality until it cries."

"I get that," she said, tone sour. "So we're at an impasse. I can help you hurt a woman who doesn't exist, and who you'd rather find a way to save, like the ridiculous hero you are, but I can't help you hurt a woman I hate and would rather see given over to the night-haunts than allowed to destroy a family and disappear to repeat the cycle. And that alone should tell you why I hate her so much, if you didn't already know. She created this situation with her damned geas. I want to see her rot for it."

I straightened, the word "hero" ringing in my ears, and turned to Tybalt. "You need to take me back to Oberon," I said. "I know how I'm going to do this."

"He loves her," said Tybalt. "I wouldn't help someone destroy you, even if you somehow became a monster of her magnitude."

"If I became a monster of Titania's magnitude, I'd expect you to destroy me yourself," I said. "And you and the Luidaeg both know I'm going to try to kill her for what she's done to Stacy and what she did to Jessica. That's not up for debate. Oberon, though? Oberon *doesn't know me that well*. He's catching on, but he hasn't witnessed any of the really stupid shit we get up to when our backs are against the wall. All I have to do is ask for help without telling him exactly what I'm going to do with it."

"This is a dangerous game, October," said the Luidaeg. "Attempting to deceive my father is not a good idea."

"Do you have a better one?" I demanded. "We're standing here trying to workshop a perfect solution while a monster runs around with my best friend's face and tries to kill members of my family! If your dad doesn't like me going after his precious Queen of Flowers, he shouldn't have let her kill Jessica. He shouldn't have let her kill Stacy."

"You should still try to find a different way," she said.

"Are you going to stop me?"

She looked at me sorrowfully, but she didn't move. Her hands stayed by her sides, and her eyes stayed green. When she spoke, her teeth were blunt and human. She didn't like what I was doing, but she wasn't going to oppose me, either, and under the circumstances, that was about as good as I could expect.

"Good," I said, and stepped into Tybalt's waiting arms. He stepped backward into the shadows, pulling me with him, leaving the sea witch behind. Alone.

The way she always seemed to be.

THIRTEEN

WE STEPPED OUT OF the shadows, me shaking ice out of my hair, Tybalt not even out of breath. Oberon was gone. His throne was still there, rooted to the reception room floor, and Arden was circling it with a frown on her face. She looked up at the sound of our footsteps, frown melting into relief.

"Nolan came back with Walther and the Browns," she said. "I was starting to get worried that the two of you had run into trouble."

Meaning Titania. I would have been worried too. "Are they someplace safe?" I asked.

Arden nodded. "I sent them to the orangery. All the conservatories are warded to keep out people who aren't in the company of a member of the household. It's old magic from before we had decent produce sections in the grocery store, back when we really needed to worry about citrus thieves—Mom's magic, or I would have already had it dismantled. I just can't bring myself to throw anything of hers away."

My throat was tight, even as my flesh was thawing. It felt like I still couldn't breathe. "Titania is supposed to have been the strongest of the Three when it came to illusions and wards," I said. "We can't count on the wards keeping her out if she comes back. Where's Oberon?"

"You mean now that he's done damaging my floors?" Arden hooked a thumb toward the balcony doors on the far side of the wall. "He went outside to brood in peace. You can probably catch him if you hurry. He seems to let you see him most of the time."

She almost managed not to sound bitter about that. Almost. Still, this wasn't the time to work through that particular social wrinkle, and so I just bobbed a shallow bow and took off for the balcony, Tybalt in pursuit.

We were almost there when she called, "Your father's with him."

Simon was alone with Oberon? Great. A wave of unease swept over me, followed quickly by a wash of shame. He hadn't sold himself to Evening for power; he'd done it for August. The temptation might be there. He wasn't going to give in unless he felt like it was the only way to keep his family safe.

I still felt vaguely as if I had abandoned an alcoholic at an open bar. I paused only long enough to nod again to Arden, then ducked outside.

The balcony was low stone, gray and so clean it was almost gleaming. No small feat, given that it had been more than halfway swallowed by a vast blackberry bush, its strangely thornless creepers twining around the posts and balusters and, from there, working their way up the wall. Not content with stealing their thorns away, Faerie—or at least Arden's gardeners—had coaxed the bush to put out fat purple fruit and vast white flowers at the same time, scenting the air with a perfume reminiscent of her magic, while also distinctly other.

It was late afternoon in the mortal world at this point, but time runs differently in the Summerlands, and from the looks of the sky, it was sometime in the early evening, twilit and kind. Oberon and Simon were standing at the balcony's far end, their hands resting on the rail between patches of creeper, their eyes turned toward the rest of the garden.

I hurried toward them. "Sir," I said, when I was close enough not to come off as yelling at someone I really, really didn't want to offend. "I need you to help me find your wife."

Oberon turned his head, pendulous and slow, looking for the first time as if the weight of his antlers mattered to him. Simon didn't move, but continued to stare out over the gardens, not outwardly reacting to my presence.

"Will you harm her?" asked Oberon.

I looked him in the eye, remembering what the Luidaeg had said to me, and took a deep breath. "I might," I admitted. Tybalt breathed sharply in at the admission, breath hissing between his teeth. "I don't know. I can't see the future."

"Some of my children could," he said. "None of them saw this."

"It seems like a lot of things got missed when they were trying to figure out the future," I said, as delicately as I could. "Lot of death, lot of suffering, whole big parade of suck. But a lot of good stuff has happened, too, and I guess this is the future we were supposed to have, or we wouldn't have received it."

"I wish I could see things as you do."

"I'm sure it helps that I haven't been around long enough to get jaded," I said. "Some days it already feels like the weight of the obligations I've collected along the way will squash me flat. I can't imagine having centuries more to carry. It must be so exhausting. But please. She'll hurt the children if I don't find her."

"Then what do you need me for? I can tell you at a glance what your bloodline is built for. Finding a person, especially a person who's been casting illusions recently, should be nothing to you. The smell of them will be a beacon to you."

So Oberon could see the way we were designed? That just made me crankier about the fact that he'd gone off and left us all to our own devices. The least he could have done was stick around until Mom was old enough to train, so he could have made sure she didn't screw everything up the way she had.

It did at least explain something about how all the other Firstborn had been able to master their own magic, and guide their children toward doing the same. It wasn't like they'd had access to a big book of tips and tricks for guiding a new type of fae toward self-actualization.

"Every time I breathe her magic, it shuts mine down," I said.

"Ah." He looked away, back toward the gardens. "It doesn't, really, you understand. Mine could. I could snap my fingers and tell your magic never to listen to you again, and it would be so. But her gifts are more subtle, and more terrible for being so. She plays and preys upon the humanity in you. It leaves a stain, even if removed in its entirety."

I wanted to scream and shake him and order him to get to the point. Now that I was moving again, it felt like things that had always been urgent had reached a sudden immediacy that demanded action. I also wanted to grovel and back away. He was a god. A literal god when compared to someone like me, who wasn't even Firstborn. He could wipe me from the world if he wanted to. My particular combination of healing and hardheadedness makes me effectively impossible to kill via normal means; this was someone who, if he really set his mind to it, could easily find a way. I kcpt my mouth shut.

"Your magic remains even when you brush up against her own," he continued. "To truly bind it is an act more intentional. She can set your magic to devouring itself, if she wishes. A ward is a kind of binding, and it makes sense that her children would remember her for those, rather than for any of the . . . less pleasant gifts she carries."

"Yeah, well, I don't want her to *do* that," I said sharply. "I want to live. That means I need a way to stop her."

"Ah." Oberon looked at me levelly. "Do you understand what you ask me for, granddaughter?"

"Nope," I said, brightly. Tybalt put his hand over his face, but didn't turn away. If I was going to condemn myself, he was going to watch.

For his part, Oberon looked entirely nonplussed. "What?"

"Just what I said: nope. I'm asking you to help me stop a woman who is basically a god from doing whatever the hell she wants, and I'm asking because I know you can, and I have no idea what fulfilling that request looks like. Maybe you give me a gun. Maybe you turn me into a boulder. Dealer's choice, really."

"I would prefer the dealer not choose anything inanimate," said Tybalt. "Please, sire. I prefer my lady to keep breathing."

"You really don't know, do you?" Oberon looked at me for a long moment before he sighed. "Annie told me Jenny failed to prepare our daughter, and that our daughter failed in turn to prepare her own children. I thought surely she must be exaggerating out of her dislike for the line that cost her the presence of her mother."

"Nope," I said, again. "The Luidaeg is pretty fond of me, or as fond as she is of anyone who doesn't live in the ocean. She tolerates me, if nothing else. She doesn't tend to exaggerate where I'm concerned." The way he'd worded that made me wonder, somewhat, whether Titania had managed to keep the weight of the chains she'd placed on his eldest daughter a secret between her and the Luidaeg—and why the Luidaeg had allowed that secrecy to stand.

Faerie is built on a foundation of falsehoods and hidden truths, and we'd be healthier if we started talking to each other, but sometimes it feels like we don't want to do that because once we start, we can never shut up.

"I do not want to do this," said Oberon. "I love her. For all that she's a terror to you, she was a treasure once to me. I don't want to help you harm her in any way."

"I knew Tybalt loved me when I asked him to kill me before I could hurt the people I loved, and he agreed," I said, as gently as I could. "It took a while for me to admit to myself that I'd asked out of love, and he'd answered the same way, but I knew. If she used to be better than this . . . She's hurting people, sire. She's destroying the world she helped to create. I have to stop her."

"Very well, then," he said gravely, and reached up, gripping the forward prong of his left antler in one hand. It was sharper than it looked; blood seeped out between his fingers as he tightened his grip, smelling of bright wildness and all the forest green. Blood shouldn't have been able to smell like that. It wasn't even his magic. It was *him*, as if all he was—all he could ever be—was magic itself, raw and rare and ravenous.

Then he twisted his hand, and with a loud snap, the prong broke off in his hand. He lowered it to the level of his chest, bringing his other hand up and beginning to knead the antler like it was clay. It yielded before his fingers, becoming a blood-streaked lump of yellowed ivory.

"There was a time when I would have been forced to strike you down dead for even asking this of me," he said, almost casually, his hands still working. "When my ladies were both here and home, and we tried to maintain balance between us. We swore no oaths, but still, it was known that we could not be used as weapons, one against the other."

"She swung first," I said quietly.

His head jerked up, and he blinked at me. Then he looked back at the lump in his hands and went back to working it, smoothing away its lumps and ridges. "That shouldn't matter. Faerie is our trinket to dangle like a star on a string, and all that it contains is meant for our enjoyment."

"You said you'd have to kill me for asking," I said, carefully. "I still don't know what I asked. I wanted help. You could have just handed me a pair of nose plugs and wished me good luck."

He shot me a weary smile. "I dislike being called upon to do this. If I'm going to do it at all, I'm going to do it properly, for the sake of the child she's killed and the woman you've lost."

He sounded so complacent that I wanted to scream. "Children," I said instead.

"Pardon?"

"I said children." I looked at him as levelly as I could. "You bound her five hundred years ago, and told her to move without a trace, which meant she couldn't leave any Firstborn behind when she shed her skin and moved along to her next incarnation. I promise you this isn't the first time. If you were to call all the night-haunts, I'm sure we'd find a dozen families and more who'd been wiped out by their own mother as soon as they were old enough to be thinking about children of their own. Only not, because they would all have been so young when they died that they've long since faded and been forgotten."

"I don't think—" protested Oberon.

I interrupted him, causing Tybalt to flinch in anticipation of the response my insolence was likely to inspire. "No, you never did, did you? How many Firstborn, *sire*? How many innocents? How many pieces of Faerie that never got to grow into the pillars they should have been? She destroyed them because you put her in the position to do so. Because you *compelled* her to do so. This is your fault."

"Then it seems only right that I should assist in its undoing," said Oberon solemnly, and opened his hands to show me the rough pot he had sculpted out of his own antler, complete with lid. He held it out toward me, clearly expecting me to take it.

I did. When the King of Faerie offers you something, you accept.

"Hold it open," he said, and I did that as well.

Turning his hand so that his palm was directly above the mouth of the jar, which was no larger than the jars of pureed pears I used to buy for Gillian, he ran the edge of his opposing thumbnail over his skin. It parted easily, and blood gushed forth, fast and dark and smelling all the more strongly of the green. It was almost overwhelming. My knees shook, threatening to buckle.

"Stay as you are," he ordered, and my knees stopped shaking. The thought of bending them was suddenly anathema. I could no more have moved than I could have spread the wings I didn't have and launched myself into the air.

When the jar was full, he turned his hand over again and licked his palm clean, holding it out to show me the absence of a wound.

"Showoff," I muttered.

He quirked the faintest of smiles. "You'll want to put the lid on that as quickly as you can, before it attracts something," he said.

I hurried to do as I was told. This automatic-obedience thing was getting old, and illustrated just how much control Oberon could have over his descendants if he wanted to. I liked it better than the sort of obedience Eira seemed to cause in her own children. Simon had *wanted* to do what she asked of him. Quentin's parents had *believed* her when she told them blind fosterage was the right choice for them—for him. When Oberon told me to do something, I couldn't stop myself, but I also knew I was acting on someone else's orders. Still unpleasant. Not nearly as insidiously cruel.

"My blood carries no memory unless I will it so," he said. "You needn't worry about being overwhelmed by something greater than yourself."

I blinked. That was absolutely something I would have been worried about, but probably not until I was already swallowing. He smiled at my expression.

"The situation is dire, but I have experience with heroes," he said. "It will bolster and protect you from what my lady would do, but it will not overwhelm or devour you. Still, remember that the strength you carry is not your own, and do not grow to depend on it."

I looked at him blankly. "I know how to ride blood, and how to borrow magic," I said. "Sylvester Torquill taught me as best as he could, considering he thought he was trying to train a Daoine Sidhe. If you've pulled the memory out of this, what exactly am I supposed to be doing with it?"

"A sip, and my lady's magic will not be able to touch you," he said. "A swallow and your own magic will reach farther and grasp more greatly than ever it has before."

"Okay, those are real 'a dash and a pinch' directions," I said. "What's the difference?"

"You'll know it when you taste it." His broken antler was already beginning to regrow, the jagged end smoothing out and stretching into a new prong, covered in soft, velvety tissue that would die and peel away when the growth was done. Sometimes biology is gross. "You can take the necessary steps to find her now, without harm to yourself."

"Great," I said, and closed my hand around the jar. I still couldn't move beyond that. "Can I go?"

He looked quizzical for a moment before he seemed to remember what he'd done to me and nodded, curtly. "Of course," he said. "Go then, little hero, and find my wife before she destroys the family of your friend."

The tension left my legs, and I knew that I could move

them again. I started to turn away, then caught myself, looking to Simon, who had remained motionless and silent throughout this conversation. "Can you please undo whatever it is you've done to my father?"

"He's no blood of yours, little hero, whatever you've been told."

A bubble of anger formed in my chest. I narrowed my eyes. "You were *there* when he divorced my mother," I said. "You were there when August and I both made our choice. And you were there when Faerie decided on this ridiculous idea that humans don't count. If you didn't want me to call him my father, you should have made that title a little more connected to biology, and a little less connected to civility. Whatever you think about the world you helped to make, he's *mine*, and I don't know why he's standing there like a damn lawn gnome, but I don't like it. Please give him back."

For the first time since our frenzied arrival in the receiving room, I realized who else wasn't here. I blinked again, then glared. "I'd also like my squire returned, if you don't mind. I'm sort of responsible for his care and well-being, and misplacing him reflects really poorly on me."

"The Daoine Sidhe boy?"

"You should know his name by now." Oh, I liked this man less and less the more time I spent with him—and I hadn't liked him all that much when he'd just been the missing patriarch who ran out on all of Faerie.

Tybalt's hand settled on my shoulder, a warm reminder that picking this fight probably wasn't the world's best idea if I wanted to walk away from it, or if I wanted to survive to find Stacy.

"He went with the dog man to find you," said Oberon. "I'm sure he'll come running back at any moment. Leaving your kind alone in the mortal world has accelerated your idea of urgency beyond all reason."

"And whose fault is that?" I asked.

Oberon sighed. "You blame me for a great deal."

"You deserve to be blamed for a great deal," I shot back. "My father. Simon Torquill. *Now*."

"I thought you might like to converse without being overheard," said Oberon, in the mulish tone of a child being denied a dearly wanted treat. He waved a hand. The green, verdant smell of an oak forest in the summer afternoon rose around us, too dense and complicated to be comprehensible as a magical signature, too distinctly *Oberon* to be anything else. I suppose that when you're the one making the rules, it doesn't seem as important for them to apply to you directly.

Simon took a sudden, deep breath, coughing, as he jerked upright and away from the rail. He turned to face us, eyes gone wide and bewildered.

"October!" he exclaimed. "When did you get here?"

I decided to stab Oberon at the earliest reasonable opportunity.

"A few minutes ago," I said. "You were a little bit distracted by being under some sort of stasis spell cast by an asshole. It's okay. He won't be doing that again." I shifted my gaze back to Oberon as I spoke, glaring.

He sighed. "No, I won't enchant the man you claim as your father to keep him from our counsel. You have my apologies. When last I walked among my children, such an act would be civil, even expected, in a circumstance such as this one."

"Sure," I said. "Because Faerie used to be a dictatorship controlled by giant jerks, and now, we're still pretty awful, but we're not quite as bad. Good to have that worked out. Simon, Tybalt and I were about to go after Stacy. Do you want to come with us, or stay here and help Arden deal with the cleanup?"

"I . . . Where would I be of the most use?"

Selfishly, I wanted to say "with me." I wanted more backup than it looked like I was going to have, what with Quentin off somewhere in the knowe hunting for a door that might or might not currently exist. I felt bad about the thought of running off and leaving him, but not as bad as I would have if this hadn't been the definition of friendly ground. Arden would tell him where I'd gone, and he could either stay with the Browns or find May and help her get Raysel back to the house. He had options.

Simon, though . . . Simon would absolutely come with me if I asked him to, and then we'd have to deal with all the people he left behind. The issue with having allies is that your allies have allies, too, and sometimes they need to not be inconsiderate assholes and run off with their stepdaughters when their husband and wife are elsewhere, probably worried about them.

"Here," I said firmly. "Tell Arden you want to help and I'm sure she'll put you to work. Just . . . borrow a phone from somebody and call Saltmist, okay? I don't want to be the reason Dianda declares war on the Mists."

He smiled, still looking more than a little shaken. "I can do that."

"Great." I watched him go inside before I turned back to Oberon. "All I have to do is drink this and I can track her without worrying about the magic binding thing? Tybalt can't borrow blood the way I do. Is he safe?"

"As long as she doesn't target him directly, he will be," said Oberon. "His veins carry the base of Malvic, my son, and nothing of hers. She has no hooks into him."

"The Llangefni screen thing from before was infectious," I said.

"It latched on to you because of the way your mortality encourages magic to move through your body. From there, it could be spread to others whose magic moves the same. The cat cannot amplify it in the same fashion."

"Great." I uncorked the bottle and lifted it to my lips.

The contents smelled like Oberon's magic, like an entire forest impossibly distilled and concentrated into a single small vessel, a few ounces of liquid containing the essence of a whole biome. Normally, blood smells like blood to me, repulsive and appealing in equal measure, even when it's been poisoned or carries traces of a magic that should tell me not to touch it. This smelled like . . . dirt. Like grass and trees and dirt, and maybe a hint of deer urine. It didn't smell like anything I particularly wanted to be putting in my mouth.

I glanced at Oberon. He was watching me, face neutral, not judging whatever I did next. Swell. I don't like being told what to do; I like being left to walk into a situation without enough of a clue even less. If I'm not charging in completely half-cocked, I want to be as fully cocked as I can be. He knew *something* he wasn't telling me.

Then again, I was going off to potentially kill his wife, so maybe he had good reason to be a little bit reluctant to help me out.

And this whole thing was his fault, so he wasn't going to get any sympathy from me.

I closed my eyes, did my best not to breathe, and took my first sip of his blood.

It tasted like nothing. Or, no, wait, it tasted like everything, like absolutely everything at the same time, like an entire year exploding on my tongue and blasting back to clear my sinuses and scorch my throat. It was like drinking an entire bottle of menthol syrup mixed with cinnamon oil and ghost pepper extract, and I had never hated anything more, and I had never wanted so badly to take another drink of something. It hurt. It hurt and it burned and I could see, very easily, how addictive it would be to any blood-worker, however weak, because with this stuff in my system, I felt like I could do absolutely anything.

It took a physical effort to lower the bottle without taking another sip. I forced the lid into place, pushing until there was a soft snapping sound to signal that the seal was engaged. Shoving the bottle into my pocket, I turned to Tybalt.

"Now," I said. "We go now."

"If you feel the wild recede, drink again," said Oberon. I glanced back at him and nodded, then stepped into Tybalt's arms and let him pull me back into the shadows.

Darkness bloomed around us, and I very nearly laughed. The Shadow Roads were warm, the air there thin and stagnant but sweet. The dark was still absolute and all-consuming, and I couldn't see Tybalt's expression as we began our run, but I felt his hand tighten on my arm, and knew that he was confused by the ease with which I was moving in what had always been historically hostile territory. Still, we ran, and I realized that if I could breathe, I could actually be useful for a change.

Breathing shallowly in, I filtered through the traces of magic hanging heavy in the motionless air, looking for the scent of roses. It was there, buried under layers upon layers of Cait Sidhe—Tybalt and Raj and Gabriel and Samson, as well as other, less familiar cats. There were so many of them, more than I had ever seen in the Court of Cats or would ever have imagined passing through the area. I shunted them to the side as best I could and kept digging.

And there, under a layer of juniper and thistle, bright and bold and so vast once I caught hold of it that it seemed impossible for me to have been distracted by literally anything else, I found the scent of roses. It was deeper than it had been before, richer, the scent not just of ancient flowers, but of the entire world that must have existed for them to grow. It was clean water and unpolluted air and sunlight and a great garden all around them, and when I breathed it in, light flickered in the shadows, my eyes trying to focus on a landscape that had been gone for millennia.

Or maybe not. These roses had never grown in mortal soil; they were the first flowers of a newly created Faerie, of the deepest realm that carried the collective name of our entire world, and the colors that burst throughout my field of vision were things my mind had never been intended to process or to see. I tried to blink them away, recognizing the threat they represented. Even if I weren't still partially human, they would hurt me. They were reserved for other eyes than mine.

I pulled on Tybalt's arm, trying to signal that it was time for us to go back to the sunlit world. When he didn't change either pace or direction, I cleared my throat and said, "Here. This is where we need to step out of the shadows."

My voice was a profanity in a place that had never been meant for me. Wow, I was crossing a lot of lines today, and the day wasn't over yet. Plenty of time for me to piss off a few more underpinning concepts of our world, huh?

Tybalt tensed at the sound of my voice, and for the first time, I caught the whisper of his magic rising as he prepared to pull us out of the dark. It wasn't a flare, wasn't a spell being prepared for casting or an illusion being woven. No, this was closer to one of my conversations with the knowes, a negotiation with the world, couched in kindness and in a sort of strange mutual understanding that he probably wasn't even fully aware of. He'd always been remarkably accepting when I started talking to the buildings, even as he'd expressed that he didn't fully comprehend my reasons for thinking it was such a good idea. Well, maybe on some level, he actually did. Maybe we were more similar in that regard than either of us knew.

Then we were jumping out of the shadows and into the growing afternoon dimness of a familiar backyard, the grass crunching beneath our feet. Tybalt let me go, taking a few steps away before he turned to look at me.

"October?" he asked, confusion and concern in his voice. "Are you . . . What *was* that?"

"Guess the Shadow Roads like Oberon enough to let me in without a fight if they think I'm working for him," I said, feeling almost giddy. There was no ice in my hair, and my lungs didn't ache at all. I could get used to this. Which was probably a bad thing.

We have a word for substances that make you feel like you can do anything, that make the whole world brighter and better and more filled with potential, and it's "drug." Technically all medications are a form of drug, and I know that, but we don't talk about Tylenol and cocaine in the same breath. I've been addicted before. I didn't want to be again.

And that wasn't going to stop me from choosing Oberon's blood over and over, at least until this was all finished and done.

Tybalt studied me carefully before lowering his hands and saying, "If you're sure you're all right."

"I'm fine," I assured him. "The Shadow Roads just didn't want to risk kicking out the boss." I turned to slowly look at the yard around us. Anything other than the worried look that lingered in his eyes.

The smell of Anthony's blood was still in the air, simultaneously brighter and more faded than it had been before. More faded because it had been sitting out in the open for longer, and nothing holds its scent forever; brighter because with Oberon's magic boosting my own, I felt like I could follow a single drop of blood in an entire ocean. This was absolutely nothing I should allow myself to get used to.

The smell of roses running rampant dominated it all, almost obscuring even the scent of blood. I breathed in even deeper. "She came back here after we took Mitch to Muir Woods," I said. "We need to check the house."

Tybalt nodded, and followed as I walked toward the still-unlocked back door. We could still be wrong—she might not be hiding inside Stacy, and I held that hope as hard as I could as I slid the door carefully open, and heard the sounds coming from the kitchen as soon as I let go.

Music. Something poppy and upbeat. Someone was listening to the radio, which definitely hadn't been on before. I glanced to Tybalt. He looked back, eyes wide and bewildered. Anyone who would come into a house with a dead child in the living room and turn on the radio probably wasn't someone we wanted to be dealing with.

Which made it all the more important for us to go inside. I paused, hand on the door, and gave Tybalt a longer, more serious look. "If I need you to get out of there, you'll go," I said. "I'm protected. You're not, and can't be, and I won't lose you to her. I *can't* lose you to her. So if I tell you to go, you'll go, and if you can't listen for whatever reason, I'll make you go. I need you to agree to that, and promise that if I shove you out a window or something, you won't come charging right back in."

He looked horrified. "I would never—"

"Promise me. Please."

He blinked, slowly, and said, with great solemnity. "You have my word that if you bid me leave you, I will leave you, unless my will is no longer my own."

"Good enough," I said. That resolved, I eased the door even further open and stepped inside, Tybalt close behind.

The smell of pancakes and frying bacon greeted us, even stronger than the smell of roses. The smell of blood was entirely gone, stripped from the air of the house like it had never been there at all. Anything short of a Bannick scrubbing the place from top to bottom should have left a trace behind, but there was . . . nothing. Just nothing.

Someone was moving around in the kitchen. I walked gingerly along the hall toward it, one hand resting on the hilt of Oberon's antler-handled knife, half-sure of what I was going to find, and entirely sure that I *didn't* want to find it.

Then I was in the kitchen doorway, and there was Stacy,

sweet, beloved Stacy, exactly as she had always been, her hair bundled into a messy knot on the top of her head, a streak of flour down one cheek. The smell of cinnamon was bright in the air, all but drowning out the richness of the pancake batter. She had no shoes, but stood barefoot in the kitchen—exactly the cliché we used to joke about not wanting to become—wearing one of Mitch's sweatshirts. The bowl of pancake batter was tucked up under one arm, and a platter of finished pancakes sat on the counter.

She beamed bright as a beacon when she saw me. "Toby!" she exclaimed. "I didn't know we were expecting you today!"

"Um, hi, Stace," I said, trying to stay outwardly relaxed as Tybalt moved away from me, heading into the living room. I understood *why*—it was important we know exactly what was going on—but that didn't mean I had to *like* it. "I was here earlier, remember?"

"No," she said, blinking guilelessly at me. She had always been good at guileless. Better than any of the rest of us, that was for sure. "I was at the store, but I came home to make pancakes for dinner. That's still Jessie's favorite." Her voice dropped, becoming conspiratorial. "I lost my temper with her earlier, when she was telling fibs about her brother sneaking around with some girl. He's much too young to be getting up to anything like that!"

"Sweetie, he's fifteen," I said. "You and Mitch were getting frisky behind the woodpile at Shadowed Hills when you were fifteen, remember?"

Of the four of us, me, Kerry, Stacy, and Julie, I'd been the late bloomer. Paradoxically, I'd also been the first one to wind up unexpectedly pregnant. I guess that's what we call reaping the rewards of restraint. Not a proverb that's going to catch on any time soon.

Stacy blinked, looking momentarily puzzled. Then she waved it away, all smiles. "Oh, no," she said. "No, no, that can't be right. We were much older than any of my children before we got up to anything . . . before we did anything naughty like that. Much older." She turned her attention back to the griddle on the stove, flipping the pancake expertly over before transferring it to the waiting plate. "Did you and Tybalt want to stay for dinner? You know you're always welcome here."

A soft footstep alerted me to Tybalt's return, and told me how hard he was working to be considerate—a Cait Sidhe who doesn't want to be heard can walk through a field covered in fallen leaves and not make a sound. If he was stepping hard enough for me to hear it, it was because he wanted me to know where he was. I turned.

He was right behind me, all smiles and insincerity. "Forgive me, Stacy, but I need to borrow my lady wife for a moment," he said.

It had been a long time since I'd seen Tybalt smiling like that, engaging his whole face without it coming anywhere close to his eyes. I realized with a start that it used to be the only way he ever smiled, back when I'd been seeing him mostly in the Court of the false Queen, when we'd been lying to each other and to the world over and over again.

I didn't like it. I didn't have to. "I'll be right back," I said to Stacy, then offered Tybalt my hand and let him tug me into the living room. He moved smoothly, still smiling as he watched me move, and if I hadn't known him as well as I did, I could have taken it for flirtation.

Stacy clearly did. She laughed as he pulled me away, pouring another pancake onto the griddle. And then we were in the living room, and I had better things to worry about.

Better things, like the fact that there was no sign of Jessica. No manikin on the floor where her body had been, no bloodstains on the carpet or signs of the struggle that had happened here. I still couldn't smell blood. I breathed in, so deeply that the smell of roses made my head spin, and there was nothing at all.

Tybalt let go of my hand. "How is this possible?" he asked, voice low.

"She's the Lady of Flowers," I said. "Night-haunts make their replacements almost entirely out of flowers. April said that when they made a new body for January, they started with the blood she had found in the company freezers, and from there they used everything they had to hand. Which was mostly dried flowers from the ritual April had used to summon them."

Tybalt frowned. "That's a making."

"So if she was trying to clean up, if she was trying to stay calm for the sake of her own peace of mind, she might have resorted to an *un*making," I said. "Pull the spell away from the raw materials, let them crumble back into so much potpourri."

"That is . . . "

"Horrific? Efficient? Very much in line with what we know so far?" I shook my head, watching him gravely. "I don't put anything past her at this point. *Her*, not Stacy." If I thought of them as two separate entities, maybe I could survive this.

Or maybe not, because there was no way we were going to be able to force Titania back into quiescence. She was awake now. Even if we could shunt her aside for short periods, Stacy was trapped inside a body with her, and she was going to lose.

Jessica was dead. This was basically already over.

"Toby!" Stacy's voice was bright and guileless, the voice of a woman who expected her family to walk in at any moment. "Are you and Tybalt staying for dinner? Would you like eggs? I was just going to scramble them in the bacon grease, but I can do them another way if you'd prefer."

"Um," I said, brilliantly. I swallowed, both my panic and the sudden urge to take another sip of Oberon's blood, and said, "Yeah, Stace. Yeah, we're staying. It would be great if you could scramble us both some eggs. I really appreciate the offer."

"You're my girl, Toby," she said, voice still bright. "You always will be. You know that." She looked past me to Tybalt. "I hope she's relaxing about letting you love her. She never wants to trust it when it's coming from the rest of us."

"She has learned to take my affections seriously," he said, tone grave.

Stacy laughed as she stepped into the kitchen doorway. "Why are you weirdoes both being so *serious* today? It's like you think somebody died!" She sobered almost immediately, shooting me an anxious look. "Toby, nobody died, right?"

I wanted to tell her. I wanted to remind her. Because it would hurt to hear, but I wouldn't be hurting Stacy, would I? Not at this point. Stacy was just a mask she was wearing, a hollowed-out echo of my friend, and hurting Titania to make her pay for what she'd done to us seemed only and absolutely fair.

I shook my head. "No, Stace," I said. "No one died. We've just had a really long day. It was Raysel's trial."

"Oh, that poor girl." She stepped back into the kitchen, and I heard eggshells cracking as she began fixing the promised eggs. "Did they agree to wake her up? She deserves to be awake at this point."

"They did," I said. "And then we claimed offense, the way I told you we were going to, and the Queen supported our claim, and now Raysel is going to come and spend a year in my house."

"You know, we didn't get a lot of good lessons out of Devin, but of the ones he had to offer us, I think you were his prize pupil."

I blinked. "Come again?"

"He was a horrible, manipulative asshole, and we all deserved better, and nothing he did to us was fair." The distinctive sound of eggs being whipped in a glass bowl drifted out of the kitchen. "But as long as we had him, we always had a Home to go back to when we needed it. He taught us the most important thing we could do in this world was be a haven for people who didn't have anywhere else to go—and that just having someone who would open a door and say 'You can stay here if you need to, I guess,' isn't the same as having somewhere to *go*. Your mother would never have tossed you out of her tower. Julie's evil uncle would never have banished her from the Court of Cats."

Her tone didn't vary as she mentioned Julie's relationship to Tybalt. I glanced at him. He looked hurt, but not particularly angry, or surprised. That was probably for the best.

"Did you forget who I married?" I asked, mildly.

"Did you forget how much she hated him?" The eggs sizzled as Stacy poured them into the waiting pan. "He never abused her, never beat her or starved her or intentionally insulted her, but she was never comfortable in his Court, either. I wouldn't have let you marry him if he'd been actively abusive. But he wasn't good for her then. He's good for you now."

"That's a complicated form of forgiveness."

"What can I say? I'm a complicated lady." Stacy poked her head around the corner of the kitchen doorway. "Grab plates and set the table?"

"Aren't we going to wait for the kids?"

"Breakfast for dinner means we don't wait," she said. "Your eggs will suffer for it if we let them get cold. Come on, be a sport, and set the table."

"On it," I said, and moved toward the kitchen.

Tybalt watched me go. When I looked back, one last time, he mouthed exaggeratedly, "Be careful."

I flashed him a smile, pulling the little jar out of my pocket and removing the lid. The second sip of Oberon's blood was as overwhelming as the first, and it burned when I swallowed it. The smell of roses snapped back into sharp relief. I hadn't realized until that moment how much it had been settling into the background, fading into the way things always worked and always were.

That seemed to be part of the danger in dealing with Titania. She remade the world in her own image, and as she did, she became a part of the way things had always been, smoothing out and justifying contradictions, making it harder and harder to argue with them. I kept that thought in my mind as I stepped into the kitchen, where Stacy was transferring scrambled eggs onto a serving dish. She looked up and beamed at me, and she was the Stacy I had known and loved for almost my entire life, and I had no idea how I was going to do this. Whatever I might have said to Oberon, I was here to kill my friend. My friend who had never really existed. But all the memories I had of her, all the time we'd spent together, the look on her face when she'd finished doing my makeup before I got married, the way she'd smiled at me when she set Cassandra in my arms for the first time as a wrinkled and furious newborn . . . all those things were real.

Titania could take my friend away from me. She couldn't take what we'd been to one another. No one could do that, and I held to that thought as I got the worn earthenware plates down from the cupboard and pulled mismatched silverware out of the cutlery drawer, carrying it all into the next room to spread out across the table. Five kids meant it was never completely clear, even with Cassandra living in Muir Woods and Karen spending half her time at the Luidaeg's; a half-finished Lego set took up a big chunk of the middle, and a small stack of poetry books weighed down some junk mail at the far end. I looked at the books and swallowed hard, catching the faint lingering scent of Jessica's magic in the air around them.

"Hey, Stace?" I called, trying to sound casual about it. "Did you know Jessica was a Seer?"

"Oh, you mean that little game she likes to play with her books?" Stacy bustled into the dining room, Tybalt behind her. He was carrying a tray of pancakes and a platter of bacon, and looked perplexed about it. Under any other circumstances, his natural feline irritation at being pressed into helping bring out the food would have been funny. Right now, though, it was hard not to read it as another piece of evidence that Titania was rising, and giving Stacy the ability to compel others to do her bidding.

"Yeah, that," I said.

"It's not *really* Seeing, though, is it?" She put the eggs and a bowl of mixed berries on the table. "She reads a poem and then she tells you what she thinks it's supposed to mean. She's like one of those carnival fortune-tellers—not even the tarot readers, the ones who throw a handful of leaves on the table and then say they can see things in the shapes they've made. It's just a way to make herself feel special. I wouldn't worry about it."

I frowned. I had never heard Stacy talk about her children so dismissively. "Why does she need to *make* herself feel special?" I asked.

"Middle child, not as surprisingly unique as her sisters, not as popular with the other kids as her older brother, not the youngest like Andrew," said Stacy. "It doesn't matter how much we love her, or how often we tell her she's perfect exactly the way she is, all she sees is the places where she's not enough. You remember what it was to be a teenager, Toby. Feeling like we didn't measure up was our hobby."

"We were surrounded by purebloods," I countered.

"Yes, and she's surrounded by oracles and king-breakers and impossible heroes," said Stacy, and turned to walk back into the kitchen. "I know you never did it on purpose, because you never would, but you're not the most amazing thing for her self-esteem."

That stung. Even though I was sure none of this was purely Stacy speaking, it still stung. I stayed where I was, staring after her, as Tybalt moved to put an arm around my shoulders, holding me in place.

Stacy returned after a moment with whipped cream and syrup, setting them both on the table before taking her own seat and waving for us to do the same. "Come on, now, eat, eat. You love my cooking."

"That's true," I allowed, and pulled away from Tybalt, easing myself into a chair. I didn't reach for the food. I didn't trust her not to have poisoned it, and blood-magic aside, I've learned some things about putting strange things into my mouth. Those lessons started with her eldest daughter—not Cass, her *actual* eldest daughter, Eira, who had used her own blood to set a binding curse upon me, somehow exploiting a loophole that forbade her to harm my grandmother's direct descendants. If I'd been a little bit slower, or a little bit pickier about my allies, that incident could have been the end of me.

After Eira failed to kill me, it seemed almost like a waste to go off and get myself murdered by her mother. So instead, I sat there with my hands resting in my lap, close to the hilts of both my knives, and looked levelly at Stacy across the table. I wanted her to shed that face and show herself as she truly was, to manifest as Titania, so I could fight her without feeling like I was destroying something beautiful and precious. And I never wanted that to happen.

I didn't *want* to fight Stacy. I wanted to go back to where I'd been the day before, where all the things about her that suddenly seemed like warning signs had just been parts of how the world worked, unremarkable aspects of reality.

Where she was always going to be with me, always going to be my friend, and the idea of a world where Stacy didn't exist was unthinkable.

Tybalt's hand gripped my leg under the table, tight enough to provide a reassuring pressure, nowhere near hard enough to hurt. I shot him a relieved glance, and he nodded.

I looked back to Stacy. She was watching me, equal parts weary and wary, like she was waiting for the other shoe to drop. How much did she know of what was happening to her? How much was she *allowed* to know? Titania had clearly carried her back to the house when her second attack had failed, and had cleaned up the evidence of her assault on Jessica before allowing Stacy to have her own body back. Stacy was a hostage in this situation, and there was no way out for her.

It hurt to even think about. Drawing it out wasn't going to make it any better. I took a deep breath, the taste of roses cloying on my tongue and overwhelming the scent of breakfast foods, and said, "Stacy, we're here because we need to talk to you."

She blinked, all guilelessness and innocence, and tilted her head very slightly to the side. "What about?"

In for a penny, in for a pounding. "Jessica."

She stiffened, very slightly, her expression going cold around the edges. Cold and somehow brittle, like the wrong word could shatter her. "What about her? Has she been getting on the internet again? I didn't want it in this house, but after Chelsea convinced Duke Torquill to allow it at Shadowed Hills, I lost most of my argument against it. I hate to say anything that sounds like I'm judging someone else's parenting choices, but Etienne is far too lenient with that girl. Although I suppose it's easy to be lenient when you get to sweep in after someone else has done all the hard work and declare yourself as the hero of the hour for teaching the daughter you abandoned how to use her magic."

Now it was my turn to blink. Titania might be poisoning Stacy from the inside out, but everything she knew—everything she had to work with—came from the time they'd spent together.

And at this point, I had to admit that we were right. Stacy and Titania were absolutely one and the same. Stacy could never have cleaned up the evidence of Jessica's death on her own, and more, she wouldn't have wanted to. Denial, I could believe. Absolute negation of her daughter's horrific loss . . . no. It didn't make any sense for the woman I thought I knew, and that meant it wasn't something she could have done on her own.

"I'm sorry, what?" asked Tybalt.

Stacy shrugged. "Etienne knew he'd been intimate with Professor Ames. He knew there was a chance of pregnancy with a mortal woman. But he never checked in on her? He never asked her why she cut him off the way she did? He had a responsibility and he walked away from it, and now that he feels like he's getting a second chance that he doesn't deserve, he's overcompensating."

"You could say the same thing about me and Quentin," I said. "He has the internet. All the kids who hang out at my place do. That includes Karen, you know. She comes over about once a week, and she's got a smart phone."

"The sea witch insisted," said Stacy uncomfortably. "I tried to ban them from this house, and between Karen and Chelsea, it's become impossible. Jessica just *had* to have the social medias and the whole of human knowledge at her fingertips. Were we that stubborn when we were her age?"

"We were worse," I said. "But no, Jessica hasn't been getting on the internet, at least not while she was with me. I don't see her as much as I do Karen and Cass, remember?"

Jessica had been working hard to recover from her experience in Blind Michael's lands—therapy and nightlights had gone a long way toward helping her with that—but she had never been completely comfortable with me after I brought her home. I was too close to the monster who had shattered her childhood sense of safety and security. It didn't matter that I was also the one who'd killed him, the hero who'd been willing to risk myself to get her back. Children are allowed to need time to heal their wounds, and sometimes those wounds leave scars more terrible than the eye can possibly see.

At least in the last few years, she'd stopped crying every time she saw me. That had been more disturbing than I'd ever wanted to admit, and had made me reluctant to keep trying to reach her. There's being a supportive adult, and then there's being so associated with a source of trauma that every time you come into a room, you retraumatize the kid. It wasn't Jessica's fault. It wasn't mine, either. Blind Michael was dead, and even knowing that hadn't done anything to make it better.

Stacy scowled. "Blind Michael," she spat. "That . . . that *beast*."

Tybalt's hand tightened again, this time harder, less reassurance, more alarm. It would have made sense for her to call Blind Michael a monster, or a bastard, or any number of nasty things. "Beast," though . . . that had connotations in our world. That had a meaning beyond the simple insult it could have been intended as. Even if Stacy had been inclined to think that way after a childhood spent with Julie, she should never have been willing to say it with him in the room.

Titania was the one who first started the idea of cleansing the "bestial" aspects from Faerie. Hearing that word in that tone made it a little easier to think of Stacy as fading away, being overwhelmed by something bigger and crueler than she was.

"Yes," I said, soothingly. "Blind Michael hurt her, and she associated me with that hurt, and so she never came over the way her sister did, not even once she was old enough to take BART into the city by herself."

Stacy kept scowling. "He should never have been allowed to prey on children the way that he did," she said. "Not for so many years. He should have been stopped a long time ago. The children of Maeve, they think they can do whatever they want just because they're Firstborn, but they destroy what they touch."

"The Luidaeg hasn't destroyed Karen," I said, forcing my tone to stay mild. "If anything, she's kept her safe. Too many people know she's an oneiromancer. She would have been claimed by a royal Court by now, whether she wanted to be or not, if not for the sea witch standing in the way."

"And whose fault is that?" asked Stacy hotly. Her irises looked like they were starting to crystallize around the edges, throwing back the light in flecks of pink and white and red, like nothing an eye should be capable of doing. "If Antigone hadn't insisted on dragging my daughter to that ridiculous convocation, then no one would ever have known there was anything strange about her. She could have lived her life in safe obscurity, and she would never have needed to have *that woman* anywhere near her."

"Can you hear yourself right now?" I asked. "Do you understand what you're saying to me? Is there enough of you left for that?"

She blinked, hard. When she opened her eyes again, the prismatic flecks were gone, replaced by her normal, neutral blue. "Of course. I'm sorry, Tobes, what were you saying?"

"That we need to talk about Jessica."

"Oh, she's a very good girl, her little delusions about being an oracle like her sisters aside. As long as it's just poetry, well, there are worse hobbies she could have. She could be interested in taxidermy, or trying to tell the future by splashing paint on my walls or . . . or all sorts of awful things." She looked at the door into the living room and frowned. "Where *is* that girl? I made her favorite. She should be coming to dinner any time now . . ."

"Stacy!" I said, more sharply than I meant to. She swung back around to face me, and I put my hands flat on the table, finally taking them away from my knives. "Jessica isn't here."

"Is she with her father?" The question was asked with such sincere confusion that it hurt to hear it.

I took a deep breath, trying to compose myself. I'd come here to finish a fight, not to start a new one. "No, she's not with her father," I said. "She's with . . . someone else."

"Who else?"

"Jessica Brown is with the night-haunts," I said, and forced myself to keep looking at Stacy, even as the confusion bloomed on her face like a terrible flower, washing everything else aside. "I'm so sorry, Stacy, but Jessica has stopped her dancing, and I'm pretty sure you have too."

FOURTEEN

THE CONFUSION ONLY LASTED a few more seconds. Then it faded, replaced by a sour expression I had never seen on Stacy's face. The edges of her irises were crystallizing again, and that helped, at least a little; it was easier to look at her when her eyes were shifting into those of a stranger, and not feel like I was attacking someone who had only ever been good and kind to me.

"You couldn't let it rest, could you?" she asked. "You couldn't walk away. I tried to let you walk away. I tried to open a safe passage between you and not doing what you just did, but oh, no, you have to be the hero. You have to be the one who solves the problems. You have to force the people around you to look at the ugly things that they don't want to see—the things they shouldn't *have* to see, because they're not heroes. Do you know why Faerie has heroes, October?"

"I don't," I admitted, staying exactly where I was. Standing up would have been an escalation. Tybalt was rigid beside me, barely seeming to breathe.

"Faerie has heroes so the rest of us won't have to see how ugly the world really is. You're supposed to be a shield, not a spyglass."

"And you're supposed to be a queen, not a parasite," I snapped. "Get out of my friend."

She raised an eyebrow, looking at me. Her expression wasn't Stacy's at all, even though the lines and shape of her face still were. "I'm sorry, what did you just say to me? Have you misunderstood the situation as dramatically as all of that? Heroes do the impossible, but they don't always get what they want, and you're asking for something that can never happen. Your 'friend' isn't a body I've invaded or taken over somehow. She's mine. She's me. She's made of me, and she never existed at all, and nothing you do is going to make her anything more than a shell I wore for when I didn't have a choice in the matter. I liked being her. You were a part of that, sometimes. More often, you were a burden, one more thing I didn't want to carry but felt like I had to, because she would have done it. Because you helped to shape her into someone who was too soft to stand up to the world the way she should have. She was built to be weak. All the shells I've been allowed to wear were. But all you're doing right now is putting the rest of your precious Kingdom at risk. I hope you understand that."

"I don't," I said. "I don't see how coming here to stop you from doing whatever horrible thing you think would be a good way to announce your return is putting anyone in danger."

"Ah, but you see, my bastard husband says I'm not back to stay, not yet." She smiled, expression sharp as a shard of glass. The crystallization had almost devoured her irises, making their edges irregular, doing the same for the line where they met her pupils. "He wanted me to learn to be a 'better person,' by *his* definition. I think I'm a perfectly lovely person. Don't you?"

"Yes," said Tybalt, in a faintly dreamy voice.

"Okay, that's a line crossed." I turned to Tybalt. "Time for you to go."

"No, I don't think it is," he said, eyes still on Stacy. "I think I'd like to stay and hear what she has to say. It seems a fine way to pass the afternoon."

"You promised me," I said, warningly.

"Her husband made her promises as well," he said. "And

then he left her, again and again, for another woman's bower. It seems to me that in the presence of the Lady of the Flowers, all promises should be taken as negotiable ones."

I didn't like this. I didn't like this one bit. I stood, grabbing him by the shoulders and yanking him along with me as I turned him to face me. He blinked, placidly. Titania might have rendered him suggestible, but she hadn't made him violent. That was a nice change. The last time he'd been mind-controlled into siding against me, he'd ripped my throat out as part of the package.

"Hey, babe," I said. "Remember when you used to kiss me to mess with me? We're gonna go for a little bit of that now, so you'll hopefully be less pissed when I shove you through that window we were talking about outside."

"What?" he asked, in the same dreamy tone.

I jerked him forward and kissed him, hard, molding my body against his until he started to properly respond. In the end, I didn't even need to stab him. I just bit his lip while we were locked together, clamping down and holding on as he tried to pull away. It felt like a violation, probably because it was. It was also the fastest way to get him away from a woman who was going to do much worse.

The taste of his blood filled my mouth, bright and bitter and filled with memory. I'd already known he thought this was a bad idea; feeling it from the inside didn't change that. He could tell Titania was starting to cloud his mind; his thoughts shifted as she worked her way into them, turning against him, turning ashen and cruel. Good. The fact that he knew it was happening meant he was less likely to be angry with me.

There was surprisingly little in the way of deeper memory. It felt like the blood was giving me specifically what I needed, instead of overwhelming me with whatever happened to tumble into my way. That wasn't the way my magic normally worked, and it was probably going to be one more thing for the list of things to bother me later once I was out of active mortal danger.

I only needed a few drops of blood to reach for his magic, something I'd always been afraid of before, due to a strong dislike of involuntary shapeshifting. Right now, with Oberon's blood lingering in my system, I felt like there was no magic I couldn't manage, and so I pulled Tybalt's into me, and reached for the Shadow Roads, which I could suddenly find with perfect clarity. They were right there, like curtains hanging in the air all around us, and the thought that I had ever missed them before was virtually laughable. I pulled them open and pushed him away at the same time, sending him stumbling into shadow. Then I closed the curtains between us, and he was gone, and I was alone with Titania, still draped in the face of my friend, watching all of this like it was a production orchestrated purely for her amusement.

"I saw the potential in your grandmother when she was presented before me," she said, almost carelessly. "Human to the core, not a drop of fae blood anywhere within her, but she burned with a fire that humanity would have seen extinguished as soon as anything else. How she yearned, that Carter girl, how she *hated*. Hated what was expected of her, hated what she was offered, hated what she was denied. She wanted restitution from the world for the crime of forcing her to exist within it as a transitory thing."

"After she broke Maeve's Ride?"

"No, silly child, before." Her smile was contentment personified. "When my best beloved girl brought her before me, cobwebs covering her eyes and fairy wine mazing her senses, so it must have seemed a dream if it was anything, and told me she had found the tool with which she would shatter our chains. She said she'd had the knowing of how from the mouths of our Seers, and seen them slaughtered to cover her tracks, and who cared? They were all of the blood of beasts. No Seer had ever been born of my bloodline. I was proud of that." For a moment, her smile faltered, and the edges of her irises seemed to smooth, becoming more human. "It seems pride will always be my downfall."

"Wait, Eira brought Janet to meet you *before* she broke the Ride?"

"Of course she did. My girl never acted without my approval, not once. Unlike so many of our children, she was never willful, never disobedient, and she knew the only way to be rid of my sister was to pass her into another reality entirely. The Heart would do. It could beat with her cradled inside, and I could have our Oberon, and the whole wide worlds beside him."

I blinked, very slowly. "Eira brought you my grandmother."

"Yes. I set the love of Tam Lin, which had been an ember brought on by a moment's meeting in the woods, into a bonfire that would have devoured her had she not used his flesh to slake the blaze." Titania smiled with Stacy's face, and it was a terrible thing to behold. "I broke the Ride. I may never have the credit for it, but without me to give guidance to my daughter, and through her to Janet, my sister would have Ridden as she had done so many times before, and the boy would have been lost, and Faerie would have continued on as it always had, unchanged and unchanging."

"You're gloating," I said, more amazed than horrified.

"I am, I suppose." She shrugged. "I'll have to go and kill the rest of the brats soon enough. Harder this time. How dare my bloodline finally start throwing Seers, after I had worked so hard to eliminate them from our midst? How dare it betray me so?"

"Yeah, kids have this nasty habit of being their own people, no matter what we want," I said blandly, and set my hands back on the hilts of my knives. "But please, keep talking."

"Why?"

"Because I came here to save my friend and stop you, and you've told me, in no uncertain terms, that she can't be saved." I looked at her coldly. "The longer you talk, the easier that is for me to believe. The more I believe it, the easier it's going to be for me to kill you. So please, keep talking. If Stacy's really gone, she won't blame me for doing whatever I have to do in order to save her children."

"Please," said Titania. It was a dismissal, not a plea. "I've had dozens of children. Hundreds, maybe. I lost count before this country was born, before Camelot had fallen. What are five mewling brats sired by a half-human man? They're *nothing*. Their destruction costs Faerie *nothing*."

"Jessica was going to be a veterinarian when she grew up," I said. "She was scared of horses after what happened to her, but she thought being scared of them wasn't a good enough reason not to take care of them, so she was going to work with as many kinds of domestic animal as she could be trained for. She knew that the broader she made her knowledge, the shallower it would be, but she also knew she had more time than even the best human vet could hope for, and she was going to change the world. She liked silly movies where people started singing for no good reason. I once saw her act out half of *Shrek* like a one-woman show just to get on her brother's nerves. And she didn't like me very much, because I reminded her of a really terrible thing that had happened to her, and that was okay, that was *fine*, because it wasn't her fault and it wasn't my fault and it was just the way the world was going to be. She loved me anyway. She loved her mother and her father and her siblings, and she was the only Jessica Brown in all of Faerie, and knowing she was Firstborn doesn't change any part of that, and now she's gone, and we're less because of it. *Faerie* is less because of it. You cost Faerie *everything* when you took her away."

The smell of roses was getting stronger. This tactic of "talk to Titania endlessly because you know you can't take her in a physical fight" wasn't going to work forever.

Then she blinked, and when she opened her eyes, the crystallization was gone. It was just Stacy, looking back at me, broken and battered and terrified, but undiluted. "Toby?" she whispered.

"Yeah?"

"Jessica's dead, isn't she?"

I pulled out the little bottle Oberon had given me, taking another furtive sip of his blood before I answered. If this was a trick, if Titania's magic was gathering in the room because she was getting ready to launch an attack, I was going to be ready.

The smell of roses was no stronger than it had been before. Putting the stopper back in the bottle, I tucked it away in my pocket and swallowed.

"Yeah, Stacy, she is. I'm sorry."

She looked at her hands like she'd never seen them before. "I didn't kill her. I know no one's going to believe that, but I didn't. *She* did. She's still here, and she's so much bigger than I am that I don't think I can hold on for very long, and I think she's always been here."

"That sounds right, yeah." I moved around to her side of the table, breathing in the smell of pancakes and bacon—fresh enough to overwrite the roses, if only for a moment—in order to fold her into my arms. She clung to me like she was being blown away by a hard wind, and this was the only way she could stay where she belonged, shaking like a leaf.

"I'm sorry," she moaned, and pressed her face against my arm. "I'm sorry, Toby, I'm sorry for every bad thing I ever thought or did or said to anyone, and she shoved me to the side when Anthony came in, she pushed me out of the way like I was nothing, and she was going to hurt the boys, but then Jessica put herself between her and them, and she hurt Jessica instead, and she used my body to do it. She hurt my baby with my body, and I'm almost glad I don't get to stay, because I can't live here anymore. I can't live inside a body that hurt my little girl."

"No," I said. "Stacy, no. Don't give up. We'll find a way to fix this. Oberon is in Muir Woods. I can call Arden, have her bring him here, and we'll make him clean up his own damn mess."

She sniffled, tilting her face up to look at me. "He's not going to choose me over his wife, and you know it. She's going to win, and he's going to choose her, and I'm going to disappear, and I'm glad. I don't want to live in a world where I killed my baby."

"Stacy . . . " I leaned forward, pressing my forehead to hers. "I'm not letting you give up."

"I'm not giving up," she said, and pulled back, almost laughing. "I'm asking you for help. I'm asking you to be a hero. I'm asking you to kill me."

"What?"

"I know that's what you came here to do. Well, I'm giving you permission. This may be the last time I get to be in charge. It's not safe for me to go to wherever my children are. She'd be there, and she'd be able to get them through me. So we need to end this. Please. Kill me."

I pulled away from her, straightening up, horrified. "Stacy, I—"

"Came here perfectly prepared to kill the Summer Queen, didn't you? I see you taking little sips of something that I'm guessing protects you from her. You sent Tybalt away. Well, no one's protecting *me*. This is *how* you protect me. You stop her from hurting anyone else."

I stared at her, speechless.

"How many times have I bailed you out of trouble? Even when you didn't want to be saved, I was always there to save you. Even when you said we should all walk away and let you fall, I was standing by, because you were my friend. Please, Toby. Please. Be my friend one more time. Finish this."

The air still smelled like breakfast, without a trace of blood, but the roses were working their way back. She wouldn't be able to hold on much longer. I exhaled slowly, putting my hands on the hilts of my knives, and looked at her as levelly as I could.

"I love you," I said. "I love you more than I love myself, Anastasia Brown. You were the best part of me, and I hate that she's been lurking inside you this whole time, but she never touched you. She never tainted you. You were perfect. And I'm so sorry."

I drew my knives and lunged for her, silver in my left hand, antler in my right, tears blurring my vision.

Stacy smiled wanly as I moved, and for a moment, it seemed like this was all going to end so much more easily—so much more horribly—than I ever could have hoped for. Then she blinked, and when she opened her eyes again, they were pink and white and crystalline with prismatic shards that broke the light into terrible rainbows. She smiled. She didn't move. She didn't have to move, because I wasn't moving anymore.

Because the bowl of mixed berries she had placed on the table was suddenly a riot of briars and clinging vines, wrapping themselves around me like the tendrils of some terrible beast, stopping me where I was, keeping me from reaching her. I snarled and tried to break free, which only made them twine tighter, pulling me back.

Titania stood, still wearing my best friend's face, still not quite the dazzling woman whose blood Jessica had refused to remember. Talking to the night-haunts wouldn't have made any difference, I realized abruptly, the same way someone might remember they'd left the oven on in the split second before a car accident took memory away forever. Jessica hadn't been able to fully perceive Titania's face, and so the night-haunt that swallowed her memory wouldn't have been able to see it either.

Huh. For once, when I'd decided not to do the ridiculously dangerous thing, I'd been making the right decision. That was nice to know, even though I was about to have my own ass handed to me by the literal Queen of Faerie.

She stepped toward me, smile still on her face, as cold as any smile had ever been. Looking at her, I could finally see where Eira got it.

"So my husband set you up to kill me," she said. "I suspected, when I saw you taking little sips of something you shouldn't have been able to get in this world. Do you know what will happen if you do that for too long? He may have tried to warn you, but I doubt he fully understands the consequences of his own choices. He never has. The poor man gets lost so easily when I'm not with him."

I struggled against the vines, glaring at her. They drew tighter still.

"I'm sure you know that I can't kill you, or you would never have dared to come here on your own."

My surprise must have shown in my face, because she blinked, and then laughed, sounding absolutely delighted.

"You *didn't* know! Oh, October. I've known you since we were children—you in fact and me in fancy—and sometimes your willful plunge toward self-destruction still finds a way to surprise me. I can't kill you. I can't even do you harm, not directly. If you'd eaten the pancakes I made for you, you could have made yourself safe by making yourself mine, but I couldn't force you to eat even if I wanted to. When my damned husband bound our precious girl to stay away from your bloodline, he bound me as well. Me, his queen! Who he should have chosen above all others! But he dallied with the Carter woman, who refused to remove herself as a broken tool was meant to do, and when she got with child, he bade me to do her no harm. *He*, who crossed outside *our* marital bed, bound me against harming his mistress!"

"So suddenly you care about fidelity?" I asked. "I know how many of the Firstborn weren't his."

Titania snorted. "I never kept my lovers long enough for them to inconvenience him in any way," she said. "I got what I wanted and I cast them aside, but he was *keeping* her. Said my sister's last gift had been to the girl, and that he wanted to understand why Maeve would react with kindness through her anger. Said he had to know her to know how he was going to repair the damage done to us all. Said she was *important*. I raged and I roared and I demanded satisfaction, and so he sent the girl and her child away to keep them safe from the harm he could not prevent me doing, but I could no more raise a hand against either one of them than I could raise a hand against you now."

I pulled against the vines, which still refused to let me go. "This feels pretty raised."

"You attacked me," she said coolly. "I'm allowed to defend myself when someone attacks me."

"You're wearing Stacy like a sundress," I snapped. "*She* asked me to kill her. You're collateral damage."

"And you have killed her, little rosebud," said Titania, voice going sugar-sweet and cloying. "This is all down to you, and was always going to be. I look through the eyes of the masks I wear as through a clouded mirror. Everything is dim and distorted and controlled for the most part by their desires, but I can nudge. I can push them in the ways I want them to go, providing I allow them the freedom to grow into people I would never once have chosen to become. And when she met you, when I knew you for the bitch's bloodline, I nudged her toward becoming your friend. I whispered in her dreams every night that you would be her dearest of companions, that you would enrich and enhance her life in every way known, and she loved you because I convinced her to."

I stared at her. Her smile grew broader.

"I'm sorry. Was she one of the most important relationships in your life? One of the people who convinced worthless little changeling you that you were somehow worthy of love? And you see, this is why my husband always loses. You say 'Do no harm' to a hero and he sets his blades aside. You say the same thing to a villain and she starts looking for loopholes. I can cut you to ribbons without raising a hand or enchanting you in any way."

I pulled against the vines again, eyes narrowed. "Stacy was her own person. You may have whispered love in her ears, but she still chose to listen, and she still loved me. You can't taint that. You can't unmake what we were to each other."

"Can't I?" Titania stepped closer, and her smile was all the crueler because the mouth that wore it was so familiar. "Here's what you're going to do for me, descendant of the great betrayal. You're going to return to this insipid body's equally insipid husband, and you're going to convince him to remove his children from the dubious safety of your Queen's halls. You're going to bring them back here. And you're going to let me have them, all four of them, so I can shed this face and move on to the next accursed life my husband would condemn me to. You can't destroy me. You can move me forward another forty years, and make me a problem for the future. Until the children die, my geas is unfulfilled."

"I won't," I spat.

"Then I'll destroy everything you love that doesn't belong to you," she said. "The boy, you consider him a son, do you not? Well, Faerie doesn't. Faerie says he's mine. And the cat. He may be of Malvic's line, but Malvic was of my keeping in his cradle, and I can have the cat as well, if I desire him."

I stopped pulling against the vines for a moment, stunned by the revelation that the Lady of Flowers was so damaged, so fundamentally broken, that she had been willing to somehow warp an infant Firstborn to give herself a hold on his descendants.

She turned away from me, holding up her hand and

studying her fingers like her manicure was more important than anything she was saying to me.

"The kitten as well, and the bird—and the little Torquill child you pursued so assiduously. All of them. Every person you love, save for yourself and . . . well, no. You don't love your mother. Or the other babe she bore. Or the mortal woman who lay with my husband. Your Fetch, I suppose. I've not tried to harm her. I might not be able to. She filled her belly with your blood in her own remaking, and so she could be considered to be under my husband's protection. It doesn't matter." The glance she tossed me over her shoulder was filled with nothing but poison.

"I can have them all, and no one can stop me. Bring me the children I need to destroy, and I'll leave your family alone. You have my word. Keep them from me, and enjoy the fruits of your own harvest."

She walked away then, leaving me alone in the tangle of vines. I struggled against them, unable to break free, until I heard the back door slide closed with a bang, and knew I was alone. Then, and only then, I sagged as much as the clasping vegetation would allow, and sobbed, helplessly. I couldn't let go of my knives. If they fell into the bramble, I wasn't sure I'd ever find them again, and I needed them. So I held them fast, and I cried, and I waited for the world to start making sense again.

I was still crying when the scent of pennyroyal and musk overwhelmed the lingering smell of roses.

"October?" called Tybalt.

I sniffled, trying to catch my breath so I could call out. Not quickly enough. The next thing I heard was a sharp inhalation, and then he was rushing into my field of vision, eyes wide and worried.

"October! What has she done to you?"

I sniffled again, mustering a watery smile. "Just tied me up a little. For the record, I'm still not into bondage."

"I figured that out when you didn't attempt to introduce it into our private activities," he said, extending his claws and beginning to slice through the vines holding me. "I would never have been the one to volunteer it. Cats think poorly of being constrained."

"Good to know it's not going to be a fight in the future." I sniffled again, trying to clear my sinuses. "Titania got away."

"I figured that out as well, when I got here to find you alone, crying and confined, with no body on the floor. Did she harm you?"

"Turns out she's not allowed. I don't think anyone ever taught the Three how to have self-control without a compulsion spell to do it for them." He continued to slice until I could move my arms again, sliding my silver knife back into its sheath before beginning to cut the vines away from my legs with the antler knife. They shrank away from its touch, showing more awareness than I expect from vegetation, and they charred around the edges where I cut them. "Oberon bound her not to hurt Janet or Janet's descendants before he banished her from herself. So she can't hurt me."

"Meaning she threatened to harm me," said Tybalt grimly.

I looked up to meet his eyes, shocked. He looked calmly back at me.

"If you told me that someone wanted to destroy me, and I wasn't allowed to stop them myself for some reason, I would turn my hand against whatever they held most dear," he said. "It's not a difficult conclusion to draw. I am her best wedge."

"Not just you," I said. "You, and Quentin, and Rayseline, and everyone, except for Gillian and maybe May." But she hadn't named Gillian, had she?

When I had removed myself from Gillian's heritage to protect her, had I rendered her vulnerable to something ancient and terrible? Oh, oak and ash, was being related to me enough to put her in danger *again*? She was barely coming around to the idea that I might not be the most terrifying thing she'd ever met. I didn't know if our fragile relationship could survive another blow.

I shuddered, tears bright in my eyes, and kept cutting. The best way to protect my family was to destroy Titania. She wasn't just threatening to eliminate the Browns; at this point, she was threatening to wipe away everything I cared about, and I wasn't going to let her. No matter how poorly she'd been treated by Oberon, none of that justified the things she was trying to do now.

"She wants me to bring her the Browns, or find a way to bring her to them, so she can slaughter them all and fulfill the terms of Oberon's geas," I said, voice gone flat and cold. "Once she accomplishes that, she can disappear again. Turn into a new iteration of Stacy, grow into someone else entirely, and have a fresh new life." Turning Titania into a functionally powerless member of the society she had helped to warp into its current shape would have seemed like a fitting punishment, if not for all the innocents who would be hurt or destroyed along the way. If she'd been purely a closed unit, incapable of harming or involving anyone else in her self-destruction, it could even seem like a reasonable, proportionate response to what she'd done.

But she wasn't a closed unit. No one ever is. If we let her complete this loop of her binding, if we let her go back into Faerie and vanish for another round, we'd have done worse than feeding the four remaining Brown children into the meat grinder of Titania's demands. We'd have condemned another generation to this level of destruction.

We could be better than this. We *had* to be better than this.

We just had to figure out how.

FIFTEEN

IT TOOK ME AND Tybalt working together about twenty minutes to get me cut completely free. The vines he slashed through with his claws writhed back into position and resumed grabbing at me within seconds. The ones I cut away with my antler knife stayed charred and withdrawn, apparently afraid to reach out again. The more time passed, the heavier the smell of roses became, as if Titania were preparing to re-manifest.

With the last cut, I fell forward, no longer held upright by the bramble. Tybalt was there to catch me before I could hit the ground. He wrapped his arms around my waist and crushed me against him, holding tight, shivering. I blinked, hugging him back.

"Hey," I said. "Hey. I'm okay."

"You always are, aren't you?" He pulled back, enough to see my face. "I understand why you had to push me away. I could feel her working her way into my mind. She wasn't commanding me to do anything against my better interests yet, but she was influencing the way her words landed. Given time enough, she could have turned my thinking entirely to her desires."

"Why is it I can feel a 'but' coming?"

"Because you could have come with me." Tybalt looked at me gravely. "It was obvious she wasn't going to lay down quietly and allow herself to be destroyed, but by presenting you with a situation you thought you might be able to talk your way out of, she locked you into a pattern of negotiation. If she has Stacy's memories to pull upon, she knows you better than I do."

"Not something that many people can say these days."

His smile was fleeting and shallow. "Indeed. But, October . . . when you opened the shadows and pushed me into the dark, the shock cleared my head. We could have retreated and regrouped, together."

"I'm sorry." I ducked my head, unwilling to meet his eyes. "I was hoping . . . " Hoping what, exactly? I'd been hoping to convince Titania to go away, to give Stacy her body back and let my friend find a way to go back to living her life. I'd been hoping to stop her. I'd been hoping for the impossible.

Or I guess I'd been hoping for some flicker of evidence that my friend was still there, and that, at least, I had received. Stacy was clinging to existence as hard as she could, but she wasn't going to be able to hold on much longer—and she didn't want to. Even if we somehow found a way to seal Titania away, she would always be a lingering threat to everything Stacy cared about, and so there was no way to save them both.

Given a choice between surviving as a shadow of herself and saving her family, I already knew what Stacy would decide. It made perfect sense, because it was the same thing I would have decided.

I lifted my eyes back to Tybalt. "I was hoping there might be a way out of this."

"Is there?"

"If there is, I can't see it. I'm sorry I pushed you away. I'm protected from her magic and physically almost indestructible. If she'd lashed out against me, I could have survived it. If she'd lashed out at you . . . I can't survive that, Tybalt. I'm sorry, but I can't."

He scowled. "And yet you'd ask it of me. Sometimes I wonder if you'll ever be able to stretch your sense of martyrdom to include the existence of people who care about you."

"I'm trying." The smell of roses was getting too thick for me to tolerate. I sneezed, then blinked at him. "Can't you smell that?"

"Smell what?"

"Titania's magic. It's overwhelming everything." The vines had mostly obliterated the table when they sprouted from the berry bowl. I gestured to the wreckage. "Breakfast was enchanted, of course. She wanted us to eat it. So, you know, don't eat the floor bacon."

Tybalt gave me a withering look. "An unnecessary instruction."

"Just being cautious. Raj would eat the floor bacon." I pulled the jar out of my pocket and took another sip, the taste of loam and forest green settling in the back of my throat. The scent of roses receded.

"Yes, but as we're invoking the children now, Quentin would not," said Tybalt. "The boy has far too much understanding of his own dignity. He should have been a cat."

"I'm sure he would have been happy, and wildly destructive, as a Cait Sidhe," I agreed. With the scent of roses gone, the smell of pancakes was almost overwhelming. My stomach churned. "We need to get back to Muir Woods. I need to talk to Oberon. Can I get a ride?"

"For you, my lady? Anything." Tybalt took my arm with exaggerated civility that felt like a lingering comment on the way I'd pushed him away before, and together we stepped into shadow.

Again, the air was balmy and breathable. It would be far too easy to get used to the Shadow Roads welcoming me as a trusted traveler, not pushing me away as an outsider. I tried to focus on matching Tybalt's stride, running through the darkness toward the unseen outline of Muir Woods. If I looked into the blackness, I could see thin threads of magic spreading out around us like a spider's web, coruscating with colors, bright lines of life and energy directing our steps. We could go anywhere from here. We could run forever, and the shadows would be happy to have us.

No wonder Cait Sidhe were so migratory, territorial

without being stagnant about it. Most people find a home and stay there. Tybalt had been King of Cats in at least three places he'd already told me about, and had lived in at least two more without taking a throne, and now he was in San Francisco, and while he was happy with me, we might reach a time when he was agitating to move to Australia or something.

Hopefully not for a good long time. I loved my city, and expected that I always would, even as the mortal side of it was changing into something I barely recognized. The changelings of my generation were going to find ourselves as out of touch as our pureblood parents, in less than a quarter of the time.

The run was so much easier when I wasn't trying to hold my breath at the same time, and in no time at all, we emerged into the receiving room at Muir Woods.

It was, for once, entirely empty. I let go of Tybalt's hand and turned, blinking at the unoccupied throne in front of us. "Okay, that's a little odd."

"What time is it?"

"I don't know. Around seven?"

"So the rest of the court will have risen by now, and everyone is no doubt settling in for their evening meal." Tybalt shrugged, looking at me wryly. "The sky is falling, but the sky is always falling where you're concerned, little fish. The rest of the world carries on; the courtiers must be fed."

"Okay, fair enough," I said, and started for the door. "Come on. Dining hall's this way."

"You assume the knowe will not have moved it since the celebration of our marriage, or that I will have forgotten the path?"

"I assume the knowe is feeling charitably toward me after the conversation we had earlier, so yeah, it's either not going to have moved the room *or* it's going to give me a decent pointer on how to get there, and being cool with knowes is sometimes the only thing I've got going for me," I said. "Let me have this."

Tybalt laughed, shaking his head, and followed me out of the receiving room.

The knowe at Muir Woods was huge, as befitted a royal

knowe, easily twice the size of Shadowed Hills, which had previously been the largest knowe I'd ever spent a substantial amount of time in. The best mortal comparison would be the old English manor houses, built less to be a single-family home and more to be at the functional center of a small community. Arden was still building her staff, hiring slowly and cautiously to avoid any of the dangers of running a formal Court, like "oops, all infiltrators" or "whoops, that guy you just hired was secretly loyal to the deposed former monarch," or my personal favorite, "now your housekeeping staff is made up entirely of people who think changelings are dirty, and judge you mercilessly for allowing them into the knowe."

Eventually, when the knowe was fully up and running, she'd probably have more than a hundred people living here full-time, not including the courtiers who set up camp in visitor's quarters and simply refused to leave. As chatelaine, Cassandra would find herself with more and more draws upon her time, until she either stepped down or dedicated herself entirely to the service of the Queen. For the moment, however, it was possible to walk the halls and feel like you were walking through a ghost town. Even including the people who'd come to see Raysel's trial, the ones I'd brought with me who were still hanging around, and the Browns, we were probably looking at maybe a hundred warm bodies inside the knowe.

Maybe that was why the route to the dining room was so linear. The hall led us straight to a long flight of stairs, winding its way down from the dubious "ground level" of the main floor into the depths of what would have been a canyon if it had actually existed in the mortal world. We reached the bottom at what was probably the equivalent of roughly sea level, stepping off the stairs and into a long open-air corridor lined with trellises dripping with thornless blackberry creepers. The twilight sun cast dreamy shadows over us, crisscrossing our bodies with bands of gold and charcoal.

As always, the stripes looked remarkably natural where they fell on Tybalt's face, sketching out the stripes he didn't have in human form. I matched my pace to his, moving a little faster than was comfortable but a lot slower than the urgency of the moment wanted me to.

"Loggia," he said.

I blinked at him. "What?"

"This type of outdoor hallway. It's called a loggia. From the Italian, I believe, although all the Romance languages blur together after a while. They spent so much time stealing and twisting words from one another that it could have come from the Sardinian, or the Dalmatian."

"Now you're just making things up because you know I don't know enough to argue with you," I said. I appreciated the attempt to lift my spirits, at least slightly, even as I knew it wasn't going to work.

Tybalt held up his hands. "I swear. Dalmatian was spoken in Dalmatia, which corresponds with the area that I believe they call Croatia today."

"And let me guess, you were King of Dalmatia at one point?" Being married to a man with centuries of impossible stories and random trivia is delightful, but also occasionally exhausting.

"No. I just thought you might like to know where the spotted dogs got their name."

I smiled at him, a little sideways. "Thank you for being a giant nerd."

"And thank you for being willing to recognize that nerdhood is more than merely skin-deep," he said, smiling back.

Thanks are generally verboten in Faerie, to the point where we'll dance around gratitude like it's a venomous snake and we're afraid of being bitten. This is partially because thanking someone implies a debt—and in Faerie, it's not as easy to discharge a debt as just saying "It was nothing" or "Don't worry about it." And it's partially because we're all ill-mannered assholes playing at civility. Doesn't really matter, though, since thanks are technically allowed between immediate family members. Spouses or long-time lovers, children, parents, and siblings.

Dean thanked me for bringing him a sandwich about a week ago, and I damn near dropped the plate. Getting two unexpected stepbrothers as an adult is second in strangeness only to the fact that the elder of those two stepbrothers was already dating my squire when our parents got hitched, and while he and Quentin are eventually going to need to break up, neither of them is anticipating doing it any time soon.

Even if they viewed Quentin's majority and subsequent return to Toronto as a hard stop, that still gave them nine years to spend together. That was longer than any of my early relationships had managed to last.

Thanking Tybalt still felt weird and a little subversive, and from the look he was giving me, he felt the same way. I reached over, letting him take my hand, and we walked that way down the remainder of the hallway—sorry, loggia.

It ended in a wide, trellis-bounded veranda, mainly lit by large glowing beehives that buzzed with pixies coming and going in an endless chiming of wings. Small round café-style tables filled the area, each of them seating four people, save for a spot near the front where someone had pulled two of the tables together to form a space big enough for Mitch, all four Brown children, and the Luidaeg. Mitch didn't look thrilled to be eating with the sea witch. The Luidaeg didn't look like she cared whether or not he was happy. She was talking quietly to Karen, her arm around the girl's shoulders, her posture curved to comfort.

Servers moved between the tables, refreshing drinks and family-style platters of what looked like a reasonably straightforward seafood-focused menu.

Simon was the member of my party nearest to the entrance, sharing a table with Patrick, Dean, and an anxious-looking Rayseline, who seemed incapable of looking at Dean directly. He was taking a malicious glee in this, and kept nudging her and pointing to things on the other side of the table, clearly asking her to pass them.

I stepped up behind him. "Can we not break my cousin?" I asked, in as academic a tone as I could manage. "It's only that I just got her, and I want to wait at least a week before I void the warranty."

"Toby." Dean turned to face me, everyone else at the table doing much the same. "Is everything okay? The Queen wouldn't tell us where you'd gone, just that it was hero business, and she took Quentin to her table with her, so we can't even grill him for details."

"Interesting that you'd target Quentin, since Simon was there when I left," I said, gleefully ignoring the frantic "stop" gestures Simon was making. He glared at me. I smiled in response. "No, everything is not okay, but I'm not sure how much I'm allowed to say right now, or how much it would be smart to say."

"Since when have you been overly concerned with what is or is not a smart thing to say?" asked Patrick, but from the sidelong look he was giving Simon, I could take a guess at how much had been omitted when he was explaining things to his husband.

"I need to go talk to the Queen, but Raysel, are you okay?" I looked at her closely. "Are they being nice to you?"

"Queen Windermere made my parents leave when they refused to stop trying to convince me to go with them," she said, looking down at the table. "She says it would be an additional insult for me to go to Shadowed Hills after she's said that I'm not allowed."

"It would be," I said. "I'm sorry if this isn't actually what you wanted when you asked me to take you for a year's service." There was also the possibility that she had forgotten doing that in the first place, since she'd been asleep at the time. Dreams are weird.

Raysel looked up sharply, golden eyes wide with alarm. "You're not going to release me, are you?" she demanded. Her voice was loud enough that several people at neighboring tables turned to look in our direction. So much for making a quiet entrance. "You *promised*."

"I did," I agreed. "I promised when you were elf-shot, asleep, and still trying to adjust to your new normal, and then there wasn't any way to discuss it with you between waking you up and needing to make the claim of offense. So if you've changed your mind, you only need to say."

"I haven't," she said firmly. "I didn't want to go with them, and then, the way Mom kept looking at me, it was like I was a total stranger, and not just a Daoine Sidhe. I can't . . . I can't *do* that. I can't spend every night with someone who wants me to be somebody I don't know how to be."

"I understand better than I wish I did," I said. "No one's going to make you go to Shadowed Hills. If we don't finish dealing with the current situation soon, I'll ask Quentin and May to take you home. We have a room all ready for you."

Raysel looked at me warily, as if she was trying to find the falsehood in my words. When she didn't find it, mostly because it wasn't there, she relaxed slightly, looking so much like a dog that had been beaten every day for years that it made me want to put my current crisis on hold, walk over to Shadowed Hills, and slap Luna myself.

"Really?" she asked, voice small.

"Really," I assured her. "Quentin says he's not going to let you have the Wi-Fi password until you've been there for three days without stabbing anyone, but since you haven't had time to get addicted to phone games yet, that should be fine."

"I . . . " She sagged. "Good. Three days is good."

I wasn't sure how to extricate myself from the conversation. Fortunately, I didn't have to be. The smell of blackberry flowers and redwood sap rose behind me a beat before a hand landed on my shoulder and Arden's voice said, in my ear, "Great, you're back. Now you can report *to your Queen*. Oh, and kitty, you can come too."

SIXTEEN

ARDEN PULLED ME THROUGH the portal she had created, holding it open long enough for Tybalt to step through after us, looking entirely unruffled by this disruption. We were back in the empty receiving room. Oberon's throne was still there, although the leaves were brown and curling around the edges. It wasn't going to last forever. The damage to the floor was probably going to be another story.

Another portal flickered into being a moment after Arden's closed, and Nolan stepped through with a platter of finger sandwiches in his hand and Cassandra close behind him.

"She insisted," he said, looking to Arden. "I told her she should be staying with her family, and she reminded me, with inappropriate vigor, that as she is the chatelaine and this business impacts the knowe, she has every right to attend upon you if she so desires."

Arden looked at Cassandra, unimpressed. "You know, when I was a kid, the household staff was much more willing to listen to the nobility."

"When you were a kid, the bra had yet to be invented," countered Cassandra. She took the platter from Nolan and walked over to me, thrusting it into my hands. "You have to eat. It's important."

"Why?"

"I can't tell you." Her mouth twisted unhappily. "If I tell you, you'll change what you do, and if you change what you do, things will go much, much worse for you. So I can't tell you, but you're going to eat as many of these sandwiches as you can stomach, and then you're going to eat two more, because you're going to bleed a *lot* before you get to eat again, and you need something to use when you're building back all that blood."

I took the tray, blinking at her. "You're not normally this specific about what's going to happen, even in your nonspecific way," I said.

"Yeah, well, I'm not normally in the middle of a massive crisis involving my whole fucking family, and my sister's not normally dead," she snapped. "I can't See *that woman* directly—even the air shies away from her, it's like she's the original evil enchanted mirror or something—but I can See the wreckage she leaves in her wake, and there's a lot of it. Something really, really bad is going to happen if you don't stop her soon, and it's going to hit all of us. That makes it enough my business for me to See."

"Aren't oracles useful?" asked Arden, almost abstractly. "Can't pick lottery numbers, can't tell you not to wear the white dress on a night when the chefs are serving cioppino, can make dire proclamations with absolutely no guidance to go with them. What *happened*, Sir Daye?"

Meaning she wanted the formal report rather than the colloquial one. Too bad for her that the two are effectively one and the same where I'm concerned. "Went to Oberon for help stopping his wife," I said, blandly. Everyone here knew he was back, even if I had never seen Nolan directly interact with him. "He gave me a very temporary form of protection, but didn't want to otherwise help me. Where is he?"

"Wandering around the grounds, while steadfastly refusing to go and look for her himself," said Arden. "To be honest, it feels like he wants to pretend none of this is happening."

"A position I can sadly understand," said Cassandra.

So could I, and that was really the problem. "After speaking to Oberon, I went back to the Brown house, hoping I could find a trail there to follow. I found Titania, playing at being Stacy Brown, preparing pancakes for dinner."

Cassandra winced. "Jessica's favorite."

"Yeah." It seemed best to be blunt at this point. It wasn't like I could make things better by doing literally anything else. "I was hoping . . . I don't know what I was hoping." Charging wildly off into danger had worked for almost everything else in my life, and I guess what I'd really been hoping was that it would work again here. That somehow being willing to risk myself would be enough to transform this into the sort of situation that could be handled by risking myself. More quietly, I finished, "I just don't know."

"But we know where she is now?" asked Arden.

"Not really. She said she wasn't free yet, wasn't back yet, because she hasn't fulfilled the terms of her geas. So she has to do what Oberon commanded her to do, and then disappear again, to become somebody new. She said—and I'm sorry, but I believe her, about this at least—she said there is no Stacy without her, and so we can't save Stacy. It's impossible."

Cassandra made a choked sound and turned her face away. I took the first sandwich and shoved as much of it into my mouth as I could manage, chewing fast and swallowing too quickly. "Stacy's still there, though, and still fighting, I think because she hasn't been able to arrange a perfect disappearance for Titania."

"You mean because she hasn't killed us yet," said Cassandra, voice cold.

"Yes, I do," I said. "In order to fulfill the conditions of her binding, Titania has to pass without a trace. She has to disappear into someone new, and not leave any evidence that there was ever anything odd about Stacy Brown."

"Four unexplained Firstborn from a nondescript changeling woman is certainly odd," said Arden.

"It would have been five if any of us had known how to read what the signs were trying to say," said Cassandra. "Jessica and Andrew had been having nightmares for weeks. Even if they didn't remember them when they woke up, Karen did, and she made sure I knew what was going on. We all knew we needed to be worried about something, but none of us expected it to be our own mother."

"Because it wasn't your mother," I said, more fiercely than I intended. "Stacy would *never* have hurt Jessica. Stacy's still there. She's fighting Titania. She's fighting so much harder than I would ever have thought it was possible for a person to fight against the queen of us all."

"What does Titania want?" asked Arden.

"The Browns. She wants to kill the rest of Stacy's children, so she can vanish like none of this ever happened. She can't be Titania without constraints until she's become a better person, and being the kind of person who wakes up from a long dream of being someone else and promptly starts trying to murder kids isn't what I'd call 'better.' But she can't stop being Stacy and turn into somebody new until she's erased all signs of her presence, which means not leaving four Firstborn behind." I paused, taking a slow, shaky breath.

"And she says if I don't help her finish out this stage of the geas, she's going to kill everyone I love," I said. "Well. Almost everyone. Oberon apparently bound her against harming direct members of Janet's descent. So I'm safe, August's safe, and May's *probably* safe, depending on how the magic wants to interpret the existence of a Fetch."

"Gillian?" asked Tybalt, in a tone of mild horror.

I shrugged. "I don't know. She was born a changeling, but I pulled my contribution to her heritage out after she'd been elf-shot. She still had my jawline after that, so clearly I'm still her biological mother, but when I removed the magic, I could easily have removed the protection. And it wasn't like I was going to ask Titania, 'Please, ma'am, but as you're making wild threats, can you tell me how many of my loved ones are in danger?' If she doesn't remember Gilly exists, I'm not going to remind her."

Tybalt nodded. "She can reach the Court of Cats," he said. "Her daughter, Erda, was the one who opened the Shadow Roads for our use, and while the stories of Erda paint her as the kindest of women, she was well known to be devoted to her mother, and to have objected when Oberon said the Cait Sidhe would stand alone, claimed by none among the Three, in recognition of our independence."

"So your people . . . "

"My people are not safe." He started to step away, then stopped, indecision painted on his face. "I am your husband," he said. "I am your *mate.* I stood before the sea witch and I promised to stand beside you. I should be here as you consider throwing yourself into danger."

"And you're also still a King of Cats, and you know about a danger to your Court," I said. "Go. Warn them to close the doors and keep their heads tucked down until we know what's happening. Lock the doors on the Court of Cats until Titania is no longer the wolf on the stairs outside."

Tybalt frowned at me. "You're right, little fish, but I don't want to go."

"And I don't want you to go, but I want us both to survive this, and that sometimes means doing things we don't want to do. I love you. I'll do my best not to get myself killed before you come back. All right?"

"Not in the least," he said, and ducked forward to kiss me firmly before he turned, ran, and leapt into a patch of deepest shadow, vanishing in a swirl of pennyroyal and musk perfume. I turned my attention back to the others. Arden and Nolan were watching me with varying degrees of anxiety; Cassandra was watching the air above my head, and seemed perfectly serene. I eyed them.

"What?" I asked. "I can be apart from the man for more than five minutes. Titania's teeth, I was apart from him for fifty *years*!"

"Can you please not swear by my mother?" asked Cassandra.

"Can we not call her your mother?" I countered. "She killed your sister. She's destroying your family. She doesn't get the title."

The receiving room door opened, and for the second time in one day, the Luidaeg stepped inside. Oberon was right behind her, his antler fully regrown, a dour expression on his face.

"You're not drenched in blood, so I'm going to guess things went better than I would have wagered," said the Luidaeg, letting the door swing closed and sauntering toward me. "You're also not crying, so I'm going to guess you didn't put a knife through the woman's heart."

"Hey, Luidaeg," I said, wearily. I glanced to Oberon. "No. No murder, not yet anyway. But she's made it pretty clear that there's going to be a whole bunch of it, one way or another. Either I help her wipe out the Browns, or she comes for everyone I've ever loved while she's still trapped in this liminal 'not myself, and not Stacy either' place. Can you unbind her, Sire?"

Oberon blinked. "I could," he said. "If I wanted to."

"Well, then, I damn well need you to want to," I snapped. "There are four children's lives at stake."

"Not a child," said Cassandra.

"Three children and a physicist," I amended. "If you unbind Titania so she doesn't have to kill Stacy's children to be herself again, she won't have to kill anyone."

"And the balance will still be shattered, as Maeve is absent," said Oberon. "I've called for her, to no avail. I fear she is lost to us."

"Not so much," said the Luidaeg. Everyone turned to look at her, and she pointed at me. "October over here called on Mom for help a little while back, and Mom *answered*. She's alive. She's just not showing her face right now."

"And with the way everything else has been going, she's probably somewhere nearby," I said sourly. "You know, for a family that doesn't get along very well, you guys sure do love living in each other's pockets. Better be careful or people will start to think you like each other."

Oberon looked at me impassively. "As you say. But with my Lady of Roses bound and half-aware, and my Lady of Tides still walking roads unknown, we run the risk that unbinding the Summer Queen will cast Faerie completely into chaos. I was able to bind her only because I caught her entirely unaware, and she had no time to defend against me. She won't be dropping her guard so complacently again. If I unbind her, I won't have the time to bind her again before she does as she will."

"One shot at this, gotcha," I said. "If I can lure her into an ambush, can you stop her so she can't move?"

"So you can put those blades of yours through her heart, as you did to my son?" asked Oberon. "I will not help you kill my wife, and I will not help you destroy Faerie. There is a simpler way." He looked at Cassandra, a world of meaning in his eyes.

I considered, not for the first time, the virtues of stabbing Oberon. Sure, I'd been planning for the first possible opportunity, but who was to say I couldn't *make* my own opportunity? Fortune favors the bold.

Cassandra, meanwhile, backpedaled away from him, raising her hands. "Oh, no," she said. "Faerie needs us."

"What?"

"It's getting clearer now that things are out in the open. I couldn't see a lot of things before, because there was a shadow over Mom, standing in the way. The shadow's gone now. So's Mom."

"Oracles cannot chart the movement of the Three," said Oberon. "We are beyond you."

"Charming," I said. "Cass, continue."

"Eat another sandwich and I will."

I ate another sandwich. She looked pleased with herself.

"Good Auntie. Now, as I was saying: something bad happened a long time ago, and Faerie lost almost all of her oracles, all at once. The ones we still have are trying to hold things together, but they don't have the numbers. Bringing back the Roane helped. I don't think anything short of time travel would have helped enough. There's something bad coming, and unless we can help to unsnarl it, a lot of people are going to get hurt. Really badly. You need us. Right now, I think you need us more than you need her."

She looked directly at Oberon, smiling a little. "You know *why* we can't see you? Why you've always been standing outside the lines of prophecy? It's because you're too big. When a human weatherman talks about the next few days, they don't say 'Oh and also, the sun is going to continue to be a massive flaming ball of incandescent gas.' Their forecasts take the sun into account as a matter of course. As far as the future is concerned, you're an environmental hazard, not a person. You make things too hazy to follow. When Mom was around, things got hazy whenever she was involved. Guess we know why now. But it's why we all knew something bad was going to happen this week, without knowing exactly what, or when, or how to step around it. And I'm telling you, Sire, right here and now, that Faerie is making oracles because she needs us. She needs us to see what's coming next. And she needs that clarity of vision a hell of a lot more than she needs the woman who murdered my baby sister in cold blood."

"You are a child," said Oberon ponderously. "It isn't your place—"

"We're *all* children compared to you!" she protested. "The *Luidaeg* is a child compared to you!"

"Guilty," said the Luidaeg, who had the audacity to sound faintly amused, like she had always wanted to watch a college student verbally smack down her father.

"And I've *been* here, living in this version of Faerie, while you've been off playing human and escaping your responsibilities," said Cassandra. "You stepped out on us because you didn't want to be alone, and you *left* us all alone! Our whole culture is the island from *The Lord of the Flies* right now, thanks to you! So if you don't like it, tough. You should have been here. My siblings and I, we're Seers, yeah. All four of us. All five of us, yesterday. And as a Seer, I'm telling you Faerie needs us, and it doesn't need her."

"You said the future treats the Three like environmental hazards?" I said. Cassandra looked at me and nodded. "Okay, that's easy enough to follow. But Cassie . . . if you can't see them clearly because they're too big for that, what happens if we take one of them away? What happens if you *kill the sun*?"

She paused, a complicated expression crossing her face. "Okay, so maybe we can't kill Titania," she said. "But Faerie can't afford to lose us right now, either." She lifted her chin, turning back to Oberon as imperiously as any queen. "You'll have to find another way."

He sighed, heavily. "An unbalanced Faerie is a nightmare the likes of which you have never dared to dream. There is a reason I was willing to raise a hand against my own queen, when she should have been able to feel completely secure in my bower."

"So we can't kill her, we're *not* letting her have the kids, and we can't allow her to unbalance Faerie," I said. "Is there anyone else who could unbind her? Get her pinned down and let you enchant her again while she's still disoriented?"

"You could," said the Luidaeg.

I turned to stare at her, and for a long, terribly moment, no one said anything at all.

"Look at the little hero, Dad, and tell me what her line was built to do," said the Luidaeg.

Oberon turned to stare at me, and I abruptly found that I couldn't move. Couldn't even blink. All I could do was stand there and struggle to bear up under the sheer weight of his regard. It wasn't easy, despite the fact that it literally wasn't possible for me to do anything else. I wanted to collapse into a boneless pile, and instead, I could barely breathe.

"Don't break her," chided the Luidaeg.

Oberon frowned. "The blood is there—a living hope chest, to replace what has been broken. An instinctive understanding of the balances and interactions between the different strains, necessary for the doing of what she's made to do. Sensitivity to magic. More than I would have thought advisable."

"Because it isn't," said the Luidaeg. "When she was younger, I used to worry she'd walk into an illusion and have a stroke where she stood. It's too much for one line to carry, but it's hers, and she has to contend with it. Look *deeper*."

It felt like telling him not to break me and then to look deeper in the same breath was a contradiction, but I couldn't say anything. I was just trying to survive the weight of Oberon's eyes.

"No more illusions than the least of us, so no flowers, and little connection to the water—all she has is the blood," said Oberon. He had the audacity to sound surprised about that, as if somehow I should have picked up magic from the Queens, even though they had no part in my family tree.

"But the blood she has is more than sufficient to break the world. Is this . . . Can she truly unravel another's workings as the blood implies?"

The Luidaeg looked almost smug. "She *can*," she said. "I've seen her do it. She's like a raccoon, with their clever little raccoon hands. They can't assemble machines on their own, but let someone else do it for them, and they have the dexterity to operate what they can access."

Oberon turned to look at her, and I could suddenly move again. I took a step back, not retreating, but putting myself closer to Arden, in case a retreat became suddenly advisable. "How?"

"She finds the rough spots in the spell, digs her hands in, and pulls it apart," said the Luidaeg. "I've seen her tackle things that should have been infinitely too big for her to handle. Hell, she reversed a full Actaeon. On *herself*."

Oberon blinked, looking at me with what I wanted very much to read as a new respect. "I remember you from then," he said. "I knew you had been enchanted, I knew you had been reported missing, and I knew you could never tell me the truth of whatever had happened to you."

I looked at him sharply. "You knew you were Oberon?"

"No. But Thornton's memory is here, when I desire it. If you were to take me walking in your mortal world, you might find me to be better adapted to the age than many of the nobles who've been here all along. I simply have to . . . desire it, enough to pull it from the depths of thought. He was never me, but I was always him."

"Wait," I said. "Say that again."

"I was always him?"

"No, the piece before it."

Oberon looked puzzled for a moment, then nodded. "Ah. I see. You worry for your friend's memory. I will speak for her. Whatever my lady has done, your friend was not present when she did it."

"Good." I honestly wasn't sure whether this was better or worse than Stacy having been in any way complicit in Jessica's death. Better for her family, certainly. But maybe worse for me.

I was going to have to stop her, and now I knew that she

was as innocent as I'd hoped she was. Would I really be able to do this? And did I really have a choice? Stacy would have chosen her children over herself, a thousand times over. Could I choose any differently now?

"So that's the answer," said the Luidaeg. "You find her, or you lure her in, October unbinds her, and then you *re*-bind her before she can react."

"I would like to object to this plan on the grounds that it sounds like you would be asking my only available hero to put herself in mortal danger for the sake of detaining a literal goddess," said Arden.

I took a deep, slow breath. "Objection overruled," I said. "I've touched and unraveled enough spells at this point that I know I can disenchant her. And I'm the only one who can do it, because we need Oberon to put her back in the box before everything gets out of control. More than it already is."

"It should work," said Cassandra, firmly. "And I know how we get Titania here."

Oberon frowned. "How's that?"

"If she has any of Mom's reflexes left, she'll pick up when I call," said Cassandra. "I tell her we're ready to come home, she'll be here if she has to hotwire a car."

"That sounds like it might work," said Arden. "At the very least, it's simple. I like simplicity. Fewer things can go wrong when we keep it simple."

"All right." I looked to Oberon. "We call her, she comes, and when she goes for the Browns, I unbind her and you re-bind her immediately, to something a little less child-murder-y? Maybe with a nice, specific goal, instead of a vague, subjective, 'be a better person'?"

"I will compose my restrictions with the greatest care," said Oberon ponderously.

"And what happens after that, when I have a pissed-off Queen of All Faerie in my knowe?" asked Arden.

"If I spin the spell this time as I did the last, she'll vanish at once, off to begin her new life nestled in a safe place. Watch for news of a family suddenly taking in a foundling, or a changeling child being found wandering the fields without memory of where they came from, and you'll be able to find her before she can become a threat. My daughter here"—he indicated the Luidaeg—"was an excellent mother. Bring Titania to her, and we'll see her brought back up in better form."

"That's about ten thousand shades of creepy that I don't have the time or the energy to get into right now, but when all this is over, you and me, we're going to have a talk about grooming and ethics and how they apply to everybody the same," I said, and took a deep breath. "So I guess we're doing this."

"I suppose we are." Arden crossed to Cassandra, offering the girl her hands. "I know you hate this, Cass, but I need you to force it. Please. Tell me what to do."

Cassandra sighed and stared off into the distance, eyes unfocused as she watched the motion of the air. "Evacuate the knowe," she said, after a moment. "Everyone who's not actually a part of this plan needs to leave, or things will turn out very poorly. They may turn out very poorly anyway. Success is by no means assured, and the presence of two out of the Three means I can't See clearly enough to map any sort of safe path through. When she comes, let her come. Post no guards, offer no resistance. She needs to believe you're showing her the proper respect, or she'll hurt you."

Arden nodded. "I can do those things. Those are *easy* things. Was there anything else that would make this easier?"

"Yes," said Cassandra, looking back to Arden. "You can straight-up order October to eat three more of those sandwiches, or I'm not going to call my mother."

"Anthony has a phone, you know," I protested, taking a sandwich in each hand. "He could call her."

"He won't." Cassandra smiled thinly. "He agrees that you have to eat more."

I looked to Nolan, who had been standing by quietly for most of this. "What do you think?"

"I think a lady should feel free to eat—or not eat—whatever she likes, and it's nobody's business but her own."

Cassandra narrowed her eyes and just *looked* at me, so intently that it made me want to squirm. Then she turned to Arden. "I am the bait in this trap, but I am also your chatelaine, Your Highness. What can I do to expedite the process of clearing the knowe?"

Arden hesitated, staring off into space. It wasn't the intent staring Cass had been doing before; this was the stare of a woman who'd forgotten something, nothing more. "There was an alarm," she said, slowly. "We heard it on the night of the earthquake. If you consult your house book, it should have the instructions on finding and activating it. If the process requires someone of royal blood, either myself or Nolan can accomplish that for you. Only call."

I leaned toward Nolan, murmuring, "House book?"

"A token of the chatelaine," said Nolan. "The knowe can answer any questions she has about the structure, and help guide her to spells that have declined in efficacy and need to be reestablished."

"Huh," I said.

Meanwhile, Cassandra and Arden embraced quickly before Cass walked out of the room, brisk as anything. Nolan watched her go, shaking his head.

"Our Cassandra, Firstborn," he said. "Who would ever have thought it?"

"All of us were young once," said the Luidaeg mildly. "Now, Toby. I have a very important and possibly terrifying job I need you to take care of for me while the young Miss Brown is getting all her ducks in a row."

"What's that?" I asked.

She smiled. "You get to convince your friends and family that it's time for them to get the hell out of here."

SEVENTEEN

MAY LOOKED AT ME with the flat, affectless stare of someone who had won arguments against better adversaries than me and wasn't particularly concerned about losing this time. "No," she said.

"I'm sorry, you have to." She glared at me. I put up my hands. "If it were just you, you know I'd let you stay and face the all-dangerous, all-terrible Queen of Faerie by my side. Having an indestructible wingman is invaluable. But it's not just you."

"Quentin has the training to—"

"It's not about Quentin."

She continued glaring. I kept my hands up.

"We agreed, as a family, to give Raysel a safe place to rest and recover and see a damn therapist," I said. "We *agreed*. That means you, too. Well, Muir Woods is about to be really, really unsafe for anyone who isn't actively involved in this plan." It was going to be unsafe for us, too, but I didn't want to think about that any harder than I absolutely had to, because the only other person who might be able to play my part in this plan was August, and she was unavailable for a lot of reasons. They started with "She's in Saltmist right now," and from there escalated through a long series of patently obvious explanations of why I shouldn't ask my semi-estranged half-sister to come up here and risk her life for reasons that really boiled down to "Somebody has to, and I don't want to do it."

May maintained her glare for another few seconds, then sighed and let it go. "And what happens if you take her into your service and then immediately get yourself killed?" she asked. "Or turned into a giant turtle or something else completely inconvenient?"

"I guess you get to deal with the Torquills trying to claim she's released, because I'm not there to argue, and that's when you get to force a ruling on the legal status of Fetches in Faerie. Either you're my daughter in the eyes of the crown, and you inherit all my debts and assets, or you're my sister, and you have the right to stand in for me on rights of insult. And either way, Tybalt will be there to help you, and as my husband, he *also* has a right to claim the remainder of Raysel's service. Just get her home, and safe, and away from all this nonsense."

"Tybalt," said May thoughtfully. "You haven't spoken to him about this yet, have you?"

"He's in the Court of Cats, making sure they understand the situation." He'd already been gone longer than I'd expected him to be. I guess the situation was reasonably difficult to explain. "Raj?"

"Was called back before we sat down for dinner," she said. "The Court needed him, and he's not his uncle; he doesn't have that kind of leeway to delegate."

"He's also not technically in charge yet." I sighed, rubbing my face with one hand. "I'm hoping Quentin will be less furious about this if I tell him he can go home with Dean for the duration."

"The lady hopes in vain," said May, voice flat. "He's going to eat your face off."

"Maybe, but not literally." Her threat reminded me of the tray of sandwiches which Nolan had ostentatiously dropped off for me before he took off to notify the first group of courtiers that the knowe was being abandoned. Cassandra was really serious about me needing to eat as many of them as I could stomach. That raised some worrisome questions about just how much blood I was going to be losing today, since I could bleed myself nearly dry without suffering any long-term consequences. How much blood did she expect me to regenerate?

And it didn't really matter, because my stomach seemed happy to receive as many sandwiches as I was willing to give it. They were pleasantly bland, cucumber and cream cheese and chicken and the occasional sharp bite of watercress. Nothing that could put a strain on an already-damaged system.

It would have been a lot more worrisome if we hadn't been standing on the verge of a terrible idea that was nonetheless the best option we had.

"Go home," I said. "Show Raysel her room, reassure her that we're really not going to send her back to Shadowed Hills, and order sushi. Jazz likes sushi."

"Does Raysel like sushi?"

"I don't know if she's ever had it before."

May's eyes lit up. "Oh, that's right, she had a formless void and then she had the kitchens at Shadowed Hills! She's probably never had *anything* good! Even if she's not down for sushi, we can get her teriyaki and tempura and blow her sheltered little mind!"

"Just don't blow it so completely that we have to give her back to her parents," I said.

May made a noncommittal noise and watched me eat the rest of the sandwich in my hand, waiting for me to swallow before she leaned over and yanked me into a fierce hug.

"I know this is Stacy, and I know how much you *want* it to be Stacy, how much you *want* it to somehow be all right again," she said, voice low, mouth close to my ear. "I know how much you want to save her. But Toby . . . " She pushed me out to arm's length, looking at me gravely. "Don't you dare die. I love her as much as you do, but I love you more. You're my sister and my family, and I need you to come home. So you come home."

I pulled away, blinking. "I was planning to. You seem more concerned about this one than I'm used to."

"Yeah, because I've met the Lady of Flowers before." May looked at me, lips a hard line, eyes worried. "Long memory, on a Fetch. Long, long memory. Longer on a night-haunt. She was never a terror, but she was a tyrant. And if you were in her way, if you inconvenienced her . . . So many of the people I remember being came to us because of Titania. And some of them came while they were still alive, in the days before Oberon bound us not to harm the living. You need to be so careful with her. She doesn't care who she destroys, as long as she gets what she wants."

"I understand," I said.

May started to speak, then paused and said, "I'll let you take this one. I'm going to get Raysel and call Danny for a ride back to the house. *Please* make sure someone calls me when this is all over."

She walked briskly out of the room. I blinked after her and reached for another sandwich.

Behind me, a smooth voice said, "Imagine my surprise when I arrived here expecting to find you with the Queen, only to be informed that the knowe was about to be evacuated, and all those not required for the successful completion of a mythical 'plan' were being bound to leave."

"Sorry." I turned to face Tybalt, a sandwich in my hand and an apologetic look on my face. "We didn't have time to call and make sure you knew the plan, but I figured you'd catch on once you got here, as long as we hadn't completely emptied the place out. How were things in the Court of Cats?"

"Hmmm? Oh, all is well among the Court. You know how the felines fare." He waved a hand, airily dismissing my concerns. "What is this plan?"

"Cassandra is going to call Stacy's phone, and get her to come here to collect the children. When she shows up, I'm going to break the binding Oberon put on her."

His gaze sharpened, and he focused on my face for the first time. "You can *do* that?"

"The Luidaeg seems to think I can, so yeah, I can probably do that. If I can't, I guess we're going to find out in the biggest, most dramatically stupid way possible. But the way I take down a spell is apparently well suited to dismantling a geas, and Oberon doesn't seem to have put as much thought into the one he cast on his wife as she put into the one she cast on the Luidaeg." If the Luidaeg had been *allowed* to tell me I could dismantle a geas lain by one of the Three, she would have told me long since. Her own geas was a burden that dragged her down every single day.

Yeah, freeing her might have meant she returned to the sea to be with the Roane, but that would have been worth it to see my friend allowed to be happy. As it was, she had to serve the people of the land, bound and forbidden to live the way she wanted to, and all thanks to Titania.

"I see," said Tybalt, still focusing on me. I took a step backward, swallowing the final bite of my sandwich.

"Tybalt? Why are you looking at me like that?"

"Like what?"

"The way Quentin looked at Chelsea when she picked them all up lunch from that Mean Poutine place in Vancouver." He was happy with Dean, but when Chelsea had popped into our living room laden with square brown fast-food containers, Quentin had looked at her like he was suddenly considering whether Dean's parents had the right idea.

Which was their business, if they decided that was the way they wanted to do things. As long as I didn't have to be the one to explain it to anyone's parents, I really didn't care.

"I'm just astonished all over again by what a creative and talented wife I have," he said, and took a step toward me.

The alarm bells that had been chiming before were getting louder inside my head, approaching storm-klaxon volume. "Yeah, well, I'm pretty innovative," I said, and dipped a hand into my pocket, pulling out the little bottle I'd received from Oberon. It was still well over two-thirds full. I wanted to conserve as much of it as possible for the actual fight against Titania, but I could have a sip now, if I needed it.

And I was direly afraid I needed it.

Tybalt scowled when he saw what was in my hand, but he didn't move to stop me. "Is this really the time to be indulging in your quest for more power?" he asked.

I paused in the motion of raising the bottle, blinking at him. "What?"

"You and I both know you accepted that only because it could make you more powerful, even if only in the short term," he said. "You've never been content with your limitations, even when you ought to be."

"Right," I said mildly, trying to ignore the sting of his words. "That verifies it. I won't say you're not Tybalt, because you probably are, but you're not speaking for yourself right now." I raised the bottle, quickly swallowing two sips of its contents, and was immediately assaulted with the smell of roses, strong and cloying and radiating, as expected, almost entirely from Tybalt. I lowered the bottle, eyes on him. "So what, the Court of Cats was already compromised when you got there?"

"The Court of Cats contains only what it means to," he said. If I focused, I could see the lines of prismatic pink in his eyes and wrapping around him like a hand. Titania had her claws in him.

"Then it needs to do some serious introspection," I said, re-capping the bottle and returning it to my pocket before spreading my arms. "Guessing she sent you here to stop any plan we might be putting in place to stop *her*, and she knows me well enough to know I'd be right in the center of it, although not well enough to know that keeping you away would have been a bigger distraction than whatever it is you're about to do to me. So come on, kitty. Let's go."

Tybalt snarled, the sound equal parts fury and frustration, like he was fighting as hard as he could against the compulsion forcing him to do this, and launched himself across the short distance between us, slamming into me like a freight train. I let the impact drive me back, not offering any resistance or attempting to get away, and was unsurprised when he shoved me again, even harder, and I tumbled into shadow.

So we were going to be fighting in the dark, were we? It made sense as an instruction from Titania: Stacy knew how much of a toll the Shadow Roads took on me, and that meant Titania did too. It was also a bad choice under the circumstances, since the mouthful of Oberon's blood I'd just swallowed was protecting me from the worst of the road's effects.

Tybalt snarled, circling me. The cold wasn't bothering me, and I could breathe, but I still couldn't see, and that was going to be a problem if he didn't make contact soon.

"How did she get into the Court of Cats, Tybalt?" I asked the darkness around me, turning to stay oriented on the sound of his voice. It wasn't as good as being able to see him, but it was better than staying completely still. "Did someone lead her in, or did she just follow the Shadow Roads and guess where she wanted to go? Stacy had never been there. Titania has probably been to the Courts before, but not this one. How much damage did she do?"

He made a strangled sound, then resumed his snarling.

"That bad, huh?" I tensed. As long as I could keep him growling, I could tell where he was.

Maybe that wasn't the only way. The smell of roses still hung around him. I closed my eyes, taking away the distraction of the dark, and reached for the spell that was binding his thoughts, the one I had seen reflected in his eyes. At the same time, I bit the inside of my cheek, hard enough to draw blood, and as it washed across my tongue, adding the taste of cut grass and copper to the loam I had taken from Oberon, I *saw*.

The space around me lit up in an array of fine threads. The Shadow Roads themselves were a magical construct. I saw the prismatic pink I now recognized as Titania, wrapped tight and tangled through the darker green of Oberon. A third line of threads was woven with the two, deep blue and pearl white at the same time, and I gasped, almost losing hold of the spell I was trying to conjure.

Maeve's magic. That was what her workings looked like. Meaning if she was still out there in the world, I knew what I would need to look for. I didn't dare reach for those threads—not only would collapsing the Shadow Roads potentially kill the two of us, but it would strand uncounted Cait Sidhe in their Courts, with no way out—but now that I knew they existed, I could try to find Maeve's magic again, to get a sense for the scent of it.

Another patch of pink moved around me, flickering prismatically, much fresher and more potent. That was the source of the roses that flavored the air, recently woven and wrapped tight around my husband's heart and head. My poor love. He wasn't going to be happy when he realized someone had tried to use him as a weapon against me. Again.

It was harder to get a grasp on the threads when they were attached to someone who kept moving. There was a solution to that, but neither of us was going to like it. I waited until he finished another loop, then launched myself at him, driving my shoulder into his chest. Tybalt hissed as we both went down in a heap on whatever served the Shadow Roads for ground. They were a dark, infinite space, but at least they had gravity: when we fell, we hit, and we stopped falling. I appreciated that.

Tybalt scrabbled to get out from underneath me, and I grabbed him by the hair, holding him where he was. The fact that I wasn't bleeding yet was a testament to how hard he was struggling against Titania's compulsions: I've seen the man fight, on several occasions, and there should have been entrails flying everywhere. Instead, he was fighting me like we were a pair of high school wrestlers and the last thing he wanted to do was hurt me.

To be fair, I didn't want to hurt him, either. My knives were still sheathed at my hips, and even as he slammed his knee into my sternum, I was trying to pin him down rather than put him out of commission. A flash of near-blinding brown and green interposed itself over the pink, and I barely had time to realize what that meant and grab the cat he'd become by the scruff of the neck before he could shoot off into the dark.

Tybalt hissed and twisted against my grasp as I stood and tucked him in against my chest. He could turn back at any time, but if he was trying not to hurt me, he wouldn't. And he didn't. Thank Oberon for that, he didn't.

"Hey, sweetheart," I said, and reached for the pink threads again, this time catching hold of them with the edges of my own magic, pulling them tight and looking for the place where they were rooted into his thoughts.

It was like grabbing for super-heated wire. I wasn't doing it with my hands at all, but I could feel the burn all the way to the bottom of my stomach, caustic acid against the surface of my magical reserves. If this was what it was like to grab something spun by one of the Three, I was going to need a *lot* more of Oberon's blood before I could tackle the binding on Titania.

Still, despite the pain, I grabbed on and held him tight, unafraid of damaging myself if it meant saving him in the process. Tybalt fought, until the moment when he didn't, which was also the moment when the lines began to break in my "hands." I yanked harder, and the web of pink shattered and fell away, leaving Tybalt limp and motionless in my arms, sides heaving with the effort of breathing.

"Poor love," I said, and leaned down to press a kiss to his forehead before looking around, eyes still closed. The web of lines making up the Shadow Roads was still intact. That was good.

Tybalt was unconscious and I had no idea how to navigate in here. That was bad.

Colored lines extended in all directions, marked pathways to the most common local destinations. I had to wonder how they appeared to Tybalt, or indeed *if* they appeared to him: he had commented in the past about letting the shadows guide him. So maybe the Cait Sidhe only ever traveled by instinct, and by following the faint scent trails left behind by the cats who had been there before them. I didn't have that luxury.

I also didn't have a single clue which of these tautly drawn threads might lead me back to Muir Woods. I turned a slow circle, trying to inventory the threads. They came in all colors, but one was as riotously red as fox fur, shot through with flecks of burning gold.

Shadowed Hills. It had to be. Technically, I was still banned from the knowe, even if formally I was just being "encouraged" to stay away. Functionally, unless Sylvester released my fealty, he couldn't turn me away when I was in crisis. More importantly, Chelsea and Etienne would be there, and either one of them could get me back to Muir Woods before Titania showed up and wrecked everything.

Cradling Tybalt against my chest, I began walking. The line stretched out ahead of me, with no clear destination in sight.

Oh, well. Why the hell not? I cleared my throat, tilted my head back, and said, "Hi. I don't know if the rules are the same for you or what, but it seems to me that you're something very much like a knowe. Fae made you, and then they used you, over and over again, until the magic that filled your walls began to turn solid and understand itself. I think you know I'm here. I think you know I'm not *supposed* to be here, and want me to get out as much as I want to leave."

There was no response—of course there was no response—but I felt an uncomfortable awareness settle across me, heavy enough to notice, like I was being studied by an entire crowd. I kept walking.

"I don't know how much influence you have here, but I've got one of your Kings, and he's in pretty rough shape, and I love him very much, so if there's anything you can do to help me help him, I would be very appreciative."

That didn't feel like enough. I took a deep breath—and was the air getting thinner? I didn't want to let the easy lure of Oberon's blood make me forget that it was a limited resource when I still had a serious fight ahead of me—and added, "Please. I know you love your Kings and Queens. Don't let me be the reason you lose this one."

The line I had been trying to follow flared a briefly brighter red, like it had caught fire for a moment. Instead of stretching endlessly into the dark, it now ended in a single flickering point, like a tiny candle. I exhaled.

"That's just what I needed," I said, and hurried toward the light, following the line to its end.

When I got there, I closed my eyes, took another deep breath, and stepped forward the way I would have stepped into a knowe, trusting Faerie to see me safely home.

The air on the other side of the step was sweet with blooming honeysuckle, and bright enough to be seen through my closed eyelids. I cracked my eyes cautiously open.

We were standing in one of the long halls of Shadowed Hills, garlands of flowers—including the honeysuckle—strung along the walls between the lower panels and the windows, everything rich and lush with polished wood and velvet. I breathed in as deeply as I could, and while I smelled roses, they were the normal blooming roses of Luna's many gardens and not the primal poison of Titania.

I turned another circle, getting my bearings, and looked down at Tybalt. He was still breathing harder than I liked, but was clearly exhausted and had fallen asleep in my arms, content to stay there for the moment. That was good. He wasn't going to be thrilled when he woke up and realized what had happened.

I started walking. The hall I was in should connect to the kitchens before too terribly long, and once I got there, I could ask the household staff for help. Melly and Ormond, the Hobs who functionally run the place, have known me since I was a little girl, and they've both adored me just about as long. They could help me lie low while someone went to fetch Etienne for me, and they wouldn't betray my presence.

And maybe I could get another sandwich. My stomach was oddly unsettled. I couldn't remember the last time I'd had this much to eat in a single day; I shouldn't still have been hungry.

Oh, well. Problem for later. The hallway curved ahead of me, and I found myself outside the familiar shape of the kitchen door. Breathing a sigh of relief, I pushed it open and slipped inside.

Melly immediately looked up from the dough she was kneading—some sort of piecrust from the looks of it, although it could really have been almost anything—and turned toward the door, her polite server's smile already in place. "If you're lost—" she began, and stopped as she saw that it was me standing in the doorway with an unconscious cat in my arms.

"I don't think I'm lost," I said, a bit more timidly than I intended. Now that I was here, in what used to be effectively my second home, I was a lot less sure of my welcome.

"Toby!" she squealed, and rushed over to throw her arms around me, mindful of Tybalt as she gave me a squeeze. "I know the Duke's been being too hard on you, but does that really have to mean the rest of us never get to see you anymore?"

"It does when he has the authority to banish me from the Duchy," I said. "Right now, if I give him space, I'm not technically breaking any rules when I *do* come to visit. If I push it, I will be."

Melly clucked her tongue and shook her head, looking at me reproachfully. "That man," she said. "He never has been able to understand something good when it's right under his nose. I'm sorry he's been being such a fool. But I hear you've been getting up to your own share of foolishness."

"Yes, and some of it's going on right now," I said. "The whole story is too complicated to explain at the moment, but I promise I'll find a way to come back and explain everything if you'll just call Etienne so he can get me back to Muir Woods."

There was a long, solemn pause as Melly looked at me. Then she bobbed her head and upper body in one unified gesture of agreement and bustled back toward her dough. "He's in-house right now, I believe. His Lady Bess rang down to request dinner in their quarters not long ago. I'll have you delivered along with the pastry."

This seemed to very much amuse her, which was a nice thing. At least one of us was laughing. Being in the kitchen was making my stomach flip over and my mouth water at the same time. I frowned, looking around for the source of the respective reactions. Onions, I realized. The smell of onions was making me want to vomit.

That didn't make any sense. I *love* onions. But someone was frying them nearby, and it was the nastiest thing I'd ever smelled. Whoever was baking bread, on the other hand? I wanted to be their new best friend, or at least their bread's new best friend, which was not the same thing and was probably a much shorter-lived relationship.

I snapped out of my brief contemplation of my surroundings to find Melly watching me with an odd brightness in her eyes. "A happy marriage so far, then?" she asked.

"I mean, apart from the danger and the disaster and the hero work, yeah," I said.

"And he supported you taking Mistress Rayseline into your home?"

I blinked. The fact that the household staff of Shadowed Hills was even more devoted to Raysel, the actual daughter of the house, than they were to me had completely slipped my mind in the chaos and need to make it from the Shadow Roads to someplace safer. "She asked," I protested. "When I spoke to her through the blood, she *asked* me to claim insult against her, so she could have a little time without any expectations, where she can recover. We're going to find her a therapist who has experience with changelings." Changeling therapists turned out to be more common than I would ever have suspected before I started dealing with Arden and Walther on a regular basis. Both of them had a strong interest in mental health and didn't think being immortal should be treated as a "get out of sanity free" pass.

Not many therapists had experience with purebloods, because not many purebloods were willing to seek that kind of help. Especially not from changelings and merlins, the two groups who seemed to make up the entire therapeutic network. Still, something was better than nothing, and Raysel was going to get the help she needed.

"I thought it might be something like that," said Melly, picking up a mason jar and sprinkling its contents over her dough, which immediately began to puff out and rise, going through its natural prove at an accelerated rate. "She's a good girl, our Raysel, and it's not her fault she's been pushed to doing some bad things. She'll be better off away from here, much as it pains me to say that. She needs the distance."

"Yeah. Simon's agreed to stay away from the house until she's ready to see him, but since she never really *saw* him while she was captive, she isn't as bothered by his presence as I would have expected her to be. I think we're going to be okay."

"See to it you are." Melly spun around to open an oven and pull out a tray of baking pastries with her bare hands. "Mind your fingers, those'll be warm for a minute yet," she said, merrily.

Hobs aren't fire fae, but they're hearth crafters, and their magic is frequently very generous when it comes to protecting them from ordinary household accidents. Like blisters when they grab hot trays without oven mitts. I still winced as Melly moved the tray to an open stretch of counter and set it down, unable to stop myself from picturing what that would feel like if it were me.

The pastries smelled delicious. Still . . . "This is a little urgent," I said, apologetically. "If there's any way we can hurry this up . . . ?"

"They'll be cool in just a moment, and as I said, I'm delivering you alongside the pastry," said Melly. "You want help, you want Etienne to put himself out for you, you'll need to have more patience than you've ever been inclined toward. I know you can do it. I believe in you. If you want *to* help, get that basket over yonder and start moving the pastries over. There's three going wanting, if you're feeling peckish."

"What are they?" I asked, retrieving the basket she had indicated.

"Cardamom-pear, cinnamon-apple, and blueberry-ginger. I didn't expect to see you today, but I still left off the strawberry. Odd, that." Melly smiled, indulgently.

I started moving the pastries from the tray into the basket, using a pair of tongs rather than my fingers. I might heal, but I didn't share Melly's affinity for touching hot metal without dropping something. "Actually, strawberries haven't been bothering me for a while now," I said. "I think that allergy was something I got from my dad, and the more I've moved myself away from him, the less it's been a problem."

Melly blinked at that, her face falling. "Oh, Toby, I'm sorry."

"Sorry? Because I can eat strawberries now?"

"Sorry because that's one more thing you should never have been asked to lose."

I looked away from her, focusing on the simple task of moving pastries into a basket—an activity complicated by the fact that I was still holding Tybalt against my chest with one arm. He seemed so fragile like this, so small and helpless. I loved him just as much right now as I did any other time, but I also wanted to keep him safe.

More, I wanted him to wake *up*. I wanted him to be here with me, to help me make Melly understand that this was urgent. But she's known me since I was a dramatic kid and, as a consequence, doesn't take much of anything I say as being as urgent as I think it is. I glanced back to her once all but three of the pastries had been moved.

"Maybe not, but I still remember him, and I'm not letting him go, no matter how much I have to lose or give away," I said, voice mild. "Now please. This is important. Stacy's family is at stake."

Melly's eyes widened, and she snatched the pastry-filled basket, clutching it to her chest. "Why didn't you say so? Come along, come."

She bustled toward the end of the kitchen, away from the door. I grabbed a pastry and followed her.

By the time I caught up with her, she had acquired another basket from somewhere, this one filled with a fresh loaf of bread, a wedge of cheese, and a pot of jam. She met my eyes, nodded, and pressed a decorative carved flower on the wall. A panel swung inward, revealing the service hall on the other side, and we hurried in.

The service halls snake all through the knowe, twisted through the body of the building like the roots of a tree, and they can be used to move from almost any room to almost any other, if the knowe is feeling cooperative and you have a rough idea of where you're going, or at least how to read the symbols on the walls.

I lived in Shadowed Hills for years without learning to navigate the service halls. It took Quentin to show them to me, explaining that they were the way he and the other courtiers could move around without being seen. It had been one of my more embarrassing moments. There weren't a lot of areas where I expected myself to know everything, but getting around Shadowed Hills was one of them.

Tybalt started to stir as we walked, finally yawning extravagantly and showing off a solid mouthful of razor-sharp teeth. He opened his eyes, blinking up at me, and squirmed to be put down.

"A second, Melly," I said, and stopped to lower him to the floor. Sure, cats are good at landing on their feet, but dropping my husband when I didn't have to seemed a little ruder than was necessary.

He walked a few steps away, stretched, and unfurled into his customary bipedal shape. "October?" he asked. "What happened? Where are we?"

"Hello, Sire," said Melly, peeking around me. "Welcome to Shadowed Hills."

Tybalt looked at her dubiously, then back to me. "Well, given that I was on my way to the Court of Cats, having left my lady safely in Muir Woods, this is not what I was expecting from my evening. What's going on?"

"I'll explain in a minute," I said, and stuffed the remainder of the pastry into my mouth before hugging him fiercely, not entirely aware of how much tension was in my shoulders until it drained away, leaving me feeling weak and shaken. I leaned back enough to meet his eyes. "Don't ever do that to me again."

"I might be better able to avoid the forbidden activity if you told me precisely what it was," he said, sounding bewildered.

I glared at him. He kissed my forehead.

"All right," he said. "Whatever I have done to so unsettle you, I promise it will not be done again."

"Good."

Melly started moving. We followed her. She stopped at what looked like a dead end, passing me a fresh pastry before she pressed another decorative flower on the wall.

"I normally would go around the front, but as we're trying not to be seen, this seems the best approach," she said, half-apologetically.

The wall swung inward, revealing a slice of the cluttered chambers Etienne shared with his wife and daughter. They were large, as befit the Duke's seneschal, and they had once been decorated with spare consideration, each item chosen precisely and with intent.

Now, they were crammed with a mix of medieval and modern furniture, one wall dominated by the television April and Chelsea had worked for an entire week getting to function within the knowe, floor a minefield of shoes, game controllers, and misplaced items. It made me happy to see it. After literal centuries, Etienne's home finally looked like he actually lived there, instead of simply existing.

"I think I hear tea!" chirped a bright voice, a moment before a black-haired head poked around the wall and into the room. Chelsea blinked wide copper eyes at the three of us, standing silhouetted in the door from the service corridor. ". . . huh," she said, finally, before turning and shouting, *"Mom!"*

"Did the kitchen forget your jam?" asked Bridget, bustling around the corner and stopping dead. She was a dainty human woman in her mid-forties, and the familial relationship between her and Chelsea was obvious in their shared features, despite her lack of pointed ears or impossibly colored eyes. She was wiping her hands on a dust rag, which she dropped at the sight of us. "October! What are you doing—Melly?"

"Found these in the kitchen, thought you could make better use of them than I could," said Melly, and set her baskets down on a nearby table clearly intended for that purpose. She had acquired a teapot somewhere along the way—hearth magic, I decided not to ask—and placed it carefully next to the baskets. I had watched this whole process, and would still have sworn she only had two arms. "I believe she needs to speak with your husband, if you'd be so very kind as to fetch him out."

"Why?" asked Chelsea. "Hi, Toby."

"Hi, Chels," I replied, semi-amused, and filched another pastry from the basket. My appetite was returning now that we were away from the smell of onions. "Is your father home?"

"Again, why? I'm guessing you wouldn't be here unless you needed to get somewhere else very quickly, and you know I can take you farther than he can."

She was right about that: Etienne was pureblooded Tuatha de Dannan, like Arden and Nolan, and could open portals between two points, but he had a normal Tuatha's limitations. He couldn't gate us directly to Muir Woods on his best day, and I wasn't counting on anyone having their best day at this point. We all seemed to be having a pretty lousy one.

"Before you get down to the weeds of this, I'm back to my kitchen," said Melly. She leaned in for a quick hug. "See that you come back as promised, with the full story," she instructed. "I'll have your supper ready for you whenever you arrive. We'll take it in the kitchen, properly, and away from prying eyes."

Then she was gone, closing the door into the service hallway behind her. Bridget walked over to collect the tea set.

"So much for a quiet evening in," she said, without rancor. "Etienne came home some time ago. Said the Queen was evacuating Muir Woods. Is that correct?"

"Yeah," I said, ignoring the way Tybalt stared at me. We couldn't keep this a secret for long, if it even was one now. I took a deep breath, and said, "Titania is back. We're trying to lure her to Muir Woods so I can help Oberon re-bind her to keep her from hurting anyone."

Tybalt kept staring. "I'm sorry," he said, in a half-strangled tone. "My ears clearly deceive me. It sounded as if, in my absence, you agreed to a plan which involved using yourself partially or in whole as *bait*."

"No," I said. He relaxed a little, only to tense again when I said, "We're using Cassandra as the bait. I'm just going to be the one on deck to tear down Oberon's binding geas."

"Just," he said, in a tone that implied he couldn't believe what he was hearing. And maybe he couldn't. I couldn't entirely believe what I was saying, after all.

"Hold up," said Bridget. "Titania? Oberon? As in Shakespeare? 'Fairy, skip hence'? Those people."

"Yeah, Mom, the Three," said Chelsea. She shot me a half-guilty look, then said, "I told you Oberon came back. He's been staying with the sea witch, because he's her dad and she likes having him around."

"No one's supposed to know that, Chelsea," I said.

"Yeah, like no one's supposed to know that Quentin doesn't really want to be High King anymore, and no one's supposed to know that Dean still tries to breathe water sometimes, so he can go back to Saltmist without feeling like he's a prisoner? Have you completely forgotten what it was like to be a teenager? We tell each other stuff." She crossed her arms and frowned at me. "We talk, and we're not stupid. We know what's going on."

"Okay, okay," I said. "Just please don't spread it around too much? Oberon wants his privacy, and he's the King of All Faerie. I don't want to see what happens if he feels like we're not respecting his wishes."

"Not sure how much I care," said Chelsea, with the airy casualness of the young.

Bridget put her hands on her hips. "Can you all *please* take a moment and explain to me what's going on?"

"Yes," said Etienne, stepping into the room. "An explanation of what you're doing here would be dearly welcome."

Fun.

EIGHTEEN

"ETIENNE," I SAID, NEAR-DIZZY with relief. "Tybalt and I need to get back to Muir Woods right now, and it's not safe for us to take the Shadow Roads."

"Wait," said Tybalt. "What do you mean, it's not safe? How did we get here?"

"Yes, how did you get here in the first place?" asked Etienne. "I know you didn't come in through the front door. I would have been alerted if you'd come through the gardens. You aren't formally banished as yet, but you walk a narrow line in the Duchess's eyes, and she will bid the Duke to release you from his service if you push her."

"And if he's willing to let me go because she tells him to, maybe it's time we free up my fealty for someone else to claim," I said, coldly. Etienne flinched, and I smirked faintly at the surprise in his expression. Loyalty is supposed to go both ways. I had always been loyal to Sylvester, and to Shadowed Hills. More and more, I was starting to feel like they were the ones who hadn't been loyal to me.

"Titania is back," I said, just in case he hadn't been close enough to overhear when I dropped that little bombshell before.

Etienne blanched. So he hadn't been. Okay. At least one person here wasn't trading texts with my squire.

"She's back, she's hostile, and she knows everything Stacy knows," I continued. Etienne looked understandably surprised at this, unlike Chelsea, who looked like this was old news. "She knew that if she wanted to get to me, the best way was by getting to Tybalt, and so she set a trap in the Court of Cats, and when he walked into it, she tied his mind in a knot and ordered him to stop me from getting in her way." I couldn't look at Tybalt as I spoke. I knew what I'd see in his eyes, and I wasn't ready for it. "He pulled us both into the Shadow Roads and attacked me. I was able to subdue him by undoing her binding, which was enough of a shock to his system that he lost consciousness for a while. I couldn't figure out how to get back to Muir Woods, so I carried him here."

"You can walk the Shadow Roads now?" asked Etienne.

"Only under very special circumstances that I don't think we're going to be repeating anytime soon. If we're going to stand around talking about this, could I have some of that bread, do you think?"

Tybalt made a small, surprised sound at hearing me actually ask for food without having it thrust upon me, and moved toward the basket without waiting for permission from any of its owners. If I wanted to be fed, he was going to feed me.

I kept my eyes on Etienne. "So Tybalt can't take us back to Muir Woods, my car is there, so I can't drive us back, and we need to *get* back, just as soon as possible. Please, can either you or Chelsea take us back to Muir Woods?"

"You say Titania is there?" Etienne shook his head. "I'm sorry, October, but no. I can't make the trip so easily as that, and I won't allow my daughter to risk herself so."

"Oh, because my friends aren't going to be putting themselves smack into the line of fire?" asked Chelsea. "Queen Windermere is evacuating the knowe. They haven't managed to evacuate Quentin. He's been texting me." She held up her phone. That explained her lack of surprise. "He's holed up in the orangery with Karen, and he says he's not leaving unless you tell him to his face that you don't need him there. So my friends are still in danger. *Everybody's* in danger. If Titania gets loose, we're all screwed."

"Teenagers were more respectful in my day," said Etienne.

"Toilets were buckets in your day," said Chelsea. "Learn to adapt."

Tybalt handed me a slab of buttered bread with cheese balanced on top. I looked to Etienne.

"Please," I repeated. "This is urgent, or we wouldn't have come here."

"The girl is willing, the risk is minimal, and she's right; if Titania gets loose, we'll all have much bigger problems," said Sylvester. I turned. He was standing in the doorway of Etienne's chambers, hands by his sides and sword at his hip, expression weary. "The knowe informed me of your arrival, October. I am sorry that you feel so unwelcome in what should be your home that you had to sneak in through a back door, and I am further sorry to have listened to words that may not have been meant for me. Sir Etienne. I understand your desire to protect your child. It's all a father should want. But a quick drop-off runs very little risk of harming Chelsea, while a failure to act could destroy us all."

"Sire—"

"Her daughter destroyed my brother," said Sylvester, bluntly. "She took him and she twisted him away from his family in ways none of us could see clearly until they were ended. She poisoned him, and because she was the daughter of Titania, none of those who loved him could see clearly what she did. And that was the child. The parent is more powerful by such a measure that we cannot measure it. We stop Titania now, while she still can be, or we don't stop her at all."

"Sylvester," I breathed, staring at him.

He looked at me without flinching. "Your husband was correct when he said I had failed the laws of courtesy as they applied to you; I should have been more to you than I was. I could say I held back out of respect for my brother's claim, but the truth is, I feared offending your mother. I feared what her anger could rain down upon my house. I regret that decision every day. I pledged to protect you when I took you to my service. I have too long allowed my wife's feelings to dictate my actions."

I wanted to believe him. I really did. But he sounded more like his brother than himself, and all I could do was stare.

Then Sylvester sighed, and sagged, and in a much more normal voice said, "Please, Toby. This isn't some ploy to get you to give Raysel back. She would have objected if she didn't want to go with you, and I want her to be safe and happy. I want that for you, too. And I miss you. So please, Etienne. I'm asking as your friend, not ordering as your liege. Let Chelsea take October and Tybalt back to Muir Woods. I'll go with them, to be absolutely sure no harm comes to her."

Etienne nodded, very slowly. "Chelsea can transport you all to Muir Woods—"

"Hold on a moment," objected Bridget.

He continued without pausing, "—but she will not be staying after you are safely arrived. Do I make myself very clear?"

"Yes, Daddy. I'm grounded from doing literally anything fun, but I'm still allowed to help," said Chelsea, and bounced over to kiss him on the cheek before she waved her hand in a lazy circle, opening a round portal in the air through which I could see the door to Arden's knowe. The smell of sycamore smoke and calla lilies rose around her. Chelsea beamed, rocking back on her heels, and gestured for all of us to follow as she stepped through.

Tybalt was first, with me close behind him, and Sylvester on my heels. The portal closed behind us, leaving us all on the other side.

Chelsea looked to Sylvester, a question in her expression. He shook his head.

"No," he said. "I promised your father."

"But Sire—"

"I don't hold your fealty, but a word from me can see you grounded for a month."

Chelsea pouted, almost impossibly casual in the face of horrific danger, and waved her hand again. A second portal opened, showing Etienne and Bridget. She stepped through, waving grandly, blew me a kiss, and allowed it to slide closed again.

"Kids," said Sylvester, in a tone that invited commiseration.

I didn't give it, choosing instead to look around us. We were standing on the mortal side of the knowe, the evening air cool and dim but not yet entirely dark. It seemed impossible that it should still be so early after everything that had happened. Shouldn't the day be almost over? But no, it was dragging on and on, marching one slow step at a time toward sunset.

My car had definitely been in the parking lot for way too long. May wasn't allowed to drive, and Raysel didn't know how. With Quentin holed up in the orangery, there had been no one to move it. Oh, well. If I got towed, it wouldn't be the first time, and that's one bill I don't mind paying in fairy gold when necessary. Hands on my knives, I approached the tree.

There were no guards on duty. That wasn't the first sign that something was wrong—this whole damn day had been the first sign that something was wrong—but it was a bad one all the same. I turned my full attention to the doors, and paused.

This wasn't like earlier, where they hadn't been there at all due to Titania's influence. Now, I could see them.

I could see that one of them had been knocked off of its hinges. It was still propped in the frame, held up by position and fit rather than any actual joining. "Oh, no," I breathed.

Sylvester followed my eye to the door and frowned. "Someone broke a door?"

"She broke the *knowe*," I said. "She's already here, and she knows it helped to hide the children from her earlier. I am so sorry." I caressed the doorframe with one hand as I got close enough, stroking it like I would a frightened horse. "I'm not a carpenter, and we need to stop the woman who hurt you, but I'll make sure Arden knows you've been hurt, and sends someone to repair you as soon as possible."

The knowe didn't answer—the knowe *couldn't* answer—

but the unbroken half of the double door swung open in silent invitation. I lowered my head, momentarily closing my eyes, and stroked the doorframe again.

"We'll be back," I said, and slipped inside, Tybalt and Sylvester behind me.

"Does she do this often?" Sylvester asked quietly, in a deeply puzzled tone.

"Yes, as you would know if you had ever spent a proper amount of time with her," said Tybalt. "She talks to buildings. They can't talk back, but they seem to appreciate the courtesy, and they show her courtesy in return. I've witnessed it too many times to discount it."

I stopped dead only a few feet from the door. The men stopped behind me, Tybalt not quite fast enough to avoid bumping my shoulder. Then he joined me in staring.

The damage to the door didn't extend to the interior. That was a small mercy. The lack of damage meant the knowe was free to redecorate as it saw fit, changing the carvings the way it always did. Only now they showed scenes of tragedy, stretching all the way back to the founding of the kingdom.

There were the Cait Sidhe of the Court of Dreaming Cats, their agonizing deaths by poison somehow captured in the wood and shown with absolutely unflinching detail. Tybalt gripped my hand, hard enough to hurt. The next panel showed Samson, bleeding out on the ground. Tybalt and I were both recognizable behind him.

Another panel showed Manuel Lorimer, cradled in Sylvester's arms, dying of the stab wound he had incurred from Oleander's knife. If that wasn't cruel enough, the very next one showed Luna in her Kitsune skin, the one I used to believe was hers in fact as well as in fiction, stretched on a bed in a room filled with carved candlelight.

"We have to keep moving," I said quietly.

Connor. Dare. My father. Gordon. January. Devin. The walls were a procession of tragedies and personal losses, not ending until we reached the reception room doors, which were framed by a single contiguous carving of King Gilad, crushed under the weight of his own ceiling, yet still clearly dead of the gaping wound in his stomach, and a woman I assumed was the Lady Sebille, sprawled on a bed with her throat cut from ear to ear. A small child appeared in each scene, Arden with her mother, Nolan with his father.

"Message received," I informed the knowe. "There's been enough tragedy. We're going to try to intervene before there can be another one."

The smell of roses wormed its way around the edges of the closed doors, making my nose itch. I dipped my hand into my pocket, pulling out the jar I'd received from Oberon. It was a little more than half-full at this point. I was probably going to need the whole thing if I wanted to tear down a spell that had been given time to fully mature and sink into the person who carried it; disenchanting Tybalt had been hard enough, and that spell hadn't been intended to last.

"Okay," I said, softly. "Tybalt, I need you to go and find Arden. You'll be the fastest."

He narrowed his eyes. "Asking me to leave again? Why, so you can rush in when you know my better judgment would bid you no?"

"No, although that's a pretty good idea," I said. "I promise I'll stay right here, with Sylvester, unless something happens that's bad enough that you being here wouldn't have made any difference."

"That isn't as reassuring as you think it is, little fish," said Tybalt dourly. He leaned in, brushed my hair back from my face with one hand, then turned and sprinted for the nearest shadow, diving into it and away.

Sylvester reached for the door. I shot him a sharp look.

"What do you think you're doing?"

"Going into the receiving room."

"Did you not hear me promise Tybalt I was going to stay right here? That means the hallway, not the room on the other side of that door." I frowned. "Don't you smell the roses?"

"October. I rule Shadowed Hills. I am so accustomed to the smell of roses that they no longer register save in their absence."

Great. "Okay, well, are they absent *now*?"

He sniffed the air, then paused, an odd look crossing his face. "No. No, they're not. Why . . . ?"

"Because she's here," I said, looking around the hall with its carvings of death and doom leering from the walls. "She's in the knowe. Don't say her name."

"Given that we swear by her, that's a tall request."

"We swear by a lot of things. Take one of the other options for a change." I let my hands rest on the hilts of my knives, not drawing them just yet, but reassuring myself that they were there, that they hadn't crumbled into dust or turned to spiders and scuttled away. Who knew what Titania was capable of? "She's here, and Tybalt is finding out exactly where I need to be for my part in this plan."

"Which is?"

"I'm going to set her free."

Sylvester blinked at me. "Come again?"

"She's been missing all this time because Oberon enchanted her to forget herself." And buried her in an identity that would be compelled to become a family-destroyer every forty years, if she hadn't achieved some nebulous degree of "better person" that no one understood apart from Oberon himself. "Every time she starts to remember—every time something triggers her to start remembering—she destroys anything that might point to who she is and disappears again."

"And this time she was . . . Stacy?" Sylvester frowned, brow wrinkling as he tried to puzzle through this impossibility. "*Our* Stacy?"

"You mean Stacy whose story never made sense if you really looked at it?" I had accepted it when we were children, because I'd been a traumatized little girl who had just discovered her mother was a fairy princess and been ripped away from the world she'd known forever. And then, by the time we were old enough to question the impossibilities of her background, it had felt somehow rude, like there'd been a period of time when we *could* ask those questions, and it had slipped away while we were playing hide-and-seek in the dusty old parlors of Shadowed Hills.

Sylvester's frown deepened. "Her grandparents were courtiers of mine when she came to live with them. I remember they were unkind to the girl. They seemed puzzled by her, like they couldn't understand how she could be theirs. But she looked like them, and when they asked for her blood to be compared to their own, the magic agreed that there was a relationship. They took charge of her. Someone had to."

"But they never liked changelings. There was no way either one of them would have had a changeling child. And Stacy never told me whether they were her mother's parents or her father's, just that they were her grandparents and they'd take care of her."

"They left as soon as she was old enough to take care of herself," said Sylvester. "Her grandfather approached me privately and told me they wouldn't be the first, if I kept allowing changelings to run wild through the knowe. He understood that you made it more difficult for me to keep the changelings out of sight, but said that higher-ranking nobles than I had been able to keep their indiscretions concealed, and I should have no issue hiding my brother's."

It was the first time he had even come close to acknowledging my complicated relationship with Simon. I gave him a sidelong look, trying to stay mostly focused on the doors as the most probable source of any danger. "And what did you say?"

"That whatever my relationship was to you, it was none of his business, and he should manage his own family without attempting to attend to mine." Sylvester's mouth did something complicated, and he shook his head, looking away. "Tybalt was right. What he said at your wedding, he was right. I failed you."

"Is this really the time?"

"Is there likely to be a better one? My own wife demands that I keep you, my knight, from my halls, where you should be more welcome than you are anywhere else in the world. My daughter and only child has chosen your home over mine, and for her sake, I'll keep my distance until I'm called for. It's not as if we can meet for apologies and cake in some human eatery, and a meeting in Muir Woods under normal circumstances would as good as state that I have lost control of my own household and must sneak about to make amends with people who should be able to depend on me."

That was exactly what was going on. I didn't say anything.

Sylvester sighed. "Luna is . . . She's trying. The skin she wore went all the way down to her bones. I don't think she understood, when she put it on, just how much it would transform her. She did it out of desperation."

"Hoshibara was still alive," I said quietly.

"Alive, and too direly injured to escape Blind Michael's lands. Two girls, one with a chance to survive if only she could get free, the other with no way of escaping."

"You're justifying and you know it," I said. "Luna asked her for permission, and that's the only reason I can forgive her at all, but Hoshibara was a *child*. She didn't know what she was agreeing to."

"Are you sure of that?"

"It's been too long. She's not with the night-haunts anymore. But I know she was too young to die the way she did."

"That's on Blind Michael, not on Luna," said Sylvester. "I'm not here to defend her, but I'm not here to blame her for more than she should carry, either. When I met her, she was living as a Kitsune, cut off from the green world she had always been a part of before, trying to navigate existence as a mammal, lost in a place where she knew no one, understood nothing, where her father's name was a curse used to terrorize children. She couldn't even tell people where she had come from without mentioning him, and if she did that, she was something to be afraid of. Her heart was beating for the first time. Can you even imagine how disorienting that must be? To have a heartbeat, when you never needed one before?"

"No, but I know what it feels like to stop having lungs, when you always took them for granted." Sylvester reddened, turning away again. I watched him closely. "Maybe if I'd known, if I'd approached Simon as a parent, or even as an uncle, rather than sneaking around behind him, I wouldn't have to know what that feels like."

Sylvester sighed. "We can't change the past. I'm trying

to apologize, October. I'm doing a poor job of it, I can see that, but . . . I'm trying. Will you please at least let me try?"

"I'm sorry," I said. "I'll let you try."

"That's all I have the right to ask of you."

"Yeah. It is." I shrugged. "You said you'd try. Keep going."

"For Luna, mammalian emotion was something new and novel, something that came with the skin she had taken, that changed the way her mind worked so completely that she didn't tell me of her true origins until she learned she was pregnant. She had never felt love before, she said, not the way she did now. She had known affection, and cared for her mother, but she didn't burn as a mammal burns."

"So?"

"So when she lost her Kitsune skin, she lost the ability to love the way we both need her to," he said. "I do my best to placate her, to cater to her needs, because she is my wife, and while she may not love me right now, or ever again, I love her completely, and I always will. I have hopes that, given time, she may recover some of what she's lost—without stealing another person's skin to do it. I want my Luna back, and sometimes I feel as if I'm living with a stranger."

Because he effectively was. Still, it was a sobering thought. How would I respond if something similar happened to Tybalt? We'd been together for so much less time than Sylvester had been with Luna, and yet I already knew that I would tear down the sky if that was what it took to bring him back to me.

"So much of what she's doing, what she's done, has been her lashing out in confusion," he said. "I may have enabled it more than I should have, because she's still my wife and I still love her, and I want to find a way for us to exist together. But you're too dear a price to pay for that, and I'm sorry."

My eyes burned with tears. I blinked them away, turning my face back to the door. "The apology is appreciated, if not entirely well timed," I said. "Can we talk about this more later? We could grab coffee or something. On neutral ground."

Sylvester jerked upright slightly, then smiled at me. "I would like that very much."

Tybalt came staggering out of the shadows, hair ruffled and clothing askew. "October!" he exclaimed, heading straight for me. "We have to go!"

"Go where? And what happened? Why do you look like you were just in a barfight?"

"Because I essentially was," he replied. "She's here. Outside the orangery. Everyone who wasn't evacuated before her arrival is either fighting for her or against her, depending on who claims their fealty."

I blanched. "All right, we—"

"We can't take the shadows," he said. I stopped, blinking at him. "You shouldn't have sent me back into them. You knew they were compromised. You knew she had her tangled briars there, ready to catch hold."

"Tybalt, what—"

"You should run now." He said it with absolute serenity, like it was the most reasonable thing in the entire world. "She can't claim anyone whose fealty is too far opposed to her—not easily. And my fealty is first to my Court, and then to my heart. Well, the Court is partially of her making, and true love's kiss doesn't break every curse. I'm fighting as hard as I can. I won't be able to fight much longer."

My stomach twisted. Titania was in his head again? I didn't have enough of Oberon's blood remaining to pull the compulsion off of both of them, and without freeing her, we were all doomed.

"You'll fix this," said Tybalt. "I know you will. Now, both of you." His lips twisted into a feral smile. "I suggest you run."

I grabbed Sylvester's hand and I ran down the hall as fast as I could, towing him behind me. There was a snarl, and I knew Tybalt had departed for the Shadow Roads.

"Light would be awesome, please!" I yelled. "Light, and a clear path to the orangery!"

The lights overhead flickered and brightened, chasing shadows away. I kept running.

Sylvester finally broke my grip and pulled up next to me, a quizzical look on his face. "Will the knowe rearrange itself to suit you?" he asked. "Is that why your visits to Shadowed Hills sometimes leave the parlors all askew?"

"Not rearrange itself, per se," I said. "It's best if you don't know too much about the layout. If I don't know for *sure* what this door connects to"—I gestured to a door that looked a little less friendly, for lack of a better word, than the ones around it. That wasn't the way—"that means it could take us just about anywhere inside the knowe, and the knowe takes advantage of that. But only if it likes you."

It was getting hard to run and talk at the same time. Running was more important, and so I focused on that, diving for a door that didn't have the oddly ominous cast of the one I'd indicated before.

A formal dining room waited on the other side, long teak table already set for a dinner that had never been served, judging by the layer of dust on the cutlery. The air smelled of old, dry potpourri, but not of roses. Titania hadn't been here yet.

I slammed the door behind us, slumping against it, gasping a little, and looked up toward the overly illuminated ceiling. "You are one of my favorite pieces of architecture," I said fervently. "If I had any way to ask your permission first, I could kiss you right now."

I pushed away from the door and started across the dining room, Sylvester close behind me.

"This is all very confusing," he muttered.

"You were a hero before you retired," I shot back. "Do what a hero does. Adapt."

Sylvester made a small scoffing noise but didn't argue, merely continued to follow me. Considering that he was my liege and normally the one giving the orders, that was a pleasant surprise on top of a day that had been built almost entirely of unpleasantness.

"Here's to tomorrow," I said, and opened the door on the side of the room opposite our entrance.

It led to a small kitchen, as dusty as the dining room. This was probably where they'd prepared private meals for Gilad and his family, when they wanted to dine together outside the view of his Court. A glimpse at the pantry as we hurried by told me the stasis spells were still holding. Somehow, the idea of eating a loaf of bread that had been baked before I'd been born wasn't as unappealing as it should have been; I was still hungry, despite the sandwiches and pastry I'd been horfing down earlier, and the brief nausea brought on by the smell of frying onions had blessedly passed.

The kitchen door let us out on a narrow stretch of muddy ground covered in shredded bark fallen from the redwood trees. The sky overhead, what could be seen between the high-arching branches, was spangled with stars and playing host to at least three moons. We were still safely inside the Summerlands, then. Good; I hadn't relished the idea of the knowe leading us to a forgotten back exit as a response to my asking for help.

It's hard to know what a building wants. Maybe the knowe wanted me to stop asking for favors. Or maybe, because I was one of the few people who seemed to care about its opinion, it just wanted to keep me safe. Either way, it was a relief to know that we'd be able to get back in when we needed to.

I'd been spending a lot of time in Muir Woods since Arden took back the throne. It helped that I'd been estranged from my liege to one degree or another since before her coronation, leaving me with, effectively, no place else to go. That doesn't mean I'd spent any real measure of that time outside. The grounds were still largely a mystery to me, and now that we were out of the main building, I wasn't sure how much help I could ask for, or receive.

Helplessly, I looked to Sylvester, and to my deep surprise, he smiled.

"Gilad hated that he couldn't figure out ways to use all the space within his walls," he said. "He wanted us to keep out of his precious trees as much as we could manage, you see, and so he tried to ensure the grounds would be as unappealing as possible. For a people whose roots lie in nature, we're remarkably unfond of getting it on our shoes."

He started walking. This time, I followed.

"But a few hundred years with Luna will teach you not to mind the mud, and I'd been with her long enough in those days to find wandering the unmanicured parts of the garden as pleasant as the cultivated ones. If we've come out where I think we have, the orangery should be just up a . . . " His voice tapered off, replaced by stunned silence as the sound of a pitched battle drifted across the field toward us.

Without another word, we resumed our run.

This patch of flat ended at a shallow hill, just where the grass began. Standing atop it looking down, we could see what looked like most of Arden's household staff making a frantic attempt to get into the glass-walled building. The door was being held by Arden herself, Lowri, and . . .

I squinted, trying to make sense of what my eyes were telling me.

But there, on the side of the defenders, was Simon. I glanced to Sylvester, trying to measure his reaction.

He looked down at the scene, thin-lipped, and said only, "He never did care for having his loyalties dictated."

Oberon and the Luidaeg were nowhere to be seen. I suppose that made sense. The one couldn't fight, the other wouldn't, and both of them would only have complicated the situation at the moment. I turned my attention to the attackers. Most were shapes I knew, people who normally moved politely through the halls or stood at attention with Lowri on door duty. A few were visitors who had come for Court and not been evacuated fast enough.

And there, at the back of them all, looking as peaceful as if this were an ordinary afternoon, as if she weren't trying to lay siege to another queen's holdings, was Stacy, her hair bundled into a messy topknot, her hands folded demurely in front of her. I hissed between my teeth and drew my knives, weighing the virtues of charging before she knew I was there. If she didn't see me coming, if I could reach her fast enough, I could end this. I could let Stacy rest in peace, without this stain on her memory.

But it was far too late for that, really. I shifted both knives to one hand as I pulled the bottle containing what I had left of Oberon's blood, trying to decide whether he was here but hiding as he waited for me to arrive, or whether I'd be wasting my only shot at untangling this if I drank my last dose now. My last hit had entirely worn off, leaving me with nothing more than my ordinary magic.

For the moment, I could let that be enough.

Sylvester looked at the scene, then at me, eyes wide and horrified. "What in the world is going on down there?" he demanded.

"Titania wants the Brown kids," I said, and gestured toward the orangery. "Except for Simon, everyone who's trying to keep her people out is from a line claimed by Oberon. Simon, I don't know. Maybe this is a trick, maybe he has some impossible way of holding her influence at bay, maybe I don't *fucking* know, I've never been in this situation before!"

"No one has, not for hundreds of years," said Sylvester. Below us, the battle continued without interruption. People were bleeding. I could smell it. But no one was on the ground yet; technically, this had become a declared war as soon as Titania, a fae Queen, asserted herself within Arden's demesne. Anyone who killed someone today would be forgiven by the Law, since killing during a war is allowed. Loopholes. Always loopholes.

They'd still be haunted forever by what they'd done. Blind Michael had deserved to die for what he did. He'd needed to be stopped, because there'd been no way he was going to stop on his own. And I still dreamt about the moment when I'd driven my joined knives into his throat, the moment when I'd decided my sense of right and wrong and need for justice were powerful enough to justify murder. None of these people needed to go through that. Especially not when their own choices weren't a part of the process. If they killed tonight, it would be because Titania forced them.

Without Simon, Arden and Lowri would have been in genuine trouble. Thanks to her long campaign against the children of Maeve and Oberon's own slowness to claim descendant lines under his own banner, the descendants of Titania outnumber the claimed descendants of Oberon and Maeve by a factor of about two to one. Far more of Arden's staffers were fighting on Titania's side. I couldn't see Quentin. I just hoped that he was still safely inside the orangery, protected from the chaos outside.

As for the Browns, it was obvious where they were.

Titania's forces wouldn't have been trying so hard to get inside for the sake of anything else.

I was still trying to make a decision when a hand grasped my shoulder and Tybalt's familiar voice purred, "There you are, my sweetling. Did you miss me?" next to my ear.

That was all the warning I got before he jerked me backward, into the shadow. It was enough time for me to catch my breath, and not much more than that.

Without Oberon's blood in my system, the Shadow Roads were as frigid and airless as they had ever been, and the lines of glowing light were gone. That was understandable, although I felt a brief pang of loss as I registered their disappearance. It had been nice not to feel like I was completely helpless in the dark.

Then I squinted my eyes shut to keep them from freezing. Having limits means knowing how to account for them.

My hands were full, and I didn't trust myself not to drop something if I tried to juggle my knives and the bottle when I couldn't see and my fingers were going numb. That meant I couldn't reach for Tybalt as he let me go and stepped away.

"I could leave you here," he said, voice low and pleasant. "I could walk away and leave you in the dark, and no one would ever find your body, and my mistress would be well pleased. But first, she would be angry, as she asked me to fetch you to her, and so I suppose this is to be a brief reunion."

Lips closer to my ear, he added, "Darling," and shoved me in the back, hard. I stumbled forward—

—out into the moonlight. Stacy, who was standing only a few feet away from where I had emerged, turned and smiled at me, sweetly.

"Hello, October," she said, and her voice was hers and not hers at the same time, the echoing, terrible voice of a goddess, and oh, I was so completely screwed.

NINETEEN

I SWALLOWED HARD, EVEN AS the smell of pennyroyal and musk from behind me announced Tybalt's return. I would have noticed his magic when I was on the hill with Sylvester, but I'd been too distracted by the smell of blood. Blood tends to overwhelm everything else where I'm concerned.

He strolled past me to join Titania, who smiled winsomely at him, the expression smug and sour and so unlike anything I had ever seen on Stacy's face that I had no trouble telling the two of them apart. She reached up with one hand, caressing his cheek, and he leaned into the gesture, eyes half-closed and content.

"Get your hands away from him," I snapped.

"Why should I?" she asked, glancing slyly in my direction. "He's of Malvic's line. No blood of mine. But as I told you before, Malvic was in my keeping in his cradle, when my darling husband proved unsuited to the challenges of a boy who was sometimes a wild beast and sometimes impossible to confine. That was what he did, you know, when we were all of us together. He created problems or he took them from my flighty sister and he dropped them in my lap, as if my only purpose were the resolution of trouble *he* had brought to my doorstep. Is it any wonder I grew bitter? Better to be bitter than to be taken for granted. So much of what he considers his own belongs to me, if only because he refused to take ownership when those things were fresh, and new, and pliable. I shall have them. All of them."

"What are you talking about?"

"Balance this and balance that. There is no balance. There is only us, the Three of us, born to power and destined to take it as we desire. We *made* you. All of you, every flawed, mewling one of you, and there's no crime in us using you as we see fit. You are our *property*, after all."

"You are absolutely the Rose of Winter's mother," I said. Even under these circumstances, I wasn't going to say Evening's name out loud. She claimed to be more powerful when she was asleep, and I didn't know whether being near her mother would make that more or less true.

Titania smiled. "Yes, I am. She may be my finest creation."

And maybe if Titania had ever once said that to her face, she wouldn't have been such a murderous disaster. And the rest of us might have a lot less to worry about.

"You came here to kill me," she said, gaze flicking briefly to the knives in my left hand. I glanced down at them like I'd forgotten they were even there.

"What, those? Nah. I'm always armed," I said easily. "Ask whatever's left of Stacy. Ask my husband, aka your new pet. I'd like him back, by the way. I'm pretty attached to him, and it took us, like, years to sort our shit out well enough to actually get somewhere. Stacy knows. She was responsible for making me look presentable for the wedding."

Titania's eye twitched. "What your little friend knew or didn't know is irrelevant, because she's not coming back."

"Would you be so firm about that if you really believed it?" I asked, almost idly. "I think you're a little bit like May at this point. All the people you've been, still buried inside you. Hundreds of years of memories that you didn't ask for, that were foisted upon you by someone else, that aren't your own but feel like they should be."

She finally pulled her hand away from Tybalt's face, eyes narrowed. "Stop talking," she said.

"Nope. Not until you give my husband back to me."

"Husbands don't have as much value as you seem to think they should," she said, sharply. "They come, they go, they tarry with your sister for a time, and they turn their back on you as soon as you're more complicated than they want you to be. You're better off without him."

"You really do remember them all, don't you?" Was taunting the Queen of All Faerie really the best idea I'd ever had? Nope. Did I see another option? Not so much, and I already knew she couldn't harm me directly. I was stalling until Oberon showed himself, trying to keep her from remembering that she could order any one of her captives to kill me on her behalf.

Or could she? Tybalt had pulled me into the shadows twice, but he hadn't even tried to slaughter me. How much of that was Tybalt himself resisting her, and how much of it was a matter of the geas refusing to let her give that order?

I tucked the bottle back into my pocket and transferred the antler knife to my right hand, arming myself properly. Titania watched this warily, staying where she was, close enough that one good lunge would put me on top of her, far enough away that she might be able to dodge if I tried it.

"Does it matter if I do?" she asked. "Those women never were. They're dead and gone and lost forever, and I'm still here."

"But you were them," I said. "How many children, Titania? How many families? How many times did you put your hands around your own baby's throat and squeeze until they stopped thrashing beneath you? Ask those women who never were how it felt to fade away knowing that they had killed their children. You really think they're okay with it?"

Not everyone views a child as a gift. Some people don't want to be parents at all—and in Faerie, that's an easy-enough reality to avoid, if that's what you want. But Stacy, at least, had always wanted to be a mother, more than any of the rest of us. She'd wanted a family that belonged to her, something no one would ever be able to take away from her, and for a long time, she'd seemed like the most successful of us all. No one could possibly have known what she was harboring underneath her skin.

Titania snarled. "Shut up."

"So more than ten, I'm guessing. More than twenty?" She glared at me. "More than a hundred, then. I'm so impressed."

"Shut *up*," she repeated, more sharply. The sounds of the battle were fading as her attention was pulled more and more onto me. I couldn't be as upset about that as I wanted to be, especially not since I could see Sylvester picking his way down the hill toward the orangery. Hopefully, Titania's attention was divided enough at this point that she wouldn't ensnare him.

"You killed so many children," I said, trying to keep my tone light. "Did it ever get any easier?"

A shadow moved in the trees behind her. I kept my eyes on her face, not wanting my attention to betray whoever was drawing near. Tybalt hissed at me, lips drawn back in a snarl, and I scoffed.

"You'd be better at that if you had whiskers right now, FYI," I said. "Maybe let go of the whole concept of bipedalism."

"You have no sense of your place," said Titania.

I smiled at her. "Give back my husband and I'll at least pretend," I said. "Until then, I don't think there's any reason for me to show you any more courtesy than you've shown me. And you understand that there's no winning this for me, right? Best-case scenario, I lose my best friend. Worst-case scenario, I lose my best friend *and* my husband *and* four more of my nieces and nephews *and* I have to watch the woman who set up her own kids to play mass murder games do whatever the hell it is she wants to do with Faerie. Which is . . . what, exactly? Oberon didn't really go around broadcasting your evil plans after he banished you. He just took himself into exile and let everyone keep thinking of you as the nice one, the sweet Summer Queen. I guess you won, in a way. I grew up thinking the children of Maeve were monsters, and the children of Titania were beautiful gifts to Faerie. So your reputation survived you being an absolute asshole."

Titania shook her head. "You know, you've always been disrespectful, but Stacy assumed you knew how to shut your damn mouth when you were talking to people who *mattered*. She figured you must have, for them to have let you live this long. Clearly she was wrong."

"It made her uncomfortable when I talked back to the false Queen, so I tried to do it when she wasn't around," I said, almost chipperly.

Titania sighed. "Yes, I can see why that would be your answer. Civility is clearly beyond you." She turned away, waving languidly. "Kill her," she said to Tybalt, almost as an afterthought.

He leapt, snarling, hands hooked into claws. I held my ground and watched him come. This was a place I'd been before, sad as that is to say. I guess when you fall in love with a living weapon, people will occasionally decide you should be on the receiving end. But I knew something Titania had apparently forgotten, or maybe Stacy had never quite understood: I knew he couldn't kill me. He didn't have the right tools.

Oberon said Faerie made what it needed whenever a new Firstborn came to be. With me, it had apparently needed the Timex watch of pushy assholes, because I can take a licking and keep on ticking. As it were.

Tybalt slammed into me, knocking me backward to the grass, his claws sliding into my shoulders and sinking in until they snagged against my clavicle. I shrieked. I may not be easy to kill, but as I have said on many occasions now, pain still hurts.

Titania screamed at the same time, high and anguished and far louder than me. My own shriek died down to a whimper and hers kept going, rising and rising, loud as a klaxon. Who knew the Queen of Faerie was also the Queen of Excessive Dramatics?

Anyone who had ever had anything to do with Faerie, that was who.

As Titania shrieked, Tybalt froze and blinked, eyes seeming to clear. "October?" he said, in a puzzled tone. Then: "Little fish, what's going on?"

"Okay, sweetie, I need you to work as hard as you can at not freaking out, and take your claws out of my shoulders, okay?" My voice was remarkably level, considering I was being pinned down by someone much larger and better armed than I was. It helped that I knew he probably couldn't kill me, no matter how hard Titania forced him to try, while I could easily kill him if I had to.

And the thought of how easy it would be to make myself a widow was nowhere near as reassuring as I wanted it to be.

Cheeks paling and eyes going wide with horror, Tybalt yanked his hands out of my shoulders and pushed himself to his feet, backing away from me. I picked myself up from the grass, retrieving my knives, and looked toward the still-screaming Titania as I slid them into their sheaths.

Blood cascaded down her arms from the ten perfect puncture wounds that had opened in her shoulders, exactly mirroring the placement of Tybalt's claws. My own injuries were already almost gone, my body putting itself back together with the dedicated speed that I had come to depend on. Titania wasn't recovering anywhere near as quickly.

That shadow was still moving through the trees toward us. I could see the outline of antlers now. Oberon was coming.

I walked toward Titania, trying not to choke on the cloying miasma of roses that surrounded her, rising from her skin, her magic, and her blood in a horrifying choral blend of overwhelming floral perfume. "You shouldn't have done that," I said. "You know you're not allowed to directly harm my branch of the family tree—and even your kid, when she ordered my own father to get me out of the way, was smart enough not to tell him to kill me."

She glared at me, tears bright in her eyes. "Oberon will kill you himself for hurting me."

"I don't think he will, since I didn't hurt you, and if he wants to threaten Tybalt, well, that will be educational for the both of us. He'll learn why that's a terrible idea, and I'll learn what it feels like to kill a god."

I pulled the bottle out of my pocket and removed the cork. The smell of loam promptly obscured Titania's roses. I was grateful for that, more grateful than I could have guessed I'd be.

"Still, you're right about one thing," I said. "Oberon

cares how this turns out. And he's not going to let you hurt the Brown kids."

I raised the bottle to my lips and downed the remainder of the contents in one large gulp. The blood burned as it traveled down my throat, and my head spun with the bright power of it all, leaving me reeling. I'd been taking sips of the stuff all day. This was the first time I'd drunk deeply, and it was intoxicating and horrifying at the same time.

This wasn't safe. This wasn't easy. This wasn't for me.

As if in answer to that thought, the red veil of blood memory descended around me, wiping the world away. I had time for one last, desperate thought—*Oberon promised me he'd pulled his memories out of the blood*—and then I was gone, swept away by the raging tide of his recollection.

I am.

That is enough of a surprise, for I have never been before. I am something new. What that thing is, I cannot possibly say. I raise my hands—I have hands, grasping appendages that I instinctively understand as a way to interact with the world—and look at them, turning them over as I try to understand their shape. How is it that I can know so much, and so little, all at the same time?

Normally in blood memory, there was a sense of duality, of being both myself as an observer and the person whose life I'm taking the smallest sip of. This time, there was only the singular "I," and the "I" in question was Oberon.

The sky is black as I turn my eyes toward it. When I see its vastness it bursts into stars, bright as anything, dazzling me. I turn away. To be able to turn is a wonder, to be able to look back at where I came from is a joy.

There, the only thing that existed before me: the great crystal spire that is my mother and my father and my family. All these things are new concepts, and every response they spark in me is equally new. I am drunk on newness. There is a crack down one side of the crystal, and this, too, is a new thing; this is what I was born from, when the Heart broke.

The Heart? Yes, the Heart. That is what I stand before. This is a new world, a world that begins in this moment, with me and the ground beneath my hooves, scant and shallow as it is, and an entire sky strewn bright with stars.

Motion, from the Heart. Motion, and a presence, and then they emerge.

Two of them, hand in hand, blinking in the blend of starlight and the aurora that pours from the Heart, incandescent and glorious. Both of them are beautiful. One, whose hair matches the light from the Heart almost perfectly, leaves flowers and green grass growing in her footsteps, setting this whole new world to life; where she walks, it blooms. The other, whose hair is as dark as the sky above us, and equally spangled with points of light, leaves patches of dampness behind her. They deepen after she has passed, until a rill cuts through the dust, flowing onward, surrounded by a wild splendor of flowers.

They are perfect, and they are mine, and I am theirs, and we come together in exultations at the very notion of life, the very concept of living. This is our world now, this is our place, and where we walk, it will grow, and when we hunger, it will feed us, and we will be eternal, and perfect, and forever.

And the light of the Heart will blanket and soothe us, always, and we will need for nothing.

I gasped, the memory shattering around me, leaving me only with the feeling of Oberon's blood suffusing my system. I could taste my heritage on my tongue like wine, every inch and angle of it; I could see Janet's ancestors, and my human father's, and see how both those bloodlines still fed into my own, even if the strength had been stripped out of them. Nothing ever truly disappeared. The ghosts were still there, too faded and attenuated to call back to life, but present all the same.

Titania wasn't screaming anymore. She was clutching her injured shoulders, blood sheeting between her fingers, making a high keening noise that set my teeth on edge. I closed my eyes.

There was no red blood haze this time. Only the tangle of spellwork spreading out through the darkness, and everywhere. We were inside a knowe, after all. It was so bright that it should have been blinding; looking at the world this way when I was standing inside a space that was also technically a spell in its own right was not good for my brain, which still wanted things to make sense for some ridiculous reason. But with Oberon's blood in my system, there was nothing I couldn't look at directly.

Including the reason I'd been hungry all week, and why the smell of cooking onions was so upsetting. I dropped the empty jar and drew my knives, watching as Oberon's shadow approached through the spellwork lines, a dark silhouette against the brightness.

Half of Titania was as dark as he was, a black velvet recreation of a woman. The rest of her was wrapped in glowing lines the color of deep forest moss, a green that verged on black but was verdant and alive at the same time. It was beautiful. It was intricate and terrible and beautiful, all at the same time, and ripping it out was going to hurt us both. I flinched in anticipation of the agony ahead. I didn't back down.

Turning my face toward the outline of Oberon, I nodded. So did he, the gesture visible mostly in the motion of his massive antlers, and I gathered all the strength I had borrowed from his blood, letting it sing through my magic, letting it fill me to the top, and I reached out, and I *pulled*. Pain blazed through me, almost enough to make me let go; it was like I had thrust my hands into a blazing fire and was trying to collect the coals. But I wasn't burning, not really, and so I kept on pulling, and I didn't let go.

Again, Titania screamed, in agony and misery and bewilderment, all at the same time. Midway through the sound, her voice modulated into Stacy's, and she wailed, "Toby, *Toby*, you're hurting me! You're hurting me! Please—please—*don't* stop."

My eyes snapped open, my mental grip on Oberon's spell nearly slipping. I caught hold of it at the last possible second, reeling it back toward me like I was pulling on the leash of a runaway dog. It was almost too strong for me. It *would* have been too strong for me if it had been any fresher, but the same time that had allowed it to sink its roots all the way into Titania's heart had weakened its cohesion. This was a centuries-old working. It was tired. I could keep pulling and let it exhaust itself.

In front of me stood Stacy, arms covered in blood, shoulders still bleeding, staring at me with wide, heartbroken eyes and a look of shattered hopefulness on her face.

"*Don't* stop," she repeated. "Please. If you ever loved me, you won't stop."

I stared at her, not letting go of the spell. Part of me admired how much better I'd gotten at doing this; not long ago, any distraction at all would have shattered my concentration and left me fumbling to recover. Now, while I was straining, I was holding on.

Stacy walked toward me, tears in her eyes. "I can feel what you're doing," she said. "And it's going to free her, and it's going to mean I'm not here anymore. I won't say you're killing me, because you're not. You're letting me go. You're saving my children. You're saving the only thing that ever mattered in the entire world, and you're doing it because you love me. Well, I love you, too. Remember that, October Daye: remember that I loved you from the time we were children, and I disappeared still loving you, and no matter what *she* says, it was always my choice. I chose you over and over and over again, even when you weren't a very good friend, even when you didn't think you deserved to be chosen. You did. You do."

The working was almost entirely gone now, unraveling in my hands. All I had to do was yank one more time and it would fall away, and Stacy would be gone.

I held it tight but didn't pull.

"This is where you let me go," she said, softly. "This is where you save my babies. I love you, and I will always love you, and I'm sorry I won't be joining the night-haunts and coming back to pester you endlessly."

I laughed dourly, the sound strained and thick with snot. "Doesn't work that way," I said.

Stacy's smile widened. "See? I knew you were still in there. I knew you would understand . . . " Halfway through the word, her voice twisted and distorted, trying to become something else. Something terrible and unwanted. "*Now, Toby, you have to break it now!*" she howled.

I couldn't tell whether it was Stacy or Titania speaking, but I wanted it to be Stacy, so badly that I did as she asked. I closed my eyes and jerked on Oberon's spell as hard as I could, and felt, rather than heard, the crystalline sound of something delicate and impossible shattering into dust. I took a half-step back to stabilize myself and opened my eyes, panting.

There was a woman on the ground in front of me, down on hands and knees, panting. She wasn't kneeling; this wasn't a woman who had ever knelt in her life, and she certainly wasn't going to start now. But she looked exhausted, and I wasn't sure she could stand.

Her hair was longer than Stacy's had been, iridescent white and filled with all the scattered colors of the northern lights. They seemed to shift and glow from within, and maybe they did, maybe they were; maybe the Daoine Sidhe came by their ridiculous rainbow of hair colors completely honestly. Her ears, where they protruded from between tangled locks of hair, were long and sharply pointed, almost a parody of the ears I was used to seeing on her descendants.

I took a shaky step toward her. "Stacy?"

Her head snapped up, and she glared at me with such ferocious hatred that I stepped back again immediately, dread sweeping over me. I hadn't really been expecting her face to be the same, not really, but there was understanding the way things were likely to go, and then there was being forced to confront it directly. This was a woman I had never seen before, except in the red-haze depths of Oberon's memory. She was beautiful, or would have been, if her features hadn't been distorted by the power of her hate.

"Titania," I breathed.

"At last," she said, and pushed herself to her feet—or tried to, anyway. She couldn't seem to find the strength. Maybe that would be encouraging later. She had limitations, even when they weren't being enforced by Oberon.

Where her hands shifted on the grass, tiny white flowers I had never seen before sprang up, their petals wide and their perfume scenting the air. It was magical, but it wasn't magic, not the way the smell of roses that surrounded her was. Even after smelling them, I didn't know what they were.

"I don't know why you unbound me, little castoff, but I do know that it was a mistake," she said. She seemed to be growing stronger by the second, an impression that was only enhanced when her next attempt to stand brought her to her feet. She looked down at the clothing she had inherited from Stacy, the bloodstained sweatshirt and the well-worn jeans, and she wrinkled her nose. "Oh, this is unacceptable."

She snapped her fingers, and she was dressed in an old-fashioned gown a few shades darker than her hair, but dancing with all the same colors. It glowed from within, as did she, and she was more beautiful than any other woman in Faerie could ever dream of being. I was vermin, mortal, less than her in every possible way; I didn't deserve to look at her. I didn't even deserve to stand in her presence.

That was a feeling I knew all too well. It was the feeling I used to get from Evening and from the false Queen of the Mists, back when I'd been more human and less sure of myself. I squared my shoulders and forced myself to look her dead in the eye. *Any time now, Oberon*, I thought. The last thing I wanted from this day's work was to be responsible for unleashing Titania on an unprepared world.

"You should never have interfered," she said, and took a step toward me, more flowers springing up in her wake. The sounds of battle had passed, replaced by the sound of someone wailing like their heart was broken. And maybe someone's heart *was* broken; maybe the fight had gone in Titania's favor. I was too far away, and too preoccupied with not getting turned into a willow tree or something equally annoying to know.

What would even happen if I were turned into a willow right now? Magic could account for a lot of things, but it didn't know everything, and I was all too aware of my own distant origins. Janet hadn't even been able to stand being in the proximity of so much transformation magic. That was where my bloodline's greatest weakness originated. The risk was too great for me to take. Even the thought of it made me want to turn and run for the hills.

It was way too late for that.

"Do you still remember being Stacy?"

Titania frowned, looking briefly bemused by the question.

"I was never her," she said. "She was never real. She was a part I was playing, however involuntarily, and now that I'm free, she's gone."

"But do you *remember*?"

Her frown deepened. "Of course I remember every awful, insipid moment that I spent living her dreary, insipid little life. It was the blinking of an eye compared to the rest of my existence, but I was present for every grueling moment."

"How can you remember Stacy's life and not feel anything about the things that mattered to her?" The world was still a web of bright lines, other people's spells stacked layer upon layer, all the way back to the foundation of the knowe itself. It was like looking at a piece of double-exposed film, only it was the entire world, and that somehow made it both more and less disorienting at the same time. I could dismiss the echoes at any time, I knew, by just closing my eyes and relaxing the part of my mind that had to stay tensed in order for me to see them. But I could never see this much, or this far, on my own. Oberon's blood was still in me, still boosting my abilities. That didn't mean it was going to last forever. Right now, it was keeping the effect going at a much higher level than should have been possible.

If I wanted to see the moment when Oberon re-bound Titania—if I wanted to know that I was safe—I needed to keep looking at the world in this distorted, disorienting way. And I needed to keep looking at *her*. Much as it hurt to know that she was wearing my friend's remade body like some sort of sweater, much as it burned my eyes to look directly at her, I needed to keep on going. So I did. I've done worse when it was necessary to keep my people safe.

In the trees behind her, I could see the figure I'd been assuming was Oberon—the black cutout in the world—start to turn away. The figure next to him, who danced with ripples of white, blue, and green, grabbed his arm, stopping him where he stood. If I judged purely by their posture, the two of them were arguing. Then the color-streaked figure pointed at me, or at Titania, and gestured fiercely, and her identity was confirmed.

The Luidaeg. Oberon wanted, once again, to turn and walk away from his commitments, and she wasn't allowing it to happen. In that moment, I could have kissed her. Happily, and on the mouth, and damn the consequences, whatever those were going to be. And there *were* going to be consequences. There were always consequences.

Oberon raised his hands. The Luidaeg let go of his arm, and the night exploded into brilliance. It was like I was staring directly into the center of a fireworks show, and not a small one, either. One of those really big ones that they have at amusement parks, the ones that keep going and going long after the smell of cordite has swallowed everything else in the world and you're sure every roof in fifteen miles must be on fire. My eyes burned looking at it. Closing them didn't help, either, since this was magical light.

Despite the pain, I still didn't dare release the effect, and that was why I saw the moment Titania realized what was happening, realized that she was being bound again, and raised her own hands to fight back.

Before that moment, I would have said the light cascading from Oberon was colorless, the burning white that sleeps at the center of a flame. The contrast with Titania's light put it into sharp relief. She was spraying pink and white across the sky, and he was meeting it with green and impossibly incandescent black. Where their magic met, it clashed, the leading edge of each spell ripping into the other like a pack of wild hounds. Oberon howled. Titania screamed.

I gasped and took a step backward, convinced to my core that this wasn't something I was supposed to see, or have seen, or understand in any way. This was only the most superficial reading of the scene in front of me, the part my mind was capable of comprehending. The reality of it was much bigger, and even more terrible.

Oberon had the advantage, on several levels. I could see that. He'd been able to start his working while her guard was lowered, and while they had both been cut off from themselves for a long, long time, she'd only just remembered. His brief head start was turning the tide.

Titania screamed again, and collapsed, still herself, face-down in the grass. The light continued to cascade from Oberon for a few seconds more before it stopped, and he slumped, the Luidaeg holding him upright. I blinked away the lingering afterimages and released my hold on Oberon's borrowed strength at the same time. The world rushed back, exactly as it had always been, save for the stranger who was the mother of . . . not all of us, but so very many, lying motionless on the ground.

Stacy was gone. She'd left no trace behind, and nothing was going to call her back. My best friend, the woman I had charted so much of my life against, was never coming back.

Tybalt stepped up behind me, and I turned, not looking at his face before I dove into his arms. If he was blaming himself for what she'd made him do, I didn't want to see it. I just wanted him to hold me.

And he did.

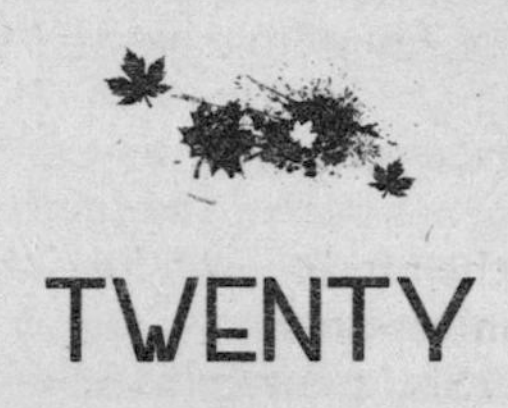

TWENTY

"TOBY!" ARDEN CAME RUNNING across the grass toward us. I pulled reluctantly away from Tybalt enough to turn and face her.

She was bleeding from a nasty cut on her left arm, but that didn't account for the amount of magic crackling in the air. She had clearly portaled over from the orangery, leaving the rest of the defenders behind. The sounds of battle had never resumed, I realized: whatever spell Titania had been casting over these people had been shattered when she lost focus. Well, that was one good thing about this night.

When your "good thing" is that the terrible thing that shouldn't be happening has stopped, there's a problem.

Arden grabbed my arm without so much as acknowledging Titania's fallen form or saying hello, yanking me toward her. "There you are," she said, hurriedly. "You need to come with me."

"What's going on?"

She was already pulling me through the portal she had opened behind her, and I had time for a glimpse of Tybalt's absolutely bereft face before it was closing again, and we were all the way on the other side of the field, in front of the orangery.

The smell of blood hit me first. It came from at least half a dozen sources, some familiar, others not. I couldn't pick out the Brown siblings in the morass. That was something of a relief. I was almost ashamed to admit, even to myself, that the absence of Quentin's blood was even more of a relief.

It was a short-lived one either way, as my traitorous nose insisted on identifying one of the injured, and one of the worst injured: he must have lost a lot of blood for the smell to be that strong. I wrenched myself away from Arden, looking frantically around the trampled field. Nolan was helping to bandage a wound in Lowri's side. Madden was passing out what I assumed were pain potions, and Jin was trying to get Sylvester to his feet. He had a gash across his chest and a bruise forming on his cheek, and I honestly couldn't say, looking at him, which side of the fight he'd joined in on.

It didn't really matter, because Simon was sprawled on the ground with a short sword jutting from his stomach. He was always a pale man—it went with the red hair—but now he was so pale that he looked waxen and bloodless. He wasn't moving. He wasn't visibly breathing.

This wasn't happening. I shouted and wrenched myself away from Arden, running over to him as fast as I could and falling to my knees on the ground by his side. I wasn't worried about hurting him worse with a little movement, so I pushed my way in close and pressed my ear to his chest.

Come on, Simon, come on, come on, this isn't how this ends . . . I thought, frantically.

As if in reward for some impossible service, his heart beat once, almost too soft for me to hear, and I jerked upright again. "He's alive," I shouted over my shoulder to Arden. "Jin! Get over here!"

Jin looked at me regretfully. "You really think I don't understand how triage works?" she demanded. "I can help a body heal. I can even force it, within limits, but I *have* limits. He's too far gone. Boy lost blood like he thinks he can compete with you."

Sylvester winced, looking surprisingly bereft.

I looked at Arden. "Is there another healer? Is there *anyone*?"

"The sea witch, I suppose, if healing is something she can do . . . but I don't have a healer yet! I was hoping I could woo Jin back from Duke Torquill, since her first loyalty was to this household, and not his." She shook her head, cheeks pale save for high spots of hectic color. "I'm sorry, October. There's no one else."

"There's me." I yanked the silver knife out of its sheath and laid my right wrist open to the bone, adding my own blood to the mixture in the air. My magic rose along with it, called out of the nothing.

If I could do this for High King Aethlin, I could do it for my own—for Simon. Aethlin wasn't nearly as skilled at borrowing magic as Simon was, and he'd been able to recover. I just needed him to be awake enough to swallow, at least a little. If he could do that, this might work out.

The smell of pennyroyal and musk swirled around us as Tybalt stepped out of the shadows, joining the crowd that had formed around the injured. No one appeared to be dead. That was a good thing.

"It was like being on a string," said Tybalt, to Arden. "She commanded, and I had no choice but to obey. I was screaming inside, and still, I did as she desired. Nothing mattered beyond making her happy."

"Yeah, that's what the others have said," said Arden, and awkwardly patted him on the shoulder. "I've never been so glad not to have a Daoine Sidhe–dominant court."

"She caught me as soon as I came into range," said Sylvester. He sounded ashamed, like the admission was somehow the worst thing in the world. I didn't want to think about that too hard. It raised questions about how that sword ended up in Simon's gut, and they weren't ones that bore examination.

I was already angry enough at Sylvester. I didn't need to add one more good reason to the pile.

Blood ran out of the corners of Simon's mouth, puddling on the ground to either side of his head. My wrist was already healed. I sliced it open again, faster this time, and pressed it back to his lips.

"Come on, you asshole," I said. "Come on. I just got you, I can't lose you yet. And August! Fuck, can you imagine what kind of bullshit she'll get up to if we make *her* an orphan? Last time she got a wild hair up her ass, she vanished to Annwn for a century and everything here went to hell in a handbasket! No, she needs babysitting, and that means you need to stick around and be her dad for as long as she wants you to. Which is going to be forever."

My wrist had healed again. I laid it open a third time as the Luidaeg came running up behind me and sucked in a sharp, startled breath.

I did my best to ignore her. This wasn't a good time to get distracted. "I knew Cass was telling me to eat because I was going to bleed a lot, but I didn't know *why*, and now I'm guessing it was so I'd have enough blood to save you, you jerk. Just fucking *swallow* already."

The Luidaeg knelt on his other side, pressing two fingers to the side of his neck. Then she looked at me and nodded. I didn't know whether the rules against lying would keep her from communicating an inaccuracy in gesture. I had to assume so. Sign language is still language, after all. I looked back to Simon's face.

"Luidaeg says you're alive, and you know we don't argue with the sea witch, so you need to live now, okay?"

The Luidaeg snapped her fingers. The sword that had been buried in his stomach turned into water, holding its form for a bare second before it fell apart, splashing over everything, leaving Simon and me equally drenched.

"That should clean the wound," she said, quietly. "That's all I can do."

"That's got to be enough," I said, and pulled my arm back, preparing to lay my wrist open for the fourth time.

Simon coughed, and swallowed.

I went instantly rigid, staring down at him for a moment before shifting my attention to the wound in his stomach. As I watched, it began to knit closed, the damage disappearing like a tape being rewound. In a matter of seconds, the blood still smeared on his skin and soaked into his sodden clothing was the only sign that anything had happened.

I turned back to his face. Some of the color had returned

to his cheeks, and while his eyes were still shut, I could see him breathing now. He swallowed again, then coughed, and finally opened his eyes.

I smiled at him, tears running down my cheeks as I stopped fighting them back. "Hey, jerkface, you can't die on me, Dianda would kick my ass," I said.

"And mine as well," he said, raspily. "I think she'd catch and jar my night-haunt just so she could shake it for the next hundred years."

"Let's not find out."

He swallowed for a third time. I straightened up and offered him my hand, pulling him into a sitting position. He looked at me, eyes slightly unfocused.

"I may have seen more than you intended," he said. "Are you . . . ?"

"I literally have not had five seconds alone with Tybalt since I found out, so please don't say anything," I said.

He looked faintly amused. "Given that the man is standing directly behind you, he knows there's something to be said."

"There's always something to be said. Are you going to be all right?"

"I am now." He touched his stomach. "I truly thought . . . Well. I thought I was going to be joining the night-haunts."

"And again, Dianda, my ass, bad combo," I said. "That doesn't even go into what Patrick would do to me if I let you die."

Simon laughed darkly, shaking his head. "Nothing good, I'm quite sure. He's far more frightening than she is."

"So let's just not, okay?" I pushed myself to my feet, not sure what was left to say, and turned to find Tybalt watching me attentively.

"What did you find out?" he asked.

"Again, we're not alone," I said. "Can it wait until we finish cleaning up this mess?"

"The more you put me off, the less I like that idea," said Tybalt, following my gaze to the orangery. "Ah," he said. "I see. Well, yes, I suppose that is rather more urgent. But we have a great deal to discuss once this is settled."

"Yes, we do," I agreed, and started toward the orangery

door. I glanced to Lowri. She nodded, indicating that it was safe for me to go inside.

So I eased the door open, and winced as a crossbow bolt embedded itself in my right shoulder like a particularly large and vicious splinter. "Hey!" I snapped. "Whoever pulled that trigger better be damn glad I was the first one inside, or you'd be getting a way longer lecture about trigger safety than the one you just signed up for."

I directed my glare at the figure peeking out at me from between the orange trees. Maybe they had been planted according to some reasonable pattern once, but the years of neglect following Gilad's death and Arden's exile had given them plenty of time to run riot, and run riot they had. In the mortal world, an orange tree takes about a decade to reach its full size. In Faerie, where the growth conditions are magically perfect, it can happen much faster. This was a forest of fruiting trees, and the air smelled so strongly of orange blossoms that it made me want to sneeze.

Not only oranges, either; they might call this an orangery, but it had clearly been designed to offer as many kinds of tree fruit as possible. Apples and peaches grew nearby, and a small grove of thorny pomegranate trees, their fruit-heavy branches drooping in a canopy toward the ground, occupied almost the dead center of the glass-and-silver structure. I grasped the crossbow bolt, grunting through my teeth, and shoved it through my shoulder, where a hand yanked it out the other side.

I turned, blinking. Tybalt was right there, a frown on his face. I probably shouldn't have been surprised to have been followed, given the circumstances, but it was still a little surprising. Pleasantly so, at least. I offered him a wan smile. He didn't return it.

"If they're planning to keep shooting at you, I will be going elsewhere," he said. "I can't force you to come with me in any meaningful way, but I can tell you that I would prefer not to leave you here, where you're being shot at, without my support."

I blinked at him. From the tangle of the pomegranates, Karen called, "Tell Uncle Tybalt he doesn't have to leave, Auntie Birdie, Quentin just didn't realize it was you."

So Quentin was getting the lecture on trigger safety? Well, that was going to be fun for both of us. "No harm done," I called back. "Maybe a little bit, to Tybalt's nerves, but he married me on purpose, his nerves must have done something to deserve it."

Quentin stepped out from between the trees, the crossbow he was still awkwardly holding pointed at the ground. There was no color left in his face; he looked, honestly, ashamed of himself. Eyes on his feet, he said, "I'm so sorry, Toby. People were trying to get inside, and Cassie said if they got in, they were going to hurt us, and then the fighting outside stopped, but the door opened, and I—I just reacted."

"That's why we haven't been training on anything that has a trigger," I said, as gently as I could. "It's a lot easier to shoot someone by mistake than it is to stab them. Sometimes shooting is the right choice, but I want you to be a little older and a whole lot better with your blood magic before we take that step. Which leads me to who the *hell* gave my squire a crossbow without my permission? I will kick their ass."

"I think that's treason," said Quentin. "Since it was Queen Windermere who handed it to me, right around the time the household staff started attacking us."

"Well, then, I will not kick *her* ass, but I will look very disapproving in her general direction and maybe tell her she's not allowed to give presents to my squires anymore."

It was nice to be talking to him like this, despite the nerves in his voice and the tight ball of dread in my stomach. It was nice to be able, even for a moment, to pretend things were going back to normal. The great evil had been defeated, or at least re-bound so she wasn't going to hurt anyone else, Arden's forces had managed to protect the orangery, Simon was alive. On the whole, we could call this day a win.

Except that Jessica was still dead, and we weren't going to get a magical take-back on that one. Even in Faerie, dead is usually a permanent condition. She had been sweet and silly and scarred and so very, very young, and now she was gone, and no matter what else happened, she was never going to be coming back. That alone would have meant this day couldn't be considered successful.

But she wasn't the only thing we'd lost.

Stacy—my dearest friend, my *first* friend, the wide-eyed barefoot girl who'd offered me her hand when I was terrified and confused and lost in the new world that I had somehow agreed to enter—was gone. And unlike Jessica, who I could probably see among the night-haunts if I was foolish enough to summon them again, or if I just hung around too long after I inevitably wound up at another murder scene, Stacy was gone forever. She hadn't died. She couldn't die, because she had never existed.

It was jarring to think about in such blunt terms, but that was the case. There had never been a Stacy. The friend I knew, the friend I remembered and treasured and would be mourning for the rest of my life, she wasn't real. She was just a pretty painted mask that Titania had been wearing, and not even because she'd wanted to. My best friend had been a punishment. I was going to be trying to digest that information for a while, and wasn't sure, quite honestly, whether I was ever going to succeed.

Quentin approached me, clearly seeking reassurance, and didn't object when I took the crossbow out of his hands and tossed it into a small grove of pear trees. Like so many rooms in a knowe, the orangery was substantially larger on the inside than it had any business being. Chelsea liked to make jokes about some British science fiction show about a time traveler with a big blue box that was also bigger on the inside. I leaned over and grabbed Quentin by the shoulders, jerking him into a hug. He came willingly enough, pressing his face into my shoulder as he embraced me back.

His hair smelled like orange blossoms—expected—and blood—less so. I sniffed, then pushed him out to arm's length, eyes narrowed. "Why do you have Cassandra's blood in your hair?"

"That would be my fault," said Walther, stepping out of the cluster of pomegranate trees. "Hi, Toby. Took you long enough to get here."

"Well, you know, traffic on the bridge, and everything going to hell, and an unexpected jaunt to Shadowed Hills and back. I'm here now." I let Quentin go, focusing on Walther. "You want to tell me why your girlfriend's blood is your fault?"

"I was trying to ward the orangery against Titania," said Walther.

I blinked. "You *what*?"

"I know, blood magic isn't my strong suit, but we were sort of desperate in here, Toby," he said. "We couldn't leave—there was nowhere to go, and if we let Titania get eyes on Quentin, we were probably going to lose him. We already knew she didn't have the same effect on her direct descendants as she did on her distant ones, so we weren't as worried about Cass and the kids, and Cass suggested we try running blood wards around the orangery. Quentin offered to help paint them, since he's Daoine Sidhe."

"Mmm," I said, somewhat dubiously. "Where are the Browns?"

"They're in here, with me," called Karen. "But shh, be careful. They're sleeping."

That was odd, given the situation. I blinked, frowned, and picked my way across the orangery, which was a maze of tree roots and fallen branches, to push the canopy of pomegranate boughs aside.

The grass that grew throughout the rest of the orangery was dead here in the shadow of the spreading, black-barked pomegranate trees. Ripe fruit dangled from the branches, their leathery skins split to reveal the ruby seeds inside. And there, on the brown-mulch ground, were the Browns.

Mitch was slumped against the tree trunk, Andrew in his lap and Anthony and Cass sleeping to either side, leaning over so that their heads rested against his shoulders. Karen was sitting nearby, her hands folded in her lap. She looked up as I entered, Tybalt and Quentin following close on my heels, and she smiled, wanly. She looked exhausted. If any of them were going to be asleep, I would have expected it to be her.

Walther was standing off to one side, glasses missing, hair mussed. He looked like he'd been running hard for most of the night. Judging by the bloodstains on his cuffs, he had been.

"Hey," I said. "What's going on in here?"

"Did you know I can help people sleep?" asked Karen. "If they need it, or if they'd be better off asleep, I can help them. They have to let me. I can't, like, walk into a museum and knock out all the guards, but if they consent, I can help them sleep."

"How I know she's your niece," said Tybalt, dryly. "Revealing a new magical ability, and the first thing she relates it to is its potential use in grand larceny."

"Are you objecting to robbing human museums now?" I asked, with interest. "Because human museums are big on robbing whoever they need to in order to make a pretty display. I think robbing them is a morally neutral act."

"Still an indication of family, in this case," said Tybalt.

"Fair." I focused on Karen. "So your family needed to be asleep, and you helped them?"

"I made them a good place where they could be safe and asleep together," she said. "I have to stay awake so it doesn't fall apart, but Walther and Quentin said they'd stand watch and let everybody else rest, so that's what they're doing."

"Okay," I said. "Can you wake them up?"

"I could, but it might be hard, and they need the rest," she said, a little dubiously. "They'll remember everything they dreamt when they wake up, though, so if you want to go in with them, that might be better."

"Okay," I said dubiously, glancing at Tybalt. He was watching me impassively, looking neither pleased nor displeased about this new development. I guess when I was asleep, he didn't need to worry about me going off and getting myself into more trouble. At least not the usual kind. I turned my attention back to Karen. "What do you need me to do?"

"Sit down and get comfortable," she said.

It would have been silly to worry about the state of my jeans when I'd already been bleeding all over everything. I sat down in the loam, leaning back on my hands. Leaves crackled beneath my palms, surprisingly sharp for being bits of fallen foliage.

"Close your eyes," said Karen.

I closed my eyes. I was definitely awake; I could smell

the pomegranate trees around us, the lingering traces of blood, and musk and pennyroyal of Tybalt's magic, and the simmering cut grass and copper of my own. Sleep didn't feel like it was coming for me any time soon.

A phantom hand brushed my brow, accompanied by the cottonwood and quince scent of Karen's magic, distant, wispy, and absolutely unmistakable.

"Time for sleep," she said, softly. "You're safe now. You can relax."

I breathed in, breathed out, and tried to relax. The smell of her magic got stronger and stronger, washing everything else away, until it was just me, the darkness inside my eyes, and Karen's voice, alone in the nothingness.

"All right," she said. And then: "I'll see you when you wake up."

I opened my eyes.

I was sitting in the grass in the Browns' backyard, next to the play structure where we'd found Anthony bleeding at the start of all this. The sun was shining bright as anything, midsummer-warm and surprisingly pleasant. I stood up.

"Hello?"

There was no reply . . . but the back door of the house was slightly ajar. I walked closer, pausing at the sound of voices coming from inside. Someone laughed. Dishes rattled. I pushed the door the rest of the way open and slipped into the house.

Like the backyard, this was the house as it would be in a completely perfect world, rather than the house as we knew it from day to day. Everything was clean and bright, and oddly soft-focused, like it was being shot by a cinematographer who had a very specific mood in mind. I walked down the hall, trying not to focus on the places where the house was strange to me, trying to focus instead on the places where it was more perfectly itself than it had ever been.

And then I reached the dining room, and there were the Browns—four of them, anyway. Anthony, Andrew, Cassandra, and Mitch sat around the table, which was ironically laden with breakfast-for-dinner, just like it had been when "Stacy" tried to convince me and Tybalt to give her the children in exchange for her own freedom. They were chattering animatedly among themselves, dishing pancakes and bacon and scrambled eggs onto their plates.

Cassandra was the first to notice me. She looked up, and smiled, gesturing toward one of the open chairs. "Hey, Aunt Birdie! I was wondering when you were going to show up. Sit down, have some pancakes. I know you must still be hungry."

I sat. "Do dream pancakes really fill you up?"

"Not in the same way, but they taste exactly like the ones Mom always makes, and that's good enough for me." A flicker of sorrow crossed Cassandra's face. That was good. I didn't want her to be unhappy, but I very much wanted not to be bursting into some bucolic fantasy and ruining everything by insisting on telling them the truth.

Anthony and Andrew had ignored me thus far, too focused on shoveling mountains of eggs into their mouths with the sort of single-minded determination that most teens grew out of by seventeen or so. I'd only enjoyed a few years of the "eating everything in sight" phase with Quentin, and I'd been surprised to realize that I missed it. Nothing like having someone around who'll always stop for a snack to make you remember that sometimes food is important.

Mitch, on the other hand, looked at me levelly from the other side of the table, his hands resting to either side of his plate. When I met his eyes, he asked, quietly, "Is it over?"

Everyone stilled. The boys stopped fighting over the platter of eggs, and turned to face me.

I took a deep breath. One of the few mercies of Faerie is that the purebloods like ritual and tradition so much that they have predetermined ways of saying almost everything from "Bob's dead" to "Bob's pregnant" to "Bob's overthrown the rightful ruler and if you don't recognize him as King right now, you're going to regret it." It's sort of like having a society run by greeting cards. But what we didn't have was "So you just found out the love of your life never actually existed, and when the person she really was managed to break through the mask, she killed your youngest daughter before she ran away."

I had never expected to need a scripted way of saying "Sorry your wife turned out to be Titania," but here we were, and I didn't want to be here, and the fact that it was happening in a dream that smelled like maple syrup and bacon wasn't making it any easier. This wasn't the sort of setting that should be disrupted like this. This was a moment that should be perfect and protected forever, the sort of thing that only gets to exist in dreams.

But Mitch was a changeling, just like I was. He'd grown up at least partially in the human world. If anyone in Faerie was going to be okay with the absence of poetry, it was him. I looked him square in the eye as I nodded and said, "It's over."

He sucked in a sharp, anxious breath, glancing to Cassandra, and then back to me. "How did it end?"

"Tybalt carried me to her." He'd done it under her orders, but it had been for the best in the end; by getting me up close, he'd put me into a position to break her hold on the situation. "She was flickering. Stacy was still there, the way a dream hangs on for a while after you wake up, and she asked me to end it before . . . before the other one could take over and destroy everything. She was fighting, Mitch. She was fighting right up until the end."

Andrew made a pained noise and hid his face against his brother's arm. Anthony stroked his hair with one hand, watching me closely.

Too late to stop now. "I unbound her—the other one. I let her out of the cage she'd been locked in for so long, and doing that meant Stacy got to rest. She didn't have to fight to keep control of her own body, and she didn't have to exist alongside the woman that killed her daughter. There was no way to save her, Mitch. I'm so sorry." Tears rolled down my cheeks, warm and wet and surprisingly real, for all that this was a dream.

"I know you would have saved her if you could," said Mitch. "I'm probably going to be angry with you for a while once we wake up and get out of here, but right now, I'm just glad you could let her rest."

"It shouldn't have ended like this," I said.

"I knew something about her was . . . I knew she wasn't

what she said she was. Too many things didn't add up, and then the kids never looked like either of us, didn't match any of the descendant lines we knew how to trace, and they could do impossible things. Changeling children aren't supposed to be able to see the future. They aren't supposed to be so powerful that the sea witch offers to take them on as her apprentices." Mitch looked away. "Time always worked a little differently when Stacy needed it to. Karen's school did a bake sale once, when she was doing human school. She forgot to say anything until the night before. Stacy started baking right after dinner. She came to bed on time. But in the morning, there were eight dozen perfect, frosted cupcakes on the counter. And she didn't call Kerry. It wasn't hearthcraft. She just . . . needed time, and so she took it."

I didn't say anything. I felt like a fool for not having noticed the things he was talking about before. I'd always been proud of the fact that I was more attentive than your average pureblood. And now my best friend's husband was telling me she'd been bending time for years, and I'd somehow never noticed? It made me wonder how many other things I'd never noticed.

"I'm so sorry," I said.

"Hey, don't be." He forced a smile. "It wasn't your fault. If . . . that other one . . . was inside Stacy, then she was inside Stacy from the beginning, before we ever met her, and that didn't have anything to do with you. All you ever did was try to be the best friend to her that you could possibly be. You got two of our kids back from a monster, and you let her do your makeup for your wedding. She'd been so afraid you'd try to do it yourself—or worse, let May do it—and wind up looking like you just escaped from a Hot Topic. You were a good friend to her, October Daye, and she loved you very much, and she was never sorry to know you. Not even when you were a nightmare given flesh and breaking all our shit."

Anthony was crying, still stroking his brother's hair with one hand, and Cassandra was staring off into space the way she always did when she was looking toward the future.

"We have to wake up now," she said. "Tybalt's getting a

little antsy. Apparently, he needs to talk to Toby about something important." She smiled at me, just a little smugly.

I eyed her. "You already knew."

"Why do you think I told you to eat a sandwich already?" She shrugged. "This has probably been the worst day of my life, and as soon as I stop trying to stay upbeat, I'm going to collapse and scream for a few hours, so that's going to be fun, for me and Walther both. I hope this hasn't scared him off."

"Don't you know?"

"I told you I can't see the future where the Three are concerned. Well, I *won't* see the future where the people I love are concerned, not unless it's something so urgent that it doesn't give me a choice. It's better this way. I don't want to know everything that's coming. It's bad for the heart to stop having surprises."

"That's very mature of you."

She looked at me and shrugged again. "I'm a lot older than you think I am, Aunt Birdie. I grew up while you weren't looking."

"I was indisposed!"

"You were a *fish*," she said, in a withering tone, and laughed. To my surprise, Andrew and Mitch joined in, and for a moment the dining room was filled with merriment to go with the light that had already been there.

There was always the light.

TWENTY-ONE

THE SMELL OF POMEGRANATES invaded my nose. I groaned, eyelashes fluttering, before I opened my eyes and pushed myself into a sitting position. All four remaining Brown children were awake now, and all four of them were hugging their father while they cried. Mitch was crying in turn, his arms wrapped tight around his family, shielding them from the world and all its dangers with his body.

If only the dangers of Faerie were so easy to stave off. Tybalt stepped into view above me, offering me his hand. I smiled a little, grasping it, and let him pull me to my feet.

"October," he began. "I'm so sorry—"

"Okay, I love you, but if you're about to apologize for being less powerful than *Titania*, we're going to have a talk about your superiority complex," I said. "I get that you're a cat. I knew that long before I married you. But when you weigh 'cat' against 'Queen of Faerie,' I'm pretty sure we all know who's logically going to win."

"And when we weigh 'changeling street rat' against 'Queen of Faerie'?"

I leaned closer, smiling at him. "Didn't you hear? I'm a hero."

If not for the sobbing family ten feet away and the fact that it would have been entirely inappropriate, I would probably have kissed him. Under the circumstances, I could just touch his cheek, delicately, and say:

"You didn't do any permanent damage. You didn't have a choice. As far as I'm concerned, either one of those things would mean you got forgiven. Both of them together means you don't have to be, because there's nothing to forgive." I stepped back. "Quentin? Fight's over. Did May get Raysel out of here before it all went to shit?"

"Danny picked them up, and then the fighting started," said Quentin.

"Uh-huh. You want to tell me why you didn't go with them? Given that you're my squire and I gave a direct order?"

"Yes, but you didn't give it to me directly," he said. "Everything was chaos. This big weird bell started ringing, and it was like it rang through the walls, you couldn't not hear it. And then Cass called her mom, and she was crying, and she said her mother wasn't coming, but someone else would be, and May said I had to go with her and Raysel, but you'd be coming back here to fight, and I know where my place is. My place is with my knight."

"That's splitting hairs and you know it."

He looked at me, unblinkingly calm. "I learned from the best."

I paused. He was right, and this wasn't the time, and it wasn't like Quentin refusing to listen to me when he thought I was making the wrong call was anything new. I'd never gone out of my way to inculcate unthinking obedience in him; I honestly wouldn't know where to start.

"All right," I said. "But the next time we're going up against one of the Three, I need you to go the fuck home the *second* you think that might be what I want you to do."

He raised an eyebrow. "What makes you think this is ever going to happen again?"

"One, Titania's still out there." I held up a finger, paused, and added a second. "Two, this has happened to us twice now, which is twice more than I *ever* expected. There's one Queen missing. At our current rate, we should run into her before the end of the year."

"I don't like that," said Quentin, paling. "Isn't two enough?"

"I would have said one was enough," I said.

"And I would have said none was more than sufficient," said Tybalt, sliding his arm around my waist. "Could we *please*, please, have a season without some life-altering revelation throwing everything into disarray?"

"I'll see what I can do," I said, leaning up to kiss his cheek. "No promises."

He sighed. "There never are."

He still looked distressed, but given how long he'd spent treating me like I was made of glass after the *last* time he'd been supernaturally compelled to attack me, I was willing to take a little distress. And that was another thing that shouldn't really have happened twice. There are plenty of people in Faerie who can reach into someone's mind and twist it around to suit their own ends. We have whole descendant lines who specialize in exactly that: Sirens can turn anyone into their one true love with a song, while Gean-Cannah prey on a similar, if somewhat baser, set of instincts. I couldn't blame him for being used against me. But wow, could he blame himself. He was remarkably good at that sort of thing.

I dropped back to the flats of my feet and reached up to touch his cheek, just above the spot I'd kissed. "Let me go talk to Arden," I said. "Can I ask you to stay here with the Browns, or would that be too much right now?"

"As I'm afraid of harming you gravely if I force you to remain in my presence, it would be barely enough," he said. "The Lady of Flowers shouldn't have been able to sink her hooks into me, not when I descend from Malvic's line. Yet she couldn't touch Simon, who is most distinctly hers. How was that possible?"

"I don't know." There was a lot that didn't make sense where the Three were concerned. I sighed and looked at him levelly. "If Oberon's out there, maybe he'll be in the mood to answer a few questions."

"That would be a change," said Quentin.

"Eavesdropping is rude," I said.

"You're having this conversation out in the open, at a

normal volume," he said. "If this is eavesdropping, I think we've changed the definition."

I turned to scowl at him, then glanced back as I realized Tybalt was laughing.

Not loudly. Not a lot. But laughing. I blinked at him. He shook his head, still laughing.

"There was a time when the appearance of any one of the Three would have been a monumental occasion, marked with awe and reverence and silent contemplation," he said. "Now, not an hour's time has passed, and you're already pecking at each other like a pair of ducks battling over the last passel of peas."

"If that's an old-timey saying, I'm really glad we have better ones now," I said, and smiled before walking over to Mitch and the kids. He and the younger three were still huddled together; Cassandra was on her feet and folded into Walther's arms, her head resting against his shoulder. She lifted it as I approached, meeting my eyes. I paused, taking a half-step back.

Her eyes, which had always been a neutral, unremarkable blue, were bleeding toward a vivid amber-gold that looked nothing like the clear honey of the Torquills, or even like the vivid topaz sported by some members of the Court of Cats. Walther looked at me and grimaced, just a little.

"I have a theory," he said.

"Nothing makes sense and everything is wrong?" I suggested.

"Well, yes, that, too," he said. "But I believe Titania's presence was enough to extend a sliver of the illusion she herself lived under to her children, keeping them from being visibly divergent from what people expected to see. She looked like Stacy Brown, and so her children looked like they belonged to Stacy Brown, at least mostly."

"No one ever could explain the ears," said Cassandra. "Lynx tufts, not common among the Barrow Wights *or* the Nixen."

"I like your ears," Walther said.

"Wasn't looking for reassurance, but I'm still glad to hear that," said Cassandra. She leaned back against him like he was a wall, grimacing. "With Mom . . . gone, and Titania not needing to hide herself, or us, any longer, there's a good chance we're all going to start looking a little different. Nothing radical. No one's going to grow extra limbs or wings or anything. But we're not going to be as similar to each other as we have been up until this point. Think of it as watching a bunch of ducklings finally molt and grow their adult plumage."

"Right," I said faintly. This just kept getting stranger, and it wasn't going to stop anytime soon. A little awkward, I added, "Do you think you can keep an eye on your dad for a few minutes? I need to go talk to the Queen."

"Sure," said Cassandra. "I was going to ask him if he and the kids wanted to stay at my place tonight. I know I wouldn't want to go home if I were them."

"Good idea," I said. "I'll be right back."

I turned and made for the orangery door before anything else could come out of left field and slow me down. I needed to talk to Arden. I wanted to check on Simon and the others. I did no one any good by staying where I was, and so I moved.

The air outside was still heavy with the scent of blood, although the smell of roses was almost entirely gone. I could find it if I breathed in sharply enough, lingering under the mingled scents of all the other magic that had been slung around during the fight, but Titania herself was gone. So were most of the combatants. Only Arden, the Torquills, the Luidaeg, and Oberon remained.

Arden smiled wearily when she saw me emerge from the orangery. "I figured we were the people you'd be in a hurry to talk to," she said. "Didn't want to make you run all over the knowe looking for us."

"I appreciate it," I said, and looked around. "Where's Jin?"

"She left some things here when the knowe sealed itself off after my father stopped his dancing," she said. "She's gone to make sure they're still in her quarters, and to see if we need anything in the infirmary. She isn't willing to leave Shadowed Hills and come home to the Woods, but she's got a few other local Ellyllon she can talk to about maybe coming here and serving as my resident healer."

I made a noncommittal noise. I knew Arden well enough at this point to read the glint in her eyes and recognize it for a scheme: if Jin wasn't a member of the Court at Muir Woods by the end of the year, I would be honestly surprised.

Arden raised an eyebrow. "Got something to say, Sir Daye?" she asked.

"No, ma'am," I said. "I am just an ordinary knight, making my ordinary way over to speak to the ordinary sea witch."

"Since I'm the only sea witch you have on a regular basis, I'll allow it," said the Luidaeg.

"So while I would love to stay and chat, Your Highness, I need to go attend to my aunt." I booked it over to Oberon and the Luidaeg, who had somehow become the less-frightening figures on this particular field.

The Luidaeg watched my approach with no visible emotion in her face. Oberon, on the other hand, looked perturbed, and concerned. I stopped, eyeing him.

"What?"

He paused, apparently taken aback by my blunt approach. Even after all this time, he still didn't know me very well. "You have tasted our beginnings," he said. "I worry for what this means."

"I thought you said you had pulled your memory out of the blood." I gazed at him steadily. "I don't know that I would have accepted your 'gift' if not for that."

"Unlike my daughter, I remain allowed to lie," said Oberon ponderously. "You had the means to kill my wife at your hand, and I gave it to you. I did not do so intending that this should come to pass. I had no idea she was close enough to interfere with our lives."

"Really?" I shook my head. "Everyone *else* is here. All the power players of Faerie have been showing up in the Bay Area since before I was born. I half-expect to find Maeve here, too. At this point, that would almost make more sense than the alternative."

"If she is, I do not know it," said Oberon gravely. "I swear to you, granddaughter, I had no idea of Titania's location, and I have just as little notion of Maeve's. The same holds true now. Titania left this knowe as soon as she awoke following her binding, and once she passed outside the sphere of my awareness, she vanished like the morning dew."

"Convenient." I hadn't come over here to pick a fight with Oberon, no matter how tempting it was. I turned my back on him, focusing instead on the Luidaeg.

Maybe it says something about me that picking a fight with the sea witch felt like the safer of my available options, but here we are. Here I seem to be over and over again, no matter how hard I try not to be. I've never met a windmill I wasn't willing to tilt at.

"Did you know." It wasn't a question.

"Which part?" The Luidaeg cocked her head. "That there was something strange about Karen, who can walk in dreams when no one has done that for centuries, who can see the future in a fantasy? Yes, I absolutely knew that. Did I know it was because she was secretly Firstborn, and a direct daughter of Titania herself? I did not. If I had known, I would never have helped you save her." She smiled, sweet as sugar. "I would have let her rot in my brother's lands before I raised a finger for one of that *bitch's* babies. I love Pete, and I've loved others of her children, although not many, but on the whole, it's best to let them die young and innocent and without blood on their hands. The fact that I helped her, and you, should tell you how much I didn't know."

I nodded slowly, accepting her words. "Okay," I said.

But she wasn't done. "Did I know your darling Stacy was secretly Titania in disguise, forced into a commoner's garb by my own father for crimes he never shared with me? I mean, apart from the fact that knowing *that* would have meant knowing the thing I already told you I was ignorant of, on what world would I have had any reason whatsoever to suspect that might be the case? I didn't even know he could *do* that. It makes me wish *he* couldn't lie, since if he could hide himself *and* my stepmother behind walls without windows, how do I know my siblings are actually dead, and not wandering lost and unaware in this horrible mockery of a world?"

She shot Oberon a glare that could have stripped paint. I blanched. That was one family fight I wasn't getting in the middle of, not for love nor money.

She still wasn't done. Looking back to me, she continued, "Did I know you could unbind even his spells? Even geasa lain down by the father of us all, without whom there would be no Faerie, would be no me, would be no you? No. But I suspected, and I hoped. I've been grooming you for decades, helping you learn your limits and exceed them, moving the goalposts every single time you thought you could go no farther, accomplish nothing more, and I've been doing it because I thought there was a chance that with the proper motivation and amplification, you'd be able to unmake something similar to the web he tangled Titania in."

It took me a moment, but I got there. Slowly, I said, "You were hoping I'd unbind you."

"Can you blame me? I can't lie, I can't harm the claimed descendants of Titania, I can't refuse to use my magic for anyone who's willing to exploit me and meet the price. She turned me into a *monster*, October." A thin thread of anguish crept into her voice. "I was always a danger to the unwary, always a predator, but I never targeted people, I never went after anyone who didn't get in my way. And then Titania said 'No, not enough, your gifts are too great, you have to serve as I say you serve,' and she made me a weapon in the hands of her own children, and she *left* me this way. I want to be free more than I want anything else in this world, and that's why I never told you, and that's why you can't do it."

I blinked. "What?"

"I'm tired, Toby. I'm so, so tired." She shook her head. "I can't lie, and I still can't tell you how tired I am, because the words aren't there. I've been bound this way for more than five hundred years. I was grieving the deaths of my children when she caught me, and I've never had the time to process their loss, not really, not without every hero and would-be despot in Faerie banging down my door. I am *exhausted*. Unbind me and I'm at the bottom of the Atlantic Ocean an hour later, sleeping a century away. Titania is back. She's limited but she's freer than she's been in five hundred years, and she's not going to stay gone for long. Unbind me, lose me as a resource, and she'll take you apart. Faerie can't afford that. So you can't set me free." The corner of her mouth twitched upward in a smile. "Anyway, I said I was the one who got to kill you, and you don't want to make a liar out of me, now do you?"

"No. I don't." I turned to look at Oberon. "Do you have anything to add here? Anything at all?"

He shook his heavy, antlered head, not quite meeting my eyes. "As my daughter says, she cannot lie," he said. "Anything I add would simply imply that I didn't trust her to tell the story on her own."

"Real nice, another excuse to stand around not doing a damn thing," I snapped.

He finally focused on me. "What?"

"You heard me. All you've done since I found you is abdicate responsibility. You're supposed to be the King of All Faerie, the one who rules without boundaries or borders, and you've been doing what? Oh, right, hanging out in the Luidaeg's apartment while we keep tearing each other apart out here. We needed you. We still need you. And you might as well not be here. You didn't want your wife running around making trouble after your *other* wife got fucked by your daughter, so you locked her in a box you thought would hold her, and you didn't think about the consequences. You did the absolute least you could do, and when that wasn't enough, way hey, off you fucked for *five hundred years*. I know you're a living god and all that crap. I no longer give a shit. You're the ultimate deadbeat dad, and you care so much when it doesn't inconvenience you, and you disappear so quickly when it does."

Oberon looked at the Luidaeg, incredulous. She shrugged. "Sorry, Dad. I love you a lot, way more than she does, and she's not wrong. You kinda suck."

"There was a time when Faerie knew what it meant to respect me," he said, and his voice was a roll of thunder in the distance, and he was the destruction of everything I held dear. I had to fight not to shy away.

The memory of Titania in the moment when they first stepped into the newborn Faerie kept me standing exactly as I was, watching him through narrowed eyes. She'd been so young, and so undamaged, and so ready to begin this wild new adventure with her sister and her lover by her side. She reminded me of Raysel, I realized. Somewhere along the line, something had broken her, and unlike Raysel, I wasn't sure she could be fixed.

"There was a time when Faerie knew who you were," I said coldly. "Now where the hell is your wife? Not Maeve, I already know you don't know where she is, but Titania. The one who killed my best friend and my niece and only didn't kill me because she couldn't."

"My Lady of Flowers has . . . concealed herself from me," said Oberon carefully. "I know not where she walks."

I stared at him. "You *lost* her? Again? I thought you'd be more careful this time."

"She is not an object, to be misplaced," he said. "She is a Queen, and walks where she will."

"No," I said. "Nope. People who want to kill me need to be watched. They need to be tracked. I need to know where they are at all times. And you *lost* her."

"He didn't lose her," said the Luidaeg. "He just didn't care enough to watch where she went."

"Is that supposed to make me feel better?"

"Not sure why you'd think that was my goal." She looked at Oberon. "Not sure why you'd think you're the only one who's run out of patience."

He frowned. "You were supposed to be on my side."

"And you were supposed to step in and say 'Hey, that's not cool, don't do that' when your wife decided to make it so that I couldn't lie, but here we are," she said.

"Can we get back to the part where you *lost* Titania?" I demanded. "Because I am really not cool with this. Can you find her?"

"No. As before, she has concealed herself from me."

I considered the virtues of walking away from all of this. Tybalt and I could move to the middle of nowhere—what

Kingdom corresponded with Ohio, anyway?—and live a peaceful life devoid of Firstborn, and long-lost Faerie monarchs, and centuries-long revenge plans. And if we did that, I'd give us a year, tops, before the boredom brought us crawling back and begging for a little recreational chaos. It wasn't flattering, but it was true.

I sighed. "All right. So we have a missing Faerie Queen, and no way to protect ourselves from her."

"I didn't say that," said Oberon.

I gave him my full attention. "Oh?"

"She still can't harm you," he said. "When I restored the bindings, I did not thrust her back into the mirrored lives—you convinced me it was cruel to innocents, if not that it was cruel to her—but I did return the injunction against hurting my Jenny, or her descendants. She can no more do you harm than my sweet Annie can tell a lie."

"Bite me," said the Luidaeg.

"Even so," he said. "She will not hurt you. She can't. Nor can she return to harm the children of her last mirroring: they are also safe from her, forever, or so long as you claim them as your family."

I paused. "Wait. Did you bind her not to hurt anyone I consider my family?"

He nodded.

"Okay, like ten percent of your bullshit is forgiven, and since that's more bullshit than most people will have time to generate in their lives, you should call that a win," I said. That was enough to protect Tybalt, and Quentin, and the Lordens, and even the assorted Torquills. My family was strange and nebulous, but it was mine, and it mattered. Even Walther would be safe, if me considering someone a member of my family was enough to protect them.

That was a nice thought. "Safe" has been hard to come by, these last few years.

"I will accept it," said Oberon, solemnly.

"You said 'bindings,' plural," I said. "What else?"

He took a breath, turning his face away from me. "She will not harm Maeve's descendants," he said. "Nor will she break down the doors to deeper Faerie, nor will she declare herself and claim control of all you've made in our absence."

"That's a start, but don't think this means I'm not pissed as hell at you," I said. "Because I am, and I'm going to be for a while, but right now, that family you mentioned needs me. Luidaeg, take your father home before I do something I'm really going to regret."

"Got it," she said, and moved to take Oberon's arm. "Come on, Daddy. Let's go. I'll explain in excruciating detail what you did wrong on the way."

He let her turn him around and lead him off, and I had never been more grateful to him for anything, and I had never felt more lost. I turned and walked back to Arden, Tybalt, and the Torquills. All three of them turned to look at me.

"Forgive me if it's inappropriate to ask this, but did you just raise your voice to *Oberon*?" asked Simon.

I nodded.

He grinned. "If not for the substantial evidence to the contrary, and the fact that it would be a dire insult to the man who sired you, I would start to suspect that you were my daughter in fact as well as in legality. Good show."

Sylvester, meanwhile, looked quietly horrified. I focused on him, raising an eyebrow. "Got something to say, Your Grace?"

"Only that in my experience, when a lone knight attempts to bait a dragon, it ends poorly for the knight," he said.

"Good thing I never manage to fight alone these days, huh?" I turned to Arden. "Okay, here's the sitch: Titania's missing. No clue where. Oberon can't find her, and she remembers who she is. All of that is bad."

Arden nodded, paling. "Yes. All of that is very bad. I don't like any of that."

"That being said, she's been bound not to harm me or any member of my family, or any claimed descendant of Maeve," I said. "That doesn't cover you or Nolan, but she doesn't have reason to be directly angry with you, so if you just don't attract her attention, you should be fine."

"Or we could marry in," she said. "How does your sister feel about arranged marriage?"

I blinked, then glanced at Simon. He shook his head, grimacing.

"Yeah, I don't think that's going to fly," I said, looking back to Arden. "Sorry."

"It was a long shot anyway," she said, sighing. "All right, we'll lay low. You should probably stay clear for a little while if you can, just so as not to attract her attention."

"Great, one more knowe I'm banned from," I said.

"The only one," said Sylvester. I blinked at him. "You saved my brother's life. You truly *are* a hero, October, and if my wife can't see it, well . . . I've made some terrible mistakes. I've allowed myself to fail the people who matter most to me."

Simon stared at him. So did I. For a long moment, none of us said anything. Finally, Sylvester mustered a wan smile.

"Please give Rayseline my love," he said. "I won't try to convince her to come home; she belongs with you right now, where she can be happy, and have the space she needs to heal. But she deserves to know I still love her, and if she wants to see me, all she ever has to do is call."

I swallowed hard as I nodded. Simon was still staring, speechless.

Sylvester turned to him. "I need more time," he said, and there was something resembling an apology in his tone. He sounded genuinely sorry, if nothing else, like he had finally accepted that he might be at least somewhat in the wrong. "I know how little choice you had in some of the actions you took. I've just been reminded of that, in a way I didn't care for in the least. But you still took them, and I need more time before I can even begin to consider forgiveness. I'm sorry. Our parents would have wanted me to be better. *I* want me to be better. But I can't."

Simon blinked, very slowly, then looked at me.

"Did I die?" he asked, in a polite tone. "Because it seems very much as if I must have died. This cannot possibly be happening."

"Nope," I said. "Raising the dead, sort of an unanticipated specialty of mine." Not that he had actually been dead—I didn't think. If he had, then I needed to have a serious talk with the Luidaeg about where, exactly, my capacity for healing both myself and others would top out.

Limits are good things to know, and to have, at least right up until the question is "respecting your limits" or "burying a family member."

Simon nodded. "So I've heard." He looked back to Sylvester, offering him a very shallow bow. "I can extend you as much time as you require. I've grown tired of being an only child. With September unavailable, I suppose that means you and I must eventually find a peace between us."

"Given that the other option is our father finding a way to return from the grave and shake us, that seems very true," said Sylvester. They both laughed. I had never heard them laugh together before.

It was a beautiful sound.

Tybalt's hand settled on my shoulder.

"Delightful as this all is, if we're done with the mopping-up and the aftermath of the latest disaster, I believe you promised to tell me something which is better said in private," he said. "Is now acceptable?"

Sylvester looked puzzled. Simon smiled the small, secretive smile of a man who had already ridden my blood and knew far too many of the secrets it contained. Good thing this was the only thing I could think of that no one else was supposed to know yet.

"Now is *lovely*," he said. "Please, don't let us keep you any longer."

"Appreciated," I replied. "Sylvester, I'll come by Shadowed Hills tomorrow afternoon, so I can catch you up—and yes, I'll call first to make sure Luna doesn't meet me at the door with a knife in her hand."

He grimaced. "Much as I wish it weren't necessary, I can't fault the logic."

"Okay. You have a way home?"

Sylvester looked surprised, then nodded. "I can call for Etienne if Queen Windermere is unable to loan me the Crown Prince," he said. "I thought I would stay until my niece arrives. August is coming from Saltmist to take her father home."

"Great." Impulsively, I stepped over and hugged him, firmly, holding on until he brought his own arms up and hugged me back. I tucked my head up under his chin, briefly closing my eyes. "I missed you," I said, voice low.

"I missed you, too," he said.

I let go and stepped back, smiling at him as I went. His eyes were suspiciously bright. I didn't say anything. I could feel the tears clinging to my own lower lashes, and if I said a word, we'd both wind up crying.

"All right," I said, turning to Tybalt. "Get me out of here?"

"Without question," he said, and pulled me with him into the shadows, which were dark and cold and airless, but still somehow warmer than they had been, and we were gone.

TWENTY-TWO

WE STEPPED OUT OF the shadows and into the dimly lit confines of our bedroom. I shook the ice from my hair and shot Tybalt an amused look.

"When I said to get me out of there, I assumed we'd wind up in the Court of Cats or something," I said.

"Why in the world would you assume that when home was right here, waiting to serve as a perfectly lovely option?" he asked.

"You know, when you put it like that, I have no idea." I smiled at him, offering my hands.

Raising his eyebrows, he took them. "Why am I concerned that whatever it is you're about to say will be in some way distressing?"

"I genuinely hope it's not going to be," I said. "I mean, we've talked about it before."

"We've discussed a great many things." He eyed me warily. "Many of them involve knives, blood, and screaming."

"I think two of those are likely to be involved, at least eventually." I took a deep breath. "I'm pregnant."

He frowned.

That wasn't the response I'd wanted. I tried to tug my

hands away. He clamped down harder, stopping me, and kept frowning.

"I'm sorry," he said. "I do believe I must have misheard you."

"Um, if what you heard was 'I'm pregnant,' you heard correctly," I said. "We've talked about this. You said you wanted to have kids. Did you not? Want to have kids?"

"You said we would have to wait until you had finished risking your life in a casual fashion," he said.

"I said I wasn't willing to start *trying* until I was finished risking my life in a casual fashion," I corrected. "Apparently, the universe had a different idea."

His face slowly relaxed into neutrality. "You're pregnant."

"Yes. That's what I've been trying to tell you."

"And you told Simon first."

"He was dying. I shared my blood to save him. He must have picked up the thought from what he was swallowing."

"So you didn't tell him?"

"Not intentionally, or using actual words."

"A baby." He was starting to smile, his voice warming as the news sank in and made it past the first layers of stress and confusion. Then his eyes widened. "But before, when I—"

"You mean, when Titania." I freed one hand, reached up, and touched his cheek. "You didn't do *anything*. She forced you, and I'm fine. I'm fine, and the baby's fine, and we're both going to be fine."

He put his hand over mine, keeping it in place, pinned to his face. "You know how my first wife died."

"And you know I'm basically unkillable." I stepped closer. "Can we try to be happy? Please? For me? For us? So I can be in a decent mood and not totally terrified when I go to tell Quentin and May? Oh, ash and oak, and Raysel. Is she going to think we don't have room for her? That we want her to lea—"

His kiss cut me off mid-word, stopping me from going any farther down that particular spiral. I held on to my tension for a few seconds, then allowed him to pull me closer, kissing him back with as much enthusiasm as I had. That turned out to be a fairly large degree of enthusiasm. He slid his arms around me, tugging me along as he backed up and sat down on the bed, still kissing me.

When he finally paused, it was to smile at me with melting affection, still holding me close to him. "A *baby*," he breathed. "*Our* baby. I've never been a parent before."

I thought of Raj, and didn't contradict him, just leaned over to rest my head against his shoulder. "Our baby," I agreed. "I guess it's time to start talking about names. Oh, and there's that whole Sleeping Beauty story thing. Do purebloods have any weird 'Hey we have a baby now' traditions that I need to know about?"

He wrinkled his nose. "Well, there won't be a christening, if that's what you're asking. There will be a party, however, to present the infant to the local nobility, and to allow them the opportunity to provide gifts. It's traditional for the Firstborn of the parents to be invited. They never attend, of course."

"Except that in my case, they actually might," I said, and groaned.

"That's a problem for tomorrow," he said, leaning down to kiss me again, slow and deep and loving.

That was when the wards on the house were ripped out from underneath me. I screamed, jerking away. It was a sudden, violent loss, and it hurt like someone was slamming shards of glass into my skin. Only unlike actual shards of glass, there was no way for me to pull it out, and the pain continued, even though a physical injury would have healed before Tybalt had time to pull back and stare at me.

The pain continued. I kept screaming. The bedroom door slammed open, and May burst into the room, eyes wide and wild.

"Toby?" she demanded, a note of shrill terror in her voice. Her eyes snapped to Tybalt. "What's wrong with her? Why is she screaming?" Then: "What did you *do*?"

"Nothing," he said, sounding horrified. "I was kissing her, and she just—"

I tried to catch my breath, tried to stop screaming, and could do neither. Somehow, it seemed as if my lungs, despite being agonized by the lack of air, had an infinite capacity for screaming. Quentin lurched into the doorway behind May, staring at me, eyes wide, a short sword in his hand. Jazz was close behind him, visibly horrified.

All we needed was Rayseline and we'd have the full household. Not that it was doing any good, and not that I needed someone else here to witness me wailing. She deserved to be allowed time to settle in and adjust to being awake again before we went lurching into another crisis.

Well, she wasn't going to get it. I finally managed to stop screaming long enough to catch my breath, and in the quiet that followed, I heard the sound of footsteps on the stairs. I looked to May, gasping, "Is that . . . Raysel?"

"She's asleep in her room," said May. "She was exhausted. I know that seems odd, given the whole 'cursed to sleep for a century' thing, but magical sleep and real sleep aren't the same thing. She's fine."

I swallowed another painful breath. "Someone . . . on . . . stairs."

She gave me a horrified look, then whirled around, paling as she stared at whoever was coming down the hall—whoever had ripped their way through my wards. "You can't *be* here," she gasped.

I tried to stand. Tybalt didn't let me go.

Quentin turned. "You!"

I tried to stand again. This time, Tybalt released me, standing in near-unison, putting his hands on my shoulders. I drew my knives, keeping them low to my side.

The smell of roses wafted down the hall, light and effervescent and entirely at odds with the growing tension in the room. I stepped forward, and Tybalt allowed his hands to drop away.

"Quentin," I said, very quietly.

He came the rest of the way into the room, moving to stand beside me. May stayed where she was, staring down the hall.

"Child of mine," said a new, terribly familiar voice that sent shivers running up and down my spine. May stiffened. "Child of mine, you cannot stand against me. Stand aside."

May cast an agonized glance in my direction, then moved

out of the doorway, clearing a path for the woman who appeared where she had been standing. Titania stepped into the dim rectangle of light coming in from the hall, looking flatly in my direction. She wasn't frowning. She wasn't smiling, either. She was looking at me the way I'd look at a spider I found unexpectedly in my bathtub, something unwanted and small and unwelcome in my space.

"You can't hurt me," I said, wishing my voice wouldn't shake. "You can't hurt any of us. You're not allowed to harm my family."

"True, child," she said. "But you forget how young you are. You forget how much more time I've had to play this game. So much more time than any of you. Only the distorted child of mine comes anywhere near to me, and hers is a dilute and unwarranted claim to her age. I know the way of ward and wording. I know the roads through riddle and restriction. Do you truly think my husband can stop me from doing anything I want to do?"

"Get out of my house," I said.

"I can't hurt you." She finally smiled. "But I can make you someone else's problem."

The smell of roses grew stronger, until the air was too thick for me to breathe without sticking in my throat. I couldn't feel my fingers. I couldn't feel my arms. I couldn't feel anything at all, and then the light was red, red as roses, red as blood, and then there wasn't any light at all.

Everything went away, and the space after the sentence was blazing white, and silence.

TWENTY-THREE

LIGHT CASCADED THROUGH MY bedroom window, silvery bright and warming. I yawned and rolled over, burying my face in the heap of lacy pillows Mother insisted I keep on the bed. She said a proper lady should never leave room for anyone to assume that she'd been joined by some unworthy suitor during the day, and so long as the pillows never touched the floor, my virtue would be unblemished and understood.

Sometimes I thought there was a reasonably decent chance my mother might be making things up to mess with me.

The light continued cascading into the room, bright enough that there was no way it was being filtered through curtains. I groaned and sat up, pushing my hair out of my eyes as I blinked at the world. "I wasn't ready to rejoin you," I informed it.

The world persisted in existing.

Groaning again, I slid out of the bed and padded toward the window. The curtains, which I knew had been closed the night before, were standing open and letting in the early-evening air. Mother must have aligned the moonrise to her mood again. That, or she thought it was time for me to be awake and getting on with my night. That was considerate of her, even if it made me want to crawl into the closet for another few hours of sleep. But Mother wouldn't have opened my curtains. She didn't like to come into my room after I was in bed; said it was inappropriate, and that as a grown woman, I should have been able to put myself to bed.

"August," I muttered, leaning over to grab the curtain and jerk it shut.

The light mercifully dimmed.

My older sister was more rebellious than I—a dire consequence of having no human blood to make her recognize the privilege of her position—and my room, being closer to the ground, was all too often her chosen pathway out into the world. She had been refining the skill of creeping through the room and climbing out the window since we were children, and no longer woke me with any sort of regularity. That didn't make it something I approved of.

Mother kept us in the tower to keep us safe. Mother loved us. Mother loved us like the precious treasures we were.

Mother would forgive me if I went back to bed.

I turned, eyes half-closed, and walked over to collapse onto the mattress. I had been so *tired* lately, and for no reason I could possibly see. If it was still bothering me after a little more sleep, I could talk to Mother.

Or I could talk to August right now, as she came bursting into my room and ran over to drop down beside me on the bed, the drapes rustling with the motion. "Are you going to get up *tonight*?" she demanded.

I hit her with a pillow.

"Violence! Really, October, where did you learn such a terrible reflex?" She picked up another pillow and pressed it over my face, leaning on it with all her weight as I squirmed and shoved. "You've been spending too much time with Father, if you're going to be so *aggressive*."

I managed to get my hands against her stomach and shoved her away. She tumbled back on the bed, laughing. I sat up, glaring at her.

"I was still asleep, you wrecking ball," I scolded.

"What's a little suffocation between sisters?" she asked.

I hit her with another pillow.

August grinned. "There's my baby sister," she said. "Vicious and overly aggressive and terrible."

"Better than pushy and invasive and awful," I said.

She leaned over, catching me in a hug that was more like a headlock.

I considered squirming, then gave it up in favor of hugging her. When August was in one of these moods, the best thing was to give in and let her move things along as she desired. I would be able to get a nap before sunrise if I let her haul me out of bed now. Besides, she was my sister, the only friend Faerie had intended me to have, the only companion with whom I had been provided. Changelings might be necessary for the stability of Faerie, born to be obedient and biddable, but we could never marry, never settle in households of our own. I would live with Mother as her dutiful daughter until such time as she tired of me, and then I would go with August to serve her when she married or set up her own household elsewhere. I would never have been born had not Mother been doing her duty to provide a loyal handmaiden of her own blood for my sister.

My existence was a gift, but I must always remember that August was my superior and deserved my cooperation whenever it could be given without going against our mother's wishes.

Still, I had to know. "You went out my window again yesterday, didn't you?"

"That awful *cat* was lurking around the garden again," she said, with a pout. "I've driven him quite away, and we should have peace, for now. But we may need to update the wards."

"You're too good to me," I said. For her to have passed up a day of dancing in the glade with her other friends in order to protect her useless sister was a gift beyond all measure.

August kissed my temple.

"You need to value yourself more, October," she said. "Father wants to see us in the garden before we sit to breakfast."

"Then I should rise, and dress," I said. "But I'll be there."

"Good girl," she said, and let me go, rising. "Best sister."

"No, *you're* the best sister," I said, smiling up at her. "I love you."

"I love you too, goose girl," she said, as she made for the door. "See you in the garden."

Then she was gone, and I was alone with the moonlight and the slivers of my dreams. I yawned, stretched, and got off the bed. Time to begin another night.

Had any changeling ever had a better life, or a better family? I thought not.

And I couldn't imagine ever wanting anything more.

Read on for
a brand-new novella
by Seanan McGuire:

SUCH DANGEROUS SEAS

We all that are engaged in this loss
Knew that we ventured on such dangerous seas . . .
—William Shakespeare, *Henry IV, Part II*

Cailleach Skerry, 520

THE CHILDREN WERE LAUGHING outside my door, their voices high and sweet and pure, ringing like the chimes of morning along the twilit beach. Not that morning ever came here; in Cailleach Skerry, it was always truest twilight, untouched by the searing of the sun. I had no need for such mortal affectations here, and would not until one of my children chose to lay down with a human—I thought Firtha might, since no matter how far into the future I looked, I could see nothing of her children. Sure, she might be one who never chose to be a parent, or she might be one of those who never chose to know another physically, but changelings can confuse the issue. They come and go so quickly that unless a Seer knows when to focus their attention, the child in question could be born and buried before the vision became clear in one direction or another.

It didn't matter one way or another. I loved my wild, impudent youngest daughter completely, and always would, whether she chose to carry on the line or no. Her siblings were doing well enough in that regard. The Roane multiplied with each passing year, my father's hope chests had pulled the mortality from their veins, and one day, they would fill the seas.

One day very soon, because I had taken the youngest of them for Moving Day. The seasons were turning, the Queens exchanged their Courts, and my descendants would have the time to tarry without their descendants begging their time or the children of Titania harrying their steps. Titania's handsome sons and daughters would be too busy attending upon their mother to try my family's patience for at least the next set of seasons, and we would be plentiful in those days of peace. Such had it always been. Such was the tide that turned our sweet and subtle seas.

Seated on the table's edge and secured with ropes of living kelp, my youngest grandson reached for me with chubby, webbed fists, his mouth open and working in silent plea for another bite of breakfast. I dipped the spoon once more into the thin fish soup all the children had been given for their morning meal. Near to two dozen there were in total for this interlude, ranging in age from thirteen and sliding into the long, slow adulthood of the immortal to precious Ulchel here at my table, who was not yet two years of age. His father, Aulay, was counted among my favorites.

Mothers are not meant to play favorites with their children, but they all do, even if most of them refuse ever to admit it. I did my best to love them all the same, and they made it easy on me, sweet and strange and seabound as they were, but of my boys, Aulay was easily my favorite, having the most of his father in him, and of my girls, I thought I might love Firtha most of all.

Spooning thin soup into Ulchel's mouth, I laughed at his expression of intense concentration as he worked to taste and swallow at the same time. He was too young to know what it meant to savor something, to recognize that because it was good, it should be eaten slowly, for it might never come again. To him, the world was still sweet, delicious and kind and meant to be devoured as quickly as it could be.

Some of my siblings question why, if we are meant to live forever, we even possess the urge to reproduce. It seems an odd thing to have in common with the mortals who teem in Earthly lands, the only life we have ever found not as part of Faerie. They age and die; it only makes sense that they should want to pass their history and beliefs along. We have no such need. We are eternal.

I am an odd one, for I argue that our very eternity is what makes the need so impossibly great. History feels less important to preserve when it seems that it can never be forgotten, and the things that make life so gloriously good become easily dismissed when they will never go away. We see the world made new and bright and full of wonder through the eyes of children. We will always need them.

Not all my siblings are suited to parenthood, and I have nothing but respect for those who realized such before they could commit the endless crime of bringing a new life into the world when they had no intent of caring for it. The urge to reproduce is strong. The urge to parent is not always as powerful. Some of my brothers and sisters had barely come into the world before they were abandoned to their own devices. I was a parent long before I had children of my own, for I could not leave those babes for the world to devour.

Faerie would be far less had I not been willing to sacrifice my own peace for the sake of Titania's unwanted children. She had borne and left far too many infants, walking away from them without a glance behind. But oh, how I had loved them. Some were no relation to me at all, while others were brothers and sisters, bound by a father in common, and all were welcome in my cradles. Not a one of them had ever made me regret their raising, not even when their true mother beckoned and they could not help but go.

Out of all my brothers and sisters born to Titania, only Amphitrite had ever been able to resist her call, I think because the nature of the Lady of Flowers was so inimical to the sea. It was a mystery to me when the girl was born, and is a mystery to me now, that any child of Titania's should be called to the water. But then, the children of Maeve are often called to the roses, and Titania claims them entire, so perhaps it was only fair.

When next I tried to deliver soup to my grandson's waiting mouth, he gurgled and slapped the spoon away, flailing and angry. I laughed, putting the bowl aside.

"All done eating, my little Prince of the Western Sea?" I asked. "Shall we to the beach, to join your cousins at their play?"

He waved his hands at me, indicating his desire to get down from the chair. Laughing again, I stood and scooped him into my arms, letting him latch on to my hair. The babies always seemed to love my hair. I wore it long and loose mostly for them, giving them something they could cling to when we moved from place to place.

Their parents complained, at times, said that *their* hair was less like the living water, and so hurt when it was pulled upon. But they never bade me stop, and our relationship was close enough that I thought it was more than just the fear of a Firstborn's wrath keeping them from interfering in my relationship with my grandchildren. They let me be as I was because they loved me, and that was enough for them.

We were a family. That was enough.

The children came running when they saw me emerge from the house with Ulchel in my arms, their feet soundless on the sand, their mouths overfull of words like pearls, which they spilled in all directions, eager for my attention, my focus, my approval. They had been patient while I fed the baby, for they remembered being in his place, and knew I would tolerate nothing less, but they could be patient no longer.

"Grandmother! Grandmother! I saw a *shark*!" Tibbe made a great chomping motion with her arms, showing her teeth at the same time, as if that could demonstrate the accuracy of her words. "It was swimming off the shore, proud as anything! It was so big it could have swallowed me right entire up!"

"No shark you find here in Cailleach Skerry would ever dare to harm a child of the Roane," I assured her, handing Ulchel off to one of the boys, who balanced the baby expertly on his hip and moved toward the back of the crowd, all of them bright-eyed and innocent and ignorant of a world that worked any way other than this, other than long days spent in endless twilight under the caring eye of their grandmother, who would never let anything harm them. Other than sweet seas and the love of their parents and storms, yes, storms and sharks and the ever-present threat of Titania's influence on the waters, but at the end of it, Cailleach Skerry. Safety always won out.

Safety would always, always win.

If I could stop time, I would stop it there. Perhaps that is selfish—perhaps I should pick a point further removed, the moment when the plan was first conceived, the hour when the first conspirators were recruited—but I don't know those points. I know my grandchildren in the gloaming. I know the way they looked at me, absolutely confident in their safety.

I know that they will never look at me that way again.

Tibbe was the first to scream, abandoning her sharky pantomime and clutching the sides of her head as the wails were ripped from her throat. She sounded like she was dying. I jerked upright, shock and horror racing through my body, and pushed through the other children to reach her. She was still screaming when I got there.

"Tibbe? Tibbe, what's wrong?"

Her screams continued, seeming, impossibly, to increase in volume and resonance, until I realized . . . she wasn't screaming alone. All the other children were screaming with her, and not in the playful manner of young creatures trying to startle their elders. These were screams of pure grief and terror, all save Ulchel's. The boy was howling, yes, but more in shock than anything else.

I whipped around. He was on the ground, his little lip bloodied from the impact, and I couldn't even be angry with the child who'd dropped him—Suanach, one of Merraid's sons—because the older boy was clutching the sides of his head and screaming along with all the others. A collective vision had come upon them, swallowing them in its urgency and its horrors.

In Cailleach Skerry, nothing comes for me unless I allow it to. I looked at the screaming faces of my grandchildren, and I did the only thing I could possibly have done.

I closed my eyes, and I let the vision come, and I saw my babies slaughtered in the sand at Eira's bidding, and I became a monster as I ceased to be a mother.

I became a monster evermore.

Brocéliande, Albion, 523

There are things about that day I had forgotten almost before they finished happening. Little things, like a fight over the privy or the burning of a slice of bread. Things that don't really matter when they're happening. Things I would happily bleed for the opportunity to recall. I have envied my father's claimed descendants for many things in my time. The ability to ride their own memory at will with a drop of blood is the greatest of them.

Every moment of that morning is locked within my veins, captive in the living memory my body carries but will not share with me. It is unfair beyond all measure that Eira, may she rot as mortals rot, may she melt away into decay and pestilence . . . Eira could witness every moment of that day as through my eyes if only I would bleed for her. Eira could have the last good things I am denied. Eira, who deserves nothing good ever in this world or any other.

Eira, who will burn.

There are things about that day I had forgotten, dismissed as unimportant, even before it became the most important—and the worst—day of my long and lonely life. I can't have them back again with wanting or with wishing, and even if I were willing to bleed for my sister's sorcery, I would never be able to trust a single scrap of the accounting from her lips.

So I shall have her life instead, and perhaps that can serve as memory enough. I won't forget a moment of that, of this much you can be sure. I'll bleed her as white as the snow she fancies so fair, and leave her marbled corpse for the night-haunts to devour. Perhaps I'll sit and wait for their arrival. It's been too long since I've spoken to my sister's descendant line. They must be very lonely.

They didn't ask to be as they are. They requested their

natures no more than any of the rest of us did, but they must live with them, even as the rest of us must live with our own.

And it's not as if any of my own children will look back at me through their eyes.

Brocéliande loomed before me, a glowing confection of a castle that had no place existing this close to the mortal world, or bending it so unreasonably. The foundations, such as they were, stood rooted an ocean away in Paimpont Forest in fair Brittany, but the towers stood in Albion, tall and proud and impossible, ignoring the distance between their roots and their branches. If ever Titania peeled her magic from the site, it would crumble and collapse, done in by its own inherent contradiction.

In Albion, the castle could be approached from the mortal world, with no need to make the transition through the Summerlands, or even through the neighboring skerries. It was a tidy trick, extravagant and cruel, and a beautiful reminder to us all of how much less we were than our parents. I cannot say with certainty that I am the most powerful among us, and so I will not say it, although I do believe myself to be; it is, at best, a question between myself and Eira, and given her fondness for running mewling to her mother at the first sign of my displeasure, it seems likely that my strength is greater than hers. If someone else is greater than I, I do not know of it.

The creation of Brocéliande, however, would be quite beyond me. That I can perceive the spells that build and bolster it is a testament to my power: my children never could.

The flags that flew above the castle told me that Eira was in residence, as I had hoped she would be. It had always seemed a likely thing, this being the time of year when she would generally retreat into her mother's company; the spring thaw weakened her as only drought could weaken me, and she loathed the touch of summer. That did not make it honest truth.

My inability to think, even in silence, that I had known she would be here only fanned the embers of my rage. She had stolen so very much from me. My home, my family, my control over my own mind. I *would* have my satisfaction.

Killing Eira would not break the bonds I labor under, would not free me from Titania's frozen reins, but one will come who *can* release me, who *can* unbind me. I have Seen her, distantly, in the cracked and broken mirror of the future. Eira's death will change much about the form she carries—Eira is to do something terrible in the years to come, something so brutal and unforgivable that I could not See it clearly even as I approached Brocéliande, and that terrible thing would result in Faerie gifting us with a new bloodline, one intended to repair so very many of the failings of the past—but not everything. We were flawed. We were failing to live up to what the Heart required us to be. She would come whether Eira died this day or not. Perhaps in a different form. Perhaps sooner, or farther in the future. But she would come, and one day, she would set me free.

I would not be bound forever. With that thought in mind, bright and perfect in its undeniable truth, I lifted my chin and strode toward Brocéliande.

Fair Brocéliande, fairy castle in the enchanted wood, place where one day a man named Arthur would be crowned, if the future continued along the track it was currently taking, where terrible things would happen and blood would water the forest's roots. But where we could, if we were quick and clever, still be worthy of the best of us.

I had no way of knowing how the day would end, which told me one truth more: that Eira's mother was almost certainly in attendance.

The Seers who are less powerful than I—my own descendants, the others who carry the gift of prophecy in their bones—find their eyes are clouded when I, or my siblings, enter the scene. We are too vast for them to see; the future does not share our faces. And that is only fair, and right, and because I see that it is fair and right, I dare not object when the same future will not show me the presence of our parents.

Compared to my descendants, I am a bonfire set beside a candle. Compared to my parents, I am a bonfire set beside the sun. Their light blazes too bright. It blots all else away. No matter how hard I looked at the hours ahead, how closely I tried to map the movement of the close and closing future, there was nothing but stillness, as perfect as a pearl. There was no future I could see. And as my death was the one thing I knew I would be able to see even in the presence of my parents—my death, when it came, would shake mountains—that meant not that I died today but that one of our parents was present.

I didn't dare to hope for Oberon. In a conflict between myself and Eira, he might choose either one of us, but he would always endeavor to be fair when he possibly could—and in this case, I could see no way she could convince him she was the injured party. My sister was a master manipulator, to be sure, but even a master has their limits, and "I orchestrated the slaughter of my sister's children, then beguiled my mother such that she bound said sister's tongue most cruelly" was sure to be beyond hers.

No. I could not hope for Oberon, and Maeve never tarried at Brocéliande when her sister's children were in residence. That left Titania, the rose of poisoned thorns, for all that her flag did not fly above the castle. That meant that I was going into battle with a heavy disadvantage laid upon me, and would be hard pressed to walk away unharmed, much less the victor.

But I would not die this day. I had Seen too many things that happened in the far distant future, too many events that required my presence. Whatever happened in Brocéliande, I would survive it, and as Eira and her mother had already stolen the lies from out my mouth and replaced them with only the bitterest of truths, I could see nothing left for them to do to me.

I had fought direr battles against worse odds, and the screams of my grandchildren still painted my dreams in crimson every time I closed my eyes. I squared my shoulders, set my eyes upon the wall, and stepped onto the bridge that would carry me to the castle.

It was solid stone beneath my feet, half quarried from the earth of Albion and half from the deeper, more dangerous mines of Avalon, and as I crossed it into the Summerlands, the deck under my feet began to glitter as if each individual brick had been crafted out of captive starlight. I raised my foot in the mortal world. I put it down in Faerie, and the bridge blazed beneath me, silver-bright and effortlessly beautiful. The beauty was reflected in the castle, which gleamed and glistened in the low twilight that blanketed the land. It was flawless. It was forever. It was everything Titania had intended it to be, and only the fact that I had Seen a great war waged here, a war that would change the face of Faerie forever, was enough to keep me from hating it as utterly as I loathed Titania herself.

She was no mother. She was a monster, and like all monsters, she begat more of the same. I was a monster now as well, thanks to her dearest daughter, but at least I had the sense to see it, and to realize that monsters should refrain from making more when they could. The world has monsters enough, and not nearly the number of heroes needed to fight us all. When everything is said and done, all that remains will be monsters, and the deep, unforgiving chambers of the sea.

When this is done, I think I will go there and sleep a time. A millennium or two should be enough to let the world forget me. What's forgotten is by its very nature forgiven, and I wish forgiveness almost as much as I wish for peace. When this is done.

The bridge stretched out beneath and before me, longer now than it had been when I stepped onto it, back in the mortal world. If I turned and went back the way I had come, only a few steps would carry me back to the simple safety of human lands, and Brocéliande would stand unchallenged. The stones knew me for a threat against their mistress, and their Lady was present, flag or no: the castle only blazed this bright when Titania was in attendance, when Titania's desires held sway. They would protect her, as they could.

Fortunate, then, that we have no King or Queen of stones; flowers, blood, and water, those are the divisions that govern our magic, although I've sometimes thought it would be better stated as thorns, blood, and water, since all three of our parents carry roses in their hearts, but only Titania and her descendants seem to take pleasure in causing pain.

But as the stones have no masters, I knew the bridge itself would not fight me past a point, and that point was well within my grasping. I reached out with my magic, water to the core, only slightly seeded by the blood of my father, and soothed the jagged edges of the angry wards that sought to keep me out, whispering words of peace and comfort. Every one of them was true, as was required of me. I was not here to harm Titania, I told the stones; I doubted I could do so if I tried. I was so much less than her that if she raised a hand against me, I would be struck down and destroyed without a second thought on her part. I could no more threaten her than a mouse could threaten a tiger, than a hen could threaten a dragon. I was harmless.

I was here to slaughter their mistress's favorite daughter if I could, and to break her if I couldn't, but Faerie has never been willing to believe that harm to others could be harm to the self in any way. If it were, Eira would have been punished for her actions against me, rather than flattered and forgiven because she had done me, myself, no actual harm. But I told the stones truly that I had no intention to attack their mistress, and they believed me. Bit by bit, the distance ahead of me reduced itself to something more believable, and I was able to continue on, until I stood before the gates, until only a thin wooden barricade kept me from my destination.

The gates did not swing open at my approach. Brocéliande was not intended to be receiving visitors at this moment, then, which was no surprise. Eira has never been the most social of my siblings; she enjoys worship and adoration, but not the casual interactions that come in a healthy Court. Even Kings and Queens must, at times, allow themselves the opportunity to be seen as people rather than only crowns. Eira would prefer never to be known as anything beyond perfect, and in her mother's presence, perfection was too clearly outside her reach. Even if she had come to Brocéliande with the intent to call a Court and bask in the adulation of her descendants, those plans would be put on hold until such time as her mother sought another bower. That was no hardship for my sister. So long as she kept her Court closed in Titania's presence, she could have her mother's full attention—the only thing she desired more than admiration.

I didn't have the time for this. I scowled and narrowed my eyes, focusing the full strength of my magic on the gate.

"I am Antigone of Albany, first daughter of Oberon and Maeve, Firstborn to the Roane, claimed by Oberon himself when the year turned and my mother turned him from her bower, and Brocéliande is mine as much as any other's," I said, tone imperious. "You have no right to ban or bar me from my own property."

The gate trembled like a living thing as my words clashed against the simple locks Eira had thrown into place. She knew I was coming. She had always known I must one day come. After what she'd done . . .

I was like the tide. I was only the inevitable.

There was a time when I had hoped my sister and I might be friends. We were similar in age, after all, with her being the first daughter born to Titania and I the first of three born to Maeve. Had Annis, Annie, and I been more alike in face, we might never have known who the true First was. But we did know, and Eira hated me for it from the moment she understood my position in our family.

How she hated. She had no reason to fear me, save that I was more powerful than she, and I had never once turned that power in her direction, nor sought to harm her. But my distance had never been enough to grant her peace, and when she orchestrated the destruction of my children, she had convinced herself it meant I must now be set against her. She had sent the children of the ones who killed my darlings to seek my mercy, expecting me to slaughter them for their impudence, and instead, I had granted them what they wished in the most terrible manner I could. I had not sought to destroy the Daoine Sidhe, nor to raise an army against them, as I was sure she had hoped I might do.

Had I declared war in response to her cowardly attack, she could have convinced her siblings to stand with her against me. Eira was no match for me alone, but with the other children of Titania behind her, she might have been able to destroy me. As long as I lived, I would be first among our father's children, and first among us all for power. She could never be as great as she desired while standing in my shadow. The death of the Roane had been intended to lure me onto a killing field, a lamb for the slaughter and her hand on the sickle. And when I failed to rise to the bait she had dangled before me, when I had set myself to the creation of the Selkies and the charting of the tides that every day rose a little higher, swallowed a little more of Cailleach Skerry, I had thrown her careful plans into disarray.

Eira was a grand planner, even a subtle one, but she was never once a deep planner, nor was she well equipped to handle the changing of her intended outcomes. When I had failed to behave as she would bid me, she had panicked and run to the one person who would always listen, always believe her, always take her side: her mother.

What she had expected of Titania, I do not know. Perhaps it had been exactly what occurred, in which case, my sister was, and is, a greater fool than I had ever supposed, for binding my tongue would do nothing to stop me committing sororicide. It was in truth that I wanted Eira dead. It was in truth that I had commissioned the knife I carried from my sister, Alswn, who had known my intention without my ever once telling her it was intended to be used in the murder of another of our siblings. What reason could a daughter of Oberon have for carrying a blade of blended iron and silver, if not to kill one of the other First?

The hilt was carved from antler shed by our father some seasons before, that Alswn had been keeping for just such an occasion. I had given her no instructions regarding ornamentation, but the dark eyes of seals peered out at me from between ropes of scrimshaw kelp and pearls, not quite the image of my children, but close enough that it hurt me to look too closely. Alswn knew. She had never asked, and still she knew, and I had spoken no lies when I told her what I wanted, and Titania's binding had only delayed me for the few years it took me to remember the shape of my own voice, the ways to shape speech to suit my bidding.

Lies were pretty, convenient things, and I missed them

badly. They came to me only when I spoke to the Selkies, or to my few remaining blood descendants. Even my own siblings compelled the truth from me. Even empty air demanded it. In my most charitable moments, I wondered if Eira's own addiction to falsehood might have made this seem like a way to force me to keep company with my kin, preventing me from isolating myself as I had been so intently doing. This question was always followed by the much less charitable assumption that if she had wanted us together, the best and only thing I could do for them was to stay away. Her first attempt to destroy the Roane had failed, after all, coming close without ending their line entire. Were she to try again—were I to call them all into one colony of seals, Roane and Selkies alike, gathered in a single place—she could end them forever.

Perhaps I deserved nothing more than to see my bloodline destroyed and my better days forgotten. But the Roane deserved more. The Roane were innocent. The Selkies, born in slaughter and repugnant in my sight as they were, were innocent. And my dear Ælfweard, long dead and buried, forgotten by all save myself and the sea, deserved more. He deserved waters teeming with his children, thriving with the babes he'd given me and the babes they'd given in their days.

I loved him when he was by my side, and I loved him when he left me, and I love him still. And perhaps it was that love that made it possible for the children of the ones who killed my children to slip into their skins like cradleclothes. There was nothing of the mortal in me, not a drop of humanity, but Ælfweard had been a human man before I called him to Cailleach Skerry to live with me and love me. Time had not been able to catch or claim him there, frozen as my shores were in the stillness I commanded of them. Time had not been able to *see* him, and for a century and more we had been together as man and wife, the human with the laugh like a promise and the Firstborn daughter of the sea who placed his children in his arms for him to name and adore.

And then one day, I had come home from a brief journey into Emain Ablach to find him gone and our children crying at the table, weeping in the absence of the father who had always been more reliable and present than the tide. It had taken most of the night to coax the story out of them, the Siren who had appeared offshore almost as soon as I was gone, singing to my Ælfweard until he followed her lure into the water, where the Kraken she rode upon had snatched him up and carried him away. They had fled to the border of the skerry and beyond, into waters where the Roane could not go, and by the time I returned, they had been so long gone as to be little more than memory.

The Sirens are descended from my sister, Raidne, but she has not been seen in centuries, and in her absence, her descendants do as they will. They lack the heart or ambition to rule beneath the seas, nor would the Merrow look kindly upon such a challenge, and as Amphitrite still swims among her descendants, the Sirens have never seemed inclined to challenge. They scattered instead, and sell their services to any who will pay them.

Finding the Siren who lured my Ælfweard away was no difficult thing. She had taken the payment she received and gone to celebrate her good fortune—and what good fortune it had seemed, that all she had to do was sing a single human man away from a deserted stretch of skerry to be paid in such riches as she had never seen. She had believed herself set for life, prepared to establish her own stronghold against the roaring seas, perhaps even to pay one of the First to build her a skerry of her own.

Instead, she had turned to find the sea witch close behind her, my anguish and anger dripping from me like seafoam, and when she had tried to run, she had found me there to block her way, keeping her from finding peace or protection anywhere in all the seas. Had Raïdne been present to intercede on her behalf, she might have gotten away with what she'd done, might have gone back to the tides unharmed.

We do not live in that happy world. I had her, and I had my answers from her, and when I left her, I left her living, for it is unfair for such as us to destroy those who are so very far beneath us. Her strength could never have matched my own. But as I would never again have my Ælfweard, she would never again have the sea. It would not claim her if she tried, save as a deep and watery grave.

She flies on feathered wings now, and while her voice is yet alluring, her sisters know her not. I have Seen her when I closed my eyes, finding her way among the Kingdoms of the Air, and she might yet be happy there, if she is careful, if she can set her longing for the deeps aside. She can confuse the mortals utterly, by setting Sirens in the sky as well as in the sea, and I feel Raidne would forgive me, if ever she returns to us. If she yet lives.

My Ælfweard does not. Human men are not meant to stand outside history for a century's time. Young he was when first I met and courted him, and young he was in Cailleach Skerry, and young he was when my sister Eira paid a Siren girl too young and foolish to see how unwise her actions were to lure a human man away. Young he was yet when that Siren delivered him into Eira's arms.

That, alone, is the reason I spared her. Raidne is gone. It doesn't matter if she would have spoken for the girl; the girl stood before me alone and criminal, deserving of whatever punishment I selected for her shoulders to carry. But Eira tricked her into doing something less than clever. Eira presented her with riches and let greed dictate her choices. Eira never explained. And when the girl lured Ælfweard away, she had no means of knowing that time would be lurking, looming behind my love, ready to swallow him whole.

She handed him to Eira a young man. By the time I arrived, less than a day's time later, he was withered to the bone, ancient beyond his own mind's capacity to carry, babbling with delirium and wetting himself without the ability to control it. He sobbed when he saw me, clutching at me with skeletal hands, the ancient horror who had been the father of my children, and when I told him I would take him home, he crumbled into dust in my arms.

I did not see Eira there. I cannot truly state that I know her to be responsible for the death of Ælfweard, and so I cannot accuse her. But the Siren girl described her to perfection, and he died with the scent of snow and roses on his skin, returned to dust as all mortal flesh must one day be. Like my children, he was never to appear among the night-haunts. Like my children, she saw to it that he would be lost to me forever.

For Ælfweard's sake, I could not gather my remaining descendants to my side, for that would make them too easy for Eira to destroy. And destroy them she seemed intent to do. Anything to do me harm, to make me less, to force me to place myself where she could break me.

She did not kill my children, but she orchestrated their slaughter, and I would never forgive her for that. And when I had gone to confront her, to ask her why she would do such a thing, why she would harm innocents, she had spat at my feet and told me they were no better than changelings, with humanity in their veins even if it had been massaged into immortality by my father's own hands, that they deserved to go as all mortal flesh must go. I had lunged for her then, furious beyond measure, ready to enter the wizard's duel that seemed our only remaining avenue of conflict, ready to end the night with one of us broken before the other. By strength alone, I would have been the victor, but Eira had antagonized me beyond the point of cunning; had she met me fairly, she might actually have been able to defeat me.

She did not meet me fairly.

Instead, she had turned triumphant to the curtains behind her throne, and she had shouted as loud as a village bell, "You see, Mother? She would attack me for nothing more than the death of a mortal man who was fool enough to listen to a Siren's call!"

"Odd, that you remember Ælfweard when you forget my children," I spat in the moment, and ever more in memory. I had not understood the situation. I paid dearly for that failure. I am still failing now, and will be until the impossible is accomplished, and Titania is dead or one who can unmake her bindings is discovered. Faerie makes only what she needs. Why would Faerie ever have need to undermine her own daughter so dearly? "Face me, sister, for you must answer for your crimes."

And then the curtains had pulled apart and Titania had stepped into the room, and I had finally begun to understand the depths of my mistake.

I cannot lie. I may never lie again. And still I cannot repeat the words of the binding she placed upon me, for they were spoken in a language I did not know and could not comprehend. They fell upon me like a cloying mist, sticking to my skin, enveloping me in the smell of roses, and all was the gleam of Titania's eyes, and the crushing weight of brambles piled into towers, brambles such as must scrape and snare the moon, snatching it from the sky. When she stopped speaking, I was rubbed as raw and defenseless as a newborn child, and she had looked at me with twice as much disdain before she turned to the daughter she loved best in all the worlds and said, in a voice as soft as sunset, "It is done, beloved. Now see it to she stays out of trouble."

Then she had walked away, leaving me alone with Eira, bound and broken on the floor. And Eira, laughing, had walked a circle around me, a smile on her lips and malice in her eyes.

"Will you slay me now, sister?" she had demanded. "Will you rise and break me?"

I had given her no answer, save for the silent pleading of my eyes, the shifting misery of my injuries.

She had prodded my hip with the toe of her foot, then resumed her circling. "Father says our games have grown too violent of late," she had said, and her voice was acid and honey wine. "He says he would prefer we not slaughter one another in the fields simply out of spite. I am enjoined not to harm those claimed by his other wife, nor to raise hand directly against you."

I had rolled onto my back, staring up at her, as silent as a stone.

"But there's nothing to say I can't work through others," she had said, and smiled as she stepped away. "You're beneath me, sister, and if not for Father's commands, I would have your heart for my collection. Never come before me again."

Then she had walked away, and left me on the floor of her temporary palace, and even as my own hatred had begun to fully blossom in my heart, I had finally understood why she hated me so, and why I had never been able to change it, no matter how hard I tried. She hated me because she could not imagine a world in which I was more powerful than she and would not inevitably seek to destroy her.

Had she left me alone, with my tides and my children and my lover and my skerry, I might never have troubled her. Would have been forgotten by the greater part of Faerie over time, as I would never have seen the need to stir beyond my borders for any cause other than my family. I could have been a sheathed sword, and she, out of fear of my sharpness, tore my sheath away. Now I was a naked blade, and I was going to have her heart, as our father had forbidden her to have mine.

I was going to end her.

The door shivered beneath my hand, wards and locks falling away one by one, worn down like stones before the tide. I narrowed my eyes and kept pushing. This was no spell, no working, no enchantment on my part; this was only and entirely power, poured into the cracks between what Titania had woven. The strongest foundation cannot stand forever against the sea. I knew it. Titania knew it. Eira knew it.

So my power poured into the substance of the castle, filling wood and stone alike, until there was a sound like ice cracking on a frozen pond, and the warding dropped away. The gates swung open, and I stepped inside, into the echoing great hall of Brocéliande.

Here, too, the stone gleamed from within, lit by a brilliance that had no business this near to the moral world. The floor was polished marble as transparent as the air, and when I glanced down, I could see into the firmament itself, the flashes of deep fire buried in earth, the opalescent sheen of gems that shouldn't have been so polished but had been by the presence of Titania's ever-flowing power. Arrogance is a hallmark of the fae, all of us, myself included, but for true hubris, you need to look to the Three. They have always been as gods. They don't know any other way to be.

Banners covered the walls, the personal seals of each of Titania's children, their coats of arms on bold display. None of my mother's children were represented among those banners. Nor were the less-favored of her own; look as I might, I couldn't find the yellow acacia flower and green moth sigil of Acacia, or the downward trident and kelp of Amphitrite. It was a gallery of the descendants she termed worthy of her love, and it made me like her even less, which was no small feat, given the existing depths of my dislike.

When Mother holds her own formal Court at Caerleon—something she avoids whenever possible, finding it terribly limiting—she hangs all our banners on the walls, even the arms of those who have failed her in some way. She is still our mother, and we are still her children, and she casts none of us aside. For Titania to flaunt her favoritism so blatantly seemed like a transgression against her own descendants, and it curdled in my stomach, bitter and unpleasant.

I continued onward, down the length of the grand hall, toward what should have been the far wall. There was nothing there, only a misty endlessness. Titania, as Lady of Flowers, is the mother of illusions; the foundations of Brocéliande were set in stone, as it were, and even she could not shift them without Oberon's aid, but with her in residence, the appearance and tricks of the castle were entirely hers to command. I kept my chin high. I kept walking.

I knew the length of this hall, had walked it since I was a child, and yet I know I walked it more than twice over before the mist began to clear and the far wall appeared. The floor there had been raised by roughly four feet, creating a platform flanked at either end by descending stairs. At the center of the platform sat Titania, enthroned, her own crest in place of pride behind her, a tapestry longer than either of us was tall. To the right hung Oberon's crest, smaller by half but still prominently displayed.

To the left hung a blank white sheet of cloth, entirely unmarked. I stopped walking, eyes on the snowy fabric. Eira's arms were not so simple as that; were, in fact, ornate to the point of ostentation. Still, white had always been her color of choice, and this was the closest her mother could come to saying that her daughter mattered as my mother did not.

It was no mystery that Titania would see my mother

gone and a catspaw of her choice placed at Oberon's left hand, changing the balance of Faerie forever in her favor. To see it so blatantly displayed was still a shock, and it was shock, coupled with her geas, that moved my tongue to speech as I demanded:

"Stepdame, what is the meaning of this slight?"

Titania, lounging on her throne as if she had no concerns in all the world, lifted one perfect brow and looked at me, unblinking. Her eyes were rainbow pools, as opalescent as the gems beneath my feet, every color and no single color at the same time. Nothing living should have had those eyes. Even in Faerie, there are meant to be limits.

They were the color of the Heart, if not half so welcoming, or kind.

"I see no slight, uninvited child," she said, voice mellifluous and sweet. "I am the only Queen in attendance, and I hang my own crest to mark the dominance of my Court in these halls. If this fails to suit you, perhaps you should speak to your father about changing the etiquette under which all of us endure. So long as what I do here is no offense to the rules as written, I shall continue, for my comfort is what matters in this moment. What brings you here?"

To leave a question unanswered was still an itch and an ache in the back of my mind, like I was lying through silence alone. That I had heard her was unquestionable; therefore, if I declined to answer, I must be presenting some small falsehood to the world. Fortunately, I had been given the time I needed to re-learn my tongue, and I could shunt the urge aside as needed, focusing instead on what I actually *wished* to say.

"I cannot come uninvited to Brocéliande, for Brocéliande belongs to all my father's children," I said, trying to sound as patient as the tide. "The same can be said of Caerleon. Were you to call your Court's attendance there, my mother would not be permitted to prevent you, for it belongs as much to your hand as to hers."

How it ached to admit that. Caerleon was our stronghold against the marauding children of Titania, the place we retreated to when their attacks grew too vicious to endure. Those of my siblings not already fled to private skerries or gone to join the night-haunts hid themselves there as much as they did anything else, trying only to survive, and for me to remind Titania of its existence was a betrayal of my own.

Her lip curled. "*That* pile of stones and bones?" she asked, making no effort to conceal her disdain. "Were my sister to come to my beautiful Brocéliande, I would understand. How could anyone not dream themselves housed in such a place? The walls sing the praises of Faerie's glory. Caerleon is rough and unrefined. I would not be seen there for all the pearls in the sea."

"It must trouble you, stepdame, that one of the gems most suited to your desires dwells only in the depths of the sea, where you have never once been truly welcomed."

Her mouth pursed briefly, as great an expression of displeasure as she was willing to allow, then smoothed out into her usual calm neutrality. There is a certain commonality between Titania and a viper waiting for the chance to strike. They are both patient and unblinking and very, very venomous.

"I can have pearls in plenty whenever I desire them," she said. "I sometimes think it was that desiring that twisted Amphitrite in my womb. Had I not wanted something so badly, I would not have been given a daughter whose only practical purpose was to gather it for me."

Bile rose in my throat. Amphitrite was the best of Titania's daughters, save perhaps for Erda, who had not been seen in my years. Few are the daughters of Titania who choose to remove themselves from view, and most of us believe that Erda's protean nature led to her own siblings hunting her down like an animal. For the sake of what little peace we possess between us, we have not gone digging any deeper than that supposition. If we gave Malvic or Jibvel proof that their lady was gone forever, their fury might devour Faerie completely.

And Faerie might well deserve it. It was difficult to believe we didn't.

But Titania was not yet done. "Did you come here only to taunt me with what you believe is outside my reach, little—oh, what is it they call you these days, Annie? Other than your own slain sister's name, which seems an unkind affectation, under the circumstances."

"They call me 'sea witch,'" I said, through gritted teeth, unable to refuse two direct questions set so closely together. The words burned like coals coming up. "And her name was Anglides, as you well know, stepdame. That the mortals chose to call her 'Gentle Annie' does not change the name that Father gave her."

"Then I suppose I should call you Antigone, should I not? That being the name your father gave you, if you're so obsessed with precision today." She smiled at me, something that looked almost like actual warmth in the expression. Some of her children would have committed murder to see that smile directed toward them.

Some of them had.

I shuddered. "Whatever you wish to call me, stepdame, I'm sure will be appropriate," I said.

"You've been practicing," she said, and leaned back in her throne, still smiling. "I thought it might be a benefit to you, to be forced to learn how to control that tongue of yours. A liar is welcome in every Court. An honest woman is welcome only in the Courts where she can swallow poison and spit back honey without a single falter. You've done well. Better than I would have expected of you."

"Was this a lesson?" I asked, horrified.

"Everything is a lesson, child," she said. "My sweetest rose asked that you be rendered harmless, and look, I have made it all but impossible for you to raise an army against her, for who would follow a woman who never tells them the pretty lies an army needs to hear? I clipped your thorns for her, and you found a way to restore them within the bounds of your limitations. You see what a generous Queen I am? I only wanted to improve you."

Unlike me, Titania was allowed to lie. She was lying now. I could see it in the shifting colors of her irises, in the triumph behind that serpent's smile. Still, I could play along within my limitations, as she said. I bowed my head.

"If you would see fit, then, stepdame, I have improved

myself and would be more than willing to allow your instruction to be lifted from me. If you would restore the full control of my own tongue, I will be ever grateful."

Not grateful enough to spare Eira's life, of course. Some prices are too dear to pay, and some debts can only be washed away in blood.

For a moment, she looked like she might be considering it. Then she stopped smiling, eyebrow lifting again. "I can see the virtue of allowing a student the freedom to err on their own, but I have to ask, and tell you I will compel your answer if you try to dance around it: why have you come here today, child? I doubt it was merely to ask me to take back a gift freely given. Not with that knife you carry by your side."

So she could see it? Of course she could. Father would have been able to see it, and it was concealed solely by a sheath of rowan wood—enough to conceal the kiss of iron and keep it from burning me, not enough to wipe it from the world. I took a deep breath, trying to push the inevitable aside.

The inevitable refused to go.

"I came to kill your eldest daughter for what she did to me."

"And what did she do to you? I would enjoin you to speak truly, but I know you have no choice in the matter."

And there it was: the real reason this curse was so cruel. I opened my mouth. The words refused to come. They were based too much on supposition, strung on too many webs of conjecture and assumption. The merlins who had come to me with sealskins dripping bloody in their hands had been painted in the blood of their own parents, babbling a tale of treachery and immortality that sang Eira's name to the heavens, but none of them had spoken to her. None of them had seen her. The closest any came had been a boy whose mother had been on the killing field, who had promised him they would be as beautiful as a woman sculpted from snow, and as untouchable as a woman black as walnut, and as immortal as a woman made of roses. White, black, and red were Eira's signatures, and she was too vain to disguise them even when she would have been well served by anonymity, but none of them were uniquely hers. None of them *proved*.

Of my children who had been free in the harbor when Eira brought her makeshift army to the slaughter, none had survived. Not a single person could tell me what the magic of the woman who unveiled the Roane to their mortal murderers had smelled like, felt like on the skin, and the means of their execution had ensured that none of my darlings joined the night-haunts. The thing for which she was the most to blame, the thing for which I hated her most dearly, was a thing I could not yet prove enough to speak aloud.

As to Ælfweard, he had been a human man. She broke no rules by arranging his destruction, save perhaps those of hospitality, and as neither she nor the Siren had been my guests at the time, I would have been hard pressed to argue that. I tried to speak. No sound came.

I tried again, to the same result, and finally stood, silent save for the small, pained hitching of my breath, the endless hammering of my heart. I knew what she had done, I *knew* it, but in the absence of the ability to prove it, I couldn't even speak my accusations aloud.

"I thought as much," said Titania, and rose, uncoiling from her throne, her dress falling around her in a river of rainbows. "You have nothing to accuse her of, and yet you came here to end her life. Her precious, precious life. There is none dearer to me than my daughter, little sea witch. A mother's love is nothing to be trifled with. You were a mother once. Don't you agree?"

Again, her tone demanded answer, and grudgingly, I gave it: "Yes."

"I told you, Mother," said Eira, behind me in the hall. I stiffened, but didn't give her the pleasure of seeing me startle, or turn. "I told you she was coming here to hurt me. She's carrying *iron*, Mother. She intended to render me too lost to even join the night-haunts. She wanted me wiped away and forgotten."

"As if anyone could forget your arrogance," I snapped.

Titania shot me a sharp look, and I stilled, forcing myself not to move. Of the two of us, she was the greater predator, and I knew better than to attract overmuch of her attention. Moving fluidly, she started for the stairs, apparently intending to descend. In that moment, I would have given almost anything to keep her where she was.

Even as Titania moved toward the stairs, Eira moved past me, heading toward her mother. Like Titania, she was garbed in white samite that gathered and refracted rainbows as she walked, shining like a sliver of the sky. Unlike Titania, she looked almost awkward in it, too solid and defined to suit a slice of living shimmer. Her hair, a waterfall of deepest black, struck opal highlights as the light moved over and around her, and in that, she was her mother's echo.

Everything about her looked like a crude attempt to mirror Titania, doomed from the first to fail, as she could never once have hoped to match her mother's impossible beauty, her impeccable brilliance. It was almost enough to make me feel sorry for Eira, in a distant, fleeting way. She had set herself against an ideal not a one of us could ever have hoped to achieve, and, in so doing, had condemned herself to a lifetime of failure and dissatisfaction.

If only she hadn't condemned the rest of us along with her, I could even have believed she deserved to be forgiven.

Eira stopped by her mother's side, turning to face me with a smirk playing on her lips, etched deep as silver in stone. "She would see me not only dead, but destroyed. Will you stand here and allow this? In your presence, in your halls?"

"I doubt she knew I would be in attendance on this day," said Titania, patting her on the head before proceeding toward me, leaving her daughter behind. "She thought to find you alone, little rose. She thought to pluck and crush you before I could intervene. What would you have from her in recompense?"

"Her life, if you so will it," said Eira, without hesitation. She couldn't destroy me. Her mother, however, could snuff me out like a candle, and if she even needed iron—if her touch was somehow not enough—I had conveniently brought it with me. The knife I carried might be the key to my own destruction, and I wouldn't even be able to pretend that it wasn't in some part deserved. I shivered and said nothing, holding my traitor tongue as tightly as I could. No truths were going to get me out of this moment, and no lies were forthcoming.

But the future still knew me. I wouldn't die, not this day, not at Titania's hand.

"And I would give it to you, dearest daughter, but that it would upset your father, who favors the chit for some reason," said Titania. She sniffed, expressing her opinion of Oberon's poor taste in children, and began to circle me. "He would not thank me if I killed her, even for the crime of her intentions. Might, in fact, ask me the same question I set before the sea witch: why? What had she done? Intent alone is not enough to condemn her to the iron tree. She must act if she's to be hunted down and slain like the beast she is."

I said nothing, but snarled, showing her the teeth that filled my mouth like needles, like knives. Teeth have always come easily to me. If anything, it's shaping them into something smaller and more polite that seems too difficult to consider under the majority of circumstances.

"You see?" Titania waved a hand, almost airily. "She carries herself as if she should be considered a princess among the fae, as if she could ever be your equal, my dearest, but she's a beast beneath the surface. All my sister's children are, from the best to the worst of them. They'll have us dragged into the muck and mire if we allow it."

I shook my head and began to turn away. Terrifying she might be, and greater than I in every regard, but unless she wanted to force me, I wasn't going to stand here and listen as she insulted my mother and my siblings. I loved them too well for that indulgence.

Sadly, she was quite willing to force me. "We'll be having none of that, little sea witch," she ordered, and snapped her fingers in almost the same breath, and my legs refused to turn any further. I was frozen in place, no longer quite looking at her, still seeing her out of the corner of my eye, like a reflection in a halfway-clouded mirror.

Seen so obliquely, she was less beautiful and more distorted, twisted all out of true with herself, like an image cast in a broken crystal. It ached to see her so. I wished nothing more than to turn back and see her properly, which might hurt but would not send shivers of terror running down my spine. I was a small, defenseless creature in the face of something much larger and more predatory. I wanted to face her. I wanted to flee. I could do neither of those things, could only stand frozen, unable even to shy away.

Titania stepped closer, skirts a whisper of fabric around her ankles, and reached out with one long-fingered hand, running it slowly through the long river of my hair.

"A proper lady never binds or braids," she said, tone that of a woman speaking to a much younger girl, and I knew even without the power to turn that she wasn't talking to me. "A knot's a knot, whether tangled or tied. Leave your hair loose, my love. It shows any who look at you that you have either the power to keep it combed without labor, or the hands to comb it for you."

"Yes, Mother."

I resolved on the spot to start tying up my hair if I got away from here. I knew it wasn't likely, knew the future had somehow lied and my bones were going to join the deepest stones of Brocéliande, but it was something to hold to, and in the moment, that seemed like the most important thing in all the worlds.

"She's a monster, but she understands propriety." Titania's hand abruptly closed, fingers still tangled in my hair. I couldn't even wince at the sudden bolt of pain. "She understands civility. I think it's time she learned a lesson or two in humility, to match the things she already knows. She could rise above her origins, if only she were more willing to yield before those who know better than she does."

Her hand withdrew from my hair, and a moment later, she stroked my head, as a nobleman might stroke a favored hunting dog. I had never wished so badly for the ability to pull away. She took another step, placing herself firmly in front of me, and bent slightly, resting her hands on her knees, so that we were eye to eye. "Hello, little sea witch. You may speak."

And with that, I could. I swallowed, hard, rejoicing in the motion, but said nothing at all. If she wanted speech from me, it was the last thing she would have, unless she compelled it.

She frowned, very briefly. "Is that your decision, then? Stubborn to the very end."

"If this is to be the end, at least I'll face it unbeaten and unbowed," I responded, unable to help myself.

Titania's immediate smile told me the depth of my error even before the sound of Eira's laughter. "Unbeaten, are you? Oh, my dear. The beating, as it were, has only just begun."

Titania kept me prisoned in place until a full day and night had passed in the mortal world, marked only by the flicker of the candles in their sconces, which brightened to signal sunset and dimmed to signal dawn. It was a subtle thing. Had there been a Court in grand attendance, it would have been enough to keep them aware of the passage of time while leaving any stolen mortals distracted from it. Years could be taken in such a manner, doing to innocent souls what had been done to my Ælfweard, if on a smaller scale. It was no great game to reduce a young and lovely maiden to dust in a night, but to send a farmer's youngest child and dearest hope tottering home as a woman in her dotage was a glorious distraction among the crueler of our descendants.

I harbored no great love for the majority of mortals. Ælfweard had been a surprise and an exception, clever and quick, careful and kind, and I would have loved him no matter what form he wore before me. But most of his kind were barely alive long enough to register as flickers on the edge of my vision, coming and going so very quickly that they left no impression on the world. That didn't mean they deserved to be toyed with. They were still alive. They were still, far too frequently, our lovers and our servants and even our children. They might not always deserve to be treated with respect. That didn't mean we were absolved of the responsibilities of kindness. Kick a dog too often and it will bite. Humans are more advanced than dogs, no matter how many of my siblings think otherwise. Humans have numbers, and long memories, and iron, and if we didn't stop treating them as amusements, they were going to rise up against us.

I had Seen flickers of it, when the games grew too frequent and too cruel. I did not want to See them fulfilled.

While I stood in the middle of the hall, prisoned and helpless, Titania came and went at her own pleasure. Stretching languidly, she announced her intention to take her rest, and bade Eira to follow her out of the hall. Eira did as her mother commanded, shooting poisonous glances back at me all the while, and I couldn't help feeling that Titania had just spared me from a truly mortifying death.

It would be one thing to die at the hands of a sister. It would be something else altogether to be gutted like a hooked fish, unable to fight back, unable to defend myself.

Hunger twisted in my gut. I ignored it as best I could, ignoring also the growing pain beneath it. The fae are immortal, the Firstborn even more so, if immortality can be said to have gradations, but we are still beings of flesh and bone. Our bodies demand care and the basic comforts all life needs. I would never die of hunger or thirst, but I would suffer, and suffer greatly, more and more the longer I was kept separate from the sea.

Slowly, when I was sure Titania was gone for longer than it took to walk down the hall and change her mind, I allowed my own power to uncurl and expand, pressing it against the edges of the spell that bound me. As with the doors, there were gaps between the tangled strands of her web, places where I could push myself like a wedge, twisting and turning and trying to unmake.

Unmaking is a strength of the sea. It is not, sadly, a specific element of my capabilities. I would normally have been studying the spell from a distance, not from within, and holding the slow luxury of a kitchen filled with herbs and simples and ways of working the world around to my way of thinking. Unlike the doors, I didn't dare simply overwhelm the spell. It was too strong for that to be a guaranteed result if I were even to attempt it, and Titania would feel the strain against her working. She would return, and she would return angry.

No, if I were going to free myself, it would have to be through slow erosion, chipping away at the wall of her will until it crumbled in my hands. Hunger fell away, along with the needs of my current form. I couldn't change myself while tangled in Titania's net; she had a way of stopping even the most protean of us from reaching for that aspect of our father's nature. Until she let me go, I would wear the shape I had been wearing when I came to Brocéliande, and if she killed me, this was the face I would wear among the night-haunts evermore.

I pushed a little harder, worked a little more of my power into the spell, and didn't notice when the candles flickered again. I pushed harder still, and felt the first strands dissolve. They would have snapped had I moved more quickly, still taut with power as they rebounded toward their creator. This way, they simply fell into nothingness and were swept away, debris in the stream flowing outward from my core. I pushed and pushed, and more and more strands fell away, until finally I could move my own legs, could adjust my stance and listen as the muscles of my calves and hips began to shriek in indignant agony.

I bent forward, putting my hands on my knees, and panted. How great an insult would Titania take it to be if I pissed all over the floor of Brocéliande? More, at this point, how much did I care for her wounded sensibility? I straightened and began to turn, to head for the door that would carry me away from here.

Titania stood behind me, alone, a small smile on her pretty face.

"That took you less time than I had expected," she said. "Oh, you *are* a powerful one, child. The rumors I hear of you are true ones. No wonder you thought you'd stand a chance against my rose. No wonder you came here seeking vengeance."

I glared at her but didn't jump or scream. That was something to be proud of, I thought. The greatest of us stood before me, and I faced her as if I were not afraid.

I was terrified, of course. To be proud is not the same as to be foolish, although they often overlap. My mother may have claimed me, but I am still my father's daughter, and in another time, I might have been a hero, might have carried that cruel mantle for my own.

"I know, you know," she said.

I raised an eyebrow.

"I know my rose is not the fragile flower she presents herself to be, and I know she has transgressed against you." Her smile grew. "I also know you can't tell a lie, however based it is on partial truth, and you don't *know* precisely what to accuse her of. You can never convince me to allow you to kill my child, and the iron knife at your hip means you will never convince your father to release you from the muzzle on your tongue. She walks away from this place living and free and unharmed, and you agree now, of your own free will, never to harm her."

"Or?" My voice was rough and raspy from my long unwilling silence. I swallowed to moisten my throat and glared at her.

"Or you will never harm her, because *my* free will will not allow it," said Titania sweetly. "Your choices are freedom or more restraint."

I paused. "I would much prefer freedom."

"I hoped you might."

"But I am unable to lie, and that means I cannot agree to never harm her." I looked at Titania as levelly as I could. "I will kill her if I can. I could hold my hand for a time, at your pleasure, but the day will come when she is vulnerable before me, and I will strike. I will slaughter her like a sow in the dust, and I will leave her blood to the night-haunts far from any of her descendants, that even her last moments be lost."

"Will you, now."

"What she has done is so far beyond unforgiveable as to be recorded for the ages. One day, I'll have the proof I need to name her crimes aloud, and even Father won't be able to contest my right to have her heart in my hands, her throat between my teeth. When that day comes, she dies. So no, stepdame. No, I can't promise to spare her. I can only promise you I won't."

"Then compulsion is the only road left open for us." Titania shook her head, a look of profound disappointment on her face. "I had hoped, as my niece, you would be wiser than this."

"And I had hoped, as my mother's sister, that you would be kinder, but it seems we must both be disappointed today."

"Hmm. I do owe you my gratitude, for working your way out of the binding I had you under. It tells me how you'll try to wash the deeper ones away." She prowled toward me, and I took an involuntary step backward, unable to hold my ground at the approach of something so much more powerful than I. Pride has its place. So does fear.

"I don't understand."

"It was a test, little sea witch, and whether you have passed it or failed is very much determined by where you stand when the question is asked." Her smile grew back to its previous dimensions and beyond. "I needed to see how you would take something meant to constrain you apart. Or did you think me incompetent, that I didn't know how to overcome one of my sister's children?"

"I thought you considered me unimportant," I said, unable to help myself. "That if you just set me aside for a time, that would be punishment enough, and you'd go back to more interesting matters."

Whatever those were. Helping Eira with a hangnail or harassing an innocent family that had the audacity not to repudiate their changelings, no doubt. Or other, less pleasant things. Hunting my siblings in the moors and fens. Not that Titania often joined in with the slaughter; she was above it all, and preferred to keep a thin veil of deniability in place when she spoke to our father.

"Oh, little sea witch, you *are* unimportant," she chided. "You are nothing but a stone set against a mountain, and while you might have been able to resist me for a time, you've given me the key to your defenses, and told me where to lay my anchors. Now be still, and silent, and remember you brought this on yourself."

The stillness returned between one breath and the next, every muscle in my body refusing to acknowledge that they belonged to me. Even my heart stuttered in my chest, thrown briefly off its beating before it remembered it was essential to my survival and thus exempt, on some level, from any order that didn't command me to actually die.

And she wanted me alive. I could see it in the way she prowled around me, circling like a shark, smiling still. "You have never mattered to anyone but your mother, and her admiration is a weak and pointless thing, easily shattered. She's fickle, my sister. She'll forget you as soon as you stop coming to her side. You'll be one more story she never bothered to finish, and that will be a tragedy for no one. You leave no children behind, your closest sisters are gone . . . oh, your father may mourn, but he'll have me to offer comfort, and when your mother forgets your name, it can only drive him deeper into my arms. Won't that be lovely?"

Her laughter was breaking glass in a silent room, delicate and sharp. She stopped and looked past me as the sound of footsteps drifted through the room. She was already smiling, but it softened at the sight of something she actually cared about.

"Come to join us, my rose?" she asked. "It's good that you should witness this. It concerns you, after all."

Titania turned back to me. The air around us grew heavy, as if in the moment right before a great and terrible storm. It became difficult to breathe, every inhalation feeling like I was drowning in thin syrup. It was an unpleasant sensation. I am the sea witch. I cannot be drowned; the water would refuse to even consider such an indignity. My body would adapt in an instant, opening gills, sealing lungs, preparing for survival in the depths. But this was not true drowning, and so I had no resistance.

I couldn't even gasp. I had the capacity to breathe, and not much more.

With the heaviness came the scent of roses, spiraling out of nowhere, rising with every heartbeat. It was rich and cloying at the same time, more cultured than the roses of my mother, which smelled of changeability and the wilds, more dangerous than the roses of my father, which offered hope and harbor and healing. Under the roses ran ribbons of violets, woodbine and eglantine, and the bitter drift of almonds, slivered and sweetened until they became almost unrecognizable. It was a complicated, heady blend. The magic of our parents always is.

Titania moved closer to me once again, Eira watching eagerly in the background, her eyes alight with poisonous flame. Reaching out with one languid hand, Titania cupped my chin, holding my face tilted toward her. She blew, lightly, on my lips, and her breath carried the scent of wild thyme. I sneezed. It was involuntary, and so her spell allowed it. She never stopped smiling, not even as she leaned away from me again, fingers digging in more tightly on the line of my jaw.

"Pretty little sea witch," she cooed. "This is the first, and least, of my restrictions for you: Faerie springs from three wells, and they are sometimes joined, and sometimes separated, but I care for those I claim. You are forbidden to raise hand or power against any child of mine whom I have publicly named my own. Any descendant of theirs is outside your authority. You will not harm them, will not touch them, save under the conditions I give to you. Should you try, your bones will shatter beneath your skin, and they will not be restored until you win the true and uncoerced forgiveness of the one you have done harm to. Every breath will be an agony, and even transformation will not restore you. My children, and their children, are forbidden to you. Except."

"Except?" asked Eira.

Maybe the only time in her long life she had asked a question that was actually relevant to me.

Titania's smile sweetened and turned more poisonous at the same time, like the slow blooming of some terrible flower. "They call you sea witch," she purred. "A title of convenience, I think. A title of respect. Let's change that."

I would have recoiled if I'd been able. Instead, I stood silently staring, unable to even close my eyes and turn my face away. She stepped closer still, finally letting go of my face, and raked her hands through the air like she was gathering up ribbons left draped in the trees after a festival. The smell and weight of her magic both increased, until I felt they must crush me flat as a sheet of paper. And perhaps that would have been the better outcome, for me, and for the wide world beside.

"A true sea witch serves any who comes to them, out of greed and the desire for chaos," she said. "So I give you this, Antigone of Albany, yours to keep and carry, to nurture and protect: whenever you are asked for anything within your power, whether it be casting or query, you will tell the one who asks you yes. You will do whatever is requested, no matter how dangerous or disastrous it would be for the one who asks you. You may set a price for your services—witches are paid, after all—whether it be in coin or blood or favor. You may harm my claimed children when they are fool enough to come to you, but you may refuse none, and the prices you set them must be fair. Do you understand me?"

When I was silent, she snapped her fingers.

"Speak, child," she said, and her voice was cold. "Do not test my patience, for I have scant enough to spare."

"I understand," I rasped.

She smiled in satisfaction. "*Whatever* is requested, whoever requests it, you must obey." The claws of her binding sank into me then, digging all the way down to the base of my bones. I cried out, brief and sharp, like the wailing of a seabird, and Titania nodded.

"Too deep for you to erode without wearing your very self away," she said, smug as anything. "Then I'm doing my job correctly, hmm?"

"Is that everything?" I asked.

"Oh, don't you wish it were. But no, there's one thing more: save for family, save when the debts are already too deep to allow the people you treat with to escape you ever, nothing comes free. You can give the smallest token as a taste of what bound power can do, but you can't do great favors or tell great truths. Nothing comes for free, little sea witch. Not your power, and not your favors, and not your freedom. You are further forbidden to mention any of this to your father, or to my sister. It would be seeking your emancipation without payment, and so I forbid it to you."

I could speak, but I still couldn't move away from her.

My eyes burned with tears I physically couldn't shed. All I could do was stare. Behind her, Eira was bouncing on her toes, all but overflowing with excitement.

"May I, Mother?" she asked. "May I make the first request of her? Now that she's forbidden to refuse me?"

"Even my magic only goes so far, little rose," cautioned Titania. "I can allow you the first blow against her, but I cannot allow you to ask her to harm herself, or any among her descendants. The price for that would be too high, and the magic is too fresh. You might find yourself compelled to pay, rather than calling it too dear and turning aside from the bargain unfulfilled."

So I wasn't to be ordered to slay my surviving grandchildren? That was a small mercy in a day that held far too few of them.

"I just want the knife, and a favor," she said.

"If you know what you would ask, and how much you're willing to pay, then please, ask her," said Titania, and stepped aside. The bonds holding me in place snapped in the same moment, and I staggered, nearly falling face-first to the floor. My knees shook and my thighs ached as I pulled myself upright again and faced my sister.

Eira's smile was a mirror to her mother's. She looked me slowly up and down, smile spreading all the while.

"You can't hurt me unless it's the only fair price for what I ask," she said. "It's a lovely feeling. I do wish you could share it, but then, your mother doesn't care enough about what happens to you to protect you from me, now does she?"

"Eira," said Titania, almost chidingly. "She's already helpless. It's not ladylike to toy with her now."

"Sorry, Mother," said Eira, ducking her head. "She's just been so awful for so long, I didn't know when else I'd get a chance to get back my own."

I glared at her. "What do you want?" I could feel the compulsion crawling up my spine, ready to force me to go along with whatever terrible, cruel desire she wanted to voice.

Eira's smile returned as her attention slid back to me. "The knife you carry, to begin with," she said.

The fair price filled my thoughts, chasing away everything else, and my mouth opened almost of its own accord. "The blade you seek was crafted by Alswn, first among the Coblynau, made with no clear understanding of its intended use. She is innocent of all save following her nature to the fire. If you would take a knife of her crafting from my hands, you must swear never to harm her, or any of her descendants, however great their provocation."

Eira's eyes widened, and she glanced, alarmed, at Titania.

"She's allowed to ask that of you," said the Lady of Flowers. She sounded bored. I was bound and no longer a threat to her or to her daughter; she was finished with me. That was almost comforting, in a terrible way.

Nothing would ever be enough to make me matter to Titania.

"To forbid me the opportunity for self-defense, for protection, all for the sake of a knife?"

"She's allowed." Titania shook her head. "I've bound her as tightly as I can, but tie a rope too tight and it has the chance to snap. We want her confined and brought down. Any more and she might not be. So if that's the price the binding she has on her says is fair, then that's the price that's fair. She can't charge too little, or she's not being greedy. She can't charge too much, or she's not being reasonable. This is the common ground between the two."

I smirked a little as Eira swung her attention back to me, eyes narrowed in fury. "Keep your little toy, then," she said. "Congratulations, *sea witch*. First request issued, first payment declined. Don't expect to maintain that record. But I must also ask a favor of you, and you can't deny me. Are you ready?"

I wasn't. I had to be. I looked at her and said nothing, waiting for her to ask the unimaginable.

It wasn't a lengthy wait. "Your grandchildren," she said. "The ones who were with you when the unfortunate accident occurred. They're safe where they are, are they not? Well cared-for and comfortable?"

"Yes," I said, unable to stop myself. The word escaped as if it were not my own. Close behind it came a cascade that I meant truly, all the way to the base of me: "Do not ask me where they are, Eira. They are well outside your reach, and they deserve the time to heal and remember what it is to be children."

"I wasn't planning to," she said. "Leave your brats to the tides. There aren't enough of them to be a trial to me. There's no one left to teach them how to interpret what they See."

"There's me," I said.

"But that, you see, is the favor you must grant to me, for you have no choice at all." She smiled as broad as anything. "Seven years is the standard term, is it not?"

"The standard term to what?" I demanded.

"To all things in Faerie, really," she said. "But oh, your grandchildren are young. They won't understand. This is what I ask of you: for seven years, from this moment on, you will not go to your descendants. You will not join them in the sea, you will not answer their calls, and you will not speak to them, nor teach them any lessons you might feel they need to carry."

I gaped at her. This was cruelty even beyond what I could have expected. They were children. They wouldn't understand. I wanted to object. I wanted to argue.

She wanted to continue: "And when your seven years are up, and you're allowed to go back to the sea, you will not tell them why you left, nor where you were, nor anything aside from that you must now answer all requests. Choices are no longer a luxury you can afford. Do you understand me?"

"I do," I said. I wanted to fight her more than anything. The compulsion racing through my bones wouldn't allow it. It presented me the prices Faerie felt would balance that cruel demand, and there were more of them than I could have imagined, and it took everything I had to reject the first of them, to force the geas to understand that I would command it as much as possible, and not the other way around. "I understand all too well, Eira. But if you want me to do this for you, you must meet my price. That is the nature of the exchange, is it not?"

For the first time, she looked uneasy, eyes darting toward Titania in a quick, anxious gesture that betrayed just how much she disliked the idea of being held to any sort of binding cost. Her mother nodded, a small, indulgent smile on her lips. Eira returned her attention to me, taking a deep breath and seeming to draw strength enough from it to remember bravery.

Her lip curled as she looked at me and said, "I understand a bargain."

"Fine, then. For seven years, I will eschew the company of my descendants. I will leave them to the seas and to the shadow of my absence, and when I return to them, I will not answer them why, no matter how they beg and plead." The words settled around me like a net, as binding as Titania's geas. They burned and froze in equal measure.

But I wasn't finished yet. "And until the day of my return, until the moment I am reunited with what remains of my family, you will not hunt nor harm the children of Maeve or their descendants, nor bid others to do it on your behalf. You will not set your children to hunting down what's left of mine, will not beg your brothers to defend your honor, will raise neither hand nor word toward any who carries so much as a drop of my mother's blood. This is our agreement."

She stiffened, eyes going briefly wide as she felt the weight of my words settle over her. Again, she looked to her mother, and this time, Titania didn't smile. This time, Titania's mouth was a knife slash across her face, eyes blazing with the bright light of her anger.

"I understand," said Eira, and her voice was small.

I was still bound, and could not turn away. I shifted my attention to Titania.

"There is nothing I can do for you that you can't do better for yourself, stepdame," I said. "Let me go, and allow me to leave this place unharmed, and I'll keep my word."

"You won't have a choice," she said. "How dare you ask something so disrespectful of my daughter? You shame this household. You shame yourself."

"I asked only what the magic you so kindly bound me to said was fair and reasonable," I said. "She isn't bound forever, and neither am I. Both of us will be released in seven years."

I would have to find a way to prepare defenses against Eira's wrath before that happened. If I went to Amphitrite, I could begin preparing to protect them. Eira had forbidden me to join my descendants, but she hadn't even tried to forbid me the sea—she knew, even in her arrogance, that the price of self-destruction would be more than she wanted to pay. Seven years of peace wasn't so much to compel of her. I would have asked for more if I'd known how.

The magic Titania had bound me to both was and was not her own. It was a slippery thing, ancient and impartial, and it ran through my hands like water when I reached for it, refusing to be clutched except when a bargain was called for. It carried the costs, it offered them to me, but it lent me no strength, offered me no support; it would take time to learn what it was, where it came from, how to twist it to suit my needs. Avoiding the world wasn't the answer.

If I hid from everyone who might ask me to aid them, I would never learn how to control this magic, or what it was, or whether I could bend it to my own designs. Titania would get her way, at least long enough for me to learn what the magic binding me was, what it meant, and how it could be turned against her.

Titania narrowed her eyes. "You overreach."

"I reach precisely as far as you bound me to do," I corrected, politely. "I am only what you'd make of me. I am the sea witch. From now until you let me go."

"Forever, then," she spat. "Remember this when next you think to rise above your station."

"What station is that?" I asked. "Oldest of Oberon's children, first daughter of my mother? Those are stations no one can take away from me. Cut me down dead, I'll still have drawn breath before your rose was planted."

Eira made a sound of wordless rage. I said nothing. I had come here to destroy her, and her mother had striven to destroy me in her stead. Only time would tell if this could turn to my advantage.

And no matter how much time I took or was given, my children would still be dead.

"Let me go," I said again. "You've had your fun. You've hurt me. You've defended your daughter who doesn't deserve protection, and you've left what remains of my family without their progenitor. Now let me go. If you dislike the lack of civility from my tongue, remember that you stole it. All the pretty fictions Faerie thrives on—you took them away from me. They don't come back for you."

Titania's eyes remained narrowed for a long moment before she relaxed and started to laugh. She clapped her hands and I could move again, stumbling backward, out of her reach. As if she had ever been limited by something as simple as hands.

"Then leave my sight, witch, and do not trouble me again." She turned her back then. I was dismissed. Very clearly, I was dismissed.

I couldn't raise a hand to Eira. The binding upon me made it so. But she couldn't attack when my back was turned, and that would have to be enough.

I bowed my head, allowing myself to look as defeated as I felt, and I walked away.

Celyddon, Cambria, 568

The forest's boughs were good and green, damp from the rain of the night before, and they hung over me like a welcoming curtain, embracing me with their shadows. I turned my face toward them as I walked, grateful for the respite from the sun. Not that the sun of Cambria is ever blisteringly bright or unbearable, but I am a creature made for the dark depths of the ocean, caverns, and caves where the light never falls, and there are times when even the slightest touch of the sun is more than I can bear.

Forty-five years since the night Titania bound me. Thirty-eight years since my bargain with Eira expired and I was allowed to go home to my grandchildren, many of whom were children no longer but would always be infants in my eyes. Thirty-eight years since the moment when I had realized that bound or unbound, I couldn't go back to them.

I am an immortal creature, unless I am careless or unlucky enough to be killed. I can expect to see centuries pass like raindrops falling from a stormy sky, dissolving into rivers and fens. But even I was young once, and when I look to the scars that shaped me, most of them were created in my first fifty years. The cuts you receive when you are a wild, half-formed thing, those are the ones that never fully heal. Those are the things you never quite recover from.

My grandchildren lost their parents, their siblings, their entire community in an instant, and then, when they needed me most, I walked away from them and was bound not to tell them why. Even now, while I could lie to them, I couldn't force my traitor lips to form the words that would explain my absence. I had hurt them, badly, and my return would bring no comfort, for it would bring no answers.

And so I wandered. I had been wandering the full forty-five years since my enchantment, traveling the High Kingdom of Albion, seeing what could be seen, trying to understand our world as it was evolving. Cailleach Skerry was entirely gone now, swallowed by the sea, lost to the terrible tide that had risen in my absence. I could have fought the waters to call it back, but to what end? I had been happy there once. Let it be a drowned land, for I could never have been happy there again. No matter how much I might have tried.

No. Better for me to live in exile; better for me to have no ties. I walked where I would, and I avoided the children of Titania as best as I could, and I met more and more children of Maeve who knew what had been done to me, what had been demanded.

My siblings did their best to be kind, when our paths crossed. They asked little if they asked anything at all, and most of their requests were attempts to make things kinder for me than they might otherwise have been. Amphitrite, when first we met and parted, volunteered to care for my grandchildren and not tell them why I had gone away, then asked me for the cost of promising to eat and rest. She knew that I would be inclined to punish myself for being weaker than her mother, to force myself to suffer as my innocent charges suffered.

The magic I still didn't fully understand offered up a price, and she paid it gladly. For the cost of three scales plucked from her flank, she could rest knowing I would eat, and sleep, and bathe myself until next we were together.

I couldn't even resent her for the theft of one more sliver of my autonomy, for it had been done with love, which was better than could be said for what Titania had done to me. Let my sister show me care. I would wander still.

Mother was at Caerleon, or perhaps not; she might be walking the lands of deeper Faerie, visiting her children who had chosen to carve out corners for their own as far as possible from the web of interconnected domains ruled by the children of Titania. She might be three steps behind me, fading into shadow whenever I dared turn around. It didn't matter. I hadn't seen her since the day Titania bound me, and what I had Seen in the twisting currents of the future told me I would not see her for some time yet to come. She would have been distraught to see what had been done to me, what her sister was trying to make me become, and her anger would have been greater than her grief. I could not tell her. She would see it all the same.

Every time Titania or one of Titania's brood had been responsible for the loss of one of my siblings, Mother's grief had been too great to overcome, and the time when vengeance would have been forgiven by my father had been able to slip away unnoticed. If I went before her now, bound and bowed as I was, she would be nothing more than rage, and all Faerie would catch fire before her fury.

She would burn us to the ground, and we would not survive. I had Seen enough of it to know that avoiding Mother's company was the only choice open to me until this was all less new. A century or so should be enough. I'd be able to return to her side then, and while she'd still be able to perceive the bindings, I'd be better at carrying them without bending under their weight. She'd still worry and fuss, but she wouldn't be as angry, and Faerie would endure.

Faerie must ever endure.

Eira's attack on the Roane had been only the first of her salvos against those who could whisper the future. She was clever, I had to grant her that; the price of my exile had stayed her hand for seven years, during which she could do nothing but sit and seethe, and plan her next attack. The sun had barely set on the last day of our agreement before my youngest brother, Mug Ruith, had come home from the hunt to find the entire line of his descendants slaughtered, the five children who would have grown into the Tlachtgae broken like the stones they sang to, their bones ground to powder beneath the hammering hooves of Eira's host. How he had grieved, my poor shattered baby brother, how he had wept and raged and screamed his fury to the sky.

At the end of it all, he had gone to our Mother and bade her grant him vengeance, and she had said only that so long as her sister kept her hands clean, she must do the same, for the balance must not be broken. And he had set his name aside in answer, and walked from her Court, swearing never to return to her. He called himself Blind Michael now, and had carved a skerry of his own deep in darkness, where he sat and brooded, and wooed a daughter of Titania with the single-minded dedication of a young thing that has been hurt and sees no other choice.

Acacia was clever. She would go to him or not as she saw fit, and either way, she would find a path through this tangled wood. Mug—or Michael—would recover or not. If he did, he might yet be a great ally in the dark to come. If he didn't, he would be a glorious monster.

Eira seemed to be making more and more of those.

When she had tried to send her minions for the Kitsune, they had been greeted by the Nine-Tailed One. Keiko had been quick, and canny, and vicious, and had beaten back Eira's forces before she and her children retreated, bleeding, into the mountains. Her line yet lived.

The Ysengrimus had not been so lucky. The Peri had been successfully painted as incurably monstrous, driven into the desert and isolated from the rest of Faerie; the Lamia were all but gone. No whispers had been spoken of the Korrigan or the Kilmoulis in years. Even their Firstborn were silent, and I feared yet more of my siblings had stopped their dancing. One by one, Eira was closing Faerie's eyes against the future. And try as I might, I couldn't See the reasons *why*. The things we Saw were always malleable, never preordained. They could be changed. What had someone Seen in the years ahead to terrify her so?

Still, Celyddon was a comfort to me as I walked through the green, and I walked on until the flicker of a fire drew my attention and no small measure of my ire. Who would set their camp here, in this known Faerie forest? No mortal could be so careless—not unless they yearned for their own ending.

I turned toward the light, called onward by curiosity, and moved through the brush to the edge of a clearing. A small wagon was settled there, the horse unyoked and tied to a nearby tree, where it cropped placidly at the grass. As to the fire itself, a young man tended it, turning a rabbit on a spit above the flames.

He glanced up, although I knew I hadn't made a sound, and his eyes met mine, green as a shallow sea. I knew those eyes.

They were my own.

"Come into the light," he said. "I will not hurt you."

It was laughable, for him to think I worried of such. I smiled to myself and stepped forward, watching his reaction. To my surprise, he looked pleased, and nodded slightly, accepting my appearance.

"I Saw you here," he said. "I Saw that you would come before me, and that with you by my side, we might change the world."

I blinked. Whatever I had been expecting from this night, this was nothing of the kind.

"What is your name, Lady?"

I blinked again, and said nothing. I had learned, over the years, that the easiest way to speak the truth was to hold my silence until compelled.

He sighed. "But you must give me something to call you."

"Must I?" I cocked my head. "It seems I am not as yet compelled. What is *your* name?"

"They call me Emrys," he said, and offered up a shallow bow. "I will be a great wizard someday, if I can live that long. If you will not give me your name, I will give one to you instead."

"Fine, then," I said. "What's my name?"

"Nimue," he said. "As true a name as any other." Then

he smiled, and it was so like the smile of my lost Aulay that I couldn't help but smile back as he beckoned me deeper into the clearing. "In time, perhaps, you'll answer to something truer."

"In time," I agreed, and let the black-haired boy who would grow to become the wizard Merlin lead me to his fire, and we sat together in the warmth, and the future of Faerie hurtled ever on.